PRAISE FOR *TAHIRA IN BLOOM*

"In *Tahira in Bloom*, Heron delivers all the necessary elements to an artfully designed rom-com: the perfect meet-cute, a delightful arrangement, and a rich connection to roots. A masterful debut!"

—Nisha Sharma, award-winning author of
My So-Called Bollywood Life

"Farah Heron's YA debut stars strongheaded Tahira, who's pursuing her dreams as a fashion designer. Against the backdrop of a fierce flower competition, Tahira finds her true strength and shines. This heartwarming book tackles ambition and the toll it takes on family, friendship, romance, and identity."

—Roselle Lim, author of *Vanessa Yu's Magical Paris Tea Shop*

"*Tahira in Bloom* is an entertaining and compelling coming-of-age story about fashion, floriculture, and finding yourself even when you don't know you're a little lost. Never have I ever laughed at so many plant puns. Perfect for fans of Sandhya Menon, Syed Masood, and Sarah Kuhn."

—Suzanne Park, author of *Sunny Song Will Never Be Famous* and
The Perfect Escape

Tahira in Bloom

ALSO BY FARAH HERON

The Chai Factor
Accidentally Engaged

Tahira in Bloom

a novel

FARAH HERON

SKYSCAPE

☶ SKYSCAPE

Published by Skyscape, New York

www.apub.com

Amazon, the Amazon logo, and Skyscape are trademarks of Amazon.com, Inc., or its affiliates.

ISBN-13: 9781542030373 (hardcover)
ISBN-10: 1542030374 (hardcover)
ISBN-13: 9781542030366 (paperback)
ISBN-10: 1542030366 (paperback)

Cover illustration by Christina Chung

Cover design by Faceout Studio, Amanda Hudson

Printed in the United States of America

First edition

To Tony

1

THWARTED BY AN INVASIVE PARAKEET

One fateful spring day when I was only seven, I learned two things. One: I would be a fashion designer someday. I'd been filling my coloring pages and notebooks with drawings of my dolls in fabulous clothes for years by that point, but that was the first day I felt the thrill, the mind-consuming rush, of figuring out how to create actual clothes from my drawings. I'd cut off a piece of fabric from my old Eid lehenga (which didn't fit me anymore, and my sister refused to wear Indian formal wear) and wrapped it around my Surf City Barbie, because seriously . . . how gauche to live in swimwear twenty-four seven. I stapled up the hem and used safety pins to cinch the back to get it as close as I could to the image in my notebook. Seeing Barbie go from California dreamer to Bollywood glam solidified my gut instinct that day—I was born to create clothes.

And the second thing I learned? Achieving that goal wasn't going to be easy, but I'd have help and support along the way. Because that very same day, instead of being angry that I'd cut up my outfit, my parents took me to the library and showed me my first college, university, and vocational school catalogs. It was a desi-parents thing—our culture was steeped in ambition and strategic goal setting. I learned I'd be a fashion designer because my parents would help me get there. My goals were family goals. My successes all our successes. Together, we put together *the Plan* to help me start my own fashion line before I was twenty.

Yay for Eastern collectivist cultures.

Even with all that planning, none of us expected that ten years later a rogue parakeet in Paris would derail the Plan spectacularly and give me another life-changing, fateful spring day at the age of seventeen.

Once again my parents barged into my room while I was cutting fabric. After the email I'd forwarded to their respective work addresses that morning, I knew a discussion about the Plan would be coming. And it wouldn't be an easy one. But I didn't expect it to be quite this bad.

"Tahira, we need to talk," Dad said. He sat on the pink patchwork comforter on my single bed.

I stayed at my sewing machine. The last time Dad said "we need to talk" with that look on his face was shortly after I'd told them I was dating my boyfriend, Matteo. Dad had awkwardly thrown a new box of condoms at me before pantomiming with his fingers how to use them, in case I wasn't aware. Mom then told me the college dropout rates for teen mothers. Of course I already knew all that. Sex ed was pretty comprehensive around here.

"Can I keep sewing?" I asked.

"Are those the shirts for the shoot tomorrow?" Mom eyed the black, white, and gray custom-printed fabric I'd designed myself.

I nodded. The fabric had come in only that day, so I needed to hustle to get these done before my photo shoot at noon tomorrow. But I didn't mind a marathon stitching session. Sewing was my happy place.

Mom rubbed her hands together. "Okay, Tahira. Your father and I have talked, and I've made some calls. We think we have a way to get you back on Plan. Do you want to hear about the new fashion industry summer job we found for you?"

Step eight of the Plan to get me my fashion line was the one the parakeet had destroyed. I was supposed to have had an internship with a Toronto-based fashion designer, where I would work my fine ass off so I'd get a *glowing* letter of recommendation and plenty of content for my application portfolio to FIT—New York's Fashion Institute of Technology (hopefully with a scholarship; step two, already accomplished, of course, was to get straight As to help with that).

The designer I'd scored the internship with, Nilusha Bhatt, was more of an up-and-comer than at the top of the game. But she *had* been invited to Paris Spring Fashion Week after she'd hired me, so she was clearly on track to being huge.

But according to Nilusha's email earlier, two days ago, a rogue ring-necked parakeet had dive-bombed onto the oversize feathers on the designer's summer hat. Maybe to collect some bedding for its nest? Who knew? Anyway, Nilusha's Miu Miu pumps wedged into the space between cobblestones, and she nose-planted on one of those quaint continental Paris streets. Her nose was fine. But she broke her leg in three places.

I exhaled. I didn't really *want* to hear about whatever new job Mom had found now. I wanted more time to mourn the one I'd lost. I wanted to keep sewing now for tomorrow's shoot. I wanted to call Matteo again and vent about how unfair it was to lose my epic summer job because of a bird on another continent. I wanted to sketch out the cool design idea I'd had on my way back from the post office to pick up this fabric before I forgot it.

But what I wanted most in the world was success in the fashion industry, and my parents were here to help me get it. Most people who made it big in fashion, and I mean really *big*, had help from family. Maybe their mother was the style editor for *Vogue*, or their dad knew the creative director at Gucci, or they had a godmother with a house in the Hamptons next to Tom Ford's. But the only long-standing connection in fashion my family had was maybe some clout with the Spadina Avenue fabric stores, and that one sari store on Gerrard Street that gave my mom the best deals. I was *too* Canadian, *too* brown, and *too* Muslim to have built an upper hand in the style world. So my parents made up for it by teaching me how to *hustle*, times three. Thanks to them I'd had grit, determination, and Asian ambition bred into me since birth.

And that meant I had no choice, really. I wanted to be in the fashion industry, and doing what my parents asked was how I was going to get there. I pushed the fabric pieces to the edge of my sewing table and folded my hands on my lap.

"Okay," I said, "I'm listening. How do I get back on the Plan?"

~

"This sucks, Tahira," my best friend, Gia, said the next day as she stopped taking pictures of me and let my SLR camera hang from her neck. Gia, Matteo, and I were at Graffiti Alley, a long stretch of vibrant art in the alley behind a major street in downtown Toronto. It was a bit of a pain-in-the-butt location for photo shoots because we were always fighting other photographers and tourists for the best backdrops, but my Instagram followers loved seeing my designs positioned against the bright art.

"I don't get why this designer has to stay in Paris all summer," Gia continued, standing five feet in front of Matteo and me, both of us leaning on the art wall. "Can't she recover from a broken leg in Toronto?"

"Her leg is, like, *shattered*," I said. "They had to put a pin in it."

Maybe it hadn't been wise to tell Gia just now that I'd lost my coveted summer internship. I needed her attention as my photographer today. But I'd been too upset to talk to her last night.

"Anyway," I continued, twisting the simple silver ring on my index finger, "she said it's easier to just stay there with her friend to recover. Her friend's roommate is a nurse. A hot male nurse named Didier."

Matteo snorted. "She told you that?"

I nodded. "Nilusha is awesome." I'd lost so much. She would have been a great boss.

Gia fanned herself with her hand. "*Shut. Up.* A *male* nurse?" Gia was in the theater program at our school, and it showed. She was determined to be a rom-com star one day and was trying to build a platform as an Instagram influencer to help her get there. "A *French* male nurse? Why can't *I* get hit on the head with a bird?" she said, pouting. "Nothing good ever happens to me. Does this French nurse have a French Canadian cousin or anything?"

I raised a brow. I loved Gia, but she sometimes took the whole boyfriend-desperation thing too far. We'd been tight since grade nine and were closer than sisters. "G . . . this isn't about you. I'm *distraught*. I *needed* this internship."

"Well, I *need* a boyfriend." Gia lifted the camera and made a motion indicating she was going to continue taking pictures of us. Matteo folded his arms across his chest, and I rested my hand on his shoulder and schooled my face into the unbothered expression of a person who wasn't currently plotting the demise of all the world's parakeets.

We were both wearing the shirts I'd made the day before. They'd turned out awesome. After a few more pictures, Matteo asked, "So, you going to do what we talked about last night? Apply at other designers?"

"I looked, but no one is hiring anymore. Most placements started two months ago. I was only able to get the job with Nilusha because the college kid she hired flaked or something last month."

I sighed before posing Matteo and me together in a new configuration. He put on that sultry, resting smolder-face that was catapulting his popularity on social media as a teen style influencer. He also wanted to work in the fashion industry but was hoping to hit it big as a model. Or, failing that, a stylist. We'd been together four months. Matteo was actually Gia's cousin, which had made me wary of him at first. Gia put her family before anyone else, and the last thing I wanted was for a wedge to come between us if things went sour with a guy.

But so far things were great with Matteo and me. I'd called him as soon as I got that stupid email from Nilusha yesterday, and he'd been so supportive. He put things into perspective and told me there were plenty more designers in Toronto who'd love me. He totally cheered me up by helping me plan this photo shoot.

And he looked so hot today. I'd paired his cotton button-up shirt in the custom fabric with black jeans rolled at the ankles and sharp black brogues. My shirt was the same design, but I was wearing black faux-leather pants and wedge-heeled sneakers with it. We were amazing together. We were going to be labeled #PowerCouple on Instagram again.

I twisted and rested against his warm, solid back. Mmm . . . every time we touched, I felt a full-body tingle combined with a deep sense of comfort. I sighed happily.

"Slide over a bit." Gia motioned us to the right. "That bird painted on the wall looks like it's flying out of Matteo's chest." Of course. Thwarted by birds, again. I'd started to slide over when Matteo pointed at a recently vacated floral-art-covered wall.

"We can go there," he said. "The shirts will look *sick* against the pink flowers."

"No. Stay here," I ordered. "I don't want flowers."

Matteo frowned. "Why not? You see Christopher Chan's spread in *StyleFactor* magazine? Flowers are happening this season."

I shook my head. Christopher Chan was one of my favorite New York designers, but his design aesthetic wasn't mine. "Flowers are Christopher Chan's thing because he used to be, like, a florist to the stars or something. I'm not into florals." Christopher Chan might have been a major name in streetwear, but I was developing my own style, and florals were not *me*.

After a few more pictures, we leaned against a wall painted with a detailed rendition of the solar system, except with cats instead of planets. I took a sip from the bottle of flavored soda water in my bag. It was hot for the last week of June. Much too hot to be in long sleeves and pleather pants, but fashion first.

Gia had a wistful look on her face. "When you're famous, we should totally spend a summer in Paris, like Nilusha. I look awesome in berets, and I got an A in French. A little pied-à-terre, a French male nurse . . ." She suddenly perked up with an idea. "Hey, you want me to see if I can get you a job at Old Navy with me?"

I'd tried to convince Gia to work on her career this summer and take acting classes or something, but she insisted her drama classes at school were enough. And she figured that if she was Instagram famous, then the acting jobs would come easily.

Matteo snorted. "Can you see Tahira working at Old Navy? She needs fashion industry experience for FIT, not folding T-shirts and jeans."

"Dude, you work at H&M," Gia said. "How is that not just a Swedish Old Navy?"

They argued mall stores before I was finally able to interrupt them. I needed to tell them the rest of my news. I took a breath. "Actually," I said, cringing, "I won't need to work at Old Navy because I have another job lined up, thanks to my parents."

It was impressive how quickly Mom and Dad had found me a replacement job—less than three hours after they'd seen Nilusha's email. Seemed I had been wrong about them not having valuable fashion industry connections. Although it was debatable how *valuable* this experience was going to be for me.

"It's a fashion industry position, which I theoretically could use for my FIT application portfolio," I said. "My aunt bought a ladieswear boutique, like, a year ago and needs someone to do a major overhaul. You know, new look, new merchandise, new visual design—the works."

Matteo brightened. "That's actually perfect! For sure you can get into FIT with that. Where's the store? Queen West?"

"That's the catch. It's not in Toronto."

"New York!" Gia said.

My eyes widened. "OMG, that would have been awesome. But no. It's in this tiny town, Bake . . . something. Near Niagara."

Gia shook her head. *"No,"* she said emphatically. "Taking off to New York is allowed, but you *cannot* go to some shit town in the middle of nowhere all summer."

"Believe me, I don't want to," I said. "I don't have a choice. There is nothing else on short notice. At least nothing that will give me the experience I need. Apparently, my aunt has, like, three vacancies she hasn't been able to fill for summer staff. No one in the town has any fashion retail experience."

Matteo's jaw was tight. "I can't believe your parents are forcing you to leave for the whole summer."

I put my arm around his waist. "I know. My aunt's going to put me up in a garden shed or something . . . you guys know I'm allergic to flowers. What did she call it . . . a 'granny flat'? A little house in the backyard. Like a pool house or something."

Gia's head shot around to look at me. "Seriously? You'd get to live in your *own apartment*? Like, that Paris dream could happen now?"

"It's, like, the most opposite of Paris possible." Well, that wasn't true. I was pretty sure New Zealand was opposite Paris on a globe, but this place was *ideologically* the opposite of Paris. I sighed. My parents' advice was usually spot on, but I had a lot of doubts about this. My life was here, in Toronto, not out in the country. "Maybe I should talk to my parents again. There's got to be another way—Gia, doesn't that one cousin of yours work at Saks? Can you ask if they're hiring merchandisers?"

"Cousin Angela quit and joined that cult in Alberta, didn't she?" Matteo asked. Gia and Matteo had about twelve more cousins together.

Gia didn't answer. Her eyes were twinkling. "You said your aunt had more than one job vacancy?"

"Yeah, apparently. Goes to show that no one *wants* to work there."

"Maybe I should apply . . . how big is that pool house?" Gia asked, a devilish grin on her face.

Holy crap. That was an *interesting* idea. Not something I'd considered, but . . . maybe living in that nothing town would be tolerable if I had my best friend with me? "But what about Old Navy?" I asked.

She smiled wide. "You think I actually *want* to be at Old Navy? C'mon, this could be fun! Meet some country boys, take some pictures. A summer away from our parents."

Matteo wrapped his arms around my waist. "Country boys?"

I shook my head. "None for me, thank you very much." I kissed his cheek. "I prefer city boys."

He shook his head. "You *both* can't leave Toronto all summer, though."

I didn't like the idea of leaving my first serious boyfriend. He'd graduated high school (he was a year older than me) and had just started the full-time job at H&M. We couldn't see each other much because he lived on literally the other side of Toronto—Etobicoke to my Scarborough—and neither of us had a car. But we were both supposed to be working downtown this summer—his job wasn't far from Nilusha Bhatt's design studio. That stupid French bird took that from me, too.

Gia laughed, patting his arm. "It's cool. We'll come home to see you weekends."

"It's retail, G," I said. "I'm assuming I'll be working weekends."

Matteo's gaze locked onto mine. "We had things we were going to do this summer. A photo shoot at Brick Works, Toronto Islands, and . . . other stuff, too. Isn't there a way you can stay?"

His lips were smiling, but those dark eyes told another story. I knew exactly what kind of *stuff* he wanted to get up to, and yeah, I didn't like missing out on that, either.

But I wasn't worried about losing Matteo, no matter where I worked this summer. All I had to see was that look in his eyes, and I knew he wasn't going anywhere. Neither was I. We were *solid*.

"I can't think of another way. I *need* the experience." I tightened my arms around him.

Gia clasped her hands together, pleading. "So, will you ask if I can come, too?"

I sighed. Maybe, having Gia with me in our own "apartment," the summer would be tolerable. Heck, it could be fun. "I'm not guaranteeing anything, but drop me your résumé, G. I'll call my aunt tonight."

Gia clapped and hopped up and down. "Yay, Tahira! We're going to have so much fun! Should I get, like, farm clothes or something?" She tilted her head. "Would I look cute in a cowboy hat?"

I wanted to laugh, but I could see the look in Matteo's eyes. He was upset about this. I leaned into him. "The summer will go fast," I promised, "and I'll come back whenever I can." I tilted up to kiss him. I loved Matteo's soft lips. The way he let out a tiny gasp every time I made the first move. I loved that he always tasted faintly like Hi-Chews, the chewy Japanese candy that only I knew he was mildly addicted to.

"Get a room," Gia groaned, but she was laughing. She was pretty proud that she was responsible for our epic happiness.

I giggled, resting my face in Matteo's neck. Soaking in the sun and letting the deep comfort of being wrapped around *him* envelop me.

"Just for eight weeks," I said. "I'm going to miss you."

He leaned close. "I'll miss you more," he murmured, and he kissed me above my ear.

"Mmm," was all I could say.

2

THAT'S NO SOIL

"Are you still pouting, Tahira?" Mom asked as she lifted one of my bags into the trunk of her SUV. It was the last Sunday in June, five days after my photo shoot downtown, and Mom was getting ready to drive me to Bakewell, Ontario, for the summer. Sharmin Aunty was thrilled I was coming, and after a quick phone interview, she'd agreed to hire Gia, too. Gia's dad would drive her up tomorrow, since she had some cousin's baby's baptism today.

"I'm not pouting, Mom." Really, I wasn't. I didn't pout. I didn't do duck face. I wasn't that kind of influencer. "I'm in *mourning.*"

I'd once seen an interview with a fashion editor on YouTube lamenting that interns were so whiny these days that she dreaded spending her summers with students. There was no chance that editor would ever hire me anyway—from looking at her miserable interns, it was clear I had way too much melanin for her tastes. But still. I'd trained myself off pouting that day.

Mom made a disparaging sound. "You should be grateful for this opportunity with Sharmin. She didn't have to hire you. Or your friend."

Honestly, I *was* grateful. But this speech was dangerously close to one of those "Children are starving, and you're upset about losing an internship?" lectures. I'd heard it several times already, and I did my part to help the world's disenfranchised kids, anyway. I sewed most of my own clothes and avoided fast fashion like the plague.

"Tahira! Hey, Tahira!" a voice behind me called out.

I turned to see our neighbor Kayla rushing toward me, her brown ponytail bobbing behind her. She had a large black book in her hand. "Are you leaving today? I finished that sketch!"

Kayla was thirteen. I used to babysit her years ago and had babysat her brother once recently. He was a nightmare, though—I'd been avoiding Kayla's mother so she wouldn't ask me again. A few months ago, I'd helped Kayla with her application portfolio for the specialty art high school that I went to, and she still liked to show me her art.

Smiling, I opened her sketchbook. Kayla wasn't into fashion illustration, so it wasn't the same kind of stuff I did, but she was good. She did a lot of fan art of this character with silver eyes from a book series she liked in charcoal or acrylic paint and was already improving so much. I always made a point to give her tips and compliment her work, since her parents didn't care about her art at all. All they cared about lately was that she took care of her brother.

"This is amazing," I said. "The shading on the hair is so good!"

Kayla beamed. "Do you think so?"

"Totally. Are you going to add any colors?"

Kayla frowned. "Mom said I have to share my pencil crayons with Evan. He lost half of them. And he chewed one up. Or the dog did."

I cringed. I'd bought her those expensive art pencils for her birthday. They were way too good for a four-year-old.

"Tahira," Mom called out, "we need to get on the road."

I gave the sketchbook back to Kayla and rummaged in my backpack to get something. "Here." I handed her a tin of Prismacolor pencils. "Hide these from Evan. I want to see the sketch when it's done—text me a picture."

"Are you sure?" Kayla said, looking at the tin of pencils wide eyed.

"Of course." I could always order more. "Just keep them safe from your brother, okay?"

She nodded happily as she waved goodbye and headed back to her house, two doors away.

All my stuff was finally in the car a few minutes later, and Mom was pulling out of the driveway, when my sister, Samaya, came running out to wave goodbye. I waved back as we drove away.

"Did your sister tell you that she got that counselor-in-training position at that math camp at the University of Toronto?" Mom said. "The same one your cousin Abid went to. She just got the email last night."

I smiled. "Yay! I haven't seen her today." I knew how much Samaya wanted that role, but I had been out with Matteo last night, and she'd been in her room all morning. I made a mental note to call her when I got to Bakewell.

The drive was long and mostly uneventful. I pulled out my iPad Pro and Apple Pencil and sketched a new sweatshirt design to pass the time.

"I don't know how you draw in the car," Mom said. "I would get carsick."

I shrugged. I played around with adding puffy sleeves to the sweatshirt silhouette, but I wasn't convinced it was working as well as it did in my head.

"Sharmin said she got new sheets for your beds yesterday," Mom said. "She really wants to make sure you girls are comfortable. Show her your gratitude when you get there."

"Of course, Mom, I know."

"It's very generous of her not to charge you rent for the granny flat. You and Gia will be able to keep all your wages from the boutique. You'll both have lots of savings for college after this summer."

Mom was still being super enthusiastic about this whole thing, maybe because she thought she had to sell it to me? It wasn't necessary. I was still a little skeptical, mostly because I didn't know what to expect from the store, but for the most part, I was okay with this whole summer-in-Bakewell plan. I could suck it up for two months. I'd get the fashion experience I needed for my application, and Gia and I could chill with no one but my coolest aunty to supervise. I could keep designing and sewing for my FIT portfolio in my free time, and we'd find a fabulous backdrop for photos in Bakewell for my Instagram. It would be fine.

I narrowed my eyes at my sketch. The puffy sleeves definitely weren't working, so I erased them. Maybe a Juliet sleeve instead?

"Did you end up talking to Nilusha yesterday?" Mom asked after a while.

I nodded. "Yeah. She feels really bad that she had to cancel my internship. She said she would still be my mentor if I wanted. She offered to FaceTime once a week."

Mom beamed. "Tahira! That's amazing. See! I told you. It's all about networking. Even if you won't be working together, you've still made the connection. It's just as good."

It didn't seem just as good to me. Working with Nilusha would've been beyond a dream job. I was probably the only high schooler with the balls to apply, and the references, thanks to two summers working at that boutique on Yorkville Avenue downtown. It was dumb luck that she'd had an opening starting July first. Nilusha's designs were getting serious buzz in the city, and everything about her was complete *goals*. She was exponentially cool, incredibly generous, and Indian, like me. It was great that she wanted to be my mentor, but I was still sad she wouldn't be my boss.

I frowned, shaking my head at my design. The Juliet sleeves were no good, either.

"Did you see the new YouTube Marsha Logan posted?" Mom asked. "She had great tips on next-level networking and social media engagement."

Marsha Logan and Christopher Chan were some of the designers who routinely made videos on YouTube about breaking into the fashion industry. It was from watching those videos that Mom was helping me figure out exactly what I needed to do to reach my goal of admission into FIT and my own fashion brand. Mom calculated that, in addition to top internships and networking, I needed a follower count in the tens of thousands on at least one social media platform. We'd picked Instagram.

I didn't normally mind talking about my career Plan with Mom, but I wasn't feeling it right now. I'd had such a great date with Matteo last night, and I was bummed I wouldn't see him for a while. Apparently, there was no bus or train from Bakewell to Toronto—so either he'd have to borrow his brother's car to see me or we'd have to make do with FaceTime. It sucked.

I looked out the window. We'd been on the road for over an hour now, and I'd seen nothing but trees, cows, and crappy box restaurants for a while. This was practically the middle of nowhere.

What had I gotten myself into?

I slunk down in my seat. "I hope going here isn't a mistake, Mom."

"Of course it's not a mistake! I know you're upset about losing your internship, but that doesn't derail your Plan! Keep your spirits up, Tahira. Next summer you can get a job with another designer. What would your father say if he was here?"

I exhaled. It would be nice if Mom would sometimes turn off the motivational speaker and just let me rant.

If Dad were here, he would say learning to deal with whatever shit life threw in your path builds character or something, but he'd say it much more lawyer-y. I didn't normally mind their cheesy pep talks much, mostly because in the grand scheme of things, I had so much more freedom than my other Indian friends. I was allowed to date who I wanted, wear what I wanted, and work all the way downtown. The only things my parents were tough about were schoolwork and our extracurriculars. Samaya had been literally grounded last month for playing online games three hours longer than she'd practiced advanced math functions.

"You know how important your FIT application is," Mom continued. "Your father was the only child in generations of his family to go to university, and he did it with a scholarship. How did he achieve that? Not giving up when roadblocks turned up. Remember— *Janmohammads always succeed.* You aren't giving up, either. You're not going to be working for Bakewell; you're going to make Bakewell *work for you.*"

I'd heard this speech so many times. *Janmohammads always succeed.* We'd have it embroidered on a plaque on a wall, but our name was too long and Mom got frustrated by the second *m*. Samaya did once create the family motto on a graphing calculator using advanced functions, but my parents couldn't figure out how to frame it.

I looked back down at my iPad, shaking my head at the design. Right now, I couldn't see how ending up in Bakewell was *succeeding.*

Mom turned into the driveway of what appeared to be a huge garden center. I doubted we were in Bakewell yet, considering the only thing I could see was a whole lot of nothing. Fields. Trees. And this massive store.

"I called ahead," she said as she parked her car. "I want to bring Sharmin a big-ticket gift to thank her for rescuing you. She's been eyeing a backyard fountain from this place. You sit—I'll have them bring it out."

I shrugged. I kind of needed to stretch my legs, so I opened the door. "Where are we?"

"Wynter's Nurseries," Mom said. "I told you this whole area is covered with greenhouses and flower farms, didn't I? People drive up from the city all the time to see them."

I made a face. "You said farms. I don't remember them being *flower* farms."

16

"I definitely said 'flower.'"

I stepped out to look around. The gravel parking lot seemed endless and was filled with standard garden-center stuff—random plants and tacky statues. The store itself was a big greenhouse. When we got to the doors, Mom stopped. "Did you take an allergy pill?"

"Uh . . . no."

Mom shook her head. "Don't come in. You don't want your allergies acting up now."

She had a point. I was allergic to a lot of things—cats, most dogs, trees—but flowers were the worst. I could usually manage flowers outside as long as I didn't stick my nose in them, but flowers indoors were a disaster on my eyes. I didn't want to look like I had smoked something I shouldn't have when I saw my aunt.

I shrugged. "Okay. I'll walk around. Text me when you're done."

I wandered to the back of the store and was surprised at what I saw there. In the distance on the right was a massive stand-alone greenhouse. The store greenhouse was big . . . like tennis-court big. But this one was football-field big. In front of it was a really cool-looking barn thing. I'd always thought barns were red and had those round roofs, but this had a regular peaked roof, and instead of red, it was painted gray. Well, except for the lower half of the wall. It had a mural painted on it—an intricate geometric pattern made up of little triangles in shades of blue and purple, with a few bursts of green peppered in. The juxtaposition of the weathered gray walls and the vibrant mural was striking, and honestly, way too modern for out here in the country.

I was wearing some of the newer pieces I'd made myself. A pair of fitted black shorts, a loose white silk T-shirt with an embossed black zigzag across it, and a long sheer black duster cardigan. Plus, my newest purchase—red suede ankle boots. These were a killer find—I'd bought them at a vintage store in Kensington Market after we'd finished our shoot at Graffiti Alley last week.

That seemed like a lifetime ago now. Out past the barn was nothing but fields, trees, and that enormous greenhouse in the distance.

The barn *was* fabulous, though. And the light was perfect for photos—just a bit of cloud cover. I normally avoided selfies, but I *needed* this outfit against that wall on my page, and I didn't want to trust the light would be this good if I came back with Gia later. Plus, how exactly would we come back anyway? Not like either of us drove. Or had a car.

There was a bunch of crap on the ground in front of the best part of the mural—where the blues blended to deep purples. I looked at the junk—three plastic pots filled with random flowers and two large bags of soil.

Not a problem. I could move them.

I dragged the two larger pots away, careful not to get too close to the pollen-y looking flowers. The third pot was smaller, so I lifted it. Keeping my nose turned away from the offending flora, I walked it over to the other two. And that's when I noticed that the stupid pot was dripping brown water on my boots. *Ugh.* My beautiful red vintage boots.

I put the pot down. Both my feet had large spots on them. The boots were probably salvageable, but I'd need a soft brush and gentle soap to clean suede.

This was all a terrible idea. I glanced back at the gorgeous mural, then at my amazing outfit. What would Mom and Dad say?

I went back for the bags of soil. Those looked heavy. Dragging them across the gravel would tear the plastic. No problem—I'd carry them. I bent my knees, picked up one bag, and stood.

"What the *hell* do you think you're doing?" asked a deep voice behind me. And I jumped, because I always jumped when startled. But unfortunately, this time jumping meant flinging the bag of soil out of my hands. It crashed to the ground, splitting down the middle and spilling dark dirt all over my wet suede boots. Inside and out.

"Fuck!" I screamed.

There was soil literally everywhere. Halfway up my legs. On my boots. *In* my boots. Some had even managed to get on my silk T-shirt. I spun to face the saboteur who'd done this to me. Or saboteurs, I should say, because two people were coming, a guy and a girl.

"Oh my God, are you okay?" the girl asked.

I pointed at my feet. "No, I'm not okay! Look at my shoes. You two scared the crap out of me!"

They'd reached me by then, and the guy scowled at me. "Are you serious? You're worried about your *shoes*? Look at this mess!"

I stepped out of the pile of soil. I could have cleaned the dirty plant water off my boots, but now, because of these two, they were completely ruined.

I made an irritated noise and glared at the shoe wreckers. They both looked about my age, she was white and he was Black, and they were both wearing these short little green apron/tool-belt things that said WYNTER's on them. The girl's shirt had a cartoon rabbit with the phrase I WORK HARD FOR THE BUNNY under it, and the guy was wearing cutoff denim shorts and an even stranger T-shirt—pale orange, with a picture of a Stormtrooper mask made completely out of colorful flowers. Below the mask were the words, THESE AREN'T THE PLANTS YOU'RE LOOKING FOR.

Where did these two buy their clothes? Was this the work uniform around here?

But their faces were quite cute. Her lips were downturned with concern, but her eyes sparkled playfully. The long, curly auburn hair, fresh face, and happy eyes were all a bit . . . wholesome. She was very pretty but had kind of an Anne of Green Gables country vibe.

The guy, well, he still had that killer scowl on his face.

"Care to tell us what you're doing here?" he asked.

I tried to shake the dirt off my boots, but it was a lost cause. "I was trying to move this stuff so I could get a picture for my Instagram. You two work here?"

The girl pointed at her apron. "Obviously."

I did kind of feel bad for them, both for those shirts and for the soil everywhere. "I'm sorry about this mess. I can help clean it up. And I'll pay for the dirt—"

"Can you not *read?*" Flower Stormtrooper Shirt asked, arms folded across his chest.

I frowned. What was he talking about?

He pointed at a sign that I hadn't noticed on the wall of the barn. A camera and a phone with a red line through them.

The redhead smirked. "I can help you decipher it—we keep the signs to a kindergarten-level comprehension. No pictures!"

Okay, so maybe she wasn't so wholesome after all. Anne of Green Gables in the novel had a temper, but she wasn't *mean.*

"I can't take a picture of a wall?" I asked. "Is this place, like, IDK, a CIA front or something?"

The girl snorted a laugh. "This is Canada! It would be CSIS, not CIA. However . . ." She peered at me through long lashes, pure mischief on her face. "I'm not denying anything." She pinched her shirt and lifted it to her mouth, pretending there was a microphone in it. At least I thought she was pretending. "Code red. She's onto us. *The red bird has run out of seeds.* I repeat, *the red bird—*"

Flower Stormtrooper Guy smacked her arm. "Can you be serious right now?"

I was in agreement—I wasn't in the mood for this girl's annoying brand of humor right now.

"I can credit this place in my pictures to make it up to you," I said. "I have over twenty thousand followers."

Flower Stormtrooper gave me a glassy stare. "Do you think we care how many mindless zombies you managed to attract with your bloated-ego thirst traps?"

Wow. Way to rub salt in my wound. Or rather, dirt. I wasn't posting pictures of myself on Instagram to make people *desire me* or something. I was building my brand.

"Excuse me?" I asked.

He waved his hands with agitation. "We've had enough of people like you coming out here to take pictures for your precious social media. We don't need any more trampled lavender fields or beheaded roses. Last year someone took down a seven-foot sunflower stem outside the garden center when they grabbed it because a bird flapped near them. And now we have to clean up all this manure!"

Sunflower stems were seven feet tall around here? After the parakeet thing, I kind of understood being afraid of a bird. But he was being *rude.* Even after I'd *apologized.* I offered to help clean up. I offered to pay for the spilled—wait, *what?*

"What did you say this was?" I looked down.

The redhead flipped her hair over her shoulder and smirked. "Sheep manure."

"Manure?" This was *manure,* not soil. Literally, shit. I closed my eyes.

"I mean," she continued, "it's composted manure, so it's mostly sterilized. C'mon, you look like the type to bathe in curated poop at one of those fancy spa places. Manure is no big deal."

Flower Stormtrooper scowled again. "It is a big deal that there is manure all over the gravel."

I glared at them sharply. "Can you stop saying that word?"

The girl chuckled. "Would you prefer we called it sheep shit? Poo? Excrement? Softened turds?"

Honestly, I would've preferred they both stopped talking.

I sighed. I was far from home, covered in poo, and had completely lost my will to fight back. "I just wanted a picture."

"Well, this isn't your personal photo booth," said Flower Trooper. "It's a *business,* and we need to work, not argue with wannabe *influencers* or clean up your messes." He took a deep breath, preparing himself for more. "No trespassing, no moving stock around to suit your whims, and *no pictures*. Now please leave so we can clean this up." He snorted at my shoes, shaking his head.

I didn't need to be told twice. I walked toward Mom's car. Which was gross, because I could feel the squish of manure in my boots with every step. I wanted to vomit.

"I don't want to be here. I don't like your fucking town!" I called out without turning back.

Two feet from the car, I unleashed a series of sneezes that I swore pulled a stomach muscle.

I really, really didn't want to be in Bakewell.

3

TINY HOUSE OF PINE

I had no choice but to leave my poop-covered boots on for the fifteen-minute drive to my aunt's. There were six other pairs of shoes in the trunk, but I wasn't about to change, or even go barefoot, until I took off (and burned) these socks and scoured my feet clean. All I could do was wipe the suede with a napkin while Mom tried not to laugh. I gave her a much-deserved pout.

I texted Gia that there was no way my first day in Bakewell could get worse—there was only uphill from here.

Mom pointed out the window. "Look, we're in Bakewell."

Yup. There was the town welcome sign. A large carved wood monstrosity with the words WELCOME TO BAKEWELL, FLOWER CAPITAL OF ONTARIO surrounded by painted wood flowers. It was speared next to a highway overpass on a little patch covered, of course, with real flowers in shades of . . . well, all the shades. So many colors. Too many flowers, if you asked me. I was glad I'd packed the Costco-size bottle of antihistamines. I'd need them.

I added to the text.

We may have made a colossal mistake.

Gia didn't respond. I texted Matteo, but also, no answer. They were probably still at that baptism.

A few minutes later, Mom turned onto a street, saying, "Here we are, Tahira."

The street looked kind of weird. Since this was the so-called flower capital of Ontario, it was no surprise that all the houses had pretty, well-maintained gardens. But they were spaced farther apart than I was used to, and they were all different sizes and colors.

Mom pulled into the driveway of a standard, small redbrick house with a green lawn and a nice garden out front. "This is Sharmin Aunty's place," she said, but I couldn't help staring at the house next door. It was also redbrick with a beige garage, but it was twice as big as my aunt's place and had a massive, overstuffed garden with weird winding paths and a large statue of . . . was that a rabbit? About four feet high and made of twigs and flowers, it was perched in the middle of the yard and surrounded by enough flowers to make the overpass look like a barren field.

Way. Too. Many. Flowers.

I imagined an overly nosy garden-obsessed retiree lived there. Hopefully they'd stay out of my and Gia's hair this summer.

"Come, let's say hello before we bring in your things," Mom said, taking the path to Sharmin Aunty's front porch.

"Sabina! Tahira! You're here already?" Sharmin Aunty floated out the door, her long, flowy summer dress dancing in the breeze behind her.

My aunt (Mom's cousin, not her sister) was a couple of years older than Mom, so probably in her early fifties. She'd always been the *Why walk when you can sashay?* type. She'd worked in the lingerie department of a posh store in downtown Toronto for years, which was great because she'd kept me stocked with Dolce & Gabbana Light Blue fragrance with a new bottle every Eid since I was twelve. After her ex traded her for a Mercedes-AMG GT a year ago, it was no surprise to the family that Sharmin Aunty promptly bought her own store with her divorce settlement. That had always been her dream. Though why she bought one in the middle of nowhere was anyone's guess.

We did that desi kiss-on-both-cheeks thing, and then Sharmin Aunty took me by both hands. "Let me look at you, Tahira. So beautiful. I think you're even taller than the last time I saw you. When your mother reminded me that you're applying for college, I nearly fainted. The girl who used to rummage through my purse looking for lipstick is not allowed to grow up." She put a dramatic hand to her forehead. "I feel like an antique. Now I'll be taking makeup tips from you!" My aunty smiled at me. "Come, I'll show you the main house first."

"U-um," I stuttered.

Mothers, of course, never felt secondhand embarrassment for their daughters. "Tahira needs to wash her feet. There was an incident at the nursery."

"Of course, of course," Sharmin Aunty said. "Let's go to the flat first, then. Did you go to Wynter's?"

"Yes," Mom said, beaming. "We got you that fountain!"

We went back to the car, where there was much squealing, thanking, and insisting Mom was much too generous while I stood there, trying to hide my impatience to rid myself of manure.

After we finally grabbed my things and headed to the backyard, the total explosion of flowers that greeted us there didn't surprise me. What was a shock was that the massive space behind the houses wasn't divided into separate backyards. No fences at all. I could kind of make out some property lines between Sharmin Aunty's yard and several of the houses on the one side because of different lawn-mowing habits, but there was no hint of a property line at all between her yard and the flower-vomit house's yard. In fact, a stone patio with a low table and wicker outdoor sofas was positioned right between the yards, exactly where I would have thought a fence should be. Seemed my aunt was close to the garden-obsessed lady. Privacy was going to be in short supply here.

25

Also, I wasn't sure what I'd expected from this "granny flat," but I wasn't seeing anything that resembled an apartment in Sharmin Aunty's yard. There were two structures—a cool-looking wood and glass greenhouse on the neighbor's side and, closer to my aunt's house, a yellow shed with a red screen door and one window. It was . . . *little*. God, that couldn't be the . . .

"Here's the granny flat!" Sharmin Aunty said, wheeling my suitcase over the uneven stepping-stones leading to the yellow shed . . . er . . . flat.

"It's charming, isn't it?" she continued. "I bought this house from Joanne and Leeland Langston when they moved to a farm last year. Leeland's mother lived in this flat for years—she's in a nursing home now. She's almost ninety-nine years old!"

"It's so adorable!" Mom said.

In front of the teeny structure with a wide-open door was a little concrete pad with two old lounge chairs.

"I've been airing it out all day. Here, let's let in some light." She pulled open the window curtains. I had my sewing machine in one hand and a duffel bag over my shoulder, and I was pushing my dress form (whom I'd named Ruby) on her wheels. I put the sewing machine on a pine table a few feet into the room, put Ruby on the pine floor near a pine ladder, and dropped my duffel bag on the pine-backed sofa. The pine table on the pine floor was a bit much, but the pine walls, pine coffee table, pine chairs, and pine cabinets needed an honorable mention, too. As a whole, it was . . . a lot of pine. The place was more like a small wooden living room than a "flat." Not that I knew what a flat was—but I'd expected something like a bachelor apartment.

"You or your friend can sleep here. It's a daybed," Sharmin Aunty said about what I thought was a sofa with, you guessed it, pine legs and many, many pillows. One of which had a wood-grain print. "It's only a single, but there's a loft with a bed up there." She pointed to the pine ladder / steep staircase thing at the end of the room leading to a plat-form that covered about half the square footage of the place.

"Just like when you used to sleep on the top bunk when you were a girl!" Mom was still being super enthusiastic.

"Bathroom is here." Sharmin Aunty walked three steps to a sliding door on a heavy iron rail near the ladder. "I know it's a bit snug, but I think you'll be comfortable."

"This will be fine, right, Tahira?" Mom asked.

I gritted my teeth and nodded. "It's cute as a button," I said. "Gia and I are tight; we'll be fine." I opened the duffel and pulled some clean clothes out. "I'll just go . . ." I squeezed past Mom and Sharmin Aunty and went into the bathroom.

The bathroom was remarkably lacking in pine but was also teeny. All I needed was water and soap right now, and thankfully it had that. After scrubbing my feet red under the tap in the shower stall, I dried off with one of the towels from the shelf above the toilet and put on fresh socks and a clean shirt. I checked myself in the mirror. The shirt was another one of my own designs—a short-sleeved and collarless button-up. Down one side I'd appliquéd the letters *HOT*, which stood for House of Tahira, the name of my someday fashion line. I tied the hem into a knot and returned to Mom and Sharmin Aunty.

"Tahira," Mom said, pointing out the window, "Sharmin was show-ing me some of the improvements to the garden since I was last here. It's quite a change."

"It's really cool," I said, nodding. I couldn't comment on any of the changes, though. This was my first time visiting. Between school, fashion show committee, photography club, and my evening sewing classes, I hadn't had a chance to come up here with Mom before. Also, I was the last person to judge the aesthetics of a garden.

Sharmin Aunty led us outside. "All this is Rowan's and Juniper's doing. They'll be thrilled I got the fountain we wanted." She pointed to a patch of dirt over by the patio. "They're putting a new flower bed there. The ground is giving them trouble, though. The soil here is rich clay—great for growing but hard as sin to dig out. Come. Let's get some chai on back at the house."

"This couple, Rowan and Juniper, they own the house next door?" Mom asked as we followed Sharmin Aunty up the path.

Sharmin Aunty laughed as she slid open a sliding glass door into the main house. "Couple? Oh no. Rowan and Juniper are about Tahira's age. Their parents own the house."

Mom beamed at me. "That's wonderful! You'll have friends right next door!"

I nodded noncommittally as I stepped into the kitchen. Honestly, I didn't need friends in Bakewell other than Gia. Work at the store, then work on my portfolio. That was the plan. Not hang out with country folk who put four-foot rabbits on their front lawn.

"I ended up hiring Juniper in the store part-time," Sharmin Aunty said as she put some mugs on a tray. "Her father wanted her to work at the nursery with Rowan, but June was adamant she didn't want to work there. You'll like her—she's a sweet girl. Last week, I took her to the jamboree in the town over to watch her brother and their friend in the rabbit obstacle trials, since their mother had to cover for the other doctor in town. You should have seen the little bunnies hop through hoops! I can't imagine how long it took to train them."

What? What was with this rabbit obsession? These kids sounded weird. Clearly, I wasn't in Kansas anymore. Or rather, I was a lot closer to Kansas than I'd ever been.

"You'll have to keep the rabbits away from Tahira," Mom said. "She's allergic."

Sharmin Aunty laughed, patting Mom on the arm. "I know, I know. You told me her entire medical history." She winked at me. "C'mon, let me show you around while the tea brews."

The inside of the house was really . . . well, country. Wagon wheel coffee table, dried flowers everywhere, and a lot more wood than I expected.

Not as much pine as the granny flat, but still. My coolest aunty had gone full-on backwoods bumpkin since moving out here. The house was bright, though. And it smelled like masala chai, just like my home.

"It's a bit small, I know," Sharmin Aunty said as she showed me the living and dining room. "But I've had so much fun furnishing with antiques. I even picked up one of those old-fashioned sewing tables for you."

I smiled. "Thank you."

"I'll have Rowan and Juniper bring it out from the garage. Oh, and here." She handed me a stack of linens that were on the dining table. "I bought new bedding for the loft bed, but with my back there's no way I could set it up. Do you mind, Tahira?"

I smiled. "No problem. I'll do it now. I want to unpack some of my stuff before Gia gets here, anyway."

I took the sheets and went back out the kitchen door to the granny flat. I took stock inside for a moment, looking around without having to praise it just to be polite. The apartment was minuscule, but it wasn't *that* bad. The window was huge, so the space was bright at least. There wasn't much storage, but I could probably fit my sewing supplies under the table. I put the new sheets on my bed in the loft, then climbed back down and started unpacking my sewing machine and supplies.

I had just dug out my cookie tin filled with scissors, machine needles, bobbin thread, and other notions when my Instagram notification went off. I checked my phone. Of course—it was Sunday, and I had an alert set up for the Indie Fashion Weekly roundup. The account was run by the *DashStyle* fashion blog, and every Monday they posted a prompt. Emerging designers like me could post an outfit or a fashion illustration inspired by the prompt, along with the hashtag #IndieFashionWeekly. Then on Sundays the *DashStyle* people picked about five highlights of the best entries and posted them on their page. I wasn't entirely sure who picked the posts that got highlighted, but it was a major boost for an indie designer's visibility. I'd been doing the prompts for months, but my work had never been picked as a highlight.

I sat on the sofa and opened the page. The prompt this week was gray scale, which was so perfect for those shirts I'd made for that Graffiti Alley shoot. The photo I'd hashtagged #IndieFashionWeekly had over three hundred likes. For sure I'd be highlighted this time.

But I wasn't. My stomach clenched. Why wasn't I there? What was I doing wrong? I texted Matteo.

Tahira: Do you actually think I'm a good designer?

He wrote back immediately—which was so sweet of him because I was pretty sure he was still at that kid's baptism.

Matteo: Of course. You're amazing.

Tahira: I didn't get featured on the Weekly Indie thing again.

Matteo: Ugh. You'll get it next time. We can build up your profile, get you more followers. I'll help you babe. Anyway, can I call you later? I'm still in church.

Tahira: No worries. Talk soon. Tell G I'll see her tomorrow.

I rubbed the back of my neck as I stared at the picture of Matteo and me in our gray and white shirts. I had a healthy twenty thousand followers on Instagram. Maybe that wasn't enough to catch the attention of this style blog?

I checked out the accounts that had gotten profiled this week. Most had more followers than me, but their designs weren't really better than mine. Okay, maybe that one was pretty spectacular—but I could see puckering on the seam on one of the others.

So maybe it wasn't my platform, or my talent. Maybe there was something else I was missing. A certain . . . spark. *It factor*. Originality.

I worked hard. Really, really hard. But without that certain *something*, it was all for nothing.

I sighed, chewing on my lip. This was ridiculous. My day had already been bad enough. Self-loathing wasn't going to help with my Plan. I grabbed my iPad and opened the illustration of the shirt I'd been working on in the car. And it hit me.

Bell sleeves.

I quickly erased the Juliet sleeves and drew new sleeves that were tight around the upper arms and widened under the elbow. Yes. It was *perfect*. I could do this. No more self-doubt allowed. Only confidence that the Plan would work.

After putting away my iPad and the rest of my sewing stuff, I hurried back out to the yard, where Mom and Sharmin Aunty were having tea.

"Sorry I took so long," I said. "I was finishing a design."

Sharmin Aunty waved me over. "Tahira. Come meet Juniper!"

A girl stood up from the garden on the far side of the patio. She held a trowel. I guess she'd been crouched, digging.

When she saw me, she squealed with glee, and, well, the only way to describe the way she headed over to me was she bounded. Like Bambi.

"Yay! You're here, you're here!" She stopped in front of me and wiped the dirt off her hand. "I was so excited when Shar told me someone my age was moving in all summer! I'm Juniper Jessica Johnston." She shot her hand out to me. "Terrible, right? My parents think alliteration is sooo cute. I go by either June or Juniper, and I honestly have no preference. I'm sixteen, my pronouns are she/her, and I'll be in grade twelve in September. Ooh, I forgot. I have something for you." She grinned and skipped off toward the greenhouse at the far end of the yard.

Juniper was a bit too perky but still kind of adorable. Tight curls in a low ponytail and wide, dark, round eyes. She was wearing cutoff black shorts, an open flannel shirt with a fitted black camisole under it, and a ribbon choker with a heart locket in the middle. Also, she was Black, with smooth medium-brown skin. In fact, her skin tone, eyes, and cheekbones were exactly the same as the grumpy nursery guy's . . . and Sharmin Aunty said Juniper's brother, Rowan, worked at the nursery. Which meant he was probably Mr. Flower Stormtrooper.

Great. I'd be living next door to *that* guy all summer. I'd been wrong. It *was* possible for my day to get worse.

4

SO THEY'RE NAMED AFTER TREES?

"S he is probably going to give you flowers," Sharmin Aunty said as Juniper disappeared into the greenhouse. "I should have told you: June likes to give meaningful bouquets to everyone."

"What a thoughtful neighbor," Mom said. "Tahira, don't get the flowers too close to your face."

Sharmin Aunty nodded. "Juniper and Rowan are both so thoughtful. I'm so lucky to have such great neighbors here. Bakewell's not completely white, but they are one of the only Black families in town. They've had to deal with some intolerance and microaggressions . . . not a lot, but any is too much. The kids are so well adjusted, though. You'll love living next to them, Tahira."

I was sorry to hear about the racism, but honestly? I doubted this guy was going to be happy to see me here, assuming he *was* the "These aren't the plants you're looking for" guy.

Juniper reappeared then, holding a bundle of flowers wrapped with a yellow ribbon. I took them, keeping my eyes and nose away from the blooms.

"This is a welcome bouquet," Juniper said. "I used chrysanthemums and sunflowers to symbolize friendship. Did you know that sunflowers are really called helianthus? I added some daffodils to symbolize new beginnings. Their real name is narcissus. Oh! I hope you don't think I'm calling you a narcissist! Although it's the white ones that are commonly called narcissus . . . the yellow ones are daffodils, even though the scientific names for both are narcissus. They're one of the earliest spring flowers—that's why they symbolize new beginnings." She beamed, proud of her arrangement.

"Thank you," I said. They were kind of pretty—I liked the yellow with the deep burgundy. The girl could have had no idea I was allergic to flowers, so this was a nice gesture. A little weird, but nice. "I . . . um . . ."

"They're lovely," Sharmin Aunty said, taking the bundle from me. "I'll put them in my kitchen so Tahira can see them when she comes in for dinner. Come have some chai, Tahira."

I sat on the outdoor sofa while Juniper went back to her digging. Sharmin Aunty asked me some questions about school and my sewing classes. Mom was, of course, glued to her email on her phone, even though it was a Sunday.

Mom suddenly stood. "There's a crisis in the Ottawa hotel. I'm going to have to call in. I'll go inside; you keep catching up." She headed to the house.

I sighed. Mom was always on call if an HR emergency came up at the hotel company she worked at. She was a workaholic, like Dad. It was a Janmohammad family trait.

Juniper turned from her digging so she could face me. "What grade are you going into?" she asked.

"Twelve. I just turned seventeen," I said.

"Same grade as me! Except my birthday's in December, so I'm still sixteen."

She seemed younger than sixteen to me. Small-town kids just weren't as sophisticated.

"My brother Rowan's eighteen," Juniper continued. "He's going to university in September. He's excited you're here, too."

I stifled a snort. That wasn't likely.

"Do you have any brothers or sisters?"

I nodded. "Yeah, a sister, Samaya. She's a year younger."

"I wish I had a sister. You'll miss her this summer—hope she can come up for a visit."

I shrugged. "We're not really close." I mean, I liked my sister fine, but it was hard to relate to her since we had nothing in common. She went to a high school that specialized in math and science, while I went to the best art-focused high school in the city. Still, I did need to remember to call Samaya tonight to congratulate her for getting that math camp position that she wanted so much.

"I'm trying to dig out this garden bed before Row gets home," Juniper said. "He's been in a shitty—sorry," she said, glancing at Sharmin Aunty. "He's been in a *bad* mood all week."

Sharmin Aunty snorted. "You know you don't have to sanitize your language for me, June. Is your brother okay?"

"Yeah, it's just the usual. Dad and him were"—Juniper made air quotes with her fingers—"'discussing his options' again this morning. More like Dad was talking and Row was sulking." Juniper turned back to me. "Dad refuses to see that we're not little kids who want to be just like him anymore. He still calls us his 'little saplings.' You'd think he'd be okay with his oldest sapling wanting a career in gardens."

I must have looked confused, because Juniper grinned. "Rowan and I are both named after trees."

Ah. Cute.

"Tahira is a cool name," Juniper continued, dropping her trowel and joining me at the table. "Do you ever shorten it? Because I don't want to call you something you don't like." I shook my head, but Juniper was still talking. "It's funny—we're kind of a flower family since my grandma was a florist, but Dad used to work more with trees when he was starting out in botany, so we got tree names. But now he's working at the nursery, and Rowan and I are all about gardens and flowers. Can you imagine if Dad named us after flowers? We'd have been Chrysanthemum and Clematis. Chrissy and Clem! Maybe we would have fit in here more . . . did Shar tell you I'll be working at Lilybuds with you this summer?"

I cringed. I'd been making a genuine effort not to think about the fact that the store I was depending on to get fashion experience for FIT was called Lilybuds. Terrible name.

Sharmin Aunty picked up the teapot. "Can I pour you a chai, June?"

"Ooh, yes, please. Is it from Hyacinth's?" She grinned at me. "Hyacinth's is this café downtown that has custom tea blends and these amazing Bakewell tarts. Did you know that Bakewell is named after a village in England? And Bakewell tarts are named after that village. Hyacinth's Bakewell tarts are sooo good. I want to see the real Bakewell one day. There's this big house there that was used as Mr. Darcy's house in the *Pride and Prejudice* movie. Not that I'm into Jane Austen or anything; I'm more of a contemporary or urban fantasy reader myself. But I hear the gardens are spectacular. Row and I want to go one day."

I raised my brow. On one hand, I liked Juniper's innocence, and she seemed nice enough. On the other hand, considering I'd be both living next door to and working with this girl, it kind of sucked that we had nothing in common. Also, her chattiness might get exhausting after a while.

Sharmin Aunty and Juniper started asking me about my art school. It got a little intense, with both of them peppering me with questions about what courses I was taking and what programs they offered, so at a lull in the interrogation, I stood.

"This garden is so pretty. I'm going to look around," I said. I pulled out my phone as soon as I was ten feet from the patio and texted Matteo.

Everything in this town has flowers on it. People drink tea from flowered teapots and train rabbits and fantasize about visiting gardens in England.

When there was no answer, I tried Gia.

The backyard we're living in makes your Nona's garden look like a parking lot. Flower overkill.

But even for flower overkill, I had to admit it was impressive. The garden had three clusters of plantings, each with different flower varieties in them. Even though there were so many different types, the colors in each bed were all coordinated. In one corner was what I assumed was a vegetable garden, based on the round cage things like the ones Gia's grandmother used on tomato plants. In front of the greenhouse was a big weathered-wood workbench with some trays of plants on it. Maybe Juniper was planning to plant those in the garden where she was digging.

As a whole, the garden was very full, very colorful, and it was obvious a ton of work had been put into it. It was probably even more work to maintain. Honestly, if someone was into the whole English country garden vibe, this place would be a dream. I knew more than a few Instagrammers who would kill to do a photo shoot in the wildflower-looking spots near the greenhouse. Me? I was worried about sneezing. I was normally okay outdoors, but this was far from a normal amount of flowers.

Sharmin Aunty turned to me when I was at the back of the yard. "Everything you see is Rowan's doing. He redid all this last summer. He has a real eye for landscape design."

Interesting.

My phone vibrated with a call in my pocket. Probably Matteo. When I looked at it, though, it was Gia calling.

"I'm going to take this inside." I rushed into the granny flat and accepted the call. "Hey, Gia. What's up?"

"Is the pool saltwater or chlorine? That turquoise suit I bought in Miami will fade with too much chlorine. It's really for the beach."

I plopped on the sofa/bed thing. "What pool?"

"The pool at the house."

"What house?"

"Your aunt's house. Did you forget I'm moving in with you tomorrow?" Gia giggled.

I frowned. "There's no pool here."

That made the giggles stop. "Yes, there is."

I glanced out the window to where Sharmin Aunty and Juniper were sitting and not swimming at all. "Seriously, Gia. No pool. Just flowers. We did buy a fountain on the way up, but you wouldn't fit in it. By the way, do *not* stop at the garden center right outside town."

"Stop messing with me, Tahira! There *is* a pool! You said we'd be living in a pool house!"

"I said 'granny flat.' It's like a pool house, but without a pool in front of it. It's a guesthouse."

"Why'd you call it a pool house if there's no pool!" Gia was really distraught about this lack of pool. Which was fair. I'd prefer a pool to flowers.

"Gia, you misunderstood. There's no pool here. I mean, there is probably a pool somewhere in town; it's not *that* small. I don't know where—"

"But I was going to spend the whole summer sunbathing by the pool!"

"I thought you were coming here to work?" I loved Gia, but I wasn't about to pick up her slack if she just wanted to lie in the sun instead of working.

"Of course I'm going to work, but when I'm not working, I wanted to be sunbathing. But now the pool's gone . . ."

"It's not gone; it was never here! Besides, you don't actually need a pool to sunbathe. It's just sitting in the sun." As a brown girl, I didn't do a lot of intentional tanning, but as far as I knew, you needed UV rays, not water, for the process.

"You're supposed to dive in when you get too hot!"

"Like you'd dive into a pool, Gia. Not when you spend five hours a week on your hair."

"Seven. But seriously, I'd like the option if I wanted to."

I laughed. "Well, maybe we can put a kiddie pool outside the granny flat." Although, honestly, I wasn't exactly sure there'd be space. Maybe next to the patio?

"Ugh, fine, there's no pool, but do we seriously have to call it a 'granny flat'? Especially since I already said 'pool house' on my Insta."

"Gia, you're being ridiculous." From my view on the daybed, all I could see was the pine wall in front of me, brightly lit by the window behind me. All this wood didn't scream "granny" to me. Then again, it didn't scream "pool house," either. It looked like a cottage in the country, but smaller. "Call it a Bunkie," I said. "Or an outbuilding. A tiny house. A—"

"There! That. *Tiny houses* are cool. There's a whole Netflix show about them. There was even this Instagram model who lived in one. Or was that a camper van? What are those silver trailer things called? Anyway, maybe I can do a whole 'Gia in a Tiny House' series in my Insta. Might help me finally break five thousand followers."

I laughed. "Be warned, though: there's a ton of pine in here."

"Not a problem for me. Chris Pine is my favorite Chris. I love that whole dad vibe."

I laughed again. Gia was constantly ranking actors named Chris. Today she liked Pine; tomorrow it would be Evans.

"Tell me everything about the tiny house," Gia said. "I don't want any more misunderstandings."

So I did, not holding back on the extreme spatial limitations of it. Gia did perk up when I described the garden, though. She didn't share my flower aversion.

"Ooh, that's why you were texting about my nona's garden! You think I should pop out and get another floral romper? I only have two."

"Juniper and Rowan are probably the only ones who'll see you in the garden, and they won't care what you're wearing," I told her. "They—"

"Wait, what are Juniper and Rowan?"

"They're trees, apparently. Also, the names of the neighbors. Sixteen and eighteen."

"Wait, there are *neighbor teenagers*? They cool?"

"Yes and no. Juniper seems all right. Very . . . talkative. She's a bit naive but nice enough. She'll be working at the boutique, too. But Rowan, her brother, he's another story—pretty sure he hates me."

Gia paused a few seconds. "He cute? Single?"

I rolled my eyes. "I told you he *hates* me. You can't go after someone who hates your best friend."

"But if we dated, then he'd have to like you, because I wouldn't put up with any boo dissing my bestie. This is all in service to you, T."

"Gee, thanks, G."

"So, he *is* cute, then?"

"You do *not* want to go there. Seriously. He hates influencers."

"Ah! I like a challenge! And you owe me after I found you a boy-friend, even though I've been looking for one forever," Gia said.

"Gross. It's not like *you* could have dated your cousin."

"Still." Gia paused. "Sucks there's no pool—he could have seen me in a bikini all summer. Although maybe he still can—where does one buy a kiddie pool? Because I *need* to find a way to tear you away from your *fashion* this summer. You're getting a little two-dimensional—like your drawings."

"Ooh, savage." I laughed. I already missed Gia, and we'd only been apart a day. She never failed to make me laugh. I could be a bit intense and focused at times, which was why we got along so well—we complemented each other. Gia sometimes needed a little push to keep the hustle in her life, and she reminded me to have fun sometimes.

"Ugh. Mom's yelling for me," Gia said. "She's in full-on panic mode about what food we're bringing up. She's trying to figure out how to make a porchetta with no pork. I should go. Warm up that influencer hater for me, will ya? I'm going to need a country boy to corrupt."

"Ha ha. Love you, G."

"Love you, too, T."

Smiling, I ended the call with Gia and opened the door.

"What the hell! Thirst Trap is now in *my* yard?" said a familiar voice.

Ugh. Rowan Johnston was home from work. And he *did* remember he hated me. Wonderful.

5

THAT JAW, THOUGH

Ugh. I was alone in the backyard with Rowan Johnston's frown. And the rest of him, of course, but his disappointed scowl that I was in his precious garden was the defining feature of the space right now. Still wearing that ridiculous *Star Wars* flowery shirt and frayed shorts, and holding a metal shovel, he glared at me from beside the flower bed.

Ignoring him, I walked to the patio, sat on a sofa, and scrolled my Instagram. I didn't want to give him the satisfaction of seeing me squirm after seeing him.

Rowan huffed with displeasure. Finally, he spoke. "I should have known. *You* are Shar's niece. This is just adding to my already crappy day."

"Wow," I deadpanned. "Small-town hospitality is even more welcoming than I expected." The sarcasm dripped from my voice.

He stabbed the shovel into the dirt, leaving it standing next to him. "Do you know how long it took me to clean up the manure from the gravel?"

I *did* feel kind of bad about that. I sighed. "I *am* sorry I made that mess. That's why I offered to clean it and to pay for it. But you and your sidekick were incredibly rude. Whatever happened to 'The customer is always right'?"

"You weren't a customer! You weren't going to buy anything. You're an *influencer*. You think your presence alone is something we should be grateful for!"

He said the word "influencer" like some might say "street rat." Whatever. I could've told him I was there with my mother—an actual *paying* customer. Or that influencers are actually entrepreneurs—and it was super cool to be able to inspire people while making a bit of money from sponsorships. But I'd encountered his type before. He thought there was a negative correlation between a girl's IQ and her Instagram follower count.

I turned my cheek and looked back at my phone. He grunted his displeasure again and went back to digging.

Juniper came out of her house with a box of cookies and headed toward the patio. "Oh, hey, Row. When'd you get here?"

"Five minutes ago," he said, not looking up from his mound of dirt.

As Juniper sat across from me and offered me a cookie, Mom and Sharmin Aunty reappeared from my aunt's house with more snacks. Indian chevdo and some chips and salsa.

"Rowan, did you meet Tahira?" Sharmin Aunty asked as she sat and motioned for us all to help ourselves to the snacks. "She'll be working at the store with Juniper all summer."

Mom sat next to me and handed me a small bowl.

Rowan sighed. "Leanne and I had the *pleasure* of meeting her at Wynter's today."

I glared at Rowan. I disliked the fact that we were stuck together as much as he did, but unlike him, I wouldn't broadcast my displeasure to everyone.

But focusing on him, even like this, caused a problem. It made me notice that Rowan looked different in his own garden. His dark, wide-set eyes were darker. His cheekbones higher. His jawline sharper. His skin glowed more, and his lips seemed soft. I'd thought both he and his friend were pretty attractive when I first saw them, but right now? Rowan wasn't just cute; he was *stunning*. Exquisite. Even in that dumb shirt. If it weren't for his personality, I would *love* to photograph this guy. He was, like, *model-level* good looking.

Mmm, yes, I could see it. Smoldering eyes, disinterested glare, scowling mouth . . . wearing . . . my cropped gray men's T-shirt with the leather epaulets? Matteo hadn't looked right in it—my boyfriend was unfortunately short waisted. What shoes would I put on Rowan? Retro-style Jordans, or even black leather Pumas. Anything was better than those beat-up Chucks. What color were they originally, anyway? Blue? Gray?

And . . . I was probably staring too long there. He managed to raise one brow at me while still scowling. This guy *really* needed to be in front of a camera.

I turned away, helping myself to some chevdo.

"Tahira's seventeen," Juniper said to her brother. "She's got one more year of high school, like me."

"Half," I said. "I'm on track to graduate early with honors."

Rowan looked at me. And I mean really looked . . . like he couldn't quite figure me out. I guess he was entitled, considering the analysis of his appearance I'd just done. Then he turned away without saying anything—clearly deciding I wasn't worth the mental energy to decipher.

Rude.

"Rowan's graduation was last week," Juniper told Mom and me. "He was backup valedictorian. What did you call it, Row? Understudy?"

"Salutatorian."

"It's such a weird word. I think they made it up at our school."

"Rowan's best friend, Leanne, was valedictorian," Sharmin Aunty said. "Her parents are Joanne and Leeland, who used to own my house."

I shrugged. So, Grumpy and the Sunshine Girl were smart, so what?

"We're hoping Tahira gets many awards when she graduates," Mom said. "Art awards definitely, but hopefully academic, too."

"Rowan," Sharmin Aunty said, "if you have a second, could you help bring a table out to the flat for Tahira and her friend to use?"

His head shot around to me. "There are *two* of you?"

"Yes, my best friend, Gia, is coming tomorrow. You'll get the pleasure of both our company."

Rowan glared at me again. No problem; I could glare, too. I even bit my lip with a flash of amusement, which probably annoyed him more.

"Well, everyone," Mom said with a smile, standing. She wiped her hands on a napkin. "I really should get on the road. I need to stop at the office on the way home."

After Mom said goodbye to Rowan and Juniper, she thanked Sharmin Aunty again and told her to call if I gave her any trouble.

"Tahira, come walk me out," Mom said, and she and I walked around the house to her car.

She hugged me when we got there. "I know this isn't what you wanted this summer," she said, "but I also know you'll make the best of it."

I sank into the hug. I really was going to miss her. "I think it will be okay," I said when I let go. At least I hoped it would be. Even if I wasn't entirely happy to be here in Bakewell, that didn't mean I wasn't going to do the absolute best I could to make the summer a success. I needed the fashion experience too much.

Mom put her hand on my cheek. "You'll be amazing, Tahira. I know you can accomplish anything. I'll miss having you around this summer. You girls are growing up so fast." She opened the car door. "Oh, and go to jamatkhana in Niagara Falls with your aunt when she goes."

"I know, Mom." Jamatkhana was an Ismaili Muslim place of worship, and we went to prayers regularly at one in Toronto. Mom didn't have to nag me now; I didn't mind joining my aunt for prayers here, too.

"Okay. Love you, Tahira."

"Love you, too, Mom." I smiled and waved to my mother from the driveway as she drove away.

～

As expected, Gia made an *entrance* when she arrived Monday morning. With a fresh spray-on tan and hair in perfect tousled waves, she clomped up the driveway in brown suede cowboy boots and a frothy pink floral dress that barely covered her butt.

I stood on the porch, laughing. "Gia, what *are* you wearing?" She'd always been more adaptable with her style choices, but this was way more country than I'd ever seen on her.

"You like it? I figured, when in cow town, right? Taylor Swift says we're all supposed to be cottagecore these days."

"This isn't even a cow town."

Gia's father was behind her, carrying aluminum trays and bags that I knew would be filled with food. Gia's parents were the type to constantly offer everyone around them meals, or salami. After I refused the salami a few times, they figured out I was Muslim and started buying beef salami, and they officially became my favorite friend-parents.

"Tahira! This little town is so charming!" He kissed both my cheeks. "I did some research on Yelp, and you'll have to order pizza from the place on Main. Their reviews are the best." He smiled at Sharmin Aunty, who stood behind me. "I'm Joe Borroni. You must be Sharmin? We spoke on the phone."

After introductions, we went inside. Mr. Borroni presented Sharmin Aunty with two beef salamis, three homemade frozen lasagnas, and six big jars of homemade red sauce.

While the adults talked about living arrangements, Gia's dietary restrictions, and other parent-type stuff, I picked up two of Gia's bags, leaving her with three (she'd brought even more than I had), and took her to see our new home.

"Oh, wow, this is stun-ning," she said when we got to the backyard. "You said the garden was overdone. This is magical."

I scrunched my nose. "You don't think it's a bit much?"

She shook her head. "No! It's amazing. My Instagram is going to be so good this summer. Maybe I'll finally get some sponsorships. Okay, I watched tours of tiny houses on YouTube the whole way here. Show me the house."

I pointed to the granny flat.

"Oh." She frowned. "I thought that was a shed."

I laughed as I stepped up to the door of the flat. "You ready?"

She nodded, so I opened the door.

She frowned. "It looks really . . . flammable?"

"It's like living in a sauna but without the warmth," I said, dragging her bags in.

She stepped inside, her cowboy boots reverberating on the pine floor. "Or a tree house."

I nodded, agreeing. "A woodpile."

"Is this all of it?" she asked. She dropped a bag on the daybed, which was still made up to look like a sofa, with its floral bedspread and wood-print cushions.

"Pretty much." I pointed to the back of the tiny house. "There's a tiny bathroom back there—thankfully not made of wood. That ladder leads to a sleeping loft with another bed."

"I'm not climbing that. I can't even wear platform shoes."

"I figured as much." Gia wasn't a heights person. "I slept up there last night; it was fine." Mostly fine. I woke practically at dawn from what sounded like eight dozen birds in the yard. I had been told it would be quieter out in the country. It wasn't.

"Oh, I forgot, I brought something to decorate!" She pulled a framed photo out of a bag. It was of the actor Chris Pine, in his gray-bearded phase. "You said it was pine themed."

I laughed. "Love it. Makes all this seem . . . intentional."

She leaned the photo on the table. "It doesn't matter what the place looks like, anyway," Gia said. "We get to *live* here. Just you and me. It's going to be *lit*."

I wasn't sure how "lit" it would be, considering I knew only Gia plus four people in town, and one of them was my fiftysomething-year-old aunt, and another found me as palatable as rotting roadkill, but sure. If Gia wanted to delude herself that this would be a party summer, I wasn't going to be the one to burst her bubble.

The plan for the day was for me to spend the rest of the morning getting Gia settled in and unpacked. Then Juniper would meet up with us late morning, and the three of us would walk together to Lilybuds at noon for our first day of training.

Finding space for all Gia's clothes was a bit tricky since my stuff was already everywhere, but somehow, we managed to get her stuff to fit. In every corner, under every piece of furniture, and even hanging from the walls were clothes, shoes, accessories, and hair products, but you could at least walk around the tiny house. And you could barely see the pine anymore. Mostly.

After unpacking, I put on my most *retail sales associate* outfit: my black high-waisted dress pants with a paper-bag waistband and a blouse I'd made myself—pale gray with bold red stripes around the sleeves. I'd sewn it out of the softest French jersey, and I loved the way it draped over my body. I put my hair up in a half bun on the top of my head and started on my makeup.

My phone vibrated with a text as I was doing my eyes. I checked the screen—Matteo. We'd talked on the phone until late last night, and I was still feeling warm and fuzzy from the call.

Matteo: Hey baby, Good luck at your new job today!

Tahira: TY! You're the best. You on your way to work?

Matteo: Yeah. On the subway. About to go underground, I'll call you tonight. Miss you.

Tahira: Miss you, more.

I heard a knock on our door. I hadn't quite finished gluing my false lashes on (they were short and "professional" looking), but I went out so I could be there when Gia met Juniper.

"Wow, Tahira was right. You *are* adorbs," Gia said.

Juniper was in a calf-length black pleated skirt and a sleeveless white collared blouse. Her hair was in a higher ponytail than yesterday, and she had pale gloss on her lips.

"Thanks!" she said. "You're Gia, right? That dress is amazing! I love that shade of pink. I'm Juniper Jessica Johnston. You can call me June or Juniper." She held out three small pink flowers. "I had Row bring rain lilies from the nursery for each of us . . . you can wear it as a boutonniere, or put in it a vase, or whatever. They symbolize big expectations, so I thought they'd be good for the first day at a new job."

"Ooh, pretty!" Gia took a flower and promptly found a pin to affix it to her hair. I took a flower, too—but didn't know what to do with it. It was just one flower, but I didn't want my eyes watering.

"You don't have to keep it if you don't want to," Juniper said as she slipped her flower into the elastic holding her hair. "Shar told me you're allergic. It still works if you just look at it."

"Still works for what?" I asked.

Juniper shrugged. "This is something my grandma did. She said smelling, or even seeing, the perfect flower could change your day. That's why I gave you the welcome flowers. Did you know red tulips mean deeply in love? Like, real love, not just passion, like roses. And tansy flowers are given as a declaration of war? Grandma once had a bride ask for tansies in her wedding bouquet. Can you imagine? Grandma called it a declaration of divorce. Are y'all ready to go?"

"In a minute." I handed Gia my flower, and she slipped it in her hair with the other one while I headed back to the bathroom to finish my face. I could hear Juniper telling Gia her pronouns, her age, her grade, and her favorite books. Clearly no one would be bored during slow moments at the store when Juniper was working. This girl saw every silence as an opportunity.

"It's super cool that y'all are here this summer," Juniper said as I slipped on my white platform sneakers. "I screamed with joy when Shar told me you were coming. I've never had a friend on the street. Row had Leanne, but she moved."

"Aren't you and Leanne friends, too?" I asked.

Juniper fidgeted with the locket necklace she was wearing. "Not really. She and Row have been best friends since practically kinder-garten. I'm just the kid sister." She put her hand on the door. "It's a twenty-minute walk to the store, so we should probably go."

"Ready," I said, grabbing my blue suede hobo with my phone, iPad, and lipstick.

"So, your brother has been best friends with a *girl* since he was five?" Gia asked as we walked down the street. "And they're not together?"

Juniper shook her head. "Just friends. Leanne calls Row her brother."

Gia grinned. "Ah. Give them time. Friends to lovers—I love to see it."

Juniper scratched the back of her neck before pointing out the nearby flower-themed playground. Had Juniper been on the receiving end of the same snarky rudeness this Leanne had shown me at the nursery? It wouldn't surprise me, and it would explain Juniper's current uneasiness.

"I just started an Instagram for books," Juniper said, "but I don't have many followers yet." After our chat yesterday, I was kind of used to Juniper's habit of changing subjects quickly. "I want to learn to take better pictures. You have an Insta, right? How many followers do you have?"

"About twenty thousand," I said.

Juniper nodded. *"Impressive."*

"Mine's nowhere near that high," Gia said. "Tahira is the *real deal.* I keep telling her she needs to get on TikTok or Twitter—"

"Instagram is enough," I said. I was better off focusing my efforts on one platform and honing my craft during the time I would otherwise be maintaining multiple accounts or editing videos. I spent hours a day either sewing, drafting, or researching trends and techniques, and there wasn't time for much else.

Although maybe I *should* have been working harder to build my platform—I still wasn't getting the recognition that I needed. Maybe with more followers across different platforms, I'd get on that #IndieFashionWeekly page. Or maybe my designs just weren't innovative enough, and I should've been working harder there.

We turned onto a busier street, and Juniper pointed out a drugstore, a small grocery store, and the building where her mother worked. The town was laid out like most small towns I'd been to, but it was way more . . . colorful. Many of the buildings had brightly painted moldings and doors, and the store signs were super vibrant. There were flowers everywhere. Hanging in baskets from ornate lampposts and dangling from the edges of the awnings on the patios. There were window boxes on most buildings, planters on the boulevards, and even long boxes filled with flowers on the tops of the fence railings.

"Who takes the pictures for your Insta?" Juniper asked.

"I usually take them myself," I said. "Unless I'm modeling."

"Lately she's been modeling with Matteo a lot, so I take the pictures," Gia added. "The *power couple* gets a lot of attention."

"Who's Matteo?" Juniper asked as she waved at an older man and woman across the street.

"My boyfriend," I said. "He's Gia's cousin. He's trying to build a following as an Instagram model."

"Ooh," Juniper cooed. "That is sooo cute that y'all work together! I prefer girls myself, but there's slim pickings around here, so I'm single. Your boyfriend should've come up here, too. But Lord, there would *not* be room in that flat. Can I model sometime?"

Gia grinned. "You should put her in that oversize blazer you made, Tahira. She has the height for it."

Juniper nodded, smiling. "I know I'm not really, you know, *pretty* pretty, but models are more *interesting* than pretty, right?"

Gia shook her head. "Shut up. You're totally pretty pretty. You'd be great."

She *was* pretty, and if I was going to be here all summer, I would need someone other than Gia and me modeling. "Have you modeled clothes before?" I asked.

Juniper shook her head. "Rowan was in the school fashion show last year, but I didn't even try out. I'm such a dork at school; I would have been laughed off the stage."

Rowan had been in the fashion show? Clearly, I wasn't the only one to notice that his outside was much more attractive than his inside. But I didn't want to talk about Rowan—mostly because I didn't think it was right to call him a douche canoe in front of Juniper, and those were the words that came to mind when I thought of him.

Maybe I could try Juniper's conversation quick change. "What's that building?"

"The library and community center. I wanted to work at the library this summer, but Mrs. McLaughlin only hires college kids. Ageism, right? I've read more books than that Adams girl . . . but I guess it's good—the library booth is the most boring booth at the festival—and I'd have to be there all day because Mrs. McLaughlin thinks she's too important to stay put. Did y'all bring any books up with you?"

"Just some sewing books," I said. The sidewalks widened after we passed the library, but there were more people walking on them. I squeezed close to Juniper as a woman with a massive stroller approached. Juniper said hello to her as she passed.

"That's Yolanda Torres," Juniper said. "She's the head of the festival this year."

"Oh, look how pretty that little courtyard is!" Gia said. "This whole town looks like a postcard. What's the deal with this festival?"

"No one told you about the festival? The Bakewell Festival of Flowers is massive. It's at the end of August, and there's a midway with rides and games and food trucks. Last year there was an arepas truck from the city. Oh, and they have this custom ride with spinning flowers. It's on the logo for the festival. There are also all these contests, you know, best garden, best flower arrangement. The biggest is the Bloom— that's the floral sculpture competition. This year they've partnered with some hoity-toity horticultural association, so it's an even bigger deal. They did this winter ball in December to raise money, so the Bloom prize is epic now. Not that I want to enter. Row will, of course. He came in second last year."

Juniper kept describing this community fair while I kept looking around on the way to the store. This must've been the downtown core, if you could call it that. The buildings were two stories tall and were more tightly packed together, and they were somehow even brighter and more flowery. We walked past a small specialty-food store, a hardware store, and an antique shop. Plus two banks, a bookstore with a front window filled with gardening books, a Chinese restaurant, some sort of bistro, an auto garage, and a large clock-tower building with a big, manicured garden in front of it.

"So how come you two ended up coming here, anyway?" Juniper asked as we passed a store that looked like it sold only plaid things.

"I was supposed to be working with a designer this summer, but the job fell through." I told her about Nilusha, the bird, and the lost internship.

"And I came along because I can't have a summer without Tahira," Gia said. "Don't worry, T, we're going to get so much new content to make up for losing your job."

Juniper looked at me, tilting her head. "That sucks about the internship. This is why you really don't want to be in Bakewell, right?"

I turned to Juniper. How did she know I didn't want to be here? It wasn't like I'd ever said that—aloud, at least. I smiled. She was perceptive. "Nothing against Bakewell; it's just . . . the experience with the designer would have been better for my college application. I'm trying to get into FIT."

"Is that an art school?" Juniper asked.

"It's a fashion school in New York."

Juniper's eyes widened. "Sounds intense."

"You'll get into FIT," Gia said. "You have *twenty thousand* followers. You're, like, ridiculously talented." Gia was my biggest cheerleader, but honestly I didn't think she understood how stressed I was about this. Everyone who made it big in fashion had big platforms, but they also had connections, talent, and all the right kind of experience.

And maybe expecting to get that experience from a town with less people living in it than I had Instagram followers (but more flowers, apparently) was a bad idea.

I rubbed my palm. *No.* No self-doubt now. No second thoughts. I didn't have any other option but to be here. I had to make it work.

Juniper pointed ahead. "There's Lilybuds."

I saw the store for the first time, and it took all my self-control not to make a face. It wasn't very big, and it had large windows on either side of the door. Above the door was one of those oval wood-carved signs like the welcome sign into town. Was there some sort of Bakewell discount on those or something? **LILYBUDS** was in cursive writing in the middle, surrounded by pink, purple, and yellow flowers. Looking in, I could see the window display, complete with mannequins in floral dresses, and more batik than at one of those Thai beach photo shoots. Fixing this place up was going to be a *serious* project.

"Is everything church-picnic wear?" I asked, trying not to frown but probably failing.

"The stuff in the window's not great," Juniper said. "But Shar got some new things in recently that are pretty cool. I'm saving up for the black linen overalls. Anyway, should we go in?"

Whether I wanted to be here or not, I *was* going to turn this store around and put my own personal stamp on it.

I took a breath. "Yes. Let's get started." I opened the door.

6

LILYBUDS AT LAST

G irls, you're here! Look at you three!" Sharmin Aunty said as we
came in. "So fashionable. My customers are going to *love* you. I
hope you had a pleasant walk."

I put on my smile, ready to lay on all the praise for Bakewell, but I
didn't really have to. I forgot I had Gia the Positive with me.

"It was lovely!" Gia said. "This town is not just cute, but *cu-ute*. So
picturesque. I can't wait to check out the little shops and restaurants!
The bookstore was just darling!"

Sharmin Aunty chuckled at Gia, then turned to me. "What about
you, Tahira? What did you think of Bakewell?"

"I think this is going to be an awesome place to live, Sharmin
Aunty." I was pretty proud of that enthusiasm, to be honest. It sounded
real, at least to my ears.

"It's a wonderful little town. Tourists will start invading heavily next
week; then it will really pick up. And you don't have to call me Sharmin
Aunty here. Everyone calls me Shar. You too, Gia. I'm Shar, okay?"

"Okay," I said.

"Excellent." Sharmin Aunty—*Shar*—nodded. "Why don't you
three look around a bit while I finish this paperwork. Then I'll give you
the grand tour and train you on the computer. Sound good?"

We split up to look around Lilybuds. After a few minutes, I was just as underwhelmed as when I'd first peeked in the window. Walls painted boring beige. Gray, industrial carpeting. And the clothes? Yeah, the stock was clearly leaning into either the Sunday-church crowd or the new-age-hippie crowd. Except with more flowers. Because this was Bakewell—flowers were a given.

Shar's official tour took about five minutes. Stockroom in the back, small bathroom. And the selling floor.

"I usually showcase merchandise by color," she said, "but I like to change out the front stock often. Like these." She held up a long, daisy-printed skirt. "I've had them since April, but I sold three yesterday because I moved them here with the yellow tops."

I nodded. She didn't need to tell me about the power of merchandising.

Gia flipped through some dresses on a rack. "Do you sell any, you know, casual stuff? Streetwear?" she asked.

Shar looked confused, so I elaborated. "Denims, maybe some cords, graphic tees? Urban looks?"

Shar shook her head. "I carry primarily dresses and skirts. Florals do well because that's why people come to Bakewell. No jeans or T-shirts, other than the festival T-shirt."

"I heard they're not doing a festival shirt this year," Juniper said.

"Really?" Shar asked. "Why not?"

Juniper shrugged. "Not enough people bought them last year. The BFF logo is kind of lame. The art is, like, from 1988 or something."

I raised a brow. "BFF?"

"Bakewell Flower Festival. Mom said the acronym predates texting, so we can't complain."

Gia snorted. "But who even says 'BFF' anymore, anyway?"

Exactly. I tried not to roll my eyes.

It didn't matter what I thought about Bakewell or Lilybuds—I was here for a purpose. I pushed my hair behind me and mentally got to work on the reason I'd been hired—to rebrand Lilybuds. "I'm excited to get started with the changes to the store. There's this exclusive line out of Copenhagen we should look at—I think it's going to be a big deal next year."

"Ooh, Søren Anker! Good call, T," Gia said. "They have this bag that—"

Shar put her hand up. "Copenhagen! Heavens! I'm sure that's not right for my little shop."

"Oh, are you trying to keep to Canadian lines?" I asked. "That's cool. Buy local and all that. Nilusha Bhatt might work. What are the price points you're looking at? Maybe we can get her to make an exclusive capsule collection." I pulled out my phone. I could use my connection here. This would be great for Shar and Bakewell as a whole.

"Don't get ahead of yourself, Tahira," Shar said. "I'm happy you're here to help me choose some new pieces and freshen up a bit, but I'm not looking to change suppliers. I've built good relationships with my wholesalers, and they have a large selection. We could bring in new hats!"

Hats? I looked over to a rack near the counter that already contained hats. Straw ones, with flowers on the brim.

I bit my lip. *Stay positive, Tahira.* This might not be all bad. If these wholesalers really did have a large selection, maybe I could find things that had a bit more city cool and a bit less flowers?

"Do they have a catalog or something?"

"They're online." Shar stepped behind the counter and motioned me over. On the computer, she brought up a website—Brandon's Apparel Wholesale. "I buy a lot from here, but I have two more that I also use. Ooh, these are new!" She opened to a page of long dresses, miraculously not floral. Still not what I was envisioning.

"I could see these working," Gia said, leaning over me to see the screen. "Or wait, look at that one!" She pointed to a flowery thing on the sidebar. "So Coachella, right?"

59

"Oh my God, yes!" Juniper nodded vigorously. "I totally saw dresses like that from the footage from the Coachella music festival last year. I want to go to one of those big concerts one day."

I gave Gia a look. She knew this wasn't my aesthetic. She wasn't really helping here.

"How about I look at these later," I said. "I should start by making a plan for the store. Maybe make some sketches?"

"Sounds like a great idea," Shar said. "I'll show Juniper and Gia the computer system." She switched to the point-of-sale program.

I grabbed my iPad from my bag and started at the back of the store, making notes on the things I would change. Definitely a coat of paint to start. Clean white walls would make a world of difference. Maybe new flooring, too. Ebony hardwood would look good. Or slate tile. I stood in the center of the space and looked toward the back, imagining a customer seeing the store for the first time. Maybe a feature wall there? Everything was so cluttered now, but that was an easy fix—reduce the stock on the floor so the key pieces would stand out more. And definitely hide at least half the florals.

After making copious notes and a few sketches, I connected to the store's Wi-Fi and pulled up the website for the wholesaler. I took a closer look without any commentary from the others. Could I make any of this work? It sucked I wouldn't be able to bring in any *real* designer lines, but after seeing Bakewell, I suspected Nilusha Bhatt would probably be wasted here. I found some solid high-waist twill skirts with buttons down the front that had potential. And the linen overalls Juniper had mentioned in many colors—I actually liked those. I might even be buying myself a pair.

I grinned. It wasn't all bad. I could make this work.

~

Despite a few hours of training and a few minor rushes of customers (I figured five people in the store at once was a rush), I managed to make a long list of ideas and a few rough sketches for my proposal for the new Lilybuds. I was excited, but I kept my ideas to myself. This project was for my FIT application—I didn't need it done by committee. I would compile it all tonight and present it to Shar tomorrow. Hopefully we could start implementing some of the changes by the end of the week.

Late afternoon, Juniper took me to the famed Hyacinth's to pick up coffees for everyone. Gia stayed with Shar at the store in case there was another rush of customers. On our way there, Juniper said, "They make the best chai frappés."

I wasn't thirteen and didn't live in suburbia. I didn't drink frappés. "Do they have flat whites?"

Juniper shrugged. "Probably."

Hyacinth's was, of course, floral themed. But the outside patio had comfortable cushioned bench seats and chic black umbrellas. I could see a significant amount of time being spent here in my future. As we waited in line at the busy café, a few people came in after us and stood behind us. But two people, what appeared like a woman and her daughter, came in and looked right at Juniper, and then the girl headed straight for us instead of the back of the line with her mother. She was tall, about our age, and exactly what others would call an all-American girl, or all-Canadian, I supposed, which meant white, blonde, blue eyed, and nonthreatening. She had on a striped nineties-style T-shirt and white jeans and sneakers. Her hair was in long curling-iron waves and she had pink lips. Her mother was an even blonder, but older, version of the girl, wearing a blue and yellow floral sundress I recognized from Lilybuds.

"Oh *great*," Juniper said quietly, clearly irritated that she had the attention of these two.

"Hey, Junebug," the girl said, planting herself beside Juniper. "Love that skirt; the whole look is so unique!"

"Hey, Addison," Juniper said uneasily. "This is Tahira. She's working with me at Lilybuds. She's Shar's niece from Toronto. Tahira, this is Addison. She's in my grade at school."

Addison's eyes traveled from my shoes up to my hair. Her expression made it clear that she wanted me to know exactly who was queen bee around here. "Nice shirt," she said sarcastically.

I rolled my eyes. *Just terrific.* Bakewell had mean girls. "Um, thank you?"

Addison turned back to Juniper and flashed a smile that looked faker than her "Longchamp" bag. "So, Junebug, did you think about what I asked?"

Juniper's jaw clenched. "Do you mind *not* calling me Junebug?"

"Everyone calls you Junebug!" Addison stepped closer. "I really hope you'll agree to help us out—for old times' sake. Our team needs you!"

Juniper glanced at me briefly, then at her feet. "I said before, I don't think I'll have the time. I'm working this summer. And you're not even really asking me to be on your team, are you?"

"I'm asking you to be our coach! That's more important than being on the team! Really, I would love to let you join, but with Sadie, Cameron, and Kelsey, there isn't space. And Kelsey and Sadie are dying to go to New York. None of us have ever been, and you went last year. You wouldn't want to go with us, anyway. You're too awkward for the stuff we want to do. It's totally not your scene. We're going to go dancing and—"

"Excuse me," I interrupted. I couldn't figure out what exactly Addison wanted June to coach her for, but if she thought *negging* was the way to convince June, she'd be dealing with me first. "Juniper said she won't have time. I've been hired to do a complete rebrand of Lilybuds, and she'll be helping me." I mirrored the once-over the girl had given me, making it clear I was as unimpressed by her fashion choices as she was with mine. "This town could use a style makeover, to be honest. I've got my work cut out for me."

That got me a death glare from the mean girl, which was fine. I'd rather her wrath was on me than on Juniper. Juniper may have been naive and a little too earnest, but that didn't mean she deserved to be bullied or manipulated by a classmate.

"Tahira's a designer," Juniper said. "She has her own clothing line and everything. And twenty thousand Instagram followers."

Addison's posture changed instantly. She stood straighter and stopped glaring at me. "Oh, cool! I was on the fashion show committee at school!" She smiled at me. "Welcome to Bakewell. You meet Flower Power yet?"

"She's talking about Rowan," Juniper told me.

I raised a brow. Had this girl been negging Rowan, too? "Briefly. In his backyard."

"Ah, in his natural habitat. Let me guess—his clothes were caked in mud and his eyes were on the flowers instead of you. Don't feel the need to spend more time with him—he's just as dull with longer exposure."

This girl was so irritating she almost made me want to defend Rowan Johnston, and that made her even more annoying. It was time to lose Addison; plus, we were close to the front of the coffee line. "Well, it was lovely to chat. I'm sure I'll see you around, Alison, wasn't it?"

"Addison." She beamed. "We should chill. I can show you the cool side of Bakewell. We'll talk later, Junebug. I still have time to convince you!"

~

As we headed back to Lilybuds, Juniper pulled a reusable folding straw out of her bag and plunged it into her frappé. "I should probably tell you," she said, "Rowan dated Addison."

Now *that* was unexpected, although it did explain her warning me off him. Why did she deem the plant nerd worthy of her, anyway? They were both annoying, but their snobbishness seemed to be aimed in different directions. He hated superficial people, and she was as superficial as they came. I was weirdly disappointed in *him* that he hadn't seen through Addison's phoniness.

"I can't see it," I said.

"They were together awhile, but she's changed. You going to hang out with her?"

I snorted. "Unlikely. What is it she wants from you?"

"To help her and her friends get ready for the Bloom. I'm pretty sure she wants me to do all the work, and they'll take the credit."

"What? That sounds . . . wait, this is that contest?"

"Yeah, the floral sculpture one. Addison was on a team with Rowan last year, and they came in second. But this year the grand prize is a trip to New York, thanks to all the money they raised at the Snowbloom Ball. Addison realized they don't have a chance without Row."

"Why is she asking *you*, then?"

Juniper shrugged. "I mean, I'm not Rowan, but I know my way around flowers. I worked with my grandma all the time. Row and I have been gardening and flower arranging since before we could walk."

"Then why won't Addison actually let you on her team?"

Juniper laughed, shaking her head. "You can only have three or four people, and she doesn't want to displace any of her squad. Don't worry, I'm not going to do it. Addison McLaughlin doesn't have anything on me." She paused, biting her lip briefly. "Hey, what's your Insta? I want to see your designs."

I narrowed my eyes. My senses were tingling that Addison once *had* something on Juniper, but Juniper didn't want to share that with me. I had no intention of getting involved in the drama here, but I made a mental note to watch out for this mean girl and make sure she left Juniper alone.

We exchanged Instagram handles, and I took a look at her feed while she held the tray of coffees. Her pictures were nice, but just books. I made a second mental note to give her some camera pointers to reduce the glare. In fact, with a bit of help, I bet I could get Juniper's follower count high enough to make Addison show her some respect. This was a game I knew, and I knew how to win it.

7

WAY HARSH, PLANT-BOY

After we had some of Shar's amazing chicken curry with chapati for dinner, I washed dishes while Gia went back to the tiny house to call her parents. When I was done, I found Gia lying on one of the lounge chairs in front of our place with her eyes closed. Although I supposed they were a little bit open, because as I approached, she said, "Sup, T."

I chuckled. "Whatcha doing, Gia?"

"Need to maintain this color to pull off the boho look."

I cringed. "You're not really going to keep with this flower-child vibe all summer, are you? Plus, it's evening."

Her eyebrows shot up high. "There's enough sun—I tan easily. And *yeah*. Of course I am. I told you, cottagecore is huge this season. I'm embracing it. You hanging out for a bit?" She pointed to the empty lounge chair next to her.

"Can't. I want to pull all my notes and sketches together tonight and show Shar tomorrow."

"Ugh, Tahira. You can't be all work and nothing else this summer. We're supposed to chill."

"You *knew* I was coming here for a purpose. I'm not sure why you expected it to be a party summer."

"I know, but sometimes you have to stop and smell the roses, or something."

I snorted. "I'm allergic to roses. And you're starting to sound like a true Bakewell-ite." I frowned. Bakewell-er? Bakewell-onian? "Anyway, the sooner I get it done, the more time I'll have to chill with you later." I was headed for the door when Gia stopped me.

"Hey, why didn't you tell me sheep-manure guy was so hot?"

I cringed. I shouldn't have told her about the whole manure incident. "You met Rowan? My condolences."

Gia nodded. "He and Juniper were just here to bring over a sewing table. We now have thirty percent less floor space. And ten percent more pine. I don't think the guy liked *me*, either."

I didn't doubt it. If Rowan thought I was superficial, Gia came across as ten times shallower. But anyone who knew her—like, really *knew* her—knew there was more to her than that.

Gia had her own type of kindness—a way of putting people at ease around her, no matter what. Like when she reassured Juniper she was pretty when we were walking to the store. She was also one of the most generous people I knew. She used to let me share her lunch money all the time back before I had a job, because I used to spend all my spare money on fabric. And she never went on vacation without buying gifts for all her friends. She was always so *positive*. Honestly, sometimes I kind of wished I was more like Gia—not in the whole "expecting life to be a party all the time" way, but more like . . . she made life seem so easy. Effortless. She made friends quickly and always trusted herself. I had no doubt Gia would one day be the style influencer with a huge platform *and* the rom-com star she wanted to be.

The part of Gia people saw first, her attitude . . . her *shallowness* . . . was mostly fake. It was a persona—she put it on because she wanted people to think she was fun, lighthearted, and influential. But someone like Rowan wouldn't even try to get to know her and see the real Gia. He was the very definition of a "judge first, get to know later" guy.

"You going to make a move on him?" I asked. I really hoped she wouldn't. I'd already decided to pretend Rowan didn't exist all summer, and it'd be awkward if my best friend was dating an invisible guy.

She snorted. "I thought about it, but nah. I'm no masochist. He did nothing but grunt when he met me. Oh wait, he sneered, too—when Juniper told him I took pictures for your page. I'm positive there are guys in this town who will worship me the way I deserve. He's a looker, though. Too bad about the personality. He's nothing like his sister."

"I know. Juniper is—"

"She's too much." Gia shook her head, chuckling. "She told me the full plot of two books in the time it took to bring a table in."

I laughed. "Only two?"

"She's just so *wholesome*. Giving us flowers, going on and on about that county festival. She'd be eaten alive in the city. Seriously. Bully magnet."

I shrugged. "I suspect she may be dealing with that here." I told Gia about the run-in with Addison.

"Holy shit—that's some nerve to ask for help without actually letting her on the team. The Bakewell locals sound terrible. I know—let's adopt Juniper. We can even do a makeover montage. That'll show them."

I snorted. "Gia, this isn't a teen movie plot! Juniper seems to have a real issue here."

"It is a movie plot! We've got mean girls, the plucky book nerd with a heart of gold, even a Hallmark-esque small-town setting." Gia put her sunglasses on and lay back. "We can help her. We can pretend it's *Clueless*, and she's our Tai."

I laughed. Gia was low-key obsessed with the nineties teen classic *Clueless*. "I suppose you are as lily white and blonde as Cher."

Gia shrugged. "My blonde comes from a bottle, though." She stood. "That reminds me: it's getting late and I still need to wash my hair. You do your work, T, because then? We need to make some *fun* happen this summer. There's got to be a beach nearby. Heck, I'd settle for the kiddie pool you promised."

~

I kind of wanted to just chill and maybe watch a show or something after the long first day at work, but instead I set up my sketchbook on the new sewing table and started redrawing the rough sketches I'd made in the store. After about twenty minutes, I realized this wouldn't work.

"The light is crap here," I muttered.

I had a pretty good drafting light in my room back home, but the tiny house had only a ceiling fixture with one bulb.

"Tell me about it. I can flat-iron my hair blindfolded, though, so I'm good," Gia said.

Gia was sitting on the sofa-daybed thing, a mirror balanced on her lap and a flat iron in her hand. I'd tried to get her to do her hair in the bathroom, but she claimed there wasn't enough elbow room.

"Sketching is impossible in here." I could see the rough sketches on my iPad, of course, but I'd wanted to make better pencil-and-paper ones to show my aunt.

The smell of burning hair wasn't ideal to get my creative juices flowing, either.

"Go to Shar's," Gia said.

At dinner Shar had said she planned to marathon a show after we finished cleaning the kitchen.

"She's watching that show with the vigilante priest. I need quiet."

"You're such a princess, Tahira. Go outside. It's brighter out there than in here."

True. And natural light was better than anything else. I packed my sketchbook and iPad into my backpack and went outside.

The sun was still bright, and the antihistamine I'd taken earlier was still in full effect. I set my things on the patio table, propped my sketchbook on my lap, and resumed working.

I had a basic three-part plan to improve Lilybuds. Part one: reduce the amount of stock in the store so the good stuff could be seen. Two: replace a large portion of the floral prints with new pieces. I knew this was the flower capital of whatever, but you could buy flowery crap anywhere in this town—Lilybuds *needed* a different vibe to stand out. And that brought me to step three: change the damn name. Because Lilybuds? *No.*

I was a realist, though—I wasn't going to throw out the name altogether. Definitely needed to get the word "buds" out of there. Honestly, I was amazed the store wasn't overrun with potheads with that name. Just "Lily" might work. It was still a flower, but it was also a name, right? I played around with modern lettering and came up with a quick prototype: LILY. Just like that. The word alone with a period after it. Black lettering on a white background. No wood-carved sign. No flowers.

I made some more sketches of the outside of the store with the new name and logo. The store was going to be so . . . *arrestive.* People everywhere would talk about it. I was *so* getting into FIT.

I started a new sketch of the store's back wall, imagining it with designer wallpaper. Maybe even Arabic-tile style as a nod to the Muslim owner of the store? We could put a few waterfall-style clothes hangers to display key pieces for the season, but the wall itself would be the focal point, with the new logo in the middle.

After twenty minutes or so outside, my hand was cramping. I wasn't done, but a ten-minute break would make all the difference. I stood and stretched.

The sun was setting, and the dimming light cast an almost otherworldly orange glow over the garden. A soft hum filled the air, blending with the slow trickle of the fountain Mom had bought. It was in the back of the yard, near a bed of wispy white and deep-pink flowers. I headed over to take a closer look.

The fountain was basically a big concrete block with a clear glass bowl in the center. Inside the bowl sat a black sphere with water cascading from the top. The low sun reflected in the dribbling water, making it look like gemstones cascading over the sphere. I took some pictures with my phone. I didn't even need a filter to get that warm ethereal vibe. Too bad Gia was in no state for pictures now—her new boho look was perfectly suited for this mood.

But a good photographer didn't waste light like this. Since there were no flowery-dress or scarf-in-hair-type people around, it would have to be me. I peeked behind the fountain and held my phone out in front of me, checking to make sure the sun's rays illuminated only half my face. The whole look was so compelling, even though I was normally selfie averse. It wasn't that I didn't like having my face on camera or anything. I mean, I modeled my clothes all the time—I was clearly not camera shy. It was just . . . selfies were so cliché. I was trying to project a professional image—and having someone else take my pictures added to that. Plus, selfies weren't great for outfit shots. It was supposed to be about the clothes, not my face.

But taking pictures and not sharing them on social media was fine—it was good photography practice. I had snapped only a few shots when a voice nearly made me drop my phone in the fountain.

"Great. Thirst Trap is at it again."

Rowan. Because of course. I'd tried to take selfies only twice in months, and he'd witnessed both times. He put a plastic tray filled with colorful flowers on the cluttered workbench near his greenhouse. I slipped my phone in my pocket and glared. "Is your only purpose this summer to annoy me?" I said.

He snorted as he grabbed this weird metal mesh thing and laid it in front of him. "*You're* the one in *my* yard. I'm trying to get some work done here."

He was wearing a ridiculous shirt again, pale blue with a weird cartoony-looking plant on it that said PLANTS ARE PEOPLE, TOO. With more cutoff shorts, and . . . holy crap—*Crocs?* Dude was being seen in public in plastic clogs? I guess this wasn't really public, but still.

I shook my head. Supermodel good looks. A smoldering, swoon-worthy scowl. And dressed like a vegan preschooler.

I sighed. "You're going to have to learn to share your yard this summer. Channel that inner kindergartener—shouldn't be too hard, considering your outfit."

I sat on the sofa, put my sketchbook back on my lap, and reached into my bag for my colored pencils to add some details to the sketch of the back wall, but they weren't there.

"Damn it, I forgot I gave away my pencil crayons," I said.

"You're drawing?" he asked.

"I'm *drafting* plans. The tiny house wasn't bright enough, so I came out here." What was *he* doing, anyway? He appeared to be stuffing this green sludgy stuff into the wire mesh.

"Why'd you give away your pencil crayons?" he asked.

"A girl on my street needed them. Her brother lost all hers . . ." I shook my head. Why was I telling him this? "Don't be nosy, Plant-Boy," I said. I shut the book quickly. The sketches would have to be black and white. The point was to *reduce* the garish colorfulness of the store anyway. I'd started putting my charcoal pencils back in their tin when my phone rang, making me jump again. Two pencils dropped to the ground, rolling under the table. Ugh.

Maybe it was Matteo on the phone, though? I checked—it was my mother. I accepted the call.

"Tahira! I want to hear all about your first day at the store," Mom said. I glanced over at Rowan, but he'd moved to the far end of his workbench and was focused on whatever he was doing there.

"Hey, Mom. Everything was good. I'm working on the rebranding plans right now."

"Oh, that's great! I'll leave you to it. I know you'll do a thorough job. We got a package in the mail for that scholarship I was telling you about, the one for South Asians in the arts? I think it only works for Canadian universities, though. I'll read through the documentation and see if it will work for FIT. Because—"

"I know, Mom, I know. FIT is the best, so that's where we'll start. No need to say it again." I glanced over at Rowan. I didn't like the idea of him hearing me sounding like a petulant child to my mother. But he didn't seem to be paying attention to me. "I'll call you tomorrow after I show all this to Shar . . . min Aunty."

"Okay. Love you, Tahira. Good night."

"Night, Mom." I disconnected the call.

I leaned down to get my fallen pencils and then put all my stuff in my backpack.

"I like to draw out here in the evening, too," Rowan said, suddenly, still standing over by the workbench. "The light is perfect."

Okay, so that was weird to hear him say something with no venom in his voice at all.

I stood and turned to look at him, blinking. He was smiling, and wow, it changed his face. His jaw didn't look so sharp. His eyes less intense. With that expression and the otherworldly glow of the evening, the guy looked *soft*. Still exquisite, but approachable. The colorful flowers on the bench seemed to glow around him. Framing him. Such a shame he cared more about photosynthesis than photography. It would have been a lovely shot—if he'd been wearing decent clothes.

"You draw?" I asked. "I'm impressed. Plant-Boy is full of surprises."

With his eyes slightly downturned, he chuckled lightly. And his cheeks pinked a bit. The guy could do bashful-cute, too?

At this point, I didn't care that he looked like he shopped at Dollarama and the Disney Store, or that he had the personality of a garden slug . . . I decided then that, one way or another, I *had* to get pictures of him on my page this summer. He would look so amazing in my clothes, and Matteo wasn't around to model.

Rowan shook his head, that small smile still on his face. "I'm glad to keep you on your toes."

"I wouldn't have thought you were the artistic type, based on your clothing choices, that's all."

"I can't believe someone who wore high-heeled boots to a garden center claims to know who I am, based on my clothes."

"You saying you didn't like my outfit that day, Plant-Boy?"

"What I'm saying is I'm not surprised that you're judging someone without knowing them. You get the manure out of your stuff, or is eau de sheep poo your permanent aroma now?"

That was it. I wasn't going to let the most judgmental prick I'd ever met call *me* judgmental. "You're doing the same thing! You don't know a thing about me!"

"I know plenty about you." The venom was back in his voice. "You, and *influencers* like you, only care about how something *looks*. You don't give a shit about what's behind the surface, or the work that goes into making the pretty things. You just want to use everything around you for your quest for fame."

I snorted. If almost anyone else had said that to me, I might have been hurt. But Rowan seemed determined to misunderstand me, so why bother caring? The toxicity in his voice when he spat out the word "influencers" made me wonder if an Instagrammer had kidnapped his puppies or something in his past. It sounded like there was some serious trauma there. I might have felt sorry for him, but no. He certainly wouldn't have any sympathy for me.

I narrowed my eyes as I took two steps closer to him. "What is it about Bakewell and people making quick judgments on anyone new in town? You don't want people invading your precious village and upsetting the equilibrium that keeps you and your type on top?"

"My *type*? What the hell are you talking about?"

I gave him a pointed look. "I met your ex today. That's some taste you have there."

He frowned, still stuffing the green, fuzzy stuff into his wire mesh. "Addison?"

I nodded. "Two sides of the same coin. Addison thinks my Instagram following makes me *worth* her time, and you find me *worthless* because of it. Neither of you see that I'm more than that. By the way, you should tell her to leave Juniper alone. And now I'll leave you alone."

"Wait, Tahira," he said with a sudden urgency as he dropped his handful of green stuff on the bench. "What did Addison do to June?"

So, he *did* know my name. "She was harassing her about that flower contest. Does every interaction in this town have to do with foliage?"

He swept his hand over his head. "I *told* Addie to cut that out. Was June okay? Addie didn't call her any names, did she?" The big-brother concern in his voice surprised me. He hadn't struck me as empathetic.

"She called her Junebug, which seemed to irritate her."

"Addison didn't say anything else nasty, did she?"

"She made a crack about your sister not being cool enough for New York City." I stepped closer. "Why don't *you* enter the contest with June so Addison will leave her alone?"

He huffed. "That's actually what I want." He indicated the mesh-wire thing he was fiddling with. "I asked her to be on me and Leanne's team, but she said no. I figured I'd try the flower-symbolism thing that June's into to get her to change her mind."

I looked at the flowers on the workbench. "What are you using?"

"I found this driftwood last week, and I couldn't get the idea of using it in a floral arrangement out of my head. I figured June might like these irises and lisianthus for their meanings." He pointed out the flowers. "The irises are for trust, I think. And the lisianthus are for admiration and respect. I'm not sure I was using the right book for their meanings, though. Honestly, this whole idea of choosing flowers as symbols isn't normally how I design arrangements. I usually just use what works, appearance wise." He narrowed his eyes at the arrangement, like he wasn't sure it matched the image in his brain.

The driftwood was this gnarly, twisty thing, and completely bare of bark. The metal mesh was built up on one side with the green stuff wedged into it, and the flower stems had been poked into the green stuff. It honestly shouldn't have looked this good—it was just dried-out wood and dead flowers. But it was *beautiful*. Modern. The twisted line of the wood continued on with the unusual shape of the iris flowers. And the pale, papery petals of the lisianthus grounded the whole thing. I wasn't sure what I had expected when I heard the Johnston kids were into flower arranging, but I'd assumed it would be more like what my nanima did with plastic flowers from the craft store. Or maybe like the centerpieces in weddings. I'd heard them mention a "flower sculpture" competition, but I assumed it was more like flowers in vases.

But this? This was actually *sculptural*. And compelling. I stepped even closer. I couldn't deny it . . . I went to an art school—this was *art*. And Rowan? I was no floral-sculpture expert, but I could see the weirdo was like some sort of floral savant. No wonder Addison was pissed her ex wasn't going to help her win that competition.

"Juniper is as good as you at this stuff?" I asked.

He chuckled. "Careful, Thirst Trap. I think you just complimented me."

I rolled my eyes. "I'm just trying to figure all you people out. Addison was, like, totally negging Juniper to get her on her team, and you—you're researching flower meanings to convince her. As far as I'm concerned, both are manipulative."

His nostrils flared. "I'm not manipulating her; she's my *sister*. I want her to . . ." He paused. "I'm trying to protect her."

"Okay, so, that's admirable and all, but you should be letting Juniper do what she wants." And I suspected all Juniper wanted to do was read books. And maybe talk about books. Photograph books. "This *is* cool, though." I gestured to the flower arrangement and sighed. "I admit, I am impressed."

He snorted. "High praise, coming from you."

"Actually, it is." I shook my head. The guy's flower talent was distracting me from my point. "Honestly, I can't see how you and Addison are the slightest bit compatible, but whatever. I'm not going to pretend to understand the love lives of the hayseeds and flower children. Wait, what did she call you? Flower Power?"

He huffed. "Addison and I are *not* compatible. That's why we're not together. I'll talk to her. Get her to leave June alone."

I waved my hand and headed back to the table to get my backpack. "You do that."

"Tahira, wait. I need a favor."

I turned back to him, one eyebrow raised in question. What could I possibly do for him?

He walked around the workbench and came closer to me. I couldn't make out his expression anymore because it was getting dark and the bright colors in the sky had dimmed. "You'll be working with June this summer, and for some reason she really likes you. Can you just, I don't know . . . keep her safe from people like Addison?"

"You want me to protect your sister from your girlfriend?"

"*Ex*-girlfriend. Look, June's . . . she's dealt with a lot of crap at school, and she took our grandmother's death last year pretty hard."

I winced. June talked so warmly about her grandmother—I hadn't realized she'd died recently. "Oh. I'm sorry. Is this the grandmother who taught her about flowers?"

Rowan nodded. "She lived here with us for the last five years, and June and her were close. Anyway, June's head's in the clouds lately. I don't want people like Addie taking advantage."

I didn't want that, either. I slipped my backpack straps on. "I didn't like the way your *ex* was talking to Juniper. No one is going to bully my coworker on my watch. Gia and I have already decided she will be our teen-comedy sidekick."

He snorted. "*Mean Girls?*"

"*Clueless.*"

He laughed out loud. "Well, you certainly have Cher's pout mastered."

Huh. Rowan Johnston knew *Clueless*. "I don't pout," I said.

"You're pouting right now. You'll tell me if Addie harasses her again?" he asked.

I shrugged. Getting involved in Bakewell drama when I wanted to focus on work was probably ill advised, but I didn't want June disrespected by a snobby brat.

"Fine. Good night, Plant-Boy."

I left the beautiful douche canoe alone in his garden.

8

TEARS, PEP TALKS, AND DIGGING GARDEN HOTTIES

I ended up texting Matteo for a while from my sleeping loft when I got back to the tiny house. Gia was watching something on her phone from her bed with headphones. Matteo had a lot of ideas for elements to add to my proposal for Lily, but since the store didn't carry menswear, I wasn't sure I could use any of them. I promised I'd hire him as a consultant if we ever sold clothes for guys and then said good night. I still had a crap ton of work left, and between my mother, my boyfriend, and the grumpy plant nerd in the yard, I'd had enough distractions for one night. I stayed up late writing by the light of my phone to finish the proposal. It was fine—my body was used to little sleep when I was designing or sewing, anyway.

The Lilybuds schedule normally had one person (usually Shar) opening the store at ten, with one or two people joining at noon, since that's when most of the customers came in. But on Tuesday, Gia and I both opened with Shar since some tour buses were going to be passing through town on the way to some immersive flower experience. The tour-bus ladies (because most were older women around Shar's age) came soon after we opened, browsed for what felt like hours, and bought barely anything. Waste of time, if you asked me. When we rebranded the store as Lily, people wouldn't drop in while passing through town—we'd be a destination in itself.

After the crowds died down, it was finally time to show Shar my proposal. The three of us stood around the counter, and I pulled out my sketchbook and handwritten notes.

"Wow, this is impressive," Shar said, flipping through my sketchbook to look at the five detailed mock-ups I'd made. "You're so professional. I don't think you'll have a problem getting into that school of yours."

I smiled. The positive reinforcement kept my nerves tamped down as I went through my proposal. Gia had seen most of it this morning, so she jumped in here and there, but this project was *my* baby. I couldn't wait to see it come to life this summer.

I went through it all—the sketches of the inside of the store, the new logo, the sketch of the exterior, and some sample products from Shar's wholesalers that fit the store's new vibe. I'd even sourced some new suppliers with similar price points but more on-trend stuff. After showing Shar the last sketch—the one of the back wall with the new logo and geometric wallpaper—I stilled, biting my lip. My aunt had been awfully quiet as I was talking. I was scared all of a sudden—she did like the proposal, right?

Finally, she spoke. "Wow, Tahira. This is impressive. Really. You did all this since yesterday?"

"Yeah, while we were here and then last night."

Shar shook her head. "You're a remarkable girl. Truly. But . . . I think you may have bitten off more than we can chew. I appreciate your vision, but this is too much."

I blinked. "Too much?"

She put her hand over mine. "I think this plan is too ambitious for my little store. New sign, new fixtures, turning over all the stock . . . it's more than I'd planned. And the cost! This is Bakewell, not Yorkville Avenue in Toronto. We have a more mature clientele who, for the most part, like the store as it is. I was thinking more a freshen-up, not an entire redo."

She didn't like it.

I closed my eyes and took a breath. I'd been rejected before. Loads of times. I didn't get the job in the denim section at that luxury department store. Someone else's design was picked for the finale of the school fashion show last year. Other than Nilusha, no designer had even called me for an interview for a summer job. Plus, #IndieFashionWeekly rejected me every Sunday. This shouldn't have hurt so much.

I wasn't cut out for this career.

My heart was beating heavy in my chest. I wasn't *supposed* to get rejected here. Shar was my *aunt*. This was Bakewell. This was supposed to be the easy way to get the experience I'd lost when that damn parakeet ruined my life. But I had still failed.

If I couldn't even do this, why did I think I could handle FIT? Or the fashion world?

Gia gave Shar a pleading look. "But you could be sooo cool! You could attract younger customers!"

"The older crowd is my bread and butter, and I can't afford to make them feel uncomfortable," Shar said.

"But why can't younger people be the store's bread and butter? The Toronto boutique I used to work at managed to make a killing with younger customers," I said.

"There aren't a lot of younger people around here. They certainly don't spend enough to make all this worthwhile."

"What about just changing the name?" Gia offered.

I looked down at my sketch. What was the point of using the cool, minimalistic name and logo if the store was the same old country-clothing store?

Shar shook her head. "Maybe in the future, but not this year." She reached over to the edge of the counter. "Changing the logo now would cost a fortune in marketing." She put a glossy sheet on my open sketchbook. It was a flyer for the Bakewell Festival of Flowers. "We're a sponsor for the festival, and most of the promos are already printed."

Yup. The damn oval with flowers and the name "Lilybuds" was printed on the flyer, along with McLaughlin's Hardware (Addison's family?) and the Book Nook.

"That bites," Gia said, hunching her shoulders and resting her elbows on the counter. "This could have been awesome. Tahira is talented."

Shar smiled with encouragement. "She's *so* talented. I'm in awe. Let's have a compromise, shall we? How about we bring in a few of these pieces?" She pulled out my list of products. "We can set up a little corner—maybe five feet or so on the back wall. A younger line within the store. You could even call it your name—Lilies."

"Just Lily, with a period," I said, voice shaking. A small corner of a store with mass-produced wholesale clothes was nothing impressive. This wasn't getting me into FIT.

Shar continued flipping through the pages in the sketchbook. "I think we can work with a lot of your ideas. Fresh white walls and less clutter would make a big impact. How about this—come back to me with a scaled-down design plan with no new fixtures or major construction. Include a small new section with some of these trendier pieces. We can still do amazing work here, just on a smaller scale." She tapped the sketch of the back wall. "This is impressive. Really. You're going to be a force to be reckoned with soon, Tahira, but let's walk before running, at least here at Lilybuds. Can you still use these sketches in your college application?"

I shrugged. I supposed I could, but without the follow-up photos of the plan implemented, what was the point?

"Don't be discouraged, beti," Shar said. Then she smiled at the sketch of the back wall. "This reminds me of the mural at Wynter's."

I cringed, looking at my drawing. Yup—the "designer" wallpaper I'd drawn did kind of look like that stupid purple and blue mural on the barn at the nursery. The irony wasn't lost on me. This moment also felt like a sack of poo had been thrown on what was supposed to be the start of an amazing summer.

Gia tilted her head, smiling at me with encouragement. "I totally want to help pick the pieces for a new line. It'll be awesome."

Gia was a good friend. I closed my sketchbook and put on a smile. I had to at least look optimistic. Pouting not allowed. This job was the only one I had this summer, and I still needed a reference.

"It's no problem," I said slowly. I put the sketchbook back in my bag. "I can totally rework this plan. It's a process, right? I'll draft simpler ideas tonight."

"Oh, that reminds me," Shar said, grinning. "Rowan stopped by the house on his way to work this morning. He brought an extra drafting light for the flat and some colored pencils for you."

"Rowan brought them?"

She nodded. "He's so thoughtful. I'm going to miss him when he goes to university in September." She looked at her watch. "I'll take my lunch now. You girls hold down the fort."

I sighed, putting my bag behind the counter. Rowan wasn't being nice; the light was probably just so I would stop sketching in his precious backyard. But that didn't explain the pencil crayons . . . was that payment for protecting Juniper? Honestly, it didn't even matter right now. Not when my entire summer plan had just crumbled to the ground and I had to regroup.

Again.

～

Since the store was dead, and Juniper was coming in later to close anyway, Shar said I could leave after Gia's lunch break if I wanted to. Clearly, she could tell I needed space to process the humiliating rejection this morning. I was grateful—I always thought best when walking alone in downtown Toronto. Hopefully downtown Bakewell would do in a pinch.

It was a downright glorious sunny day, which was kind of rude, considering my mood. The streets were quiet, and I barely passed anyone as I made my way up Main Street toward home. Since I was alone, I allowed myself a good old-fashioned, adolescent-angst pout, because none of this was fair. The stupid parakeet, Nilusha's broken leg, the manure on my red suede boots, Rowan Johnston's smirk, and finally, Shar rejecting my plan for her store. I worked hard—and hard work was *supposed* to pay off. Yeah, connections and talent and all that mattered, too, but if I made a plan and stuck to it, I was supposed to succeed.

Janmohammads always succeed. It was the family mantra. But apparently, I was the one to disprove it.

I closed my eyes for a second, trying to will away the tears. Last time I cried like this, my false lashes came clean off, and I didn't want to scare the Bakewell kids playing at the flower playground. I pulled out my phone and called Matteo as I walked. I needed to hear his voice. I needed him to tell me it was going to be okay. But of course he didn't answer. He wasn't allowed calls at work. I texted him to call me when he could.

What was I supposed to do now about my FIT application? On the drive out here, Mom had said I needed to find a way to make Bakewell work for me while I worked for Bakewell.

Ugh. How, even? I called Mom.

"This isn't going to work," I said. "I need to come home."

"Tahira . . . what happened? Are you crying?"

"Shar hated my proposal."

Telling Mom should have helped. It normally felt like a weight being lifted when I told my parents my problems. But I'd told them only disappointing news lately.

"Do you want me to talk to Sharmin?" Mom asked. "I can try to convince her to let you do your plan."

I exhaled. "I . . . I don't know." I'd rather not get what I wanted because my mommy stepped in—although that was how I'd gotten this job in the first place. "I mean, if she thinks she'll lose business, I have to deal, right?" The store was her livelihood—and she knew what her customers wanted. "Painting the walls isn't going to get me into FIT, though. Should I just come home?"

"And do what? We looked. There are no other suitable positions on short notice. No, you must stay and make this work. FIT is the most prestigious fashion school in the world. You know how competitive it's going to be to get in. And even once you're at the school, you'll be competing against all your classmates for every opportunity there. You can't just leave when it gets hard."

But what if I'm not good enough to compete at FIT? In New York? I didn't dare say that to Mom. She wouldn't allow it. I was a Janmohammad. I needed to succeed.

"It's about how you sell it, Tahira," Mom said. "Do this smaller project for Sharmin. Get a great reference letter. And use your spare time to build up your portfolio so that it stands out in your application. Design something that goes viral."

It was what I loved the most—designing. I turned onto Shar's driveway. "Mom, I've been trying. I post new designs weekly, and none of them go anywhere. I might not be cut out for this."

"Tahira, none of this. What do Janmohammads do?"

I sighed. "Succeed."

"Right. *Succeed.* We're *always* cut out for this because we *work* for it. You are incredibly talented, but talent alone isn't enough. Maybe you need to do some more creative thinking. Why don't you call that fashion designer of yours?"

"I can't call Nilusha now. We're supposed to FaceTime on Thursdays for our mentorship." Today was only Tuesday.

"Tahira! You need to be more proactive! She said she would mentor you; this is what mentors do!"

I was in the backyard by then. I dropped my bag on one of the lounge chairs outside the tiny house and flopped on the other one. Mom was right, of course. Even though she was kind of famous, or at least getting there, Nilusha had been incredibly kind the few times we'd talked. It was she who'd insisted on weekly calls. I felt awkward phoning her now, but I was desperate.

"Fine. I'll text her," I said. "But if she tells me to go back to Toronto, I'm leaving this place."

"And take Gia with you, after convincing your aunt to hire her? You can't abandon Sharmin like that; you made a commitment."

I sighed again. I was completely and utterly stuck. "All right, Mom. I'm texting Nilusha now."

"Good girl. You can do this, Tahira. All your hard work *will* pay off, I know it. Love you, beti. I'm praying for you."

"Love you, too, Mom."

After asking Siri the time in Paris right now (a respectable 8:30 p.m.), I sent a text, asking if Nilusha had a minute. A FaceTime call from her immediately showed up on my screen, and I turned my chair for a glare-free video before answering.

"Tahira, darling!" Nilusha, as usual, looked fabulous. Black turtleneck, small purple glasses frames, hair in a perfect messy bun. Honestly, I could only dream of looking that flawless while recovering from surgery.

My voice stuttered. "I h-hope . . . I mean, I'm sorry to bother you . . . I just . . . I need advice."

"It's absolutely no bother. I feel terrible that we can't work together this summer, so I'm always here for you. I'm so *over* being stuck here in France."

"Being stuck in Paris can't be that bad."

Nilusha laughed. "True, true. I was able to go to Les Puces de Saint-Ouen yesterday. Didier pushed me in a wheelchair. Those little shops are *not* accessible, but it felt good to get out. You should see the antique brooch I found. *Wait.* Who is the young man digging behind you? Where are you?"

I turned, and yup, it was Rowan. Wearing big headphones, so I doubted he could hear me. Also, terrible ripped denim cutoffs and a misshapen, pink T-shirt.

I settled back in the chair. "I'm in the garden at my aunt's house. This is where I'm staying for the summer. Don't mind him; he's just the garden dude next door," I said to Nilusha, lowering my voice, just in case.

"The gardener? How very *bougie.*"

Her expression when she said "bougie" made me laugh. I really liked Nilusha. "No, no. Not the *gardener.* He's eighteen. He lives next door, he's just . . . garden oriented."

"Oriented?"

"Interested in gardens, obsessed with plants. He basically lives out here—he's like a grumpy garden gnome or something. Except, you know. Taller."

Nilusha laughed. "Well, it looks like you're as fortuitous as me this summer. I have Didier the handsome French nurse, and you have the garden-oriented boy next door."

"The grumpy, judgy, garden-oriented boy. Anyway, I have a boyfriend back home."

She shrugged. "Situations evolve. Okay, sweetie, tell me your problem. Are you having issues in that teeny town of yours?"

I told her about Lilybuds and the rejection of my rebranding proposal. Nilusha listened carefully, asking questions along the way. It felt weird at first telling her about my failure, but she was so easy to talk to and encouraging.

"Sweetie, I understand why you're upset. It sounds like you did an incredible amount of work for this project."

"I did. I hardly slept last night. It was all for nothing, though. If she'd only wanted a coat of paint and maybe bring in some T-shirts or something, why ask me to put together a proposal for a whole rehaul of the store? She could have gotten Addie McLaughlin to do it."

I think Nilusha could hear my disdain for Addison in my voice because she snorted. "Do I want to know who Addie McLaughlin is?"

"No. I wish I didn't." I was sulking. I was angry. I needed to stop—I was talking to *Nilusha Bhatt*.

"Look, Tahira, I get why you're upset, honestly, but you need to see this from your aunt's perspective. Rebranding is a *massive* endeavor. She must know her client base, and what they want, or she wouldn't be afloat as a small business. This is the most important thing to remember as a designer—yes, we're artists. But we're also in the business of making customers happy. Without them, we have nothing." She smiled, tilting her head. "Finding the balance between art and customer satisfaction was the hardest lesson I learned when I was starting out. Push the envelope, be innovative. But don't forget to know your market."

"Yeah." She was right. I didn't want to be one of those artists with my head so far up my own butt that I thought my vision was 100 percent flawless. But still. This stung.

"What about this small capsule collection?" Nilusha asked. "That sounds like an opportunity. You can do all the market research, buying, and merchandising from scratch."

We talked about the potential experience from building this trendier line, and she even offered to look through the wholesalers to help me pick pieces.

"I would love to see the sketches you did," Nilusha said. "Is your sketchbook handy?"

"You want to see them now?"

"Yeah. I'm not doing anything else. I want to see these ideas of yours."

I pulled out the sketchbook and laid it open on the chair. Flipping through the pages while holding the phone camera over the book, I explained my vision to her. Her warm praise felt so good.

"This is excellent work," Nilusha said. "I can see some of this working in Toronto or something."

"But not here."

"I don't know the market there. Hey, what's that? There's a flower festival?"

The flyer for the Bakewell Festival of Flowers was still between the pages. I cringed, turning the camera back to me to tell her about the festival, and how obsessed everyone was with it.

"It sounds *darling*. I love those country farm places. Last year my girlfriends and I went up to one of those flower farms to take pictures in the lavender fields. You wouldn't believe how amazing it smelled."

"Could be around here. It's all very picturesque, if you're into that kind of thing." Obviously, she couldn't have gone to Wynter's—Rowan and Leanne would have chased them out with pitchforks for daring to take a picture. I opened the brochure to show Nilusha some of the pictures of the flowers inside.

"OMG . . . Tahira, zoom closer, will you? I see something interesting."

I did.

Nilusha laughed in surprise. "Ha! This is amazing! Did you even read the prize for this sculpture competition?"

"Yeah, it's a trip to New York. That's why everyone wants to win."

"Tahira, the prize is a trip to New York to enter the AHA Grand Floral Cup."

I picked up the flyer and took a look. "What's that?"

"Hang on, I'm googling this," Nilusha said. "Your little garden competition feeds into the American Horticultural Association's biggest annual event."

"Am I supposed to know what that is?"

"Yes, yes, you are. The Grand Floral Cup is a *massive* televised floral competition that happens in New York every year. Even people that aren't into flowers pay attention to it. It's like the Westminster dog show for flowers. Plus, *Christopher Chan*."

That got my attention. Christopher Chan, one of the hottest designers in New York right now, had a background as a posh florist or something, but these days he was doing really cool stuff with streetwear. Matteo was always going on about his menswear line. The designer was also an instructor at FIT—and honestly one of the reasons I wanted to go there. "What does Christopher Chan have to do with any of this? I mean, he uses a lot of botanical prints, but—"

"Tahira, he's a judge in this."

"Wow. Does that mean . . . ?"

"Whoever wins this little competition will get to go to New York and meet Christopher Chan. You are aware he's also on the selection committee for FIT, aren't you? Hell, even if you don't win, entering would be amazing. This would stand out, if he saw it on your application."

"But I'm applying for fashion design, not floral design."

"Tahira, lesson two for today—*design is design*. Line, color, form . . . the principles aren't that different. Christopher Chan used to be a floral designer, and now he's one of the top streetwear designers in the world. *You need to enter this.* I overheard him talking about it during Fashion Week, back when I could still walk. I'd stepped into this teeny tea shop because they had the most beautiful madeleines in the window, and who should be there but Christopher Chan, talking to Eda Meurisse from *Vogue*. I quickly put on my Fashion Week lanyard and sat at the table next to them, but alas, I'm a *nobody* to Christopher Chan. He wouldn't stop talking about this flower competition, though—he sounded obsessed. Oh, I'm still *dreaming* of the madeleines. I'm going to ask Didier if they'll deliver."

I didn't even know what a madeleine was. "There's no way I can enter a garden thing. I don't know a thing about flowers, and I'm extremely allergic to them. My aesthetic isn't really naturals, you know? I'm not into flowers or foliage—"

"Adapt, Tahira. Take an antihistamine. Ask your garden-oriented hottie next door to teach you. *Design is design.* This could be the break you were looking for. Actually, not 'could be.' This is *Christopher Chan.* You must reach for this connection."

I exhaled. "Okay."

Flowers. It always came back to bloody flowers around here.

9

A DREAM TEAM IS BORN!

Every instinct in my body told me that entering the Bakewell Bloom flower sculpture competition was a bad idea, but I couldn't exactly claim Nilusha Bhatt was my mentor if I ignored the first big piece of advice she gave me.

Holding in a sneeze from just thinking about it, I opened the Bakewell Festival of Flowers website on my phone and found the page for the competition. After scrolling through pictures of last year's winners, I realized two things. One: Rowan's gift with floral design wasn't unique around here. Many of the large architectural entries were amazing. But the second thing? The dried-out flower rabbit on the Johnstons' front lawn was Rowan's Bloom entry from last year, and it was spectacular—when it was fresh. Filled with vibrant flowers in so many colors. It was lush, interesting, and . . . alive. The lines, the color gradients—it didn't look like a rabbit but like some sort of magical forest god.

I frowned.

It was slightly annoying that the guy was a wicked talented artist. His work stood out even among the rest of the serious flower skills people had around here.

And yup, the Bloom grand prize was a trip to New York and entry into this Floral Cup in late October. The New York competition was huge—they averaged over three hundred entries—and it would take serious hustle to catch the attention of Christopher Chan there. That wasn't a problem for me: Hustle was practically my middle name. (Actually it was Huma, but close enough.)

But I needed to *win* the Bakewell competition first, and as I saw it, there were three roadblocks in my way. One: this was a team competition, and I had no team. Two: I knew nothing about flowers, floral design, or flower sculptures, and I was sure YouTube could only take me so far. And three: the whole allergy problem. I sneezed again. The antihistamines I took daily wouldn't cut it. I wondered about the feasibility of flower arranging from inside a big plastic bubble. But honestly, problems one and two were the biggest. I needed a new Plan.

Rowan was still across the yard wearing headphones. He had said he was entering the competition with Leanne, so there *was* room on his team for me, even if June agreed to join, since teams could be three or four members. But . . . of course, *no*. I wouldn't subject myself to being on a team with someone who hated me.

I needed my *own* team. Who would I recruit to join me? Gia, of course. Too bad Matteo wasn't here because he'd totally do it. Shar? Maybe. But her back problems would probably be an issue. Juniper was the obvious choice, but she herself had said she didn't want to enter, and the last thing I wanted was to be yet another person begging Juniper to be on their Bloom team.

But maybe Juniper would join with me? Maybe the reason she'd said no to Rowan and Addison wasn't that she didn't want to do the Bloom, but that she didn't want to play second fiddle to her flower-genius brother or be anywhere near Addison "Wannabe Regina George Mean Girl" McLaughlin. I mean, *I* didn't want to be on a team with either of them.

I texted her and invited her for tea after dinner, since I'd learned that was something she loved when we'd gone to Hyacinth's together.

Yes! Want me to make the tea? I have some of Hyacinth's chai blend. Or maybe the lavender chamomile tea bags they sell at the nursery? What time? Where should we meet? In the backyard, I assume. OMG one day I'm going to have to take you to the fields behind the nursery—although that's better for a picnic, not just tea.

I chuckled. Juniper texting was just like Juniper talking. I wrote back with a time and told her I'd take care of the tea.

I headed to the tiny house to call Matteo to eliminate any possibility of Rowan possibly eavesdropping. My mood was already monumentally improved after talking to Nilusha, but Matteo made me feel even better. He was supportive and kind and comforted me about what had happened at Lilybuds. He said I'd definitely done the right thing by getting advice from Nilusha, and he loved my idea of entering the flower competition.

After the call, I did a quick Google search and settled into my bed on the loft to read everything I could about floral sculpture. If I was going to do this, I was going to do it like a Janmohammad. I was going to give it everything I had.

A few hours later, Gia got home.

"T, come down here so I can hug you," she called up.

"Why do you want to hug me?" I called back, confused. My brain was mush from all the floral design theory I'd just binged.

"Your beautiful dreams were *crushed* today! Destroyed! Your future was squashed like an ant on a sidewalk! You must be *devastated!*"

I'd been feeling okay since I had a new plan, but when she put it that way, I felt kind of sucky again.

"I've been so distraught all afternoon!" Gia continued, her voice so melodramatic that I fully expected her to have a weak wrist on her forehead. "Tell me, my sweet, unfortunate friend, how can I support you in this difficult time?"

"First of all, you can stop calling me your 'unfortunate friend.'" I poked my head over the railing of the loft. "G, what are you wearing?"

She stood there in purple tie-dyed overalls.

"I bought them from the store." She grinned, looking down at herself. "You said you liked the overalls there."

"Okay, but the ones I liked were black linen. Not . . ." I tried to identify the fabric. "Rayon batik. Purple, at that."

"I'm trying a new look, remember? This is the kind of thing country people wear, right?"

I wasn't sure, but I didn't really want to get into that right now. I nodded. "Sure. Totally rocking the rural-chic vibe. Look, I'm okay. I'm totally not giving up on FIT. I have an idea to salvage my application. We're meeting Juniper for tea after dinner to discuss it."

Gia beamed, clapping her hands together. "Yay! *Yay, yay, yay!* That's my Tahira! Always a solution for every setback. Seriously, you're an inspiration." She reached up to pat my cheek, which wasn't something I remembered my friend ever doing. "So, what's the plan?" she asked. "I'm completely on board, whatever it is."

I was about to tell her about my call with Nilusha when Gia's phone rang. She glanced at it. "Oh, I need to take this. We can chat later, right? I've been trying to find a salon around here that does hair-bond-building treatments, and this is the first one to actually return my call."

I nodded.

Gia was on the phone looking for hairstylists until dinner, while I kept up my floral sculpture research. I had a lot to learn, but I was ready for the challenge.

After dinner, the three of us sat around the low table in the yard, sipping the chai my aunt had helped me make and listening to Juniper tell us about her day.

"I went to the library before work because my interlibrary loan came in, and Mrs. McLaughlin tried to get me to start a teen book club with Addison in September, but I'm not subjecting myself to that."

"With Addison? Oh, wait, is Mrs. McLaughlin related to her?"
June nodded. "Her mother."

Oh. The clone of Addison I saw at Hyacinth's.

"I don't even think Addison wants to do this book club," Juniper
continued, "but her mother thinks she needs more extracurriculars or
something for her university application. I get enough flak for being a
weirdo book nerd at school; why ask for more? People are still making
cracks about back when I used to . . ." She frowned, shaking her head.
"Never mind that. But then Mrs. McLaughlin mentioned that Leanne
came in to check out the first Silverborn book, which is weird because
I didn't know Leanne read urban fantasy. Do you know Silverborn? It's
my favorite series. Anyway, isn't it going against some librarian rule to
tell me what Leanne is reading? That's another reason I said no to the
book club thing. Mrs. McLaughlin has no sense of privacy. Not that a
book club is some confidential meeting or anything . . . but sometimes
talking about books does feel like therapy, you know?"

"Maybe Leanne could do a book club with you," Gia said. She was
sitting on the sofa next to me, while June was across from us.

I shook my head at Gia. "Leanne was really patronizing when I
met her," I said. "I don't think it would be great for Juniper to work
with someone like that." I'd promised to keep an eye out for people
harassing Juniper.

Juniper shook her head. "No, Leanne's fine. She's just . . ." She
sighed. "Leanne's not really into books. She's going away for university
in September, anyway. She got a scholarship and everything. Thank God
Mrs. McLaughlin didn't bring up me doing the Bloom with Addison
again because—"

"Hang on, Juniper," I interrupted. "Can I cut in?"

Juniper grinned. "Of course. Otherwise I'll keep going on forever.
Mom said I talk so much because Row never did. Did you know he
didn't talk until he was almost three? He had to go to speech therapy in
Niagara and everything. I'm not telling some deep dark secret here or

anything; everyone knows. Everyone knows everything about everyone in Bakewell." She grimaced, taking a home-baked cookie from a tin she'd brought out with her. "Sorry. I did it again, didn't I? You were saying?"

My phone buzzed with a text. "One second, Juniper." I put my cup down and checked the screen. It was my sister.

Samaya: I heard half your convo with Mom earlier. You okay?

Tahira: I'm good. Just dealing with a setback. Can we talk later? I'm in the middle of something.

Samaya: No worries. Try not to let the tiger mom get to you. She really needs to lay off sometimes.

Tahira: Congrats on getting the math camp position! Let's FaceTime soon.

Samaya: TY! Later!

What had I been saying? "So, Juniper, I was just wondering . . . I saw your brother making this flower thing yesterday . . . why aren't you doing the floral competition with him and Leanne?"

She shrugged. "I can't."

Gia snorted. "They're stupid if they don't want you."

"They do want her," I said. "Rowan told me he asked you."

Juniper shrugged but was clearly uncomfortable. "I . . . I don't want to be on Rowan and Leanne's team."

Just as I suspected—she wasn't objecting to entering the Bloom, just to being on a team with Rowan. She might be willing to be on my team. But—ugh. Did I really want to sign up for all this Johnston family drama?

I remembered Nilusha's words—I must reach for this connection. "Wouldn't it be cool if the three of us were on a team together?" I tried to look like I'd just thought of the idea.

Gia laughed. Like, seriously, laughed loudly. Should I have told her this plan alone first?

I bit my lips. I was pretty sure I knew why I hadn't tried harder to tell her about this earlier. It was the same reason why I didn't tell her about coming to Bakewell until that day at Graffiti Alley—I thought she'd point out how ridiculous it was for me to even think this was going to help me.

I couldn't be insecure about this—if I wanted to enter the Bloom, I had to own this decision. "Seriously," I said. "It could be fun."

"No," Gia said, putting her cup down. "You and I know nothing about flower arranging. And you're allergic to flowers!"

Juniper poured herself more tea. "I thought you hated flowers, anyway?"

I tilted my head. "Yeah, but *you* love them. This will be a way to enter the Bloom without having to work with Addison, or the Crab Apple Tree and his Perky Smug Sidekick."

A loud throat-clearing sound startled me. A male one. "Damn it," I said. "He's behind me, isn't he?"

"Yes, along with his Perky Smug Sidekick!" a female voice said, sounding, well, *perky*. I turned . . . and yup. Rowan and Leanne. The Grump and the Sunshine Girl themselves. His shirt today may have been the worst yet—bright purple, with a daisy riding a motorcycle that said PETAL TO THE METAL. Leanne's was less vibrant—muted blue and orange bunnies. He was carrying a couple of small pots of plants, which he immediately took to his greenhouse.

"Hey, Junebug," Leanne said, sitting next to Juniper on the sofa. "How's it going?"

Juniper frowned but didn't say anything.

Gia grinned. "Ah! You're Leanne, aren't you! I love putting a face to a name! I'm Gia—Tahira's best friend. Love your hair. Those waves natural?"

Leanne nodded. "More work than it's worth, if you ask me." She ran her hand through her hair. "We're just dropping off some dahlias for Row's new garden bed; then I'm going to smoke him at *Grand Theft*

Auto. You should come play, too, Junebug. Let's show your brother that girls can loot and hijack with the rest of them." Leanne grinned at me. "Hey, nice to see you again! You get the shit out of your shoes?" Her eyes twinkled.

I rolled my eyes. "I was just . . ." I was trying to think of a way to relocate this conversation when Rowan reappeared and squeezed next to Juniper on the sofa. This guy was like a zit on my chin—always popping up when I wanted it the least.

I fully expected a scowl or glare from him. But his expression was all caring concern for his sister.

"Leanne, June doesn't like people calling her Junebug," he scolded his friend.

Leanne looked hurt. Or fake hurt. It was hard to tell with her. "But I gave her that name myself when we were kids! You don't mind, do you?" She pouted at Juniper.

Juniper took another cookie and mumbled something about it being fine.

Leanne was laying it on a little thick, and I couldn't tell if she was being sweet, or mocking Juniper. There was just something I found so . . . *off* about Leanne. She was supposedly academically brilliant, but she had the personality of a goofball frat boy. An outgoing, cheerful frat boy. I shook my head. "I can't understand how you and Rowan are friends," I said to her. "You're nothing alike."

Rowan grunted a sound of displeasure, but Leanne's head fell back as she laughed. "Row's my brother. We grew up in this garden together."

I guess if they knew each other that long, it made sense. I mean, Samaya and I were nothing alike, either. Although we weren't really friends.

"And you never dated?" Gia asked, seemingly still considering shipping Rowan and Leanne.

Leanne shook her head. "I think he's the only person in our grade of any gender I've never considered dating." She grinned. "I'm pansexual."

"Cool," Gia said. "You'll have to introduce me to some singles around here."

I frowned at Gia. "Just because she's pansexual doesn't mean she knows everyone dateable in town."

Leanne shrugged. "That's generally true, but in my case I actually do. What are you—"

"Did I hear you ask June to do the Bloom with you?" Rowan interrupted, looking at me.

"We were talking about it," I said.

"I expressly told you that my sister doesn't want to enter the Bloom," he said.

I raised a brow. "Maybe she just doesn't want to enter with you?"

He shook his head. "Why would she want to be on your team over mine? She barely knows you."

Gia frowned. "Why don't you just ask Juniper what she wants? She's right here."

I exhaled. Gia was right. My focus on getting to Christopher Chan was making me as bad as everyone else. "I'm sorry. The truth is I need to enter the Bloom for totally selfish reasons, and . . ." I turned to Juniper. "Juniper, I don't think I can do it without your help."

"Of course," Rowan said, jaw clenching. "It's all about you and your *influencing*. June, you don't have to work with her."

"Wait, Row." Juniper's brows were knitted together with concern. "What's the story, Tahira? Why do you *need* to enter?"

Juniper was kind of growing on me. She wasn't naive, just very earnest and not too cool to show real enthusiasm, which was refreshing. She was considerate, too. If she and I were alone, I would totally have told her the whole story of why I needed to enter the Bloom, and why it wasn't just about my "influencing."

But we weren't alone—and I didn't feel much like telling Grumpy and the Sunshine Girl about my failures right now, even if they weren't my fault. I told the shorter version of why I wanted to enter. "This designer I'm really into will be at the Grand Floral Cup. It would be cool to meet him if we win."

"Ooh," Gia said. "Who is it?"

"Christopher Chan."

Gia's eyes widened. "Shut. Up. You're not serious, are you?"

I nodded.

Gia's spine straightened. "I'm coming, too. Where do we sign up?"

"We still need another," I said. "Teams can be three or four people. That's why I asked Juniper."

Rowan shook his head, looking annoyed. "You're talking about June like she's not even here again. And I'm literally going to school for landscape architecture and want to make connections in New York for my future career. I'm not just looking to fangirl some fashion designer." He turned to Juniper. "If you're going to join a Bloom team, join mine, not hers."

I narrowed my eyes at him. "Fashion *is* going to be my career. This isn't just a hobby for me, either."

"But I'm her actual brother! You? You've been nothing but judgmental and self-absorbed since you got to this town, like, four seconds ago. Why would you think that would compel any of us to do you a favor?"

That was it. I did not have to sit here and put up with this. I was just about to stand and tell Gia to forget all these people—we'd find someone else in this flower town who could help without a side of nastiness—when Leanne snorted.

"To be honest, I think both of y'all have good reasons to enter, but it doesn't matter what I think; it matters what Junebug thinks. Why don't y'all put it on pause and let her decide." She smiled at Juniper. "Who you gonna help? Your brother and me, or Donatella Versace here?"

Juniper blinked. Then blinked again. Her bottom lip trembled.

Shit. We'd made her uncomfortable. Very uncomfortable. I felt terrible. This wasn't what I'd set out to do tonight. Here I was thinking Juniper was cool and we could be friends, and now I was taking advantage of her just like everyone else did.

I gave her a reassuring smile. "You know what, Juniper? It's totally okay. You don't have to do it. I'll find another way."

Everyone was silent for a few seconds.

Leanne suddenly sighed, and I don't know . . . something . . . passed over her face. Guilt? Regret? She turned to Rowan. "Did I tell you that Daphne is clearing her one-foot fences again?"

What? Where the hell did that come from? Who was Daphne?

Gia snorted. "You people need to have one conversation at a time."

Rowan seemed as surprised as Gia and I were at Leanne's odd statement. "What does your rabbit have to do with anything?"

Leanne shrugged, pushing her hair over her shoulder. "Everything. After her last agility show, she didn't seem that into jumping anymore. Fred's still gung ho, but Daphne would just sit there while he hopped over the little fences. But for the last week or so, she's been jumping again as if nothing was wrong. Drama queen."

"Still not seeing the relevance here . . . ," Rowan said.

She gave him an incredulous look. "Don't you remember? There's an agility show in Bellville the same weekend as the Bakewell Flower Festival. I said I'd be on your Bloom team again because I didn't think Daphne wanted to do another show, and I didn't want to drive over three hours just for Fred. But now I think Daphne will do it." She grinned. "She's always been more high maintenance than her sister, but man, her jumps are *legendary*. She could be a champion, if she'd stop with the tantrums."

Gia raised a brow. "Her sister?"

"Fred's a girl. I know better than to have rabbits of opposite genders."

"But you said you'd be on my Bloom team!" Rowan was clearly irritated at his friend.

Leanne tilted her head toward him. "You *know* the rabbits come first."

Juniper nodded. "You've been training them for so long."

"Look, Rowan," Leanne said. "I was totally going to stay on your Bloom team and skip Bellville. I made a commitment to you. But now that this opportunity has fallen from the sky, we can all be happy. Daphne and Fred can advance their standings, and you can be on a team with these two." She indicated Gia and me. "Both you and Tahira have a good reason to enter, and June doesn't have to." She smiled at Juniper. "Or she can join y'all if she changes her mind. It can be up to June, no pressure from any of us."

Rowan's head jerked back. "I'm not entering with these two! There is no way they'll take the Bloom seriously! It'll all be selfies and thirst traps, and I'll be left doing all the work. Not to mention they don't know a thing about flowers and—"

"Rowan," Leanne interrupted. "You taught half our team last year. You can teach them! This way everyone can stop fighting over your sister. You and the fashionista could be a great pair—you could win and have the chance to hobnob with the glitterati. Or the planterati, at least. What do you say?" She was looking at me now. "Rowan's a champion, you know. And he's a great teacher."

I sighed. I'd already seen how good he was with flowers. Rowan and I together *could* win. If we could manage to avoid head-to-head combat.

Juniper answered before I could. "I can help you train them, Row. It won't be that bad—I'll be a referee if you need it." She had a determined look on her face.

Rowan did not look impressed. He sat silently, nostrils flaring a few seconds, then turned to me and Gia. "*Fine.* Don't flake out on us. And no city-splaining my flower knowledge. Tourists always assume I don't know what I'm talking about at the nursery."

Juniper snorted. "That's just idiots who think Black boys only care about basketball and not flowers and gardens."

I shook my head. "I would *never* do that. You're the expert here. I'll bow to your knowledge."

"Yay!" Gia clapped her hands. "This will be so epic. Is there a hashtag for the competition? I'm going to document our whole process. #GiaLearnsFlowers. Maybe I should approach florists to be, like, a sponsor or something?"

Leanne shook her head. "Sponsorships are against the rules."

"Ah, well. But when we win, I'm sure the sponsors will line up to talk to me," Gia said.

"We might not win," Rowan said, frowning at us.

Leanne grinned. "With both Johnstons teaching, you've got a great chance."

I exhaled. The Plan had to come first. And Leanne was right. This was my strongest chance of getting to New York. "Fine. I'm in."

Gia clapped again. "Yay. I'm excited. Let's do this. #GiaAndTahiraInTheBloom!"

10

LESSON ONE: TRY NOT TO KILL EACH OTHER

We ended up staying on the patio pretty late while we planned our strategy, since the Bloom was just over six weeks away. We decided to meet one or two nights a week for the next three weeks starting on Friday, so Rowan and Juniper could teach Gia and me everything we needed to know to be on a Bloom team. I insisted we start from the beginning—I wanted to learn everything I could about floral design before jumping into floral sculpture. I would be at my best if I started from the basics—you need to learn to stitch a seam before making a dress.

By the time Gia and I said good night and went back to the tiny house, I was really stoked about this plan. I guess my enthusiasm was a little intense, because Matteo had to tell me to calm myself three times when we talked after I climbed up into bed.

"Easy, baby. Take a breath. You're talking faster than I can think."

I laughed. "I just want to make sure I do it right, you know? They gave me a list of YouTube flower designers to follow and some books of their grandmother's. Rowan's going to bring some, like, dying plants from the nursery for us to practice with, and—"

"I thought you were working with the girl, what was her name . . . Jupiter?"

"Juniper."

"What kind of name is that, anyway?"

"It's a tree. Rowan's on the team, too. His team came in second last year, so we're lucky to have him."

"Gia told me the guy's good looking," Matteo said.

I cringed. "Seriously, Matteo? Don't do the jealousy thing—it's not cool. I don't even like the guy. We're just working together."

"I'm not jealous of a *gardener.* I'm just . . ." He sighed. "I'm working a shitty job where they keep me in the stockroom half the day, and my girlfriend and favorite cousin are gone all summer doing fun things and winning a trip to New York without me."

He was right. I had to remember that I wasn't the only one whose summer plans had gone out the window thanks to that parakeet in Paris.

"I'd *rather* be in the city with you. And it's not all bad—those pics you posted at the Humber Bridge got a lot of likes." Matteo spent a lot of time getting pictures in different Toronto spots for his Instagram page.

That perked him up. "Yeah, and you'll never guess who liked that post—Dasha Payne!"

"OMG, really? From *DashStyle*?" Dasha was a style influencer from LA. It was her blog that ran the #IndieFashionWeekly account.

"Yup. Alyssa tagged me on one of her Instagram posts, and Dasha found it! Dasha also liked one of the shots I posted of you and I from Graffiti Alley."

"That's amazing! Who's Alyssa?"

"I told you about her. She helped me get the job at H&M. Andrew's friend. Anyway, this could be big for you and me. Alyssa said her engagement has tripled since getting on Dasha's radar."

"Good for her," I said. I meant it. Getting attention from the right people meant everything in the style industry. But I felt a wave of bitterness rise up—Matteo was getting all this attention, when I'd been effectively ignored by *DashStyle* for months. I quickly pushed it down. It was fine. So much of this was luck—being in the right place at the right time. And I was honestly really happy for him. He worked so hard to increase his visibility; it was great that it was paying off for him.

We talked strategy for his page for a while, and he promised to tag me on posts so some of that LA attention could come my way, too.

"It's too bad we don't have any new content together," I said. "I've been so busy I haven't figured out how to get home for a visit."

"I can ask my brother to borrow his car and come see you? We can go for a drive, get some pictures."

"What? Can you? That would be awesome!"

"How about on the weekend? When you working?"

I pulled up my schedule on my phone. "Gia and I are both off on Sunday."

"Perfect. I'll get Alyssa to take my shift. I had this awesome idea for a shoot . . . all we need is one of those empty country roads . . ."

We talked for a while longer about his visit. I knew that part, or maybe most, of the reason he was coming was because he was jealous of all the summer plans Gia and I were making without him, but I didn't care. I wanted to see him. I wanted things to be like they used to be, even for a day.

"Hey, Matteo?" I asked, pulling my covers tighter around me. Gia was in her bed, watching YouTube, but she had her earbuds in.

"Hmm?"

"Do you think I'm shallow?"

He chuckled. "Tahira, you're not letting those hicks call you names, are you?"

"No, I just . . ." Juniper clearly didn't think I was too vapid to be her friend, and what did it matter if Rowan did? But I couldn't forget the look on his face when I told them I wanted to go to New York to meet a fashion designer. He was, like, disappointed that anyone cared so much about *fashion*. Plus all those cracks he made about influencers.

"Those people can't possibly understand you like I do," Matteo said. "You know what you want, and you go after it. It's my favorite thing about you." I could hear the smile in his voice. "That and your hair."

I laughed, a warm comfort enveloping me. "My favorite thing about you is your arms. I wish they were around me right now."

No one got me like Matteo did. He supported me, he believed in me, and he always made me feel like there was nothing I couldn't do. Who cared what Rowan Johnston thought about me, anyway? All he had to do was teach me floral design. Before long, I'd be back in the city, where I could leave all these doubts and these Bakewell-ites behind me. Bakewell-onians. Whatever.

~

I did as much online research as I could between shifts for the next few days to prepare for our first lesson on Friday—which meant I watched YouTube videos and read the blog of every floral design guru out there. So far, I was sort of seeing Nilusha's point—floral design reminded me so much of fashion design. Watching floral designers create arrangements without preplanning, letting the shapes and colors of the flowers guide them to the finished arrangement, reminded me of draping, a technique where people designed garments by laying fabric over a dress form instead of planning them using pencil and paper. Of course, sometimes floral designs were preplanned, too. This one designer I watched on YouTube drew all his designs before making them, and I was amazed at how well he was able to imagine complicated 3D arrangements in 2D first. Honestly, I was kind of getting into floral design.

On Friday, after leaving the store at six, I found myself with Juniper at the workbench near the Johnstons' greenhouse with a big pile of . . . actually, I didn't know what that was.

"What is this stuff?" I pointed to the furry green pile.

"Sphagnum moss," Juniper said. "We're going to fill the chicken wire frame with it. Row will be here in a sec with the flowers." Juniper looked adorable in loose printed pants from Lilybuds and a white cropped T-shirt. Her hair was pulled off her face with a multicolored scarf. "Where's Gia? I figured she'd be here already since she didn't work today."

I pointed to my phone. "She just texted me—she's on her way from Hyacinth's."

My phone vibrated. A text from Mom.

Mom: Did you get the scholarship package I mailed? I checked. The scholarship can be used for a school in the US.

Tahira: Thx but haven't looked at it yet. I'm about to have my first floral design lesson.

Mom: Okay. Focus on that. Take pictures for your portfolio! And have fun!

I slipped my phone into my pocket.

Juniper was cutting off a piece of chicken wire from a big roll with some wire cutters. "Oh, I forgot," she said suddenly. She dropped the cutters, hopped over to the door to the Johnstons' house, and grabbed a mason jar from the step. "I picked some lupin from the front yard for this lesson." The jar was filled with long, slim flowers in a deep shade of purple.

"What do these symbolize?" I asked.

Clearly, I was watching too many floral design videos, because I was appreciating Juniper's flowers-for-meaning habit. I really liked the single gladiolus stem she gave me for support when I finally told her about Shar rejecting my Lilybuds plan. I was actually sorry I couldn't bring it in the tiny house.

"Lupin are for creativity and imagination." She placed the jar on the edge of the bench and picked up the wire cutters. "Did you know 'lupin' means 'wolfish'? There is a character in the Silverborn series whose first name is Lupin—which makes sense because he's a werewolf. I'm totally shipping him and the main character, even though she's supposed to be with the vampire-hunter guy. Oh my God, I just heard Lexi Greer, the author of it, is doing a North American book tour when the next book comes out! I really hope there's a Toronto stop. Mom would totally take me to the city for that. She loves that I'm obsessed with a Black fantasy writer. I would die for a signed copy."

"Isn't that the book Leanne was reading?" I asked.

The sliding door from Shar's house opened then, and Gia floated out, a massive smile on her face and an iced coffee in her hand. "Sorry I'm late! I have *news*. I met my future husband at Hyacinth's! Like, seriously. I don't normally believe in insta-love or anything, but this guy . . ." She fanned herself with her hand. "Tahira, you're making my wedding dress; Juniper, you're on flowers."

I laughed. "Gia, you're seventeen. You're not getting married."

She nodded, blue eyes dancing with joy. "Don't worry, we'll have a long engagement. Juniper, will your brother give us a deal on one of those adorable weddings you told me about that they do at the nursery? I saw some pictures in *Martha Stewart Weddings* magazine of a ceremony in a lavender field . . . but oh my God. The bride was literally wearing a toga. Tahira, you would have died."

Juniper looked confused. "To be honest, Gia, I'm surprised you found someone worth swooning over in Bakewell."

Good point. "So am I," I said. "I haven't seen evidence of a remotely dateable guy in our age group in this town. Leanne seemed to think there were, but the guys I've met are all . . ." I stopped talking. I really needed to stop insulting Juniper's brother in front of her. Especially since he kept sneaking up on me.

"We're all what?" Rowan asked, appearing with a huge bucket of flowers obscuring the design on his pale-green T-shirt.

I shook my head. "Remind me to get you a bell to wear so I can hear you coming."

He snorted as he put the flowers near the bench. "You show them how to make a chicken wire frame yet, June?"

"Nah," Juniper said. "I was waiting for you." She turned to Gia and me. "Rowan trained Addie and Cameron last year."

Gia suddenly squealed and clasped her hands together. "Cameron! My future betrothed!"

"*Cameron?*" Juniper asked incredulously. "Cameron Simons? That's your future husband?"

Rowan frowned. "Why do you think you're marrying Cameron Simons?"

I shook my head. "She's not. Gia's . . ." Gia was just being Gia. Which, granted, if you didn't know her that well, could be a lot. "She just met the guy, right, Gia?"

I gave her a look that I hoped she understood as *Can we just not with the drama right now so the hot guy wearing a* Little Shop of Horrors *T-shirt can teach us flower arranging?*

Gia nodded, but very enthusiastically, and she went on, "He's, like, the *sweetest* guy I've ever met. He bought me this coffee, and he had this adorable puppy named Ginger with him, and you know what he called me? Gigi! Like totally unprompted! I love it when guys call me Gigi. He's going to call me tonight."

"Ginger isn't a puppy," Rowan said. "She's nine. Also, *Cameron*? Really?"

"What's wrong with him?" I asked.

He shrugged. "I mean, technically, nothing. He works at the nursery. He's not the brightest crayon in the box, and he's not really a commitment kind of guy, but he's—"

Gia's phone chimed loudly. "Ooh," she squealed, looking at it. "That's him. I'm going to . . . I'll be back." Head in her phone, she went into the tiny house.

Juniper started cutting chicken wire again at the workbench. "Cameron and Leanne were dating last year during the Bloom. He's on Addison's team this year."

I shook my head, amazed. "Is everyone connected to everyone around here?"

"Yup," Rowan said. "Small town."

"Well, if he's such a dim bulb, why did Leanne date him?" I asked. "The two of you have interesting taste."

Rowan chuckled. "Leanne's not really the commitment type, either. She's not great at turning down dates. Pretty much everyone's her ex. Cameron—"

"Ouch!" Juniper squealed.

"What happened?" I asked. "Are you okay?"

"It's fine, it's fine," June said, cradling her one hand in the other. "The wire snips got away from me." She held up her fingers for us to see. There was a small cut on one.

Rowan shook his head. "Why aren't you wearing gloves? I'll get a Band-Aid." He went into the greenhouse, returning a few seconds later with a first aid kit.

Gia came back then, arms swinging and eyes dancing. "Let's get to this, because I have a date later."

"Not sure you should be dating the competition, Gia. Cameron's on Addison's Bloom team," I said.

She waved her hand. "I can be sportswomanlike. C'mon—flower arranging now, talking about my boo later."

Rolling his eyes, Rowan lifted two urn-looking pots onto the table. "Okay. We're going to start with cut-flower arranging. The Bloom is, of course, for live flower sculptures, but you need to learn the basics first. We'll make chicken wire frames like we will for the competition."

He instructed us to shape the chicken wire into balls. Gia made a face as she struggled with hers. "Ugh." She dropped it on the bench.

"It's sharp. Look, I'm bleeding. Oh God, do I need a tetanus shot? That's what you're supposed to do, right?"

I didn't see any evidence of broken skin on Gia's hands. "Gia, don't be dramatic." I tossed her a pair of garden gloves. I wasn't wearing any because I assumed working with fiddly chicken wire would be tricky wearing heavy leather gloves.

It was so typical Gia to feign a minor injury to get out of doing something she didn't want to do. Like a "twisted ankle" before we started basketball in gym class, or "sore eyes" before our grade-ten math exam. But this wasn't supposed to be something she didn't want to do. I was irked—she was my best friend, and this competition was extremely important to me.

"You're not going to get lockjaw from brand-new chicken wire, anyway," Rowan said.

"Lockjaw?" Gia looked horrified. "What the heck? That sounds like some sort of medieval torture disease. Who said anything about getting *lockjaw?*"

Juniper raised a brow. "You did? You said you'd need a tetanus shot. A tetanus shot is to prevent lockjaw."

Gia seemed so disturbed I decided to deflect. "Are those the flowers we'll be working with?" I asked, pointing to the bucket.

"No. It's a litter of kittens," Rowan said, voice dripping with sarcasm.

"Wow. I see you brought your manners again," I said. Then I sneezed. Several times.

"Row," Juniper said. "Don't be mean. We need to work together all summer. You okay, Tahira?"

I waved my hand. "I'm fine, I'm fine. I can handle it. Glad it's not kittens—I'm even more allergic to cats." I sneezed again. Of course.

Somehow, without anyone else insulting anyone, or cutting themselves with chicken wire or wire cutters, we continued with the lesson. Gia and I each put our chicken wire balls in the pots, then arranged the flowers into the wire, in what was supposed to be a pleasing design. While we worked, Rowan explained the elements of floral design: line, color, form, space, and texture. I'd of course studied that on my own the past three nights—I'd gone even further and studied eight principles of floral arranging, too. But watching someone design in a video and actually doing it myself were completely different.

It was harder than I expected. My fingers were scratched up and itchy, the stems didn't sit the way I wanted them to, or they were too weak and snapped when I wanted them to behave. Flowers lost their petals, or had too many leaves, or they didn't fill the chicken wire. Despite mainlining florists on YouTube, I felt like I had no idea what I was doing. I couldn't stop sneezing, and my eyes were so watery I could barely see. I'd taken an antihistamine, but I guess what was strong enough for walking the garden wasn't quite enough for actually handling flowers.

When I was done, I took a long look at my first-ever flower arrangement. It was unbalanced, wonky, and looked nothing like the image in my head. It was in no way good enough to get anywhere near New York City. My hands were sore, and I had a huge headache. And I couldn't stop sneezing.

It was going to be a long, painful, sniffly summer.

11

MATTEO AND THE FALLS

Our disastrous first lesson ended with Rowan handing me a roll of chicken wire to practice sculpting on my own and the phone number for his mother's medical clinic, suggesting it might be wise to find out if there were any stronger antihistamines available. I was grateful—I needed all the help I could get.

Saturday, June, Gia, and I worked, and Shar had a much-needed day off. But whenever I wasn't helping customers or arranging stock, I had my face in my phone, reading and watching instructional videos on floral arranging. Friday's lesson had taught me one thing—I had a long way to go if I wanted to be anywhere near good enough to make a splash at the Bloom.

But Sunday . . . Sunday was mine. Matteo's brother had agreed to lend him his car, and we had a full day planned at Niagara Falls with Gia. We planned a shoot at the falls themselves and one at the cheesy tourist trap Clifton Hill district. These photos would be the only #powercouple content for a while, so they needed to be amazing.

I was on Shar's front porch at ten when the blue Mustang GT drove up. My skin erupted in goose bumps even before Matteo turned onto the driveway. I was so happy to see him. He parked and got out of the car with a grin.

He wore oversize tan pants and a green and gray sweater vest over a white T-shirt, along with his usual silver chain around his neck—and he was gorgeous. Every time I saw him in person, I had the same thought—I was so lucky he was mine.

"Oh man, it's good to see you, Tahira," he said when he reached me. I was enveloped in his arms. His mouth was on mine seconds later.

Mmm . . . this. This was exactly what I needed to take my mind off the store, my FIT application, and figuring out how to be a champion floral artist in six weeks. Just Matteo's candy-flavored mouth on mine. I closed my eyes and sank into the kiss.

"You two are face-sucking already?" Gia clomped loudly up the porch stairs. "Man, I forgot how much I never see your lips unstuck together."

I pulled away from Matteo. Gia was wearing her cowboy boots again, pairing them with cutoff light-blue jean shorts and a pale-pink frilly blouse.

"Hey, cuz, what's with the boots?" Matteo asked, eyeing Gia's outfit.

I laughed, fixing my arms tight around Matteo's waist. "It's only been a week, but your cousin has already gone full-on pastoral-chic."

He smirked, then tightened his arms around me. "Glad *you're* still you."

I rested my head on his chest for a second. I wished we could stay like this for a while, but we had a long day planned.

"We good to go?" I asked. "Google says it's twenty-five minutes to the falls. But that's assuming no traffic. Might be busy today."

Gia checked her phone. "Cam's on his way. He'll be here in three."

My eyes narrowed. "Why is Cameron on his way?"

Gia had talked about nothing except her new "boo" since their date Friday night. She was quite sure he was "the one." But since this was her fourth "the one" this year alone, I wasn't expecting him to last longer than a week.

"He's coming to Niagara Falls with us," she said.

"He is? Since when?"

"Since I asked him. I told him we were going to get new pictures for our Instas, and he wants to join us. Don't worry, he knows how important your fashion shots are; he'll stay out of our way while we're doing those."

She glanced at Matteo, who just shrugged. "Fine with me," he said. "The more the merrier."

A large white Jeep pulled up in front of the house. Gia squealed with joy.

A guy who I assumed was Cameron Simons got out of the driver's side. Then Addison McLaughlin got out of the passenger side. *Okay.* What exactly was *she* doing here?

"Gigi!" Cameron said, grinning. Dude looked exactly as I expected. Blond and blandly good looking. Totally not my type, but I could see the appeal.

Gia threw her arms around him. "Cameron! Yay! You're here!"

"Hi, Tahira!" Addison smiled.

After Gia excitedly introduced everyone, Cameron smiled at Gia. "Hope you don't mind Addie tagging along; she was dying to see the falls."

I spoke before Gia had a chance to respond. "You live twenty minutes from the falls, Addison. I assume you've seen them before."

Addison shrugged. "It's been a while. Besides, I heard you were doing a fashion shoot—I thought you might need help. I took pictures for our school yearbook."

Matteo shook his head. "The Mustang can't fit five people."

Cameron waved his hand. "No issue. I can drive. I can fit five big hockey players in the Jeep; y'all will be no problem."

Gia looked at me sheepishly. She knew how I felt about Addison.

I sighed. Maybe I was being a little judgy. I needed to let this go so it wouldn't spoil my date with Matteo.

"Great." I smiled. "Let me get my things."

Once we were settled in Cameron's car (me between Matteo and Addison, in the back seat), I noticed Rowan Johnston standing in front of his garage, watching us. I shrank back in the seat, hoping he wouldn't see me. I wasn't exactly sure why I cared, but I didn't like him seeing me with Addison and Cameron after the stuff I'd said about them Friday night.

After a mostly quiet (well, not really quiet—Cameron's loud alt-rock meant none of us could really carry a conversation) drive, we were in Niagara Falls. Cameron parked in a pay lot, and we braved swarms of tourists and mist to find a spot with a good view of the falls for the first photo shoot. I'd only been in Bakewell about a week, but it already seemed weird to be surrounded by so many strangers. Weird, but good. I'd missed the hustle of crowds.

"This is awesome," Matteo said, squeezing my hand. We were a few paces in front of the others. "The last time I was here, with cousin Daniela from Cleveland, it was raining so hard we couldn't see a thing. These pictures will be epic."

"I want to get some of all of us," Addison said, jogging to catch up with us. "I'll make sure to tag you!"

"Sure," I said. Whatever. I was determined not to let Addison's social climbing bother me today.

"Are we just doing pictures here at the falls?" she asked. After I nodded, she smiled. "If you'd told me about all this before, I could have called my cousin. He works at one of the vineyards nearby. Last year I surprised Rowan with a behind-the-scenes tour of the place. He *loved* it. He spent so much time drawing the vines and the leaves. It's such a great spot for pictures, but it's not open to the public like the other vineyards around here. Let me know anytime; I'll call him and get you in."

That was actually a very generous offer. I was not interested in taking pictures of my stuff surrounded by grapevines . . . but I knew how rare it was to get behind-the-scenes access to these incredibly photogenic spots.

I smiled. "That's really cool of you."

Addison shrugged. "Seriously, though, if you ever need help scouting locations, let me know. I know the area like the back of my hand."

After finding a clearing, Matteo and I posed in front of the black wrought iron railing with the falls behind us—him standing with his feet shoulder width apart and arms crossed, and me with one arm draped on his shoulder. Gia took the shots.

We took some more of Matteo, and then me alone; then I got some of Gia, and Gia and Cameron, for her Instagram. The light was awesome, and the heavy mist in the air from the water was adding such a cool effect in the pictures. I couldn't help but be giddy. These were going to look *so* good.

"Let's get one of the four of us!" Gia said, taking my camera from me and handing it to Addison. I dropped my arm around Gia's neck, resting my head on her shoulder. Matteo had his arm around my waist, and Cameron was nestled in behind Gia. We were laughing as Addison took the picture. Eventually someone offered to take a shot of all five of us, so Addison gave the stranger her phone and joined us.

After Gia, Matteo, and I changed in the bathroom full of soggy tourists in the gift shop near the falls, we walked ten minutes over to our next location. The Clifton Hill district was filled with the absolute cheesiest tacky tourist shops, wax museums, haunted houses, and "believe it or not" emporiums. This was totally an ironic setting for a fashion shoot, and I was excited to see my designs contrasted against the garish backdrops and souvenir T-shirts.

I was wearing an outfit I'd made a few months ago—a body-con jersey calf-length dress made of a double-knit geometric print, with a color-blocked corduroy shirt over it. Matteo was wearing jeans and a shirt with Pollock-esque paint splatters, along with mirrored shades. We looked hot. The pictures were amazing. I especially loved the one with the massive King Kong hanging off a building behind us.

Spending the day with Addison was . . . not what I expected. She seemed really, genuinely interested in photography. She asked me intelligent questions about our process and was pretty good at picking out what was working and what wasn't in the shots. I even got her to take some of the shots so Gia, Matteo, and I could be together. Cameron, on the other hand, looked bored after half an hour and made unsubtle hints about his stomach growling. But Addison seemed to understand how important it was to get these pictures perfect.

"There's a bit of a glare in the ones I took at the upside-down house," she said, cringing, as I flipped through pictures on the back of the camera. "I'm sorry; we can head back over if you want?"

"Seriously?" Cameron asked. "Does it matter that much?"

Gia looked at me pleadingly. Clearly making her boo happy was as important as achieving perfection in these pictures.

I shook my head. "Nah, it's fine. I think we're good." I meant it. We had a ton of great pictures.

Matteo and I would have been fine if we headed back to Bakewell next, as we were counting on some alone time before he needed to get on the road back to Toronto. But we were outnumbered by the others, so we all packed into a small burger place for a late lunch.

"So, how're y'all liking living in the magic garden?" Addison asked me after we ordered our meals.

I raised a brow. "Magic garden?"

Cameron laughed. Clearly this was some Bakewell joke. "Last year a bunch of cops showed up at the Johnstons' to do a search," he said. "They got a tip someone was operating a grow-op."

I cringed. I wondered how much this "anonymous tip" had to do with the fact that the Johnstons were one of the only Black families in town. Was this the microaggression Shar had mentioned? It sounded pretty macro to me.

Addison grinned. "The house had been flagged because of the amount of fertilizer and soil Rowan had bought that year. It was a lot, even for Bakewell. But they didn't find any weed, of course. Rowan's, like, *allergic* to anything entertaining, so recreational drugs are beyond him."

Addison and Cameron laughed again. Clearly, they had no idea of the racial undertones of something like that. Or if they knew, they didn't care.

Me? I lived in Toronto—one of the most diverse cities in the world—and my neighborhood, Scarborough, had significantly more people of color than white people. And I *still* faced microaggressions and racism at home, not to mention Islamophobia, even though my family wasn't, like, *visibly* Muslim or anything. What would it be like to be one of the only nonwhite families in a small town?

"Kind of insensitive for you to laugh, especially since you dated Rowan. The Johnstons sound like good people," I said to Addison. She was sitting across from me in the booth of the cheesy sixties-style restaurant, with Gia and Cameron cozied up next to her.

Addison shrugged. "There is no need for you to defend the family. Rowan Johnston cares more about his garden than their reputation."

Cameron snorted at Addison. "He did care about his sister's."

Addison glared at Cameron, then nonchalantly took a sip of her soda. There was clearly a story there.

"Ooh," Gia said, eyes twinkling. "Does the Bakewell Bookworm have a juicy past we should know about?"

"Juniper?" Cameron asked. "Nah. She's just kinda strange. She used to do these weird videos on YouTube talking about books and stuff."

"Really?" Gia asked. "She didn't tell me she was a YouTuber. Was she popular?"

Addison snorted. "Ha! Using the word 'popular' to describe a Johnston . . ."

I was about to object, again questioning exactly why she'd dated Rowan if she disliked the family so much, when Matteo interrupted with a chuckle.

"Man, Tahira. You were so excited to have kids next door. Too bad they're a plant nerd and a book nerd. They sound insufferable."

Matteo hadn't even *met* Juniper and Rowan. A sourness formed in my stomach. Yeah, I hadn't exactly been kind about Rowan to Matteo, but he and Gia had to see how terrible Addison and Cameron were being, right? Didn't Gia care that they were laughing at the girl she wanted to be our "makeover sidekick"? What happened to protecting Juniper? Not to mention she didn't seem too bothered by this grow-op accusation.

"And don't forget Leanne and her rabbits," Addison continued. "She practically lives at the Johnstons'. The whole lot of them are exhausting." She turned to Gia. "Too bad you have to spend your summer next door to them."

Gia snuggled into Cameron's arm. "I'm not thinking I'll be there much."

Matteo gestured to Cameron and Addison, smiling at me. "At least you met this crew so you'll have some decent people to hang with instead of . . . what did you call them? Plant geeks?" He leaned into me for a kiss, but I wasn't feeling it.

Actually, I wasn't feeling any of these people at the table right now. I was burned out, annoyed—and so pissed that Addison freaking McLaughlin ended up ruining what could be my only day with Matteo for weeks. She'd made me want to defend Rowan. Which I didn't want to do, especially in front of Matteo. Maybe I shouldn't have been so negative about Rowan to my boyfriend. Rowan and I were on the Bloom team together now, and it would be easier to get along with him if Matteo weren't mocking him every chance he got. I needed to tell him to chill about Rowan once we were alone.

I squeezed Matteo's hand. I wished he and I had just driven alone in the Mustang so we could have left early and not had to deal with any of this pettiness. More than anything, I wanted to be back at the tiny house.

When everyone insisted on doing more sightseeing and souvenir shopping after lunch, I sort of had to go, too. But I must have looked irritated about it, because Matteo leaned in close when we were in a candy store. "Don't worry, we'll go for a drive after we get back. I need some time alone with you."

"Yes, please," I said. That was exactly what I needed, too.

After the drive back to Bakewell, I said a polite goodbye to Addison and Cameron as I got out of Cameron's Jeep. Gia hopped out, too, gave Matteo a big hug, then climbed back into the Jeep and said she was going to hang out at Hyacinth's with Cameron, which was fine with me. I had plans with my boyfriend.

Matteo drove us to this park outside town in the Mustang. On the way, he talked about his job, the new clothes he'd bought there, and some new friends he'd made. My annoyance from lunch was already fading. It made sense: Matteo and I were always best when it was just us. Too bad alone time was so rare.

After parking near a pond in the park, we found a picnic table overlooking the water and sat. The sun was setting by then, and the colors reflecting on the water were like light brushes of watercolors on dark paper. I took some pictures—not of either of us, but of the sky, the water, and the trees near the shoreline.

"The sunsets here look different," I said.

"Is it because there's less pollution or something?"

I shrugged. "I dunno."

He took my hand in his. "You okay? You seemed quiet earlier."

I nodded. "Yeah. Addison's just not my favorite person in Bakewell. She was getting under my skin."

"Really? Her and the dude seemed all right to me."

"I don't know about Cameron, but Addison's been harassing Juniper for a while. Juniper is really nice, and Addison just rubs me the wrong way." I still couldn't believe that I had been enjoying my day with

Addison—at least until lunch, when she did a great job of confirming my previous bad feelings about her.

"Well, she can't be worse than the guy that made you spill shit all over yourself."

I sighed. I didn't want to talk about Rowan. Or Addison. Or even June, right now. I leaned into Matteo's shoulder. "I'm glad we're alone now."

"Me too, baby. We got some great pictures today, though, didn't we? Those ones outside the haunted-train thing were epic. We're going to have to make sure we don't post the same ones on our Instagrams at the same time. If we stagger them, we'll have more engagement."

I nodded. It was a good idea. "I'm not going to have a whole lot of photos other than those pics for a while. Still can't find a good spot in Bakewell that's not all grandma flowers."

"You post first, then. I'll have some shots from the Flirt Skincare launch on Wednesday. Alyssa says a ton of important people will be there, and—"

"What skin-care launch?"

"I told you, Alyssa and I are going to a product launch this week. Check out the Flirt Instagram after Wednesday; I'm sure we'll be featured. The last launch we went to—"

"You've been to several launches with her? This is your coworker, right?"

"Yeah, I told you, her sister's a publicist. We went to one for a tech company last week."

I sat up straight. "You *didn't* tell me this. You work with this girl, and you go to product launches regularly together?"

"Come on, Tahira. You're spending all that time with the hot flower guy—"

"Yeah, but I'm *only* doing the Bloom with Rowan. Not working with him, and not going to parties and launches or whatever else. And I told you . . . repeatedly . . . that I don't even like the guy. There is nothing going on between me and Rowan. Can you say the same thing about you and this Alyssa?"

His jaw clenched. "I came down to see *you*, didn't I? I could've hung out with her tonight, but I'm with you."

A chill went up my spine. Neither of us spoke for a few seconds. "You *can't* say there's nothing going on, can you?" I finally said. "You two *are* more than just friends / coworkers / product-launch buddies, aren't you? What happened at that launch last week? Or after it?"

He didn't say anything. He didn't really have to. I could see the answer in his eyes.

I took a breath. "I can't believe this."

"You're the one who bailed on spending the summer with me."

"I only left a week ago!"

"Yeah, but even before that, we never saw each other! You know you're my girl, and there's no one I'd rather be with than you, but you can't expect me to sit around like a monk while you're out here having your 'Hot Girl Summer' with Gia. I thought we understood each other—we never said this was exclusive."

My hand clawed and I scraped the worn wood of the picnic table with my fingernails. My heart was hammering loudly in my ears. Matteo was *cheating* on me. "Why are you telling me this now?" I asked, my voice drenched in anger. "Why not just hide your sidepiece indefinitely? I mean, you're right—we don't see each other much. I wouldn't have found out."

He turned away and ran his hand through his hair. "I just . . . the Flirt launch. I thought you might see pictures on my Insta of me and Alyssa, so I wanted to give you the heads-up that I was going with her."

That chill up my spine? That was gone. It was replaced by a full-on fire in my chest. "So let me make sure I understand you. You borrowed your brother's car and drove all the way here—an hour and a half each way. You drag me and your cousin to one of the world's biggest tourist attractions to get pictures for *your* feed, making me style you with my designs, and making her take hundreds of shots. You make me put up with Addison McLaughlin and her jock accomplice, and you join in with them trashing the sweetest, nicest girl I've met in this town. You even act all jealous of the hot plant nerd, even though you know I wouldn't cheat. You do all this while intending to warn me at some point that I was going to see pictures of you and the girl you're banging on the side on your Instagram soon?"

He exhaled. "I wasn't going to tell you that Alyssa and I are . . . you know. Just that we'd be in pictures together. I . . . I guess I just couldn't lie to you."

I couldn't look at him. I gazed out over the water. The pinks in the sky were dimming now, leaving the sky a dull gray. "And that's supposed to make me feel better?" I said quietly.

"Tahira, please. You're right. I'm sorry. I won't go to the launch. I won't see her again if you don't want me to. We can make this exclusive. Just you and me."

Unbelievable. "Let me guess. She doesn't have as many followers as me. You're realizing that you need me for my fashion platform more than you need this wannabe socialite for her invitations. Who else are you using to get ahead, Matteo?"

He glared at me, nostrils flaring. "Is that really what you think of me? After everything I did for you? All those photo shoots? Sending big influencers your way?"

I turned back to him. "You did *nothing* but use me. *Nothing.* If you honestly think those things are why I'm with you . . ." I shook my head. "Get away from me. In fact, get the hell out of this town." I stood and pointed to his car. I was seeing red. I'd never been so angry. But I was at least clearheaded enough to add something else. "And by the way, I'm not giving you any of the pictures from today. And you *don't* have my consent to post any photos of me on your Instagram again. Ever. If you do? I'll report them. This relationship is over."

"Jesus, Tahira. C'mon. Let me take you home. We can talk—"

"I'm not getting into a car with you. Get. The *fuck*. Out of my town."

Matteo looked at me for a second like he didn't want to leave me here. Finally, he shook his head. "You're not who I thought you were. You'll never get anywhere if you don't learn to play the game. I'd be angry, but honestly? I feel sorry for you. What a waste of talent." He headed down the path toward his car.

He drove away.

And me? I was alone in a park outside of fucking Bakewell. It was almost dark.

I sat back at the table and cried.

12

THE UNLIKELY KNIGHT IN T-SHIRT ARMOR

It took me about three minutes of sitting alone with my tears to regret banishing Matteo from Bakewell. I didn't regret dumping his cheating ass, but maybe I should have let him take me home first, because now I was stuck here in this damn park in the middle of nowhere. How was I going to get back to town?

Think, think, think . . . not about how the person I thought knew me better than anyone had royally betrayed me. Not about how he was nothing but a social-climbing butt wipe willing to suck face with anyone who could kick-start his modeling career. He was cheating on me with someone for her . . . party invitations. *Don't think about that.* Figuring out how to get home was a better use for my brain right now.

There were no Ubers in Bakewell—as far as I knew. I couldn't call Shar because I didn't want her telling Mom and Dad about this. They'd lecture me about choosing my friends wisely, and they'd suggest that if relationships were interfering with my ability to work, then maybe I needed to reevaluate my priorities. I didn't want to call Gia, either, even though she could totally get her boo to pick me up. Gia was Matteo's cousin, and a tiny part of me worried that she'd be on Matteo's side since her family meant so much to her. But what worried me more was that Cameron would probably tell everyone I'd been cheated on. It was mortifying to think of everyone knowing my business, and I didn't need gossip when I was so new here. I squeezed my eyes shut. If I were in the city, there'd be loads of people who could rescue me.

I sighed as I opened a call with Juniper. She didn't drive, but she'd figure out how to get me home.

"Tahira! How was Niagara Falls? Did you go to that candy store I told you about? Last time I was there I bought this chai tea fudge that was to die for. I almost didn't buy it because I totally get that 'chai tea' is redundant, but I'd never had tea in fudge before. I swear it was the best thing I have ever put into my mouth. Did—"

"Juniper, I'm stuck."

"Stuck? Like with glue? LOL! Oh no, you're not stuck at Niagara Falls, are you? That can't be, because I just passed Gia at Hyacinth's."

"No, I'm stuck at that park near the nursery. The one with the pond?"

"You're stuck at Bell's Pond?"

"Yeah, Matteo and I were talking, and . . . he . . . left." My voice cracked.

"Oh no, did you have a fight?"

I took a deep breath. "Sort of. I mean, if you call him telling me that he's also seeing someone else a fight. Is there a cab company or any way I can get back into—"

"Shoot. I got you, Tahira. I'll call Row. He probably just left the nursery."

She hung up before I could tell her no, please anything but Plant-Boy. Ugh. Now Rowan Johnston was going to see me in this state. This day could go shove it.

～

I had no choice but to wait for my rescuer. And no choice but to think while I waited.

The sun had pretty much set, and the park was mostly empty, save for a few dog walkers and joggers. No sounds of people hanging out or talking, like if this were Toronto. Nothing to drown out my thoughts. Nothing to distract me from the realization that I was a complete idiot—at least when it came to guys.

This was on me. I mean, in hindsight, all the signs had been there from the beginning. Matteo slid into my DMs on Instagram only after I had a respectable following. Most of our conversations were about my fashion designs, or about his goals as a model and influencer. I hadn't thought anything was wrong about that since it was what we had in common. We were both so committed to our goals—so why wouldn't we talk about them?

But that wasn't the only reason he was into me, was it? I hadn't dated that much, but I thought I could at least tell when someone was sincere, and he seemed to genuinely care about me. I had no reason to think he didn't consider us exclusive. I wiped away a tear.

This was the worst possible time for this to happen. How was I going to get through what was already proving to be an enormously hard summer without Matteo grounding me? Without him reassuring me that I could do this and keeping me focused on what was important—my Plan? I just didn't have the mental bandwidth for a breakup right now. I took a long, shuddering breath. I needed to hold myself together. With or without Matteo, I needed to stay on course.

It was so weird to feel such relief to see Rowan Johnston, but my whole body relaxed when his old green car pulled into the parking lot. Hopefully he'd say something annoying and insensitive right away, which would distract me from how pissed off I was about Matteo.

I opened the door. "Hey," I said. "Thanks . . . I mean, for coming to get me."

He shrugged.

I got into the car. "I mean it: thank you for taking me home."

"It's no bother. I'm literally going to the same place."

Rowan's car was a clean older-model Subaru. Juniper had told me he'd bought it recently with his earnings from Wynter's.

I buckled my seat belt. It was super weird that I knew so much about this family, thanks to Juniper's chattiness, but Rowan himself was still mostly a mystery to me.

"Still . . . you didn't have to turn around. Thanks," I said.

He shrugged again and started the car. I leaned my head back against the headrest and cataloged all the blows life had thrown at me in the last few weeks. The bird in Paris. Losing my internship. Having to move to Bakewell. Shar rejecting my plan. And now Matteo cheating on me.

I wished I were home. Back in Toronto, not in the middle of nowhere in a car with a guy who hated me. If I'd never come to Bakewell, maybe none of this crap with Matteo would have even happened. Maybe we'd still be together.

That wouldn't be a good thing, though. Because then I wouldn't know he was using me. That he could be unfaithful just to get invitations to launch parties. I squeezed my eyes shut. I didn't want Rowan to see me cry.

I opened my eyes. "What's on your shirt?" I asked, breaking the silence. I hadn't noticed it when I got into the car, and I suddenly wanted to know what plant pun he wore today.

"What?"

"Your T-shirt. What's on it? An ironic cactus? Something floral?"

His eyes stayed focused on the road in front of him. "It says 'Pothead,' and there is a picture of flower—"

I snorted. "Flowerpots. I get it."

I remembered Addison's story from earlier about his family's suspected grow-op. Clearly, it wasn't that traumatic a memory if he was wearing a shirt that said "Pothead." Or maybe he was a total badass and giving a subtle middle finger to whoever had reported him.

He was quiet for a moment before speaking. "You into my shirts or something? I wouldn't have thought a fashionista would approve."

"I'm intrigued. They seem out of character for you."

I'd always found it fascinating when a person's style didn't match their personality. In my experience from working retail, it usually meant someone else was picking their clothes, which happened a lot at the boutique. Significant others or parents insisting they be the only ones to choose a customer's clothes. It was that, or I hadn't read the person as well as I thought I had.

He ran his hand absently over the shirt. As we passed under a street-light, I could make out that it was pale blue with rich brown print and lettering. The same shade of brown I knew his eyes to be.

"Leanne bought me a few funny plant shirts a while ago, when we started working at the nursery," he said. "And then, I dunno. I kept buying them for work. They make me laugh."

So it was a combination of both. Leanne totally seemed like the ironic-shirt kind of person, so that made sense. But honestly? I wouldn't have expected someone as grumpy as Rowan to want so much whimsy in his life. "For someone who calls me Thirst Trap, I'm surprised you wear such attention-seeking clothes."

He snorted. "I wear them to make myself laugh, not for other people. I'm sure your slick boyfriend wouldn't be caught dead in something like this, right?" There was something in his voice. Contempt?

Still, though. He'd come out here to fetch me when I was stuck.

"I do like your shirts," I said. I bit my tongue. I didn't like his shirts. Why did I say that? "And anyway," I said, leaning my head against the window. "He's not my boyfriend anymore. That's why I was stranded there."

Rowan frowned for a second, then huffed a laugh.

"Laughing at my breakup. Nice, Plant-Boy."

"I'm not laughing at you." He shook his head. "I broke up with someone at that pond once. It's a coincidence."

"Addison?"

He nodded.

Huh. So he had dumped Addison, not the other way around. After spending the day with Rowan's ex, I kind of understood why he'd dated her. Sort of. Until lunch, Addison had been easygoing, helpful, and actually pretty cool. That story she told about arranging for Rowan to see a vineyard that wasn't open to the public? As a plant nerd, he would have loved that. I'd honestly thought that maybe I'd been wrong about her. She wasn't the town mean girl, just a bit . . . brash. She just needed to learn to think before speaking.

But then at lunch. Oh boy, did I see who she really was. Definitely a mean girl and a bully. Rowan was much too good for her. Good for him for breaking up with her.

Rowan drove silently for a bit, then asked, "Were you the dumpee or the dumper tonight?"

I shook my head. "I . . . I don't even know."

"Never mind," he said. "I'm sorry. I shouldn't butt in."

I waved my hand. "No, no, it's fine. Actually, I could use a guy's opinion on this." I sighed. "He admitted he's seeing someone else in Toronto. Going to product launches and that sort of stuff. He claimed he and I were never exclusive, anyway, so I couldn't be mad, and that he wanted to give me the heads-up before I saw pictures of them together."

"*Were* you exclusive?"

"I mean, I thought we were. We never discussed it, but he always said stuff like, 'You're the only one for me' or 'No one understands me like you.' Do guys assume it's not exclusive unless it's discussed?"

"Well, I don't know what guys in general think, but I think *that* guy is an ass. That sounds pretty committed to me. You've been in Bakewell, what, a week, and he's already gaslighting you about your relationship? You sure this other fling of his hasn't been going on longer than that?"

The first time I remembered hearing about Alyssa was after I'd moved to Bakewell . . . but he did say she was the one who'd referred him for the H&M job. He'd gotten the job at least two months ago. I sank into my seat, closing my eyes. "You think I'm an idiot."

He shook his head. "No, I don't. This is his fault, not yours."

I didn't know why it was such a relief to hear that from Rowan. I stared out the window. I'd never get used to how dark it was out here. There weren't even any streetlights until you got farther into Bakewell. "I'm pretty sure he's been using me for my social media platform," I said. "And he's using this other girl for her party invitations. Honestly? I didn't expect this from him."

"If you'd expected it, you'd be as bad as him."

"You *do* think I'm as bad as him, though. I'm just a self-absorbed *influencer*, remember? You probably think I deserve it."

He shook his head. "No one deserves that. But I don't think you'd use someone just to get ahead. Look, I don't know you that well, and you seem a bit . . ."

"High maintenance?"

He shook his head. "Tunnel minded. Focused. Like me, actually. We're so focused that maybe it's hard to see what's in front of our nose until someone spells it out for us." He hesitated. "Or it's broadcasted on a shirt."

I snorted. "Are you telling me you're really a pothead?"

He shook his head, chuckling. "Only into the terra-cotta variety."

I guess we kinda had a truce for a few moments, so I decided to go in for the big questions. "Is that what happened with you and Addison? You didn't realize she was such a . . ." It was totally bad manners to call his ex a bitch while he was driving me home, so I didn't finish the sentence.

He exhaled. "It took me way too long to notice she'd changed. She'd started putting other people down to make herself look better."

Yup, she was doing exactly that about him and Juniper at that burger place. "It's not the same thing, then. Matteo didn't change—I just never realized how big a dick he always was. I should have seen it."

"He manipulated you, and none of it was your fault. You're a driven, determined, focused person, and he took advantage of that. Don't beat yourself up over it; he's not worth it. He doesn't deserve you."

I turned to him sharply. Really? Rowan Johnston being kind? "Did you just compliment me?"

He frowned. "Don't let it go to your head."

I narrowed an eye. "Seriously, though. You're good at this. I'd never peg you as a relationship/self-esteem pep talk kind of guy."

"Why, because I'm not talkative? I may not have a lot of close friends, but I'm there for the ones I have. Plus, I've been in therapy, so I know my psychobabble." Rowan's eyes never left the road in front of him.

I wasn't used to this kind of realness from my friends—not that Rowan was a friend or anything. But still. He was being so honest and open, telling me what went wrong with Addison, telling me that he saw me as focused and driven. He was more like Juniper than I'd noticed. It was disconcerting. Just like with his shirts—I'd judged him on those, and I was wrong, too.

But then again, I'd thought Matteo was being real with me. Maybe I had no concept anymore of what "real" actually was. I leaned against the cool glass of the window.

"How did you deal?" I asked.

"What do you mean?"

"When you and Addison broke up. What did you do to get over it . . . so you could go back to being so focused?"

He chuckled, watching the road in front of him. We were almost home—the wide stretches of nothing had been replaced with the houses of our neighborhood. "I kept my mind busy. I immersed myself in my job and school. I filled three sketchbooks. I relied on my friends. I ignored people who talked about it."

"Gossip, you mean?"

He nodded. "Yeah. I love Bakewell, but seriously, this town knows how to *talk*."

I was quiet for a bit. "Where are you going to school in the fall?"

He didn't look at me. "University of Toronto."

I chuckled. I really couldn't imagine Rowan in my city. He pulled into his driveway.

"Thanks," I said as I unbuckled the seat belt. "For, you know, the talk. And the ride home."

He got out of the car without saying anything, so I did the same. The sky was pretty black by now, but there was a light on above the Johnstons' garage door, so I could finally see his shirt clearly. The flowerpots each had cutesy plants in them with happy faces on the flowers. I shook my head, laughing. "Cute," I said.

He smiled, then looked up. "Clear night," he said.

I frowned. "It's too dark. There are too many stars here."

He snorted as he walked around the car toward his front door. "This is nothing. Give it a few hours, and it will seem like there's less sky than stars. I love the night skies here."

"You're not into astronomy, too, are you?"

"Nah. I don't know what they're all called, but I like stargazing to clear my head. One of the benefits of living in the country." He climbed the steps to his front porch. "Night, Tahira."

I headed toward the backyard and the tiny house. "Night, Plant-Boy."

13

SUCKY NIGHT WITH SUCCULENTS

I texted Shar as I walked through the backyard, letting her know I was home from Niagara Falls. She hadn't given Gia and me a curfew or anything, but I didn't want her to worry.

Gia wasn't in the tiny house when I got there. I kind of wished I had my best friend to talk to right now, but she was probably still with Cameron.

I headed for bed, not expecting to get any sleep. And sure enough, I spent most of the night staring at the pine ceiling three feet from my head while feeling sorry for myself.

I must have slept some, though, because Gia was in her bed when I woke at eight. I dressed quietly so I wouldn't wake her, since she wasn't working today. Being surrounded by city streets and stores always helped me clear my head, so I headed downtown for a few hours before work. There weren't a lot of people around since it was a Monday morning, and of course, this was Bakewell, not Toronto. I didn't really feel any better after wandering the sleepy town for a while. Eventually, I parked myself on a bench outside the city council building and colored in some sketches of clothes I'd made a few days ago until it was time for work. The art pencils Rowan gave me weren't the same brand I used, but they were good quality. Focusing on my designing helped—I did actually feel a bit better.

Lilybuds was pretty dead all day, but that was fine because a large shipment had come in, and everything in the store needed to be rearranged to fit the new stuff.

"I never would have thought these would work at Lilybuds, but I love them," Shar said, holding up a loose, leaf-print, unisex button-up I'd picked for the Lily collection. It was more "natural" than I normally went for, but at least it was just a leaf print and not flowers.

"Should we put them with the green high-waisted skirts?" Juniper asked. She had a good eye for merchandising. And thankfully, she hadn't mentioned anything about my breakup last night, or mentioned Rowan picking me up from the pond. I loved her for that.

"Yeah," I said. "Hey, Shar, can we move the white linen shorts there, too?"

"Absolutely! Move whatever you like. Anything to breathe some life into the stock."

For the next few hours, June and I set up the new Lily section. Rowan was right—keeping busy was a great way to keep Matteo and all the other crap going on off my mind. After about half the new stock was out, I took a step back to inspect our handiwork. The corner definitely had a younger vibe, and even the few older pieces I'd moved there now seemed trendier. But the space was missing something. It didn't look like a distinct line, like I'd imagined.

After my whole store rebrand had been rejected last week, I'd created a mock-up sketch of this new Lily section, keeping it simple, with no new fixtures and only the small circular logo on the wall that I planned to paint myself. But now I could see it wasn't enough.

"What do you think is missing?" I asked Shar while Juniper was helping a customer.

Shar came around the counter and put her glasses on. "I think it looks wonderful. I love the pop of color with the white and black pieces. You'll take pictures for the store's new social media, right?"

I had planned to photograph each new piece for the Lilybuds Insta, but I wasn't sure the whole section was ready for a close-up.

"It doesn't look enough like a distinct line within the store."

Shar tilted her head. "What about your idea of wallpaper or a mural? We could do part of the wall, just behind that section, instead of the whole back wall."

I turned to face Shar. "You'd be okay with that?"

"Sure, as long as the cost is reasonable. Designer wallpaper is probably too much, but there is cheaper stuff out there. Or you can do a painted mural. I really liked that sketch with the one that looked like the mural at Wynter's. Maybe we can find out who painted that?"

That wasn't a bad idea. I squinted and imagined a smaller mural—maybe seven feet wide and floor to ceiling, right behind the Lily racks. Like the one at Wynter's, with the interlocking triangles of purple, blue, and green. I could still paint the Lily logo in the middle of the mural.

"I know who painted that," Juniper said, joining us after her customer left.

"Great! Can you ask if they'd do a smaller version of it here?"

Juniper laughed. "I could, but you could ask, too. That mural was Rowan's grade-twelve art project."

Jesus, Rowan again? Was there anything he couldn't do? Why hadn't he told me that the art was his?

Shar beamed. "Oh, how wonderful! A small piece surely won't take him long. I'll pay, of course."

Juniper nodded. "Let's ask him tonight, since our team is getting together anyway."

Right. I'd forgotten that we had our second floral design lesson after dinner.

"Wait, Juniper, you said *our* team. I thought you were just helping Rowan teach Gia and me?"

Juniper snorted. "After that lesson, I don't think I have a choice. You and Rowan need a full-time referee. I told Row I'm officially doing the Bloom with y'all." She paused. "That is, if it's okay with you."

I grinned. "Of course it's okay with me. Two of my friends on the team is better than one."

Speaking of friends on the team, I needed to find a minute alone with Gia before that to talk to her, because otherwise? Awkward city. I didn't know if Matteo had told her what happened last night. Of course when I couldn't sleep last night, I'd carried out step one of getting over an awful breakup—I blocked him on all channels. I did snoop on his Insta first, and thankfully he didn't mention me. Which was good. He'd be nuts to take any of this out on me, because I could, and *would*, ruin him. Still. I hated that this was how this relationship had ended.

When I got home, I found Gia sunning on one of the lounge chairs outside the tiny house. "Hey, G," I said.

"Oh, hey, T. How's it going?" Her voice was a bit tight. Forced. No doubt she'd talked to Matteo.

I shrugged. "Been better. I take it you've checked in with your cousin?"

She cringed. "Yeah, he texted me. I can't believe you broke up. You okay?"

I had mostly kept Matteo off my mind all day, but every once in a while, I was hit with a wave of shame, anger, and hurt. "I'm not great, but hanging in there," I said.

"You know what part I don't get? He came all this way to get those pictures in your clothes. What a waste of time." She shook her head.

Good. I sighed as I plopped on the chair next to her. Gia understood how terrible it was that he had wasted my entire day. "It wasn't how I expected the night to go, that's for sure," I said.

Gia turned to look at me. "So that whole thing was just, like . . . spur of the moment?"

"I don't know. He just—"

"Actually," she interrupted. "Let's just *not* talk about it. He's family, and I think it's best if I just, you know, don't get involved here." She paused for a moment. "Hey, now that you won't have Matteo modeling your menswear, you want me to ask Cameron if he'll do it? He's got such a smoking-hot hockey body. You could put me and him in coordinating outfits like you and Matteo used to do."

"Yeah, maybe." I rubbed my palm. "I'm glad we're not going to let this come between us, G. I don't think I could handle losing my friend, too."

"Of course, Tahira. You're my girl, and I'm always sistas before mistas." She waved her hand. "It's totally fine. You probably won't be able to come to my nona's for dinner anymore, though, because they'll never approve of anyone who dumps a Borroni, but—"

"Wait, G. They won't approve of me dumping a cheater?"

Gia suddenly sat up straight. "Hold up. *Cheater?* Who's a cheater?"

I raised a brow. "Um, your cousin's a cheater? That's why I dumped him?"

Gia stared at me, blinking, then picked up her phone. "That's not what he said . . . ," she muttered, furiously typing.

"He's been seeing some chick," I said. "Apparently, she takes him to project launches. He only told me because she's going to be on his Insta for this launch on Wednesday. He didn't tell you about Alyssa?"

Gia kept texting for a few seconds, then looked at me. "He's not even denying it. Dipshit." She focused back on her phone. "Don't you worry—I'm blasting it on the family WhatsApp. I'll be shocked if he's still walking by morning."

I squeezed my lips together, trying not to laugh.

"I'm so sorry, Tahira. I shouldn't have automatically believed him." She leaned over to hug me, then cringed at her phone. "Ooh, the aunts are *pissed*. This is going to be good. My folks are furious, too. They're always Team Tahira. Borronis will not tolerate cheating. Oh, crap—Nona's getting involved. I'm going to peace out for a while." She put her phone down. "Don't worry, my family's got this."

I laughed. "G, you're awesome. So is your family."

"You and me, we're good, then, right?"

"Of course—we're always good," I said. We hugged again.

"Yay! Because, ugh, when I thought you'd dumped him for no reason? I wasn't sure how I was going to stay friends with you." Gia smiled widely. "That would have sucked! I mean, we've been friends so long. You're the best! Plus, like, half my Instagram traffic is because of you!" She laughed. "Anyway, Cameron told me about this awesome spot we can go for pictures; there's apparently a covered bridge just outside town."

"Cameron and you are getting close."

Gia beamed. "I like him *so* much. He's so different from city guys, you know? He bakes muffins by himself, like, once a week. And he's going to take me fishing—he promised I wouldn't have to touch any fish or worms. I've figured out how to deal with Addison, too. I told her to stop when she started going on about Juniper again last night. I don't want to hear it. Anyway, I have no interest in being alpha wolf here; I don't mind letting her think she rules her squad."

I laughed. Gia understood the teen pecking order better than anyone. And good for her for standing up for Juniper. "What about the Bloom? They're not going to try to steal our secrets, are they?"

"They don't really care enough, honestly. I think Addison's only doing the competition because her mother wants her to, and Cam's only there because Addison told him he was on the team."

"Like how I told you?"

Gia grinned. "I want to do it, remember? We're going to meet Christopher Chan after we win. This is going to be awesome for you! Plus, it's going to be a big boost for my follower count. I'll totally start getting sponsorships by the end of the summer. Why do we have another lesson so soon, though? We just had one on Friday."

"The Bloom is, like, less than six weeks away. Everyone else here has been working with flowers forever—we need to catch up."

Gia chuckled. "At least the meetings are entertaining. I love watching you and Rowan argue—you drip with chemistry, as my drama teacher would say."

"He was nice to me last night. Even gave me advice about dealing with a breakup. But I'm sure he'll be back to growling at me today."

Gia put her hands out like claws and gave me a flirty growl.

I laughed.

~

Our floral design lesson tonight was with living plants—which was what we'd be working with for the Bloom. Basically, that meant all the flowers and greenery needed to be alive with roots attached.

We were working on a small scale to start, arranging tiny succulents in rectangular metal trays. I'd bought my own slim gloves, and I guess since these succulents weren't really flowery, my allergies were behaving. My aunt had made me an appointment with Rowan and Juniper's mom, who was a doctor in town, and I suspected Rowan was keeping me away from pollen until I saw her about my allergies.

"Don't force the root ball," Rowan scolded as I tried to fit this cute little spiky thing in between puffy leaf things. "They need space."

I sighed. As expected, there was no sign of the camaraderie we'd had last night. He was full-on grumpy with me again. He barely spoke when he dropped the box of plants on the workbench, and he did his familiar scowl when Gia took pictures of me picking out the succulents I wanted to use. His shirt even had a different vibe—still plant-y, but more stylized tropical plants instead of cartoony flowers.

Leanne had joined us to help Rowan teach, though, and she made up for his sour mood by being especially perky. She'd even brought her rabbits, who she'd caged in the middle of the yard using these little fences she'd brought. They were currently gorging themselves on Rowan's grass. Leanne giggled. "Guys are always *sooo* protective of their root balls." She winked at me. "Don't even mind him—succulents are pretty hardy." She handed me some garden scissors. "You can trim a bit to make it fit. Don't look, Row—this might be traumatizing."

Gia gave Leanne a snorty laugh. "I like you."

Rowan did that growl thing that wasn't really a growl. More of a huff. "Why exactly did you insist on coming tonight, Leanne?" he asked.

"Because I had nothing else to do. Y'all are my best friends, remember?" She grinned at Juniper, who quickly looked away.

I trimmed the root ball a bit, but it still wasn't fitting. "This isn't working," I said. Leanne came around to my side of the bench to show me that I didn't need to be delicate with it. "I love succulent art," she said. "Last year my aloe Vera Wang went viral."

Rowan shook his head. "Viral in gardening circles isn't much of an accomplishment."

"Aloe Vera Wang?" Gia asked.

"There was this succulent art challenge on TikTok. Here, look." Leanne showed us a picture on her phone. It was hilarious—the plants were arranged to look like a wedding dress.

"Remember, Row?" Leanne said. "I used that succulent hybrid we helped your dad make in the lab, back when we used to go to Wynter's just to hang out with him. Before the . . . great Johnston rift."

I looked at Rowan, curious. He shrugged. "My dad works at the laboratory at Wynter's. He doesn't approve of me studying landscape architecture, so we haven't been as close lately."

It was interesting how easily he mentioned this, but I got the impression he didn't want to talk about it more. I pointed back to the aloe Vera Wang. "I kind of love that," I said.

"And you're, like, a real fashion person, so that's a big compliment!" Leanne said. "Hey, since you know clothes people, maybe you can help Junebug find someone to make her prom dress? Ever since she was a kid, she's wanted a yellow *Beauty and the Beast* dress because Belle's all into books."

"I've grown out of that," June mumbled.

"Of course you have," Leanne said. "Hey, I heard that author of that wolf series you love has a signing in Toronto soon. We should go! I read the first book and loved it!"

June didn't look up from her arrangement. "I can't go. It's the weekend of the Bloom."

"Oh." Leanne frowned. "That sucks."

"It's fine," June said. "Row, Shar wants a mural painted on one of the walls at the store. Can you do one like you did at the nursery?"

His brows shot up. "Me?"

Juniper nodded. "It was Tahira's idea. She pretty much copied it for her plans for the new section."

I winced. "I didn't *copy* it. I just . . . drew something similar."

Rowan turned to me, brows raised in surprise.

Leanne chuckled. "I could tell she liked it since she was willing to bathe in manure to get a picture of it."

Rowan was still looking at me, all puzzled like. I was pretty sure this was the first time he'd made eye contact with me all evening. I honestly couldn't figure this guy out. First, he's all grumpy, then supportive, then he ignores me, then does a double take about me admiring his art. I shrugged. "I didn't know it was yours at the time, but yeah, I wanted something like that piece for the store."

"Hey! I have a fab idea!" Gia said, clapping her hands together. "Seriously, I'm, like, *brilliant* here. Rowan can paint the wall at the store; then we'll go to the nursery to take pictures of the Lily pieces for the store's social. Because then the promo pictures will have the backdrop of the big mural, which will tie into the little mural for the store. It's, like, *cohesive*, you know?"

I tilted my head. Actually, that was a *brilliant* idea. I wished I'd thought of it. I did see a problem, though. "Rowan hasn't agreed to do the mural." And with his attitude toward me tonight, I was thinking that he'd probably say no on principle.

"He'll do it," Leanne said. "He'd do anything for Shar."

"You want to let me answer myself?" He was clearly annoyed. When none of us said anything, he sighed as he ran his hand over his head. "Fine. I'll do it; tell Shar to give me the details."

Gia beamed. "Excellent. I think all four of us girls should model the clothes. We've got two people of color, one whiter-than-white redhead, and me—sort of ambiguous Mediterranean-y. Rowan, how good are your photography skills?"

We discussed plans for the shoot while we finished our succulent arrangements. Mine turned out okay, I guess. This was nothing like what our Bloom entry would be like, but I was getting better at working with plants. And more than anything else, the night was a success because focusing on floral design kept my mind off Matteo.

I found myself alone in the greenhouse later with Rowan while we put away the garden tools.

"Yesterday I was a mess," I said quietly, not looking at him. "You really did me a solid by bringing me home. And letting me vent."

He shrugged as he slid a plastic bin off a shelf and dropped the tools in.

"You sure you're okay with helping us out at Lilybuds?" I asked. "Both the mural and the photo shoot? It would be so great for Shar."

"Yeah. Shar's been good to me." He slid the bin back on the shelf. "I'll see you later, Tahira." He left the greenhouse.

I was glad that he was willing to do this, for Shar's sake, but even though I loved the idea, I felt weird about working with Rowan on it. Doing another project with Rowan Johnston was either brilliant or a disaster waiting to happen. Nothing in between.

14

THROWN OFF BY A GRAY SHIRT

For the first week after the implosion of what I considered my most serious romantic relationship ever, I didn't mope, whine, pout, or moan about it. At least not to others. I did when I was alone, though—especially at night, when I was used to getting that last text or call from Matteo before bed. Or when I saw something amazing on Instagram and had an urge to message him about it. When my mind did wander into the memories of his lips on my neck, or the way he'd said good night in Italian, I'd remind myself that yeah, he was probably really into me, but he was into my Instagram follower count more. The strategy worked. Sort of.

Matteo, on the other hand, wasn't taking the breakup as well. Or so I'd heard—I still had him blocked everywhere. But apparently, he told Gia to tell me he wasn't seeing Alyssa anymore, and that he wanted to talk to me. She told him no. Repeatedly. Then she blocked him from being able to contact her anywhere except for the family WhatsApp, and he knew better than to set off his aunts and grandmother again.

I took Rowan's advice and stayed as busy as possible to keep my mind off Matteo. I worked a lot. Shar took me to Friday-night prayers at the jamatkhana in Niagara Falls while Gia and Juniper watched the store. But mostly, I absolutely killed it with my Bloom preparation.

After cramming all week, I'd consumed pretty much all the reputable information on the web about floral design and sculpture. I knew which plants were best as focals and fillers in an arrangement. I knew when most flowers bloomed, and which ones would survive being shoved into chicken wire. I even watched this reality show about floral installations three times through. I'd filled my sketchbooks and the art app on my iPad with hypothetical designs for the competition, using everything I'd learned about form, line, space, and color. I was hoping we'd settle on our design soon so we could start building the frame, but Rowan insisted that we needed to make some prototypes first.

I had a ton of questions as I inhaled all this information, but I had excellent teachers. We had a group chat set up for our team, and every time something stumped me—like if an African violet would work with marigolds, or if we had access to Japanese forest grass, Rowan and Juniper would hop on with answers immediately. We talked in the group chat for a while about the Bloom rules, too. The internal framework for the sculpture could be something we made or bought, and could be practically anything at all, as long as it was covered with flowers. We were allowed to build the frame ahead of time, but all the plantings had to be added on the day of the competition at the festival itself, so people could watch us make it. The judging would be focused on those principles of floral design I'd been learning about—line, color, space, scale, depth, and so forth, as well as diversity of plants. Basically, they wanted a lot of plants and flowers covering a thing in a unique and pleasing manner.

Gia was helping out, too, in her own way. While she wasn't as concerned with rules and the technicalities of the competition, she had a great eye for color, and she had some ideas for what we could make for the actual sculpture. Rowan shot down those ideas, though. Too bad—I thought a sneaker or a Birkin bag could be cool.

Monday morning, I had my appointment with Dr. Johnston, Rowan and Juniper's mom, at her clinic on Main Street. She had a million questions for me: whether I'd had an allergy test before (I had), whether I had asthma (also yes, but I'd pretty much grown out of it), and how often I took over-the-counter antihistamines (pretty much daily since getting to Bakewell). She told me about a new, stronger prescription drug, then prescribed it.

"I should apologize for not introducing myself to you yet. I've seen you in the yard with Juniper and Rowan, but I've stayed back. Juniper says I embarrass her." She smiled warmly.

I liked Dr. Johnston. She was friendly and listened, and she looked like a grown-up June.

"It's cool," I said.

"Well, I'm happy to be meeting you now, Tahira. Lord knows I feel like I already know you, what with how much the kids talk about you."

"June's talkative."

"Not just June—Rowan, too. He's been telling me about your sculpture designs. He's in complete awe of you. I should thank you for getting him excited about the Bloom again."

"What? He was already excited about it."

Dr. Johnston shook her head. "No. He was going through the motions of entering again, but he wasn't excited like he was last year. He wanted to win, of course, but the passion for the process was missing. But now he's got his spark back. I'm glad you've made his last summer before university so memorable!"

It was weird of his mother to tell me this. Even weirder to think Rowan once had a "spark" in the first place. Or that he told his mom that he liked my designs. I was flattered, of course. Mostly surprised, though. Then again, Rowan surprised me a lot as I was getting to know him better.

"Anyway, I'm glad you're here this summer." She patted my arm. "You're good for both my kids. Let me know how the new pills work for you."

~

The next afternoon at work, I was leaning on the counter, scrolling through the winners of last year's Grand Floral Cup in New York. The entries were awesome. Seriously, mind-blowing art. I *had* to win the Bloom so I could go to this thing. "Do you think I could learn to weld in four weeks?" I asked Shar.

She chuckled. "Maybe. But is it necessary? Most of the Bloom entries last year used chicken wire for the frames."

She was probably right. I sighed. But *we* needed to be more unique. Maybe I could learn basket weaving? Would straw and reeds be strong enough to hold plants?

The bell over the door rang, and a large purple plastic crate walked into the store. Presumably a person was connected to the crate, but I couldn't see them. The beat-up Chucks on the feet gave it away, though. Rowan.

Shar rushed up to help him in. "Rowan! Wonderful. You're here! Just set up to paint exactly where I showed you yesterday."

"Oh, hi," I said. I hadn't realized he was painting the mural today.

When he put the crate down, I saw something that literally made me gasp. His shirt. It wasn't brightly colored and had no plant meme in sight. In fact, today's shirt was . . . *hot*. A perfectly faded, and lightly paint-splattered, slim charcoal Henley. Holy hell. If that's what he was going to look like on campus in Toronto next year, he was going to have a devoted fan club before frosh week even ended. Again, I was positively itching to photograph this guy.

He barely looked at me and walked toward the back wall. "I'll start moving things out of the way, okay, Shar?"

"Yes, absolutely. Tahira can help you move the fixtures. The store is slow; she can be your assistant today."

I didn't mind helping. I kind of wanted to see him up close in that shirt, anyway. I went over, and we moved the fixtures near the back wall to the front of the store so the clothes on them wouldn't get paint on them.

He spread some drop cloths on the carpet and started taking painting supplies out of the plastic bin. He was being pretty quiet, and the silence felt awkward. "So," I said, "the triangles . . . do you tape them off before you paint them?" It was a stupid question. I understood how painting worked.

"I used tape for the big one at the barn, but I had to wait for each color to dry before adding the next. Shar wants it done today, so I'm freehanding the lines for this." He pulled out a printed photograph of the barn mural as reference and put it next to the containers of paint.

"Ah," I said. "The design is so great. It's perfect for the Lily collection. Like a modern juxtaposition against all the florals in the store."

He suddenly turned to me, a handful of long, narrow brushes in his hand. "What are you talking about? This *is* a floral."

"What? No." I pointed to the photo. "You're doing this one, right? It's an abstract geometric design."

"It's abstract hydrangeas. It's literally a painting of flowers."

"No, it's just . . . abstract."

He laughed, eyes twinkling with humor. At my expense.

I cringed, looking back at the picture. "Did I seriously pick a floral design as the signature backdrop for my modern, not-supposed-to-be-flowery clothing line?"

He nodded.

I leaned against the wall. "You probably thought I was so uptight that day we first met at the barn."

Using a ruler, he started drawing pencil lines that were apparently flower petals on the wall. "You *were* a bit precious."

"Yeah, well, spilling manure all over myself kind of ruined my day. And my boots."

"I was kind of an ass, too. I'm sorry. I guess I should've been flattered that you liked my painting that much," he said.

"I did. Just like I've liked your floral designs."

He turned to me, smiling almost shyly, but with real joy. His mood had completely changed again. I couldn't help but wonder if this was the *spark* Dr. Johnston had talked about. "You have another ruler and pencil?" I asked. "I can help."

We worked together to finish penciling in the triangles and then started painting some of them in the lightest blue, using Rowan's picture as a guide. Now that I knew what it was supposed to be, I totally saw hydrangeas. Specifically, blue hydrangeas in the fall, when the cornflower-blue clusters of petals darkened to a dusty purple. But of course, two weeks ago I didn't know what hydrangeas were.

"Do you paint flowers a lot?" I asked, carefully filling in a triangle with a slim brush. This was kind of soothing. My school offered amazing painting classes, but I hadn't taken them. My schedule was all math, sciences, photography, and fashion design. And figure drawing, which was where I'd learned to draw the people wearing the clothes I designed.

"Nah, this was just for my grade-twelve art project. We were supposed to do a large-scale installation that matched its surroundings. Flowers for the nursery made sense to me. I didn't anticipate that it would become a magnet for selfie-starved tourists, though."

"I wasn't the first Instagrammer who admired your work?"

He chuckled. "No."

"So, what do you have against influencers, anyway?" I probably should have asked this question before now.

He didn't look away from the painting. "They wreak *havoc* on the nursery, using it for their own purposes with no appreciation for the plants themselves. I've had to pick up wine cans and water bottles from the fields so many times. Once a group used these colored smoke bomb things for their pictures. The lawn mower was bright pink for weeks. And they always have super-entitled demands, like they want free stuff for *exposure*."

"Not all influencers are so self-absorbed."

"C'mon. It's in the definition. They want to *influence* people. They want to *personally* be relevant. Influencers are self-absorbed by design."

It was hard to disagree with him because plenty of influencers were just like what he was describing. Hell, my own ex-boyfriend was so desperate to be in that club that he cheated on me. And I myself had *wreaked havoc* at the nursery while trying to get a picture for my Instagram.

"But don't you want influence, too?" I asked, dipping my brush into the small yogurt cup of paint. "Why paint murals, or enter flower design competitions, or even go to school for . . . what was it . . . land-scape architecture, if you don't want to influence people?"

Rowan kept painting, but he seemed to consider what I was saying. "I guess I want to influence people with my creations," he said, "not for me personally. Influencers want recognition for themselves, for who they are, not for what they make."

I shrugged, smiling. "Yeah, but whatever they create, or the pictures they post, or even what they choose to wear, is a reflection of them-selves. Art reflects the artist, so why separate them? I mean, now that I've seen how much I love your painting, I see you differently."

He smiled and actually blushed a little. "Trying to butter me up for something, Thirst Trap?"

I wasn't, but I couldn't deny that smile was its own reward.

"Anyway," I said, "in my field, fashion design, the artist is as import-ant as the art. A bunch of emerging designers I follow on YouTube talk about how important platform and connections are. They put a lot of effort into curating their social media presence. Even Nilusha Bhatt—she's my mentor—her Instagram feed is as much about her life as her clothes. She literally sells sweatshirts that say BHATT across them, so people know who she is *personally*."

"But what part of you do you really want out there? The art or the artist? Do you want people excited about your actual creations, or do you just want everyone wearing clothes because your name is plastered across them?"

"Well, not my last name. Janmohammad is too long." I tilted my head. "I'm thinking of calling my line House of Tahira—and even made up some pieces with the acronym HOT appliquéd on them."

"Ah. That's why you were wearing that shirt the second time I saw you. It wasn't just to broadcast your attractiveness."

What? Did Rowan just call me hot? I shook my head. "The point is, the *artist* sells the art as much as the medium or the quality these days. You can't separate them. Influencers have learned that."

"Not always. Everyone loves their gardens but no one knows the names of the top garden designers in the world. Except other landscape architects."

"Well, that's how it is in fashion. Whether I like it or not is irrelevant."

He blew out a puff of air. "I guess I'm not cut out for fashion, then. But you have to admit, a lot of influencers are terrible."

I nodded. "Horrendously terrible. Starting with a certain Italian ex-boyfriend. Also, those people beheading roses and leaving garbage everywhere? They're not terrible because they're influencers; they're terrible *and* they're influencers. Truly great multitasking."

Rowan laughed as he swirled his brush in a pot of water.

After a short break, we moved to the darker-blue triangles. The store got busy a few times, so I had to stop painting and help Shar with customers. At seven, when it was time to close, the painting was only about halfway done. I offered to Rowan that I could stay to help him finish it, figuring we could also use the time alone with no customer interruption to discuss our design for the Bloom.

But first, we stepped out to get some pizza slices from the shop down the street after Shar left. We ate standing at the counter in the store.

"So, are you ready to take pictures of us at the nursery for the Lily line?" I asked, wiping pizza grease from my fingers.

"I'm not sure why you'd want me. I'm not much of a photographer."

"You don't have to be. Gia and I will set up the shots. We'll make it easy—point and shoot. Your sister is desperate to model, and since I haven't made any new clothes in a while, this might be her only chance."

"She wants to model?"

"She asked me to model my stuff when I first got here." Although, now that I thought about it, she didn't seem very enthusiastic about modeling the Lily collection when Gia suggested this photo shoot. "Hey, is something bothering June lately? She seemed kinda quiet that day we were working with the succulents."

"You see her more than I do. You tell me."

I honestly wasn't sure. She was chatty like normal at work, but sometimes she went quiet when we were in the garden.

"Addison isn't bothering her, is she?" Rowan asked.

I shook my head. "If she is, I'm not seeing it. What was it that Addison did to June, anyway?"

He exhaled slowly before putting his pizza down. "June never told you?"

I shook my head.

"June used to have this YouTube channel where she did book reviews and gossip about books and stuff. Last fall she got these anonymous comments on her videos. Nothing you would automatically identify as bullying or anything, but kinda . . . off. Things about the way she looked, or her clothes, instead of her content. Passive-aggressive stuff about the maturity of the books she was reviewing, or about the fact that they were mostly fantasy. Really, if you saw any of these comments on their own, you'd think nothing of it. But together . . . it became a pattern."

"Addison was doing this?"

He nodded. "It was several people doing it. One or two would start, and it would open the floodgates and others would join in. It was so subtle. I told June to delete the comments, but she left them. Honestly, they were gaslighting her so well she didn't even realize it was abuse. But it took a toll on her. Like, she had her hair in braids once, and a few people made comments about them. Not negative, but still. So she had Mom take them out. Stuff like that."

I frowned. "Addison's a bitch."

He didn't say anything for a while. Finally he spoke. "She wasn't, at first. We've known each other a long time, and she was one of the only people around here who really made an effort to get to know me. I've always been quiet, so I kind of blended into the background when we were kids. But she noticed me, you know? She was always kind of judgy, but kinder in private. Anyway, for the last few months before we broke up, she started getting more wrapped up in these *social media personalities*. You know, like, teen YouTubers? She kept bugging me to help her start her own channel. But I didn't have the time. We were all at Bell's Pond one night, and I happened to catch her on her phone making a comment on June's latest video. I had no idea she even knew about June's YouTube before that. Addie tried to reassure me that these comments weren't harassment, and they were actually helping Juniper. That all the attention on the videos was making June more popular, because of followers or something. She didn't tell us before then that it was her and her friends commenting, because she wanted to surprise us when a video went viral thanks to her 'algorithm manipulation,' as she put it. Then she said I should be commenting, too, and we could launch a spin-off show on June's channel, leveraging off her popularity. Meanwhile, my sister's self-esteem was taking a serious beating. Anyway, I broke up with Addison on the spot. I knew she could be a bit superficial, but I had no idea she was that bad. She honestly thought June's fame was more important than her self-esteem."

Boy, did I know what it was like to be blindsided by someone you thought you knew. Now I fully understood Rowan's dislike for people chasing internet fame. "Poor June. Why did they leave negative comments, though? Wouldn't lots of gushing help the algorithms, too?" I paused. "Do you think it's because she's Black?"

He shrugged. "Maybe? But June was teased for years in school. She used to be very gullible and earnest, so she was an easy target."

"She's still earnest. It's what I like best about her."

"She stopped YouTubing after I told her it was Addie and her friends behind the comments. Addie said she'd stop, but the whole thing was soured for June."

"And she's not getting the same harassment on her Instagram?"

"Not as far as I know. I'm checking it regularly."

Ugh. I felt terrible for Juniper. This explained a lot about her moodiness. A thought occurred to me. "Hey, was Cameron one of the harassers on YouTube?"

"I don't think so. It's not really Cam's style. The comments were kind of . . . subtle, you know? Cam's not one for passive aggression. Anyway, it was just Addison and the girls she hangs with who admitted to it."

"Leanne, too?"

"No, of course not. Leanne was as pissed as I was when we found out."

I was skeptical. Leanne had kinda grown on me, but there was something awfully mischievous about her. I remembered her fixation on June's bookish prom dress. "Are you sure? I mean, the commenters were anonymous—one of them could have been your best friend."

He shook his head emphatically. "Leanne would *never* do that to June. Trust me."

I wasn't so sure. My instincts were telling me that something wasn't right between Leanne and June. Maybe Rowan was too loyal to his best friend to see it. But then again, maybe I was wrong. My instincts had failed me *recently* with Matteo.

My thoughts flashed back to Addison. She was the villain here.

"I can't believe Addison expected June to teach her flower design after doing that to her."

"Yeah, me neither." Rowan balled up the paper bag the pizza came in. "Ready to add some purple to the painting?"

"Yeah, let's do this." I smiled. "By the way, I misjudged you, Rowan Johnston. Maybe it's because there are no smiling plants on your shirt, but you're an okay guy."

He shook his head, chuckling. "Thanks, I think. I hope you'll still like me when I'm back in regular clothes."

I laughed as I picked up my paintbrush.

15

BACK TO THE SCENE OF THE POO

The photo shoot at the nursery was a few days later—Thursday evening. The painting at the store turned out fabulous, and I was excited to photograph people wearing the Lily pieces in front of the full-size mural. Leanne and Rowan were working at the nursery until seven, so we had Shar drive Gia, Juniper, and me there after the store closed. The sun was setting so late lately that I wasn't worried about having enough light for the pictures, but we still needed to hustle a bit to get them done in daylight.

Juniper had been pretty quiet on the way out—I still had a sinking feeling that she didn't want to be doing this. Even though she had let me pick her outfit for the shoot, she didn't squeal nearly as much as I expected at how amazing she looked. And she barely talked about whatever book she was reading on the way.

But Gia squealed as she got out of the car in the gravel lot at Wynter's. "Ah! This place is adorbs! It's exactly as I imagined. Too bad Cam's not working today; he could have totally taken our pictures—he's really good. Eee!" She rushed toward a display of garden gnomes painted in unusual colors. "These are the cutest. We need some shots with them. Garden gnomes are my favorite!"

I was able to corral Gia away from the garden-center stuff, with some effort, and toward the barn, where Rowan and Leanne were meeting us.

I stopped short when I saw the mural again. Yeah, I'd been looking at a photo of it while Rowan and I were painting, but seeing it again in person sent the same chill up my spine as the first time. It was even more striking because there were no bags of manure anywhere in the vicinity. And because I knew the artist behind it. See? Here was proof that appreciating the artist increased my appreciation of the art.

"Hey!" Leanne waved as we got close to the building. She and Rowan were still in their work clothes. Which of course meant jeans and ironic shirts. Leanne's was pink with a picture of a realistic-looking rabbit wearing thick red eyeglasses, and Rowan's was a black T-shirt with a vintage-looking drawing of succulents. It said WHAT THE FUCKULENT? on it.

I shook my head, laughing. "Okay, that's my favorite," I said, indicating the shirt.

"I'll put it into heavier rotation," Rowan said.

"Wow, Junebug." Leanne came close to June. "You look amazing. I *love* that color on you. And your hair!" I'd put June in a long orange modern floral-print spaghetti strap dress with a purple shirt under it. I'd asked her to wear her hair out, so she had a lot of tight, defined curls skimming her shoulders. Gia had helped her with her makeup, and let me say, no one rocked winged liner better than Juniper. She was breathtaking.

Juniper took a step back from Leanne and looked down. "Um, thanks?"

There it was. There was definitely something going on that Juniper wasn't telling me. Maybe Rowan was too blind to see this vibe, but it was clear as glass to me.

I needed to defuse this. Maybe I could keep them apart until they actually had to be in pictures together? "Why aren't you dressed yet, Leanne?"

Leanne flipped her hair over her shoulder and shrugged. "I didn't want to get the fancy new clothes dirty. I don't think I'd look as good covered in shit as you did, Tahira." She grinned. "I'll go change. Be back in ten."

While Leanne was gone, I gave Rowan a literal three-minute lesson on my SLR camera. I had no doubt he could manage it—I already knew he had an artist's eye. And Gia and I were here to help.

"You got this?" I asked after showing him the focus and zoom.

"Yeah, no problem. Here, let's test it." He lifted the camera and told me to smile.

I laughed as he took the shot. It turned out pretty good. There was a big sunspot on my face, but the picture was well framed, and my expression was so happy. He definitely had an eye. I looked up at him. He was watching me intently as I checked out the photo, a tiny smile on his face. He had the warmest eyes when he wasn't scowling. So deep. I mirrored his small smile before looking away awkwardly. We needed to get to work.

The photo shoot turned out to be a bit of a challenge. Juniper seemed incapable of looking natural when the camera was pointed at her, and she was especially stiff when Leanne was anywhere nearby. Leanne, for all her easy good looks and lightheartedness, was pretty wooden, too.

"All right," I said, "let's get a shot of us tight together." I positioned us with Leanne on the end, and me, Gia, and then June next to her, all with our arms around each other. Rowan managed to get a few decent pictures. Even better were the candid ones he snapped of everyone laughing while I tried to smooth Gia's hair and keep June's dress from blowing out. I took the camera to get some shots of Leanne, and then Gia alone. The light was perfect by now, the hazy evening glow matching the urban-yet-country vibe of the Lily collection.

Leanne squeezed in next to Juniper. "Can we do one of me and June together? What do you say, Junebug? Since we're the only actual Bakewell residents in this modeling thing."

Juniper nodded before I could object on her behalf, and she was quickly enveloped in Leanne's arms from behind. Leanne rested her chin on Juniper's shoulder, and June tilted her head toward Leanne and looked straight at the camera, unsmiling. I took the pictures quickly. This picture, with Leanne's bright-auburn hair whipping around June's face, was spectacular. As good as any top fashion spread.

"I think we're done," I said after putting the camera down. After a slow start, I had no doubt we had more than enough shots to fill the Lilybuds social for a while. And I was conscious of going easy on June and Leanne—they weren't used to these shoots. I didn't want to over-work them, especially given the tension between them.

As we walked back toward the garden center, Leanne said, "Hey, wanna all go to Hyacinth's to hang out or something? Or for a walk at Bell's Pond? It's early."

I didn't much feel like running interference between Leanne and June anymore. "I can't. I want to edit these so I can start posting them tomorrow."

"Oh, okay, then." Leanne shrugged, getting into her pickup truck. "I wish I still lived in town with y'all instead of out in the sticks. Another time?"

Leanne seemed genuinely sad, but Rowan had specifically asked me to protect *Juniper* from the people bugging her. And today, that appeared to be Leanne.

~

Back at the tiny house, I did some photo editing on my iPad while Gia straightened her hair on her bed.

"Pictures are good?" she asked.

"Yeah, they're great. I didn't expect much, especially with that weird vibe between Leanne and Juniper, but the ones of the two of them alone turned out awesome."

"You noticed that, too?" Gia asked. "What's the deal with those two?"

I shrugged. "No clue, but I have suspicions. I'm going to talk to June about it when I see her next."

Gia tapped the window with her hair iron. "She's right there. Looks like she's picking herbs."

I chuckled. It certainly was weird that the people I was thinking about the most lately were literally in my own backyard.

"I'll go see if she wants to come in," I said. "Hopefully she doesn't mind the smell of burned hair."

Juniper, as expected, didn't mind singed hair at all and was thrilled to come in for a chat.

"I was just getting some peppermint for my tea in the morning," June said as she took her shoes off in the little space. "Wow! It looks so awesome here. I haven't been in since Leanne moved away. Granny Langston sure loved her knotty pine, didn't she? Oh, LOL, you put up a picture of Chris Pine . . . this is from *A Wrinkle in Time*, right? I always loved the book, but that movie was even better. I don't know why it wasn't more popular. I like how you decorated with clothes, too; is that a fashion-designer thing?"

I laughed. "No, it's because there is literally nowhere else to hang our clothes."

"Ha! It's like you're living in a closet! Reminds me of this book with a portal in a closet, not *The Lion, the Witch and the Wardrobe*, but a newer book . . ."

It was like June was a completely different person than earlier at the nursery. She sat on a chair and told us all about the portal fantasy book, and then about two more portal fantasy books, before telling us that she wasn't really a fan of portal fantasy and much preferred urban fantasy lately. "I don't think you invited me to talk about books, did you?"

I chuckled. "No, actually. We were just wondering: Was everything okay with you today?"

"Yeah, totally fine. Modeling was fun. Was I okay?" She winced. "I didn't blink and ruin the pictures, did I?"

"No, no, you looked great. I totally want you to model my own stuff at some point. But . . ." I glanced at Gia.

"You seemed uncomfortable as sin," Gia said. "Especially around Leanne."

June froze a few seconds. Then her lip quivered. "You noticed that?"

"It was obvious. To us at least," I said. "Look, if Leanne has ever done something that upset you . . . I mean, like Addison did . . ."

Gia's eyes shot to me, but it wasn't my place to tell her what Addison had done to June. I shook my head at Gia.

"No! Of course not!" June said. "Leanne isn't like Addison!"

"But you don't like her, right?" Gia asked.

June was uncomfortable. Honestly, this would all have been a lot easier if the girl were better at hiding her feelings, but she was the most unaffected person I'd ever met.

"Is it Leanne's teasing?" Gia asked. "Is that what's bothering you? Because even I think she goes too far sometimes."

June shook her head vigorously. "No. Of course not. Leanne's fine." Her voice cracked a bit there.

"Is it because she calls you Junebug?" I asked. "You hate it when people call you Junebug." Juniper's expression was pained. I'd hit the nail on the head. "You should ask her to stop," I said. "I mean, she's a troublemaker for sure, but she seems respectful for the most part. If you're not comfortable, I can ask for you, I—"

Juniper sighed and put her face in her hands.

"Now *we're* harassing her," Gia said.

I cringed. I didn't want to upset June more. "I'm sorry," I said. "It's fine. Forget it. If you have no beef with Leanne, then all is good. Let's talk about something else. How—"

"I don't have a problem with Leanne calling me Junebug," June said quietly, face still in her hands.

"What?" Gia asked.

Juniper finally lifted her face. Her eyes were wide and glassy. "I don't have a problem with Leanne calling me Junebug. Like, at all. I have a problem with anyone *other* than Leanne calling me Junebug."

It took me a second to understand. When I got it, my hand went to my mouth.

It all made sense. June was in *love* with Leanne. The evidence was all there. She couldn't seem to speak properly around her, and she put up with Leanne's constant teasing. Even going back to the beginning of the summer, when June was determined not to be on the Bloom team with Leanne and her brother. Clearly June found it uncomfortable to be around her unrequited crush. It was totally self-preservation.

Gia must have realized, too, a few seconds after me, because she suddenly turned to me and shrugged. "Honestly? I ship it."

I squeezed my lips together, trying not to laugh.

"She's pan, right?" Gia asked June.

June nodded.

"Then go for it," Gia said. "Crushing on your brother's friend is a tale as old as time. It's no big deal. Just tell her."

June threw her hands in the air, frustrated. "You don't get it. I *did* tell her. She told me she'd never see me that way."

I leaned forward. "You *told* her? When?"

"At the Snowbloom Ball in December. I've had a crush on her for, like, *forever*, and then at the ball she asked me to dance, so I thought I'd shoot my shot. But when I said something, she was all, 'Oh, that's cute,

June, but you're like my sister.' She said she only asked me to dance to shock the church ladies, but no one cared. I made a fool of myself. At least she's never told anyone. That's why I try to avoid her."

"But you're still crushing?" I asked.

Juniper nodded. She looked like she was going to throw up. She had it bad.

"Honestly, I think Leanne *is* into you, now," Gia said. "She's always, like, sitting next to you, and happy to see you and stuff. You should tell her you're still feeling it."

"She's Row's best friend." June sighed. "We grew up together. She feels bad for rejecting me and is being extra nice to make up for it."

I wasn't sure. Leanne was mighty weird around June. Hell, what about the way Leanne looked in that photo? That wasn't just guilt-motivated affection.

I pulled the photo up on my iPad and showed it to June. "That doesn't look like someone not into it."

Leanne had her usual massive grin in the picture, but there was something more than the usual twinkle in her eyes. Affection? Comfort? In fact, neither June nor Leanne was nearly as wooden as they had been in the other pictures.

Juniper shook her head. "No. Leanne is going away to university in, like, a month. All the way to Guelph for their veterinary program. She doesn't see me that way. Please don't tell anyone."

I reached over and patted her shoulder. "It's fine. If you don't want her or anyone else to know, we can keep it a secret. We just want to make sure you're okay."

"I'm fine. She's fine. Everything's fine."

Gia nodded. "Yeah, she's *fine*. Girls aren't my thing, but you have great taste, Juniper."

Juniper put her face in her palms. "This is very embarrassing," she said into her hands.

I laughed. "Don't even. Let me tell you about the time that Sohil Sharma found the secret Instagram account Gia made that was all photoshops of him and her—"

"Can we *not*?" Gia interrupted.

I laughed. "I'm texting you this picture, June. Put it away until you're old or something. Or stare at it every night when you go to bed. Then we'll never speak of this again." I texted her the picture.

I was relieved that June's weirdness wasn't because Leanne was harassing her. If June didn't want to make another move on her brother's best friend, or even talk through these feelings ever again, I could respect that. But I had to agree with Gia—I kind of shipped Juniper and Leanne. That would be an *adorable* couple.

16

IT'S A BET

O ver the next week, my time was so packed between Lilybuds and getting ready for the Bloom that I really appreciated Mom's calls every two days reminding me to get enough sleep and not neglect my social media content. Also, she reminded me to check in with Dad and my sister, which I did. Nilusha and I texted a few times, too—she helped me decide which shots from the Lily photo shoot I should use for the store's marketing. Shar and I went to prayers again on Friday night while Gia and June worked at the store. But it was all fine—I loved being so busy.

Dr. Johnston's new antihistamine was working like a dream, so I managed to make a small-scale floral sculpture honoring my destroyed suede boots using a combination of chicken wire, flowerpots, and red marigolds. Not perfect, but I was getting the hang of floral sculpture. Just like with fashion design, I found myself drawn to monochromatic, muted color schemes in floral design. Simple and minimalistic. Lots of focal flowers with little filler. It was in contrast to Rowan and Juniper, whose tastes ran more to vibrant and colorful, with lots of different flowers in busy configurations. I liked their designs, too, but mine were more *me*.

On Wednesday night, June, Rowan, Gia, and I were working on a larger piece as practice for the Bloom. I wasn't necessarily sold on the design—we were basically doing a large living sculpture of a tree.

"You say I'm self-centered, and yet you decide to make a sculpture of your name," I teased Rowan as I wrapped the trunk with brown moss. He knew I was kidding. Rowan and I had found an unlikely alliance lately, even though we hadn't really seen much of each other since the photo shoot at the nursery since we'd both worked so much. We texted daily, though, mostly about flowers and the Bloom. I'd been worried that this meeting would be weird—because of that *moment* at the nursery. After he took that photo of me, we got caught up in staring at each other a touch too long. But whatever. It was probably just because of that perfect hazy summer night. Now we were back to being slightly snarky friends.

Which was good, because I was in no way looking to start crushing on Plant-Boy right now. That wasn't part of the Plan.

He shrugged. "It's not a specific tree. It's more stylized."

I stood back. "I'm just not feeling this for the competition. A living sculpture of a tree looks too much like a . . . tree."

"The judges will love it, though," June said. "The theme this year is 'Things in a garden.'"

Only in Bakewell would they have a garden sculpture contest with the theme of things in a garden.

I peered at the bulbous head of the sculpture. "What if we only used white flowers, like those impatiens you showed me?"

"We're not going to win with only one type of flower," Rowan said.

"Well, I don't think we'll win with a tree. Or with flower vomit," I said.

Rowan gave me a pointed look. "I came in second with my 'flower vomit,' as you call it. This is the kind of thing the judges will expect—trust me."

I sighed. "I *know* this is what they expect. I want to do something they *won't* expect." I smiled because I didn't want him to think I was being precious again. "Humor me. What else is in a garden? Other than trees."

June looked around. "Um . . . us?"

"Furniture?" Gia offered. She'd barely paid attention before this, focused on texting someone. Probably Cameron.

I bit my lip. There had to be an angle I was missing here. I inspected the garden. Hose reel? Garden shears? "This is the dumbest theme in the world," I said. "Why don't we just make a freaking flower?"

Rowan raised a brow. "That's kind of the point. It's a flower sculpture competition."

I grinned, an idea coming to me. "*Wait*. I'm brilliant. Not flowers, but *flower*! We're supposed to make large living statues; why can't we make a statue of a huge flower? Covered with flowers? It's a little meta, but the whole garden theme is meta."

Rowan stopped looking suspicious and stared out into the open patch of grass in front of the workbench. I knew what he was doing—he was imagining a large floral sculpture of a flower. He was constructing it in his mind to determine if it was feasible. He probably saw something full and lush and filled with many colors. His eyes glazed over a bit as his attention stayed focused on the images in his head. He rubbed his jaw in thought. I was mesmerized watching him imagine it. I couldn't look away from his face.

Finally, a small smile appeared. "You know? I think that might be awesome."

I shook my head. "I don't *think* it will be awesome; I *know* it will be. You and me together? We can make this spectacular enough to win."

I'd been really focused on the store for the last week. The Lily launch had gone really well. Store traffic and total sales were up over last year, and the Lily merchandise was flying off the shelves. We'd had to order new stock twice since that first delivery.

But I hadn't lost sight of why *else* I was here. My Bloom entry was as important as my work in the store. I *needed* it to be showstopping. I needed to wow Christopher Chan so I would get into FIT.

"Let's sketch some ideas," I said. "I'll draw up a flower sculpture that's unique and modern with an urban edge but will still appeal to the judges."

"Yes!" Gia said. "Tahira is amazeballs. She'll make something fabulous; I promise."

Rowan put his hands up. "Hold on, hold on. Okay, I agree the flower idea is a good one, but I know what kind of flower you'll design. It will be all bare and all white or something. Let me design something, too. A flower but with actual colors."

June clapped her hands. "Ooh, let's do a bet. Why don't you both draw a design, and we'll let a neutral third party decide which one we use?"

I frowned. "Do we know any neutral third parties?" Shar was my aunt, Leanne was Rowan's best friend and maybe had a thing for Juniper, Addison was a bitch, and Cameron was a random jock smitten with Gia. Plus, Addison and Cameron were in competition against us, so we couldn't exactly show them our designs.

"Hyacinth!" Juniper said. "We can ask Hyacinth to pick which one she thinks will win. She was a judge for a few years but isn't doing it this year because she's going to Tahiti or something to get married that weekend. She used to be an interior decorator."

"There's actually a Hyacinth? I thought the coffee shop was named after the flower, not an actual person."

Gia crossed her arms. "You *know* Hyacinth! The woman with the magenta hair?"

Huh. I did know that woman, just didn't realize Hyacinth was her name. Or that she owned the café.

"I'm in," Rowan said. "What's the wager?"

There was only one thing I wanted from Rowan Johnston, and I'd wanted it since the day I'd met him. "I know what I want if I win," I said. "What do you want from me?" I fluttered my lashes playfully.

He ran his fingers over his jaw again, laughing. "Oh, jeez, I don't know. Okay, if I win you have to get me an ice cream cone. Specifically, the toasted marshmallow ice cream from Inside Scoop." That was a homemade ice cream shop on Main Street. Big lineups on the weekends.

"That's easy," I said. "I can get you ice cream right now if you want."

Juniper shook her head, laughing. "They only serve toasted marshmallow on Saturdays, and they're usually out by the afternoon. Basically, expect to have to wait in line a minimum half hour to get toasted marshmallow ice cream. It's legendary."

"Deal," I said. "It doesn't really matter anyway because I'm not going to lose."

Rowan laughed. "Way to doubt yourself, Tahira. What do you want if you win?"

I grinned suggestively. "You. I want you. Wearing my designs, modeling for my Instagram."

He frowned a second, then laughed, shaking his head. "Okay, Thirst Trap. You've got a deal."

~

Over the next few days, I researched and drew up several ideas for the competition sculpture on my iPad. I wanted to do it all alone, with no outside interference. That ended up being no problem because Gia was so busy with Cameron that I barely even saw her.

But anyway. I eventually settled on the perfect design. It was basically a stylized, narrow, white lily, done mostly with white impatiens and begonias. To represent the stamen and pistil, I used gold-colored grasses. It wasn't exactly minimalistic—it was pretty lush. But the color scheme stayed to white, green, and the golden bursts.

I thought it was great. I also thought it was very strange how much I loved it. Even a month ago, I would have hated all the flowers and greenery. This design was so Bakewell, but it was also very me. It was exactly what we needed to stand out in the Bloom.

On Friday night, Shar and I went into Niagara for prayers again. After we were back at home, I was in the tiny house adding finishing touches to the Bloom design on my iPad when Gia came in.

"I'm not here," she said. I knew she'd closed the store at seven, and I assumed she'd been with Cameron since then. "The air conditioner over the Scottish store leaked all over my head. That Hamish guy kept calling me a 'wee lassie' while he apologized. I need five minutes with my flat iron; then Cam and I are going to go hang in his backyard."

She turned to show me that the back of her head had reverted back to its natural frizzy waves instead of the intentional loose waves she made herself.

"Things still going well with you two?" I asked.

Gia nodded happily as she plugged her straightener in. "He's the absolute sweetest. You know he loves reality TV? We've been watching that dating show in Antigua. *Summer in Paradise*? But he keeps saying that *this* is his summer in paradise because of me. Sweet, right? Where can you find a boyfriend that watches reality dating shows? Not in Toronto, home of the toxic masculinity teens. You don't think I'm spending too much time with Cam, do you? I mean, you and me weren't really going to be all 'Hot Girl Summer' since you had a boyfriend when we got here . . . but—"

"No, no," I said, shaking my head. "Totally fine, G. I'm happy for you."

She waved her hand. "See! That's why I love you, T. You never get jealous or anything." She unplugged the iron. "You've got Juniper now, so you don't need me as much. Not to mention Rowan." She wagged her eyebrows. "All those thirst traps of yours actually worked. You two will have a mind-blowing summer hookup soon. Mark my words."

I straightened my spine. "What the *hell* are you talking about?"

"Rowan and you." She snorted a laugh. "C'mon, don't pretend you haven't noticed that Plant-Boy is seriously into you." She checked her phone. "That's my boo. Gotta go, T. Don't wait up." She blew me a kiss and headed out the door.

What. Was. Gia. On.

Rowan Johnston was *not* into me. I mean, yeah, we didn't exactly hate each other anymore, but one doesn't go from thinking someone is shallow and stuck up all the way to thinking they are, like, *girlfriend* material in a month. Because yeah, if Rowan *were* into me, it would be a boyfriend-girlfriend situation—he was *not* the casual-hookup type.

We were friends. That was it. We'd been texting each other light-hearted trash talk all day about this bet. He even sent me a picture of him eating the toasted marshmallow ice cream from Inside Scoop last summer.

Okay, wait. That wasn't something a guy would send a girl unless he was into her. Because eating ice cream was a pretty sexy thing. And honestly? It was a pretty hot picture.

Holy crap—it was practically a sext. Was it possible Rowan *was* into me?

I'd be on the rebound, wouldn't I? Maybe not. I hadn't thought about Matteo for a bit—and Gia said he'd stopped bugging her about me. I hadn't even been tempted to check his feeds to see what he'd been up to. I truly didn't care. I was over him.

But did I want a fling with Rowan Johnston, of all people? Plant-Boy? Talk about completely not my type. Well, physically he was my type. Physically he'd be anyone's type—I think even the Queen of England would do a double take if she saw that jaw pass her on the street.

I had to admit that, in the last few weeks, I'd grown to like Rowan. I was drawn to him. Lately, it wasn't just his jaw that I wanted to stare at, but his smile. The way his soft brown eyes laser-focused on his work when he was in the garden. The way he squinted a little bit when he painted the hydrangea in the store. That little smile on his face when he took that picture of me in the nursery.

I exhaled. It was true. I was so, so into Rowan Johnston. Not just for his looks, either. In all the ways.

Oh no. It was happening. Spending more time with him was becoming a disaster.

17

TOO MANY STARS IN THE SKY

G etting clothes ready for a weekend photo shoot was how I used to spend my Friday nights, so after I was done with the sketch to show Hyacinth, I happily altered a T-shirt to fit Rowan, just in case I won the bet and I got the chance to photograph him. The shirt was red, with faux-leather sleeves and an asymmetrical diagonal hem. I'd actually made it for myself but never worn it. It was nice to be sewing—something familiar for a change. It reminded me of my old life in Toronto.

But even though I was glad to be at my sewing machine again, part of me felt I shouldn't be doing this. If I was smart, I'd get out of this bet and stay far, far away from Rowan for the rest of the summer. I couldn't figure out how this had happened, but catching feelings for Plant-Boy was the definition of a bad idea. I needed to tamp down this crush. The Plan should be the only thing on my mind now. Not cute boys in gardens.

But I still took in the sleeves of the shirt (I *needed* those manure-bag-slinging biceps on my Insta). By eleven I was done sewing and restless. Gia was, of course, still out, and I wasn't feeling like checking in with any Toronto friends. I glanced out the window. The garden was so cool at night. The flower beds were all subtly lit, and the normally vibrant colors were dark, shaded versions of their daytime brilliance. I grabbed my camera and went outside.

I made a beeline for the flower bed near Rowan's workbench—the one with the big dahlias, peonies, and lush greens. I played around with the settings on my camera and crouched to take some pictures.

They came out pretty nice. I widened the aperture and slowed the shutter speed a bit more. It looked almost magical—like a scene from one of those movies on alien planets. I kept taking pictures, some zooming in on individual flowers, some wide shots, when a hand on my shoulder nearly made me drop my camera.

I turned quickly . . . it was Rowan.

"Jesus—I still need to get you that bell," I said, shaking my head.

He chuckled. He was so close. Illuminated only by the dim light of the backyard. The shadows painting his face in exquisite detail.

I exhaled. I had it *bad*.

"What are you doing here?" he asked.

"I could ask you the same question."

"True, but I asked first."

I took a step away from him and indicated the flowers. "Oh, you know. The garden looks awesome at night. I didn't think anyone would be out here so late. I figured I'd practice my night photography, but I can go and leave you alone . . ." I was babbling.

"You don't have to leave. I was just surprised." He grinned. "Seems I've turned you on to flowers after all."

I chuckled. "Or your mother's antihistamine has. Did you do all the lighting out here?"

He nodded. "Last year. It's all solar. The receivers are there." We walked over to a spot at the end of the garden. He told me more about the work he'd done wiring the garden, and about other plans he had for spotlights on the flower beds.

"It's impressive," I said. "You'll be sad to leave all this when university starts, won't you?"

He shrugged. "I'm not leaving Bakewell forever. My family and Shar are still here to enjoy the garden."

I picked up the camera and crouched to take a close-up of a deep-pink dahlia. "Do you plan to come back to Bakewell after graduating university?"

"I don't know. I'll be back to visit at least. My family's here, and I love Bakewell."

"You say that now, but after a month in Toronto, you'll be a city convert." I doubted that, though. I still couldn't imagine Rowan in the city. Actually, I couldn't imagine Rowan anywhere but here, in this bright, colorful garden. Or at the nursery.

He chuckled. "Do you really think someone like me will fit in in the big city?"

I turned to look at him. He was wearing the pale-orange Stormtrooper shirt he'd been in when we met, along with grass-stained jeans and flip-flops.

"To be honest, I don't think you're fitting in here, either," I said, smiling. "You march to the beat of your own drum." That's why I liked him.

He laughed and watched as I took more pictures of his flowers.

"So, what are you doing out here at this hour?" I asked after a few more minutes.

"I always come out here when I can't sleep."

I smiled playfully. "Worried I'm going to trounce you in our bet? I am *so* looking forward to you finally admitting my brilliance." Oh my God. Was I flirting?

He laughed, shaking his head. "Yeah, that's it. Totally. But . . ." He narrowed his eyes and raised one brow. "Maybe I'm excited that tomorrow you get to bathe in *my* brilliance."

That was flirty. Totally. Both of us were flirting. My stomach seemed to flip upside down at that look in his eyes. I put my camera on the workbench. "So, what do you specifically do out here when you can't sleep? Dig? Arrange flowers?"

"Stargaze," he said.

"Oh God." I rolled my eyes. "Not that again. You're a bit of a clichéd country boy, you know that, Rowan? You into tipping cows and, IDK . . . monster trucks, too?"

He laughed. "C'mon. Join me."

He got a blanket from the greenhouse, then motioned me over to a grassy patch in the yard. After laying out the blanket, he sat and patted the space next to him.

"I told you before—I'm not really into stargazing," I said, but still I sat cross-legged next to him on the blanket.

"How is anyone not into looking at stars?" he asked, leaning back on his arms so he could look at the sky. "They're just stars."

I shrugged. "The Toronto sky is nothing like this," I said.

"I know. I've been there. Many times."

Of course he had. I had a question on my lips. Would we keep in touch in Toronto after this summer? But I wasn't sure I wanted the answer.

I decided to ask an easier question. "What do you like about living out in the sticks? I always assumed people who lived in small towns were biding their time for when they could leave."

"A lot are. Most of the kids in my class fantasize about living in Toronto or somewhere like that. But I don't know. I like small-town living. It's quiet. Lots of nature. I can rely on almost everyone. I mean, it's not all sunshine and roses, and yeah, there are some profoundly close-minded people in small towns—"

"Racist, you mean." I had actually experienced a lot less racism personally here in Bakewell than I expected, but I wasn't a permanent fixture in this town and locals pretty much treated me like a tourist. And the tourists to Bakewell were about as diverse as they could get—seemed everyone loved flowers. But I knew racism existed here, and I knew it had been aimed at Rowan and his family before.

He nodded. "Yup. There are people who definitely resent a successful Black family living their best life. Just like some people don't like that Leanne is openly pansexual. But we're all still here. We have more allies than not—the Black Lives Matter protests in Bakewell were pretty big. The pride parade, too." He sighed. "I've heard racist slurs thrown at my family in big cities when we've traveled. And there are not a lot of people of color in architecture, landscape or otherwise. When I went to the campus, three people thought I was with the groundskeeping crew instead of interviewing for the landscape architecture program."

"The racism in the fashion industry is a beast, too," I said, watching his face as he looked at the stars. "And there's a lot of Islamophobia. Last Toronto Fashion Week, barely eight percent of the designers featured were people of color. All of those were doing sportswear or streetwear—there are no POC in couture."

"You seen any of that firsthand?" he asked.

I nodded, looking down at my knees. "Last year I tried out for this televised fashion contest, like *Project Runway: Junior* except on public-access TV. Anyway, they turned me down as a contestant because I was"—I made air quotes—"the 'wrong kind of Muslim.' They would have taken me if I wore a hijab so they'd get diversity points, or something. And once at school, a substitute teacher told me she hadn't heard of Muslims designing clothes, and what was the point if my husband wasn't going to let me wear any of this stuff, anyway?"

"Holy crap. What did you do?"

"Complained about the teacher to the school board and sucked it up about the show. Oh, and then I designed an outfit for my hijabi friend Ayesha to wear for the school fashion show as my own revenge. Ayesha looked hot."

He chuckled. "You're a force, Tahira, you know that? You think you're going to have to deal with that stuff at that school in New York?"

"Probably. It's an incredibly competitive school. Plus, I'm already going to have to work twice as hard there to make up for my lack of connections."

"Why do you want to go there?"

I shrugged. "It's the best. Anyway, I'm surprised you don't see even more racism here."

"There are a ton of microaggressions," he said. "Stupid stuff, you know? Like people being surprised that my parents, and my grandparents, too, are comfortably middle class, or people assuming the scholarships I was offered were all 'diversity' based. Little things. I ignore them."

"Those little things chip away at you, though. Like with Juniper's YouTube harassment. Comments that mean nothing on their own can snowball inside." I shifted and hugged my knees up to my chest. "It sucks we have to deal with this."

He nodded. "It does. But my dad says carving out safe spaces in these places is an act of resistance, and that people like us are changing the landscape. Let them hate—we'll just keep going."

It wasn't people *like* Rowan who were going to change the landscape; it was literally *him*. In a big way, or in a small, profound way, the world was going to be a more beautiful place because Rowan Johnston wanted it to be. The world was so incredibly lucky.

I shifted again and stretched my legs out next to his.

"I've been doing this forever," he said, indicating the dark sky. "My parents used to find me asleep in the backyard in the morning all the time when I was a kid."

"You slept out here?"

"Yup. Once I woke up to a skunk smelling my face."

"Oh my God, gross." I shook my head. "You won't be able to do this if you're living on campus in Toronto. If the raccoons don't get you, the drunk students will."

"Yeah, but you can't see nearly as many stars there, anyway." He lay back completely on the blanket. "Is that why you don't stargaze? I have a hard time believing you've never lain down outside to look at the sky."

"Of course I have. It's just . . ." How could I explain this? I bit my lip. "I mean, it's not that I'm scared of stars or anything, it's . . . it's just really hard to focus on them. They're just dots in the sky, and there's usually too much going on in my head to look at just that. I worry that I'm not appreciating them right."

"C'mon, Tahira. Lie back." He patted the area on the blanket next to his head. "I suspect the problem is the *city* sky. No way you'll be bored looking at this one."

I lay back and exhaled. After one second of looking at the sky, I had to close my eyes again. I hadn't been completely honest there—it wasn't that I worried that I wasn't appreciating the sky right, but more like . . . seeing so many stars together made me feel . . . alone. And I didn't like that.

But I wasn't alone now.

I opened my eyes again. In the city, when you looked at the sky, you could realistically count the stars. Here, that would be like counting the grains of rice in a gigantic bowl.

"It makes me feel small," I said quietly. "It makes me wonder if I'm actually not important. Like all the hard work I do, and my mind racing all the time with what I should be accomplishing, or my Plan or whatever, maybe it doesn't matter in the universe. I feel . . . untethered. Like there's nothing grounding me to the earth anymore." My fingers gripped the blanket tightly. "I feel like there's nothing to hold on to."

"I never would have pegged you for an existentialist," he said.

"It's not that I—" I made a frustrated noise as I turned away from the sky. I was fine—I was sure all the work I was doing was right for me. The Plan would succeed.

But when I saw that sky with thousands and thousands of stars, it forced me to think. Who was I really working *for*? Was it worth it?

Rowan's hand suddenly covered mine. He loosened my grip on the blanket and intertwined our fingers together.

"What are you doing?" I asked.

"I don't doubt for a second that you *will* accomplish all the things you want to do on your own, but . . ." He paused. "Tonight, I think you need something to hold on to," he said softly.

I smiled, holding his hand tightly as we stared at the bright night sky.

18

PLANT-BOY IN HIS NATURAL HABITAT

With the Bloom only three weeks away, we all wanted to get our design finalized so we could start building the frame, so Gia, Juniper, and I walked downtown to meet Rowan at Hyacinth's the next morning for the grand judgment on our designs. It was pretty early for a Saturday, but June and Gia were working at 9:30. Rowan and I both had the day off, but he claimed he had some errand to run before the meeting, so he didn't drive us. I didn't mind walking, but that little anxiety gremlin in my head wondered if Rowan was avoiding me after last night.

We'd held hands out in the backyard for an hour, and if I tried, I could still feel his hand in mine now. Calloused, which was no wonder, considering all the manual labor he did, and probably dirt under his fingernails. We talked about Bakewell, about Toronto, about his silly shirts. He admitted he wanted to buy some nonbotanically oriented clothes for university. I offered to help him do some online shopping before the summer ended. We talked about why I wanted to go to FIT, and how he still hadn't decided if he wanted to be a licensed landscape architect or work as a landscape designer, but he figured the landscape architecture program would be useful either way. We laughed, teased each other, and sometimes were just silent. We stared at the stars the whole time, our hands tightly connected.

It was the nicest night I'd had in Bakewell.

Everything seemed fine when we got to the coffee shop. Rowan was outside on one of the bench seats, and he greeted us like normal. He'd done his sketch digitally as well, so he AirDropped it to my iPad. June and Gia very ceremoniously took my iPad inside to show Hyacinth. They said we weren't allowed to come in and influence her decision. I sat in the seat across from Rowan. He was wearing his I CAN'T, I HAVE PLANTS shirt and had a Wynter's tote bag next to him.

"I'm nervous," I said. "Is this what waiting for the results for the actual Bloom is like?"

He seemed pretty relaxed lounging on his seat. I wondered if he was also having trouble not thinking about what happened last night. "I guess?" he said. "The judges deliberate for a while at the Bloom. Last year I left while Addison stayed and wandered the midway. She texted me the results."

"Not into rides and totally fixed sideshow games?"

He shook his head. "Nah, I wasn't feeling it. My dad and I had an argument that morning."

"Oh, that sucks. About the Bloom?" I had seen Mr. Johnston around but hadn't really met him yet. I knew that his displeasure with his son's career choice was a big conflict between them.

Rowan was obviously trying to look like this conversation wasn't a big deal, but his jaw tightened. "My dad really wants me to go into science like him. He's got a doctorate in biology with a focus on botany, and until last summer I intended to study biology, too. But I'd been taking art all through high school. And then last summer, when I redesigned the garden at home, I did all this research and even met a garden designer through the nursery. When she told me about this landscape architecture program, I just knew.

"It's the coolest thing—landscape architecture is like the perfect mixture of art and science. I didn't know there was an entire field that designs outdoor spaces with the same precision and planning they do for buildings. They take into account sustainability and accessibility, and now even social equality. There's a new movement toward creating more heterogeneous spaces—that means spaces are created from a decolonized framework to support all the diverse people using the space. I mean, they've always taken into account the diversity of plants and animals in landscape design; we should also be thinking about the diversity of different cultures and races, and how they want to utilize spaces, too. This is especially important in urban environments. Public spaces should be designed in a way to help foster community engagement. There's this one park in Boston that just opened . . . it—" He paused, smiling shyly. "Sorry. I can go on about this forever."

I shook my head, in awe. He was like Juniper going on about books—there was so much passion in his voice. It was exactly the same excitement I felt about designing fashion. About creating clothes for all the diverse people who would wear them. "Don't apologize," I said. "This is the best reason ever to apply for that program. You've told all this to your dad?"

He nodded. "I told him right before the Bloom last summer. I also applied for biology like he wanted, though. I didn't expect to get into the architecture program. It's competitive."

"But you did."

He nodded. "I got into both. I found out in May. I got a full scholarship for the biology program. Nothing at all for the architecture."

I knew the guy was smart, but I hadn't realized he was, like, full-ride smart. "So, your dad isn't happy you chose landscape architecture."

"I sent in the acceptance in early June, and we argued for about a month afterward. We've only now reached a kind of stalemate over the last few weeks."

This was why Rowan had been so grumpy when we first met in late June.

"Considering your grandmother—his mother, right?—was a florist, wouldn't he be happy that you want to design gardens for a living?"

"For my dad, it's such a big deal that I got that scholarship. I was the first Black student to get a full scholarship in biology at that school, or something."

"But he's got to see your talent in landscaping, too," I said.

Despite Rowan's easy posture, I could see that this was hard for him to talk about. He shrugged. "Maybe winning the Bloom and going to New York will show him I can still be the top."

I let out a long breath. I'd wanted to win the Bloom for my own career—for my own dreams—and this flower stuff wasn't actually my dream at all. But it *was* Rowan's. This was even more important to him.

"I wish you'd told me this before," I said, looking into his eyes.

"Why?"

"Because I would have worked even harder to win this thing for *you*."

He smiled. It lit up his face. Everything around us faded away: the street waking up, the people going into Hyacinth's to get their morning coffee, the sound of birds in the air. It all disappeared.

Because Rowan Johnston was smiling only for me. And there was more there: anticipation. We both knew we were on the way to something here—and last night was the first step to getting there. And it didn't feel like a disaster after all.

The door to the café opened.

"We got it!" Juniper came out, waving the iPad in the air. "Sorry it took us so long. That place is busy this morning! But we have a winner! The design we're using for the Bloom!"

Gia was close behind, also grinning.

I sat up straight. "Whose is it?" It didn't really matter that much, because with me and Rowan working together, it would be amazing no matter what we did. But I was curious to find out if we'd be standing in an ice cream line for an hour, or if Rowan would be wearing the shirt I made with my own two hands while I finally got to photograph that face. Those forearms. Those beautiful hands.

Juniper flopped onto the seat next to me. "Well, Hyacinth said she loved them both. She's not a Bloom judge this year, but she knows what they like. She thinks they both could win, but based on originality, she'd give a slight edge to Tahira."

"Yay!" I said, grinning at Rowan. "See? A city girl can learn to play with flowers."

He laughed and nodded. "You won fair and square. Congratulations." He picked up the iPad to study my design. "This really is awesome. It might be tricky to make these sharp corners on the petals with chicken wire, though. I think I know where we can get some brass tubing to use. There's this junkyard out near—"

I put my finger up. "Ah! Before anything else, you owe me a photo shoot. It's been too long since I've had new content on my Insta. Today, Plant-Boy, you're all mine."

～

June and Gia left for Lilybuds while Rowan and I stayed at Hyacinth's for a coffee and planned my photo shoot.

"I need somewhere that looks more urban," I said. "The barn at the nursery is good, but we already used it for Lilybuds. There's no secret graffiti wall or decommissioned subway station in Bakewell, is there?"

He laughed. "No. What about behind the library or the clock tower?"

I shook my head. "This damn town is too flower obsessed. The alleyways are all pretty." Even the auto garage had window boxes full of seasonal blooms.

"I thought you were into flowers now?"

I shrugged. I was, kinda. "Yeah, but I don't think the whole mani-cured-garden aesthetic is right for my designs. I need something more . . . industrial."

"What about the nursery itself?"

I wrinkled my nose. "Didn't I say no gardens?"

"No, not the garden center, the *nursery*. The actual greenhouse. It's flowers, but it's about the most industrial thing around here. Seriously, inside is all heavy machinery, skids, and forklifts. It's nothing like the garden center. Wynter's also has a botanical lab, too, if you want the whole science look. My dad heads it up, and he's in today finishing some research, so he'll let us in."

"Your dad wouldn't mind?"

"Are you kidding? He'd be thrilled to show off his lab. Wynter's is so much more than the garden center—it's pretty much a flower factory. Our plants are sold all over the country."

Huh. I mean, I'd seen the massive greenhouse at Wynter's from a distance, but I'd always assumed it was a bigger version of the garden center. All cutesy and florally. But it made sense—this was a flower factory.

"Oh, good. You kids are still here." I looked up. The woman who I now knew was Hyacinth was coming out of the shop. She was white, and looked to be in her thirties, and had the most perfect magenta bobbed hair. She wore black jeans with a black T-shirt that said Hyacinth's on the chest. "I just wanted to make sure I told you how much I loved both those drawings. They didn't tell me who did what when I decided. Done well, I think either design could win."

"Thanks!" Rowan said.

Hyacinth leaned in close. "You two make a good team—I'm glad you're working together. Bloom couples are the best couples . . . my fiancé and I fell in love when we were on a Bloom team together." She smiled at me. "Thomas owns the auto garage. Have you seen his flower boxes? The irony is that we're missing the festival this year because we're getting married that weekend. We're having a tiny destination wedding because otherwise we'd have to invite all of Bakewell. If we did that, I'd just want to make sure everyone has enough coffee and food, and Thom would be reminding them they were due for an oil change! Anyway, good luck, kiddos! I'm rooting for you!"

I thanked her, and she smiled and went back inside. I fidgeted with the clasp on my bag. Why hadn't Rowan corrected Hyacinth about us being a couple?

After a few awkward seconds, Rowan said, "So? Want to take the pictures at the nursery? Come see where I work. There is something else I want to show you at Wynter's, anyway."

He had the sweetest smile on his face. I couldn't seem to say no to it. "I'd love to. Let's go back to where we met, Plant-Boy."

We headed home to change first—him into the handmade shirt and me into a halter tank and fitted wide-leg trousers, both made in the same cream linen with a subtle red thread running through it. These were older pieces, and they'd been on my page before, but I styled them differently now, with chains on the belt loops and my hair down. If the setting worked, I wanted pictures of both of us together on my page, too. I was neglecting my platform, which my mother reminded me of every time she called.

Rowan had a sweatshirt over the T-shirt when I found him at his car, so I couldn't see how it looked on him. The sweatshirt was a cool gray that brought out the pale brown in his otherwise dark eyes.

I needed to stop staring.

I got into the car, schooling my voice to be light and easy. "You ready for this? I would say it's your modeling debut, but you modeled in your school fashion show, right?"

He laughed. "Yup. I'm an old hand at this." He put the car in reverse and pulled out into the street. "Only weird thing will be standing around for pictures at the nursery while the rest of my crew are busy."

"*Your* crew? Oh, wait, you're a supervisor, aren't you?"

"Yeah, but just a shift supervisor. I'm the lead for my team, which doesn't mean much because most of my team are, like, fourteen- to sixteen-year-olds."

After turning into Wynter's, he drove past the retail store and the barn to a more distant parking lot outside the large greenhouse. He parked, and we headed to the entrance. Rowan swiped his card on a pad near the door.

"After you," he said with a gallant swing of his arm, holding the door open for me. I laughed as I walked in.

And then stopped dead.

I mean, logically, I had known what I was getting into here. The greenhouse was enormous from the outside, and I'd assumed it would be filled with flowers. But in reality? I had no freaking clue.

Because what looked big from the outside was humongously enormous inside. I literally could not see the back wall of the place. It was so full. Crammed with rows and rows of flowers and plants.

On shelves, on wire benches, on skids, in urns, in buckets, were plants of all sizes, including wide plastic flats containing rows and rows of tiny seedlings. Even the ceiling was full. Rows of hanging baskets were hooked onto rails moving around the room. I didn't need to ask; Rowan could see me wondering what the heck that was about.

"They keep moving so they get even sunlight and pass under the watering hose once a day. It's all automated."

I shook my head in awe. "This is a lot of flowers. Are all commercial greenhouses like this?"

He nodded. "This is on the bigger size, but most nurseries have more than one greenhouse, while we have only the one. We also have a number of outdoor fields. And a lot of the revenue here comes from the labs. You know, propagation, breeding, that sort of thing. Want to have a look around before we take the pictures?"

I nodded. This place was enchanting. I was also very glad I'd taken one of Dr. Johnston's heavy-duty antihistamines.

Rowan took me row by row through the greenhouse, pointing out flowers and introducing me to the workers we encountered. Everyone seemed friendly, especially the other teenagers we saw (they must have been Rowan's team), but clearly a little surprised. I was pretty sure I was the first date Rowan had brought to the greenhouse.

Wait . . . date? Was this a date? No, I'd won a bet; that's why we were here. But . . . even if I'd lost, we'd be eating ice cream together now. Still kind of date-y. And we'd held hands looking at the stars for over an hour last night. That was date-y, too.

I wouldn't think too much about it right now. As we moved to the next row of plantings, someone called Rowan over and said something very technical sounding.

Rowan touched my arm. "I'll be a sec. The seedling-plug maker is acting up. I know how to get her humming again." He smiled apologetically.

I had no idea what those words meant, but wow, he certainly did. That confidence was appealing. "No prob. Go ahead. I'll be here."

I walked through the next aisle. As I leaned to get close enough to read some labels—chrysanthemums—someone called to me.

"Tahira? What are you doing here?"

Cameron. I'd forgotten he worked at Wynter's. "Oh, hey, Cameron. Just doing a photo shoot with Rowan."

We chatted a few minutes, and he asked me about Gia three times. I was delighted. He was as smitten as Gia was.

Eventually, Rowan found us.

"Hey, Rowan," Cameron said. "Can't stay away even on your day off, eh?"

"Hi, Cam." Rowan smiled, then turned to me. "My dad just texted—he wants us to come say hello in the lab."

"Well, you don't want to keep one of the double doctors waiting," Cameron said.

I didn't understand, and I thought Rowan might explain or laugh, but he just said goodbye to Cameron, and we headed out.

The lab was smaller than I expected. It reminded me more of a high school biology classroom than the sterile white labs I'd seen in movies.

"There you are, kids!" Rowan's dad wore a white lab coat and sat at a computer against the wall. His wide smile looked like Juniper's, though his face was more like Rowan's.

After Rowan introduced me, his dad asked me what I thought of Wynter's.

"It's impressive. I've never seen so much color," I said. "The lab is cool, too—thanks for having me here, Mr. Johnston."

"Ah, it's actually Dr. Johnston, but of course Misty is also Dr. Johnston, so how about you call me Grant?"

"Oh." I looked at Rowan. "Is that what Cameron meant by 'double doctors'? Because both your parents are doctors?"

Rowan sighed, sitting on one of the high stools at one of the counters. He motioned me to sit on another one. "Yeah. Cam's harmless. He's parroting what other folks say; he doesn't really get why it's a problem. It's an old nickname around here that Mom and Dad can't seem to shake."

Dr. Johnston gave Rowan a knowing look before turning to me. "Tahira, what do your parents do?"

"Dad's a lawyer; Mom's VP of HR at a hotel company."

"So you probably get this, too. When people who don't look like us remind us of our successes, like calling Misty and me 'double doctors,' even when we're not together, it's because they feel we should be grateful they gave us the opportunity to thrive. But they didn't *give* us anything—we earned it ourselves. You can bet they don't feel the need to remind white families of their accomplishments."

I nodded. I had seen this before. "Or they think you only achieved your success because of your skin color," I said. It was like the people who thought I'd gotten the internship with Nilusha only because we're both brown.

Dr. Johnston seemed impressed. "Ah, perceptive girl. I can see why my kids are so charmed." A chime sounded from across the room. "Ah! That's the centrifuge done. Want to see what I'm working on?" He spent the next half hour showing us his specimens in the laboratory's centrifuge machine and the data he was compiling on the computer. Then he showed us around the mini greenhouse where his experiments were kept. I liked Rowan's dad. He was chatty like Juniper but got to the heart of the matter right away, like Rowan.

"Now," Dr. Johnston said, pushing us out of the lab, "I need to get back to work, and you two should be out there doing what teenagers do . . . actually, never mind. I'm a biologist. I know what teenagers do. Don't do that."

"Your dad would be a great teacher," I said as we headed back outside.

"Yeah, most people here say that. He's really cool at work."

"He's not like that at home?"

Rowan shook his head as we made our way back to the large greenhouse. "No. He is. He's a good guy, honestly. I could have it worse. He's still not happy about my school choice, but it's not like he's constantly telling me I'm making a mistake or anything. At least not anymore. Dad just sees science, technology, and business as success. He thinks I'm wasting my abilities. Didn't help that I won all those science awards in school—I *can* do the science, but garden design is what I *want* to do."

"Our parents should get together for chai. My other desi friends think mine are so lax because they let me date who I want, but that's the only thing they're 'lax' about. In everything else, they're pretty typical. I mean, I appreciate that they support me going into fashion, but they can be a bit . . . intense."

"You think they're pushing you too hard?"

"I don't know." I sighed. "There is no way I would be where I am today without them pushing me, and I am grateful. But sometimes it feels like they're *only* okay with me doing fashion as long as I'm the best at it. Get the best internships, go to the best fashion school, work to make a name for myself even before I'm out of high school so I can open my fashion line while I'm young."

"That sounds . . . stifling."

I shrugged. "I mean, I *do want* to be a designer. It's all I've ever wanted. And it's an incredibly competitive field, so I can't pull it off without working my butt off. But I sometimes wonder if they'd nag less if I'd picked law or business. They seem slightly more chill with my sister and her math obsession . . ." I squeezed my lips together. I'd never really considered that before. Would they have preferred if I wanted to do something more conventional with my life?

But that wasn't something I was ready to think about. I smiled at Rowan. "I can't wait to start taking pictures of you, Plant-Boy. Are you ready?"

He beamed. "I am. You're in charge; where do you want me?"

19

THE SECRET GARDEN

There were a few massive machines at the back of the greenhouse that weren't running right now, so we decided to start there. The whole building had a ton of natural light (because, duh . . . greenhouse), and I loved the juxtaposition of the colorful flowers against the industrial-looking equipment. Rowan helped me pull some large plastic buckets of flowers to fill the empty spaces around us. With the sunbeams hitting the hanging baskets above us, these pictures were going to be spectacular. Well, mostly they were going to be spectacular because of the person who was modeling.

Rowan finally took off the sweatshirt, and I nearly passed out when I saw him in my shirt. He looked amazing. I'd told him to wear straight-leg black jeans, which I quickly rolled to above those beat-up Chucks he always wore. Nicer sneakers would probably have been better, but these shoes were more Rowan.

He preened when he noticed me checking out his outfit. "Do I meet your exacting standards?" he asked.

"You already did, but yes. You are totally doing my shirt justice."

I posed him in a few different places and took a handful of shots. Some of him leaning against the machines, some surrounded by the flowers, some bathed in sunlight. I couldn't help it; I even took some close-up shots of Rowan's face, where the shirt could barely even be seen. I had been right. He was such a dream to photograph. Except something was missing. I'd first found his face compelling when he was always grumpy. But that scowl, the frown, had been pretty much missing lately.

"Let's try one without a smile."

He made a more neutral expression. It wasn't enough.

"Pretend it's the day you first found me in your garden," I said. "Give me that face."

He laughed. It wasn't what I wanted, but I still snapped some pictures.

"Frown! Show me your range, Plant-Boy."

He tried, but it was such a comically fake scowl that I burst out laughing.

"Hey," Cameron said, approaching us. "I'm on my break. Want me to get some pictures of both of you? Gigi makes me take pictures of her all the time. I'm good at it."

Excellent. I passed Cameron the camera and walked over to Rowan.

We did a few of my favorite poses. Back to back. Standing side to side, unsmiling. Me sitting on one of the wire stands with Rowan next to me. We even did a shot like that one of Leanne and Juniper—Rowan behind me with his arms around my waist and his head on my shoulder. I leaned into him, trying to calm my racing heart from being so close. He smelled like . . . well, a bit like dirt, a bit like the bleach they used in the greenhouse, and a lot like flowers. He smelled like Rowan.

He leaned into my neck for a second and whispered, "I have a surprise for you when we're done."

I smiled. Whatever it was, I couldn't imagine it being better than Rowan Johnston wrapped around me, but I was excited anyway.

After Cameron finished taking pictures, we headed outside. I took a couple more photos outside the greenhouse, but honestly, they weren't as good as the inside pictures.

"You want me to take some of you alone?" Rowan asked.

"No, it's fine." There were more than enough pictures of me on my Instagram. I'd post the ones of us together, but this photo shoot wasn't about me. "You sure you're okay with me posting you on feed?" I asked.

"Of course. I knew what I was getting into."

"Excellent." I grinned. "Now I want to see my surprise."

"All right, then. C'mon. We'll need to drive there, but it's here at Wynter's."

We jumped in his car, and he drove around to the back of the greenhouse. I had no idea this place kept going so far back. It mostly looked like unused space, but after driving a bit, we came to a field that was like a regular farmer's field, though instead of crops, there were flowers. Not as colorful as the ones in the greenhouse, and wispier, with lots of leaves, but in the outdoor sun, the blooms looked pretty amazing.

"Wow," I said.

"This is all pretty new. Wynter's didn't do outdoor flower farming until recently. They had all this land back here with nothing to do with it. These plants are grown for cut flowers that we sell at local markets, instead of the greenhouse plants we sell to garden centers and landscapers." He pulled over on the side of the road. "Sometimes we also open this all to the public—like, have tours and let people throw parties here and stuff. But it's a pain because of—"

"Influencers, right?" I joked.

He chuckled, nodding. "Exactly. *Hundreds* of them. They swarm like ravens in the fields."

I laughed as we got out of the car. "Anyway," he said, "there's one field over there that will be open next week. But I thought you'd like to see it before the crowds invade."

He popped his trunk, pulled out the tote bag he'd been carrying earlier, and guided me to a path.

I finally saw the field, and it literally took my breath away. Sunflowers. A big field with nothing but sunflowers. There were some tall ones (these must have been the mythical ones with seven-foot stems) and some shorter ones. Some had blooms as big as dinner plates, and others were smaller. They were all in varying shades of golden yellow, with green leaves glowing against the bright-blue sky. I'd never seen anything like it. I wanted to take a picture. I resisted the urge to take out my camera so I could just enjoy this moment.

"You brought me to a sunflower field?" I said to Rowan.

He smiled, looking kinda unsure. Rowan Johnston was a lot of things, sometimes crabby, sometimes cheerful, sometimes intense, and always confident. But this? Nervous and apprehensive? This was new.

"What's in the bag?" I asked.

"Sandwiches, drinks, and tarts from Hyacinth's."

I blinked. He'd brought me a picnic in a sunflower field. Just us. Alone in this enchanting place.

"There's a clearing in the middle there," he said. "I brought a blanket."

We followed a narrow path to the clearing.

"They don't plant here in the middle so people can take pictures with flowers on three sides," he said as he laid out the blanket. "It's going to be completely overrun next week, but now we can chill here alone."

I stood watching him, speechless.

He noticed I had pretty much frozen in place. "You okay, Tahira? We don't have to stay here. We can go if you want?"

I shook my head quickly. "No, no. I want . . ." I tilted my head. "You brought me a picnic in the middle of a flower field."

"Oh, your allergies, but I thought the new antihis—"

I waved my hand. "No, no, my allergies are fine. Your mom's pills work great." I didn't know what to say, so I channeled Juniper and went with honest and earnest. "Honestly, this is the nicest thing anyone has ever done for me. I'm just . . . this is so kind. Thank you, Rowan."

He smiled so huge it took my breath away. I smiled back.

We stood in the sunflower field grinning at each other for a while like idiots before I absolutely couldn't go another moment without asking one question. "Rowan, is this a date?"

"Do you want it to be?"

Did I? I mean, yeah, there was no denying my feelings for this guy had evolved lately. Like night and day evolved. Like a complete one-eighty. He'd brought me this picnic in this amazing place, and he held my hand when the night sky was freaking me out, and he gave me his pencil crayons and a light for my drafting table and told me that being single-minded didn't mean I deserved to be treated like shit. Maybe all those things meant this could be the beginning of something amazing. And maybe I shouldn't be so afraid of that.

Matteo and I had *just* broken up, but this didn't feel anything at all like with Matteo. I couldn't even put my finger on why, but now, and all the other times Rowan and I were alone, I was completely myself. The real me.

The problem was, this me wasn't the same me I was a month ago, and that freaked me out a bit.

When I didn't say anything, he took my hand and pulled me down to sit on the blanket. "Let's just call it a picnic right now. We can figure the rest out later."

I unwrapped my sandwich. "Okay, but let me ask you . . . why did you buy this food before you knew who won the bet? If you won, we'd be staying in town and going for ice cream."

He shrugged. "I figured you'd win. Your designs are always amazing. My strength is more the execution. Anyway, if I won, I was still going to ask you to come here after the ice cream."

The caprese sandwich with tomatoes, mozzarella, and basil was delicious. The fancy sparkling lemonade was delightful. But the view was better than both of them, so I could only get through half my meal before I stopped eating to take pictures. Close-ups of sunflowers, a wide shot of the whole field. Rowan sitting on the grass, huge yellow blooms surrounding him. The pictures would just be for me—I wouldn't post them on my Instagram.

"I find it hilarious that now you're so into plants," Rowan said, grinning. "I still remember the look on your face the day we met, when I told you people come out to Wynter's to take pictures of flowers. Now look at you . . ."

I rolled my eyes. "I'm young. I'm allowed to change my mind. Honestly, before this summer, I had no idea . . ." I sat back down next to him. "Surrounded by so much *life*. It's such a cliché, but the colors, the shapes . . . I admit it. I get why you're such a Plant-Boy. I get why you want to make a career out of this stuff."

He gazed out into the field. "I know it's weird." He chuckled. "I feel at peace when I'm surrounded by . . ."

"Nature?"

"Yeah, but like . . . natural beauty that I can cultivate, you know? I feel like I have some superpower to know how to make this happen. To understand how to make flowers grow. To know their secrets. I mean, flowers are everywhere—in art, in design—"

"In fashion."

"Exactly. Green spaces, too . . . they inspire people. People feel at peace . . . they feel a connection to the natural world. I want to be the one who creates the places that make people so happy." He paused. "What about you? Why fashion?"

I thought for a moment before answering. "People express themselves in what they choose to wear," I finally said. "But clothes, mass-produced clothes especially, are created for mass tastes. Different kinds of people designing means more choices, and hopefully more people who aren't like everyone else will find stuff that speaks to their true selves. That's what I want—to make the things that people use to express themselves."

He lightly fingered the hem of the shirt he was wearing. "This shirt . . . I wouldn't have picked for myself . . . ," he said.

"Because there's no plant pun on it?"

He laughed. "Let me finish. I wouldn't have picked this for myself, but I like it. It makes me feel . . ."

"Normal? Grown up? Mature?"

"Hey," he said, laughing. "I thought you liked my shirts."

"I do. I totally do. Sorry . . . it makes you feel . . ."

He smiled. "Different, but still me. I feel like the me I am, the person I don't normally express . . . sorry, that sounds cheesy."

I shook my head. "It doesn't sound cheesy at all." I grinned. "I like you in something I made."

"I like me in something you made, too."

"I'm not sure you would have said that about me a few weeks ago."

"I know. I was wrong." His gaze was fixed on me. "I apologized before, and I'll say it again. I was such a dick when we met. I was in a terrible mood that day, and you touched a nerve, but that's no excuse. I'm sorry."

I tilted my head. "You're forgiven. Totally. I wasn't exactly my best self that day, either. I didn't want to move to Bakewell, and I judged you and everything here too quickly. I should've given this place, and the people in it, a chance."

We'd come a long way since then. When we'd met, we had made snap judgments about each other, hadn't looked beyond the surface. We were both so sure we had nothing in common. But both our first impressions were wrong.

He took a breath. "Look, Tahira. I'm going to be straight with you. I know we got off on the wrong foot, and I know I was an ass, and I know you're only here for the summer, and we're both very busy, and you just broke up with someone, and we're doing the Bloom together so it's probably not smart, and . . ." His voice trailed off.

"And what?" I whispered, leaning closer to him.

"And . . ." That little smile again. "I like spending time with you. I really like talking to you. I like . . . looking at you. And . . . I don't think I could forgive myself if I let this summer go by without asking you one question."

"Ask," I said, leaning even closer.

"Can I kiss you?" he whispered. His lips were already so close.

I could barely think with my heart beating in my ears. I had goose bumps even though it was so warm. All the objections I had to getting involved with him faded away as I gave him the only answer I could. "Yes, please."

We were both smiling when our lips finally touched. It was a small kiss. A soft kiss. A sweet kiss that tasted of raspberries and almonds from the Bakewell tart. He lifted his face from mine, and we looked at each other. I could never get enough of staring at that face.

But I also really liked kissing it. I put my hand on Rowan's waist, on the soft pima cotton of the shirt I'd sewn, and pulled him close again. He leaned in and took my cheek in his hand. And we were kissing again. Harder. Hotter. His calloused hand on my face, and his soft mouth on mine. In the wide-open air, in the middle of a field of sunflowers, Rowan Johnston's body pressed against mine.

This, right here, was all I needed.

20

THE SUMMER FLING

Two months ago, if someone had told me the happiest moment of my summer would be lying on a blanket in the middle of a field of flowers on the chest of a guy who spent all his spare time in his garden, I would have laughed my face off. But here we were, and I'd honestly never been so content. His strong body under mine, his heartbeat in my ear. When he spoke, it reverberated through my whole body, like we were one person.

We were both kind of quiet at the beginning of the drive home. I knew we should talk about what had happened in that sunflower field. After Matteo, I wasn't about to make assumptions or just play it by ear again. I was in way too deep with Rowan to risk that.

I didn't know how to start the conversation, though. Bringing up relationship talk even before our second (or third?) kiss?

It seemed that Rowan read my mind. "U-um . . . ," he stuttered. "So, are we, I mean, do you want to do that again?"

I turned to him, smiling. "Do what again? Make out with earthworms under us?"

He huffed a chuckle. "I don't have an issue with earthworms. But I was thinking more the, you know, *date*."

"So that *is* what that was, then."

He smiled.

"Can we be honest with each other?" I asked.

He took a breath. "Okay. Honestly, Tahira, I like you. I think I liked you from the moment I saw you, even though you made me a little nutty. I know the timing is bad, and I'm only here for a month before uni. No pressure, but . . . I want to go out with you again. A lot."

"Are you proposing a fling for the rest of the summer?" I asked. I couldn't promise more than the summer. I wasn't sure Rowan would fit in my life in Toronto.

He chuckled. "A fling is a good name for it."

A fling was casual. Manageable. But there was one issue with casual. "Will we be exclusive? Or will you be seeing—"

He reached over and squeezed my knee. "Totally exclusive. There is no one else I want right now."

A part of me wondered if this was a good idea, even for just the summer. The Plan, my portfolio, my online platform—all that mattered too much. I didn't need distractions. True, I'd dated Matteo without losing focus, but this was different. Matteo wasn't much of a distraction because he lived farther away from me. Rowan was literally next door. Plus, Matteo was trying to get into the fashion industry, too, albeit in a different way, so our goals overlapped. He always encouraged me, and often helped me do the things I needed to do to reach my goals.

But Rowan would support my goals and my hustle, too, wouldn't he? Was I still judging him? Assuming he didn't value the things that were important to me?

I needed to give Rowan a chance. This was just a summer fling. There was no reason to worry—I'd always been able to prioritize my Plan; this would be no different.

"Everyone is going to talk about us," I said. That was another problem. Trying to hide anything in Bakewell was futile.

"Welcome to a small town," Rowan said. "People are in our shit whether we want them to be or not."

"I don't know how you deal with that."

"Says the person who blasts their boyfriend to their 20K followers."

"That's different," I said. "It was on my own terms, you know? And now you're going to be on my page, too. Anyway, say what you will about influencers—at least we have tough skin."

He ran his hand over my bare arm while looking at the road. "Tough, but very, very soft, too."

His touch gave me goose bumps. This summer fling was a great idea. What could go wrong? "Okay. Let's do this. You and me are officially dating."

~

I was busy with a capital *B* for the next week. I was at the store almost every day, and I was writing a piece for the town newspaper on Lilybuds' new "younger" line. I posted pictures of the photo shoot with Rowan on my own Instagram page and was delighted with the fan reaction to my stunning new model.

I barely saw Gia. She'd even missed our Bloom meeting on Wednesday because she had plans with Cameron. It was fine, though, because we spent the whole time trying to figure out how we'd make the frame for the sculpture, and that wasn't really Gia's area of expertise. And I understood. I spent all my spare time with my boyfriend, too.

True to my expectation, everyone knew Rowan and I were dating practically before we even got home from our photo shoot at the nursery. Juniper squealed with utter delight and hugged me like I was marrying her brother instead of dating him. Gia smiled knowingly because, of course, she knew.

Shar was mostly happy—I mean she loved Rowan probably more than me, but she was still a Muslim Indian Aunty, so she was required to be overprotective and a little bit judgmental. And she unfortunately told my parents about this fling before I had the chance to figure out how to avoid a replay of the safe sex and "remember your focus" talk again. So I did have to hear the lecture over FaceTime (thankfully no pantomime this time), but at least Shar was able to reassure them that Rowan was honestly everything any parent could want for their daughter. Smart. Polite. Driven. Eventually, after I reassured Mom and Dad that I would keep my priorities straight and my career goals would always come first, they said they were looking forward to meeting Rowan. They sounded sincere.

On Saturday evening, June, Rowan, Gia, and I were in the backyard with a big stack of copper tubing Rowan had found, some new rolls of chicken wire, and a large pizza. We'd already been working for an hour on the frame for the Bloom. It was progressing. Sort of.

Basically, we were using lengths of copper tubing to make the outline of the narrow lily petals, which we would then fill in with chicken wire. Then we'd attached several of the petals together to make the lily shape, and we'd use floral wire later to attach the flowers and moss to the chicken wire.

But it wasn't going as well as we'd hoped. The biggest issue was how to get the lengths of copper tubing attached at the tips of the petals. When we wired the ends together, it all looked clumsy instead of clean and sleek like I'd imagined.

"What if we used copper wire?" June asked. She'd changed into loose jeans and a teal T-shirt after work, and her hair was pulled into a high bun. She was standing behind Rowan and me at the workbench, eating a slice of pizza.

"The frame won't show in the finished sculpture," I said. "I'm more concerned with the bulk added by the wire, not the color of the wire."

"Have y'all tried gluing it?" Gia asked. She had pulled one of the lounge chairs closer to the workbench to sit on. I didn't mind that she was more moral support and brainstorming at this meeting. Only so many hands would fit on the actual sculpture frame, anyway. Especially now, when we were working on the fiddly bits.

I looked at Rowan. Today's shirt had two little plant pots waving to each other. One said, ALOE, HOW ARE YOU? The other responded with, LONG THYME, NO SEE! It was adorable.

"I think we have some Gorilla Glue somewhere; should we try that?" he asked.

"It's worth a shot," I said. After digging out the heavy-duty glue from his garage, we glued the tips of the tubes together and then taped them so they'd hold until the glue dried.

"It's fast dry," Rowan said, reading the back of the tube. "We have half an hour."

We sat on the patio drinking iced tea while we waited. Rowan and I were on one couch, Juniper on the one across from us, and Gia had turned her lounge chair to face us.

"You know those pictures Cameron took of me downtown a few days ago?" Gia asked. "You have to see how many likes they got. And the comments!" She started listing some of the names of style influencers we'd connected with in the past. "My followers have been loving my flower content."

I smiled, reclining a bit onto Rowan. His arm wrapped around my shoulder. Week one of my and Rowan's summer fling had been very good. We'd lain out in the garden stargazing a few nights, but we'd also had some quality time alone in the tiny house up on my loft bed. Kissing until our mouths were numb or snuggling close, watching movies on my iPad.

I couldn't get enough of him. I loved talking to him. I loved kissing him. I loved that I'd agreed to this summer fling.

"That's awesome, Gia," I said. "I'm so happy for you." And I was. Maybe it was thanks to my shiny new relationship, but I was almost euphorically happy about just about everything this week.

"I saw those pictures," June said. "They were amazing. Ooh, you know what would be cool? To do, like, outfit shots that match book covers! There's this new release with flowers on the cover that looked a lot like that dress you were wearing. Tahira, are there fashion and book Instagram accounts?"

"I mean, probably? You could start one."

"I don't think I have enough clothes. I have the books, though."

"Tahira," Gia said, "seriously, though. You're doing yourself a big disservice by not posting flowers on your page. My engagement has tripled."

"I had flowers on my page last week." I'd posted the shots of Rowan and me in the greenhouse that same day we took them. They'd been well received, of course. Who wouldn't heart a picture of Rowan's face? "I'm trying to keep my brand consistent. I want to stick to the urban, industrial influence in my designs."

"Yeah," Gia said. "But that doesn't mean you can't photograph your urban clothes with flowers around them."

"Did you post the pictures of the sunflowers?" Rowan asked.

I tilted my head. "No . . . I thought those were . . . just for us." I loved the pictures from the sunflower field so much—I looked at them all the time. There was one in particular, where Rowan wasn't looking at the camera, but the sun was hitting his face just right. In my red shirt, surrounded by all those bright-yellow flowers. It was so stunning.

Keeping my brand consistent wasn't the only reason I hadn't posted them on my feed. Every time I thought of that perfect day—the warm sun, the picnic, and, of course, our first kiss—it was a memory I wanted to keep special. Not share with the world.

One side of Rowan's mouth upturned. "You're not ashamed of me, are you? I agree I would have looked better in one of my *own* shirts, but yours wasn't *that* bad . . ." I knew he was joking, so I poked him in the ticklish spot on his side.

He yelped, then leaned over to start tickling me back.

"Hey, now," June said. "Can y'all save that for when there are no family members around?"

Rowan laughed and sat up straight. "Seriously, though, Tahira. I don't mind if you post them. Whatever happened to artists selling themselves as much as their art? Your followers may want to see a less . . . curated side of your life."

Maybe? I had to admit that, unexpectedly, flowers—and Rowan, of course—had become a big part of my life. And he was right: I was the one who said the artist represented the brand as much as the art did. I pulled up that picture on my phone. It did kind of work for my brand, anyway. The flowers were monochromatic. And the shirt was very visible, and very me.

Why not? I quickly wrote up an Instagram post while Rowan watched. I added that picture, with a few more from the sunflower field. Honestly, I kind of liked the idea of showing him off a bit more. I grinned as I hit "Share." "Done. All my 20K followers will see how hot you looked in that field that day."

He tightened his arm around me and looked at me like he wished we were alone.

Gia groaned, looking at June. "Oh God, they're at it again, June. C'mon, guys, it's been half an hour. Let's get back to work. Because I—"

I stood. "I know, G. You have a date later." I held out my hand to Rowan. "Shall we finish our work?"

~

A week later, on Sunday night, Rowan, Juniper, and I were having tea and oatmeal cookies on the patio couches in the garden. We'd been dating for two weeks now, and things were going so well that I'd just had dinner with the Johnstons, which was awkward but fine. The weather was beautiful, and I was conscious of the fact that the Bloom was a week away. After the Bloom, Gia and I had a week and a half in Bakewell before we needed to go back to Toronto to get ready for school to start in September. I wanted as much time as possible in this garden before I couldn't be here anymore.

"Was anyone able to help you figure out how we can hold the lily petals together?" I asked Rowan. After gluing the frame, we'd tried adding some moss and flowers a few days later, but the glued petal tips snapped open. Rowan had said he would ask around at work to see if anyone had any ideas.

"Yeah, Leanne's dad said he could show us how to weld them. I don't know why I didn't think to ask him first. He's a contractor—he welds plumbing pipes all the time."

Oh. That was a simple solution. "Perfect."

"Yeah, he's free Tuesday night, so we can have our Bloom meeting at Leanne's place, and use his supplies to weld. Then we can test it again. Leanne will bring the plants we need from the nursery to practice."

"Oh." I turned to Juniper. I was pretty sure June had barely seen Leanne since the Lily photo shoot a few weeks ago, and that was intentional. I'd seen Leanne, of course. I mean, I was dating her best friend. But June was still trying to avoid her.

"You good with that, June?" I asked.

"Sure," Juniper said. "It's fine, I can go."

"But—"

"What's going on?" Rowan asked. "Why wouldn't June want to go? Actually," he said to Juniper, "Leanne said today that she thought you were avoiding her."

Juniper didn't say anything.

"Juniper doesn't need to hang out with your friends if she doesn't want to," I said.

He shook his head. "No, of course she doesn't. But Leanne *was* her friend, too. The three of us were inseparable as kids." He looked at June again. "Did Leanne do something to upset you?" He glanced at me, no doubt remembering when I'd accused Leanne of being one of the harassers on Juniper's YouTube.

"No, there's nothing," June said emphatically. "It's fine. I'll go to Leanne's. I'm not mad at her."

"June, you know you can talk to me," Rowan said.

Juniper shook her head. I thought she might cry.

I put my hand on Rowan's knee. "Rowan, leave her be."

"No," Juniper repeated. "Leanne didn't do anything wrong."

"So why are you avoiding her?" Rowan asked.

"Fine, Row." She closed her eyes and spoke very quietly. "I'm avoiding her to try to get over her."

Rowan didn't say anything. The cicadas, crickets, and the bubbling water of the fountain seemed louder when no one was talking. Finally, Rowan spoke. "Why do you need to get *over* her? You were never *under* her, were you?" His eyes went comically wide. "Right?"

I stifled a laugh. This family was really my favorite.

Juniper opened her eyes and shrugged. "I had a crush I was dealing with."

He blew out a puff of air. "Seriously, June? On *Leanne?*"

"Wait," I said to June. "Did he not know you were into girls? Did you just come out to your brother?"

"No, he already knows." She glared at Rowan. "I had a girlfriend when I was thirteen, remember?"

"But you're my little sister! You're not supposed to have a crush on my best friend!"

Juniper threw her hands in the air. "I know! I'm trying not to! But y'all keep throwing her in front of me! With that hair . . . and her laugh . . ."

Rowan's eyes were as big as peonies. I gathered he wasn't used to thinking of his sister as a sexual being.

"Rowan." I gave him a sweet look. "Your sister was honest with you about her feelings. Maybe now is not the time to go caveman big brother?"

"Oh," he said, rubbing the back of his head. "Yeah, of course. I can keep this on the down low if you want, June. I won't tell Leanne—"

"She knows," June said.

Somehow Rowan's eyes got even bigger. "She knows? Why hasn't anyone told me? What did she do . . . she better not have . . . I'm calling her." He pulled his phone out.

Juniper took the phone from her brother's hands. "Row, it's fine. Everything is good. I've just been keeping some distance. There is no need for anyone to panic here."

"Are you sure, June?" Rowan asked. "I can talk to her—"

"Rowan, don't embarrass your sister," I said.

Juniper stood, handing her brother back his phone. "Thank you, Tahira. And Row? Forget everything I just said. I'm going to bed."

She shook her head as if disappointed in herself and went into the house.

"Nice job on the overprotective-brother thing," I said to Rowan once June was gone.

Rowan still looked like he'd been hit by a truck. "*Juniper* and *Leanne?*"

"I have no idea what Leanne is thinking," I said, "but hypothetically, if they're both into it, then what's the problem? Honestly, I kinda ship it."

"It's . . ." He frowned. "Little sisters should be aromantic. It would make it easier on the older siblings."

I snorted. "My little sister has had the same boyfriend since, like, *forever*, and yet I still manage to form complete sentences. Is this because she likes girls?"

"What? No, of course not. I mean, at least she won't have to deal with teenage boys, because sometimes we only think about one thing."

"Teenage girls can be horny, too." I mean, he *had* to know that. He'd been dating me for two weeks. We may not have had sex yet, but I couldn't keep my hands off him.

He cringed. "Can we not use the word 'horny' when talking about my sister? Or my best friend, who's been like a sister to me my whole life?"

I laughed, getting up from my seat on the couch opposite him. I sat on his lap and draped my arms around his neck. "We can talk about something else. Or we can do something else. I doubt Gia will be home anytime soon."

He laughed, resting his big hands on my hips. "Yeah, let's." He leaned in to press a soft kiss on my neck, then urged me off his lap. The garden wasn't a great make-out spot, considering the windows in Shar's and his houses.

So we headed into the tiny house, which was proving to be plenty big enough for us. I was pretty sure he wasn't thinking about anything for the next hour or so except me.

21

FORGET-ME-NOT NIGHT

R owan drove June, Gia, and me to Leanne's on Tuesday night, and we all pretended that the awkward conversation from Saturday hadn't happened. I'd told Gia about it on Sunday, but Rowan and June hadn't mentioned it at all. Juniper seemed fine in the car. Chatty. Cheerful. Like nothing at all was wrong.

"Hey!" Leanne said as we got out of the car outside the Langston family farmhouse. She was wearing wide-leg jeans and a T-shirt with a picture of a rabbit wearing a floral sun hat. She handed June a small bundle of flowers that June quickly slipped into her bag.

I raised a brow at Juniper. What was that about?

The welding with Leanne's dad went fine. We then did a test run, filling the structure with flowers that Leanne had brought home. They weren't the exact varieties we wanted to use for the competition, but the lily looked so amazing filled in. And this time it didn't fall apart. Everything for the Bloom was coming together.

After we thanked Mr. Langston for his help, Leanne took the four of us over to see her rabbits, who lived in hutches in the Langstons' barn.

I poked my finger in to touch the cute brown one's head. "These really are some sweet bunnies."

Leanne pulled a smaller rabbit out of another hutch. "You want a sweet bunny? Look at this baby I just picked up yesterday. His name's Strawberry. Some moronic family got him for their kids for Easter and already surrendered him to a shelter. Isn't he the cutest?"

Strawberry was all white with dark-gray smudging around his eyes.

"This bunny does a better smoky eye than I do," Gia said, scratching the top of the rabbit's head.

My eyes started watering, so I took a big step back. Even with the new allergy pills, I couldn't handle rabbits.

"You okay?" June said, joining me at the back of the barn. Gia was now holding Strawberry.

"Yeah. My eyes are a bit scratchy. Hey, what were those flowers Leanne gave you?"

Juniper's eyes widened. "You saw that?"

"Yeah, but I couldn't see what they were."

"Forget-me-nots."

I grinned. "I told you she was into you."

June sighed, shaking her head. "No. She's just being nice, as always. She feels bad for hurting me and doesn't want me to forget our *friendship*."

"She said all that with those flowers?"

June shrugged.

I chuckled. June talked a good talk, but I doubted that's what the flowers meant. Maybe June was scared Leanne was finally making a move on her so close to the summer's end? June was going to miss Leanne when she left in a few weeks, but if they finally talked about their feelings, it would only be harder.

No matter what, the end of the summer in Bakewell was going to be hard for a lot of us.

Later, the five of us were sitting on these big boulders that were a couple of yards from the side of the Langstons' barn watching the sunset. Gia's phone rang. I was curled up on a boulder with my back against Rowan, listening to him and Leanne talk about packing for uni, and their dorms, when Gia said, "Absolutely not. Not happening. No way." She wasn't using that cutesy voice she usually used with Cameron.

I looked at her. She rolled her eyes and held the phone out. "T, Matteo is *insisting* he needs to talk to you."

Matteo. Ugh. Why was he reemerging now? As far as I knew, Gia hadn't heard from him for weeks. Most days I blissfully forgot he even existed.

Rowan tensed behind me. I put my hand on his knee.

"I'm not interested in speaking to him, G."

"That's what I told him. But he said to tell you it's not because he wants you to get back with him or anything. He has some *game-changing* opportunity to talk to you about. He says it's, like, *urgent*."

I still didn't want to talk to him. Rowan squeezed my hand. I knew what it meant—that he wouldn't stop me or be upset with me if I chose to hear the guy out. That Rowan trusted me. And that's why I took the phone from Gia—because it wasn't going to change anything at all between me and the guy I was sitting with. And honestly, I was curious what my ex had to say.

"Hello?" I said into Gia's phone.

"Tahira!" Matteo said. I couldn't help the goose bumps forming. It was so weird to hear his voice again.

"Yes, Matteo."

"Oh man, it's so good to talk to you. How've you been, babe? I've barely had the time to get any new content for my channels. I see you haven't posted anything interesting, either."

Okay, so he was still checking my social? Also, like, a week ago I posted those pictures of me and Rowan—he didn't find those *interesting*?

I sighed. This was a bad idea. I didn't want to be playing whatever game Matteo was playing. I patted Rowan's leg, then hopped off the big rock and went toward the barn for privacy. "What do you want, Matteo."

"Man, don't be cold like that. It's been *ages*, and I get a 'What do you want'?"

The goose bumps went to anger. "What do you mean, 'It's been ages'? Your sidepiece couldn't keep you warm in my absence?"

He was silent for a few seconds. Then I heard him exhale. "I'm sorry, I deserved that. I told Gia . . . Alyssa's out of the picture."

"I don't care even a little bit. What do you want?"

"I don't think you'll be so cold when you hear the amazing news I have for you."

Everyone was watching me. Rowan looked worried, so I gave him a reassuring smile. "What?" I asked.

"Dasha Payne is coming to Toronto."

"Why should I care?"

"C'mon, T, *Dasha Payne*! From the *DashStyle* blog? From LA?"

"I know who Dasha Payne is." I hadn't been reading her blog lately, and I'd stopped doing those weekly indie design challenges since I had no new designs to post and had been avoiding anything that reminded me of Matteo. "Why are you telling me this?" I asked.

"She just DMed me. She's doing a series on the hottest style cities in North America, and she wants to interview us."

"'Us' as in . . ."

"Tahira, she wants to interview you and me. She's, like, doing this big photo shoot with a bunch of designers, models, and style influencers, but then she's going to do profiles on some of the hottest names from the photo shoot. She wants you and me. As the #TorontoPowerCouple."

"We're not a couple anymore."

"Tahira, just listen—Dasha is *huge*. Like, a million viewers huge. She practically discovered Angel Torres."

I exhaled. I didn't need to be told about Dasha's influence. I took my phone out of my pocket to pull up *DashStyle*'s Insta. It had well *over* a million followers.

"We don't have to actually be a couple," Mateo continued. "She didn't even know we'd dated, only that we'd collaborated a lot. I asked her if I could bring Gia to the big shoot—and she said sure, as long as me and you were there. There's a big party Saturday night, too."

"When exactly is all this?"

"The big photo shoot is Friday. Then she's doing all the interviews in the city on Saturday. We have the time slot after lunch—she wants us to take her shopping on Queen Street during our interview. They'll have a camera crew following us, both for stills and video. Her team is getting the permits sorted out now. The party is Saturday night, at this swank rooftop bar that has a pool. Everyone who is everyone will be there."

I closed my eyes. The Bloom was Saturday. The plan was to all go to the nursery and pick the flowers to use on Friday. Then, of course, we had to be on the festival grounds by eight on Saturday for the actual competition.

"Can I just do the Friday part?"

"There'd be no point. The *profile* is the big deal. There'll be a whole article about us on her site."

"I can't this weekend. It's the Bloom. I told you . . . that flower sculpture competition I was entering?"

"Jesus, Tahira—this is bigger than any flower-arranging contest. Others would kill for an opportunity like this. This is the big leagues. The break we've both been waiting for."

I glanced over at my friends sitting on those massive rocks. They were still all looking at the horizon. The sun had painted the sky orange and pink and was casting a golden hue over the endless fields around the property.

"Tahira," Mateo said emphatically. "Think about what's important. A rooftop party with the biggest names in fashion in the city. Not flower arranging in butt-fuck nowhere. This is your dream."

Was it? I didn't even know. I exhaled long. "I can't let down my friends."

"Yeah. Your friends are *Gia* and *I*. We can't do this if you don't, and you've known us a lot longer. Think about it tonight—I'm calling you tomorrow morning for your answer. Unblock my number, okay?"

I disconnected the call. This timing sucked so bad. I leaned against the barn to think. Should I stay for the Bloom? Or would this *DashStyle* thing be a better use of my time to get my dream? Because this *was* my dream we were talking about—the dream that I'd had since the beginning of time. The Plan was my path to succeed, and everything I did was supposed to serve the Plan.

Entering the Bloom was for the Plan, but it was a sort of Plan B. This Dasha thing was closer to my original Plan A.

But it wasn't just about the Plan anymore; it was also about my friends. How could I leave Juniper and Rowan? They would never forgive me if I left the Bloom team.

I looked over at the breathtaking sunset over the farmers' fields, and at my new friends, who'd come to mean the world to me. Was all this something I was willing to give up? Even for the Plan?

22

SOFT EYES AND HARD CHOICES

I didn't give my friends details about what Matteo had said—just that he'd wanted to run an opportunity by me, but it wasn't that important. Rowan looked doubtful, but he didn't pry. So I climbed up on the rock next to him, put my arm around his waist and my head on his shoulder, and watched the rest of the sunset with my boyfriend and friends, all while trying my best to forget the decision I needed to make later.

It was pretty late when we finally packed up our things to leave. As we were getting into Rowan's car, Juniper said, "I can't believe it's already Tuesday, and the Bloom's in four days. Do we need another meeting before Friday?"

"I don't think so," Rowan said. "I don't anticipate a problem—now that the frame is welded."

"Thanks for getting your dad to help us," I said to Leanne.

Leanne smiled. "No need to thank me. You guys are in great shape. Honestly, you're way more prepared than we were last year. You three"— she looked at me, Rowan, and Juniper—"are a powerhouse. I'm only sorry I won't get to be there with you."

She glanced briefly at Gia, who of course had her face in her phone, and rolled her eyes.

I knew what Leanne was thinking. When we'd agreed to this, Gia had seemed so committed to the Bloom. She'd wanted to meet Christopher Chan as much as I did. That was before she met Cameron, but that shouldn't have mattered, should it? All this hard work that Rowan, June, and I were doing was going to benefit Gia, too, if we won.

It wasn't the first time Gia had flaked like this. I loved Gia and her enthusiasm and her cheering me on, but she wasn't the most reliable person. I had always known this about my friend, and it had never bothered me before. Now, it was annoying.

But who was I to get mad at Gia for half-assing her contribution to the Bloom? I was right now thinking of dropping out altogether. And I'd be taking Gia with me if I left. Talk about flaking.

We said goodbye to Leanne, and Gia had Rowan drop her off at Cameron's on the way home (no surprise there). Once the three of us were alone in the car, Rowan asked, "So, June, that was okay?"

"Yeah, it was fine, why?"

His gaze was on the road in front of him. "Nothing. Just . . . I want you to be happy. I know things will be tough in September. Let me know anything I can do for you." He was such a good brother. He was such a great person.

He was so different from Matteo. Rowan did respect my success, just like Matteo did, but he didn't sit around wondering how he could leverage *my* success for his benefit, like Matteo did. Like Matteo was still trying to do. Obviously, he only wanted me to do this Dasha Payne thing to advance *his* platform, not mine. Matteo wanted those millions of followers looking at *him*.

But even though I knew I was being used, I was still sort of grateful that Matteo's legwork this summer had opened up this opportunity for me. I'd spent the summer flower arranging and getting lost in Rowan's eyes. I'd been neglecting my social media platform.

I googled "Dasha Payne" on my phone from the back seat of Rowan's car. She'd been a successful Instagram model and urban lifestyle influencer for a while, but she'd really catapulted into internet fame in the last six months or so. She got a ridiculous number of hits on her blog posts, her sponsorships were numerous and valuable, and her famous friends were influential.

I'd be nuts to turn this down. Could I do both the Bloom and this? The competition was on Saturday morning—I could rush to Toronto right after it to make it for the profile. But then I'd miss the Friday photo shoot. The profile was supposed to be for people in the photo shoot. I didn't see how it was possible to do both.

Juniper went straight into their house when we got home, but Rowan lingered on the driveway. "Did you want to hang out a bit?" he asked. He could obviously tell there was something on my mind, but I wasn't ready to tell him about it yet.

It was late, and the sky was pure black. Clouds had moved in, so the millions of stars weren't even visible. The empty black sky was as disconcerting as the millions of stars.

I had a lot of thinking to do, and I needed a clear head to make this decision. Also? I maybe sort of wanted to prolong it before telling him.

"I'm beat," I said. "I think I better go to bed."

He looked a little bit disappointed. "Okay. Good night." He kissed me briefly. "Breakfast tomorrow?"

We'd gotten into the habit of eating breakfast early in the garden on days we both worked.

I nodded. "I'll be there. Good night, Rowan."

He stayed in the garden watching me as I went into the tiny house.

After changing and washing my face, I sat on my bed and tried not to cry while weighing my options. The door burst open. Gia was home already?

"Why exactly didn't you tell me what Matteo's call was about, Tahira?" she said before the door had even closed.

I climbed down the ladder from the loft so this conversation could happen face-to-face.

"Matteo called again?" I asked, plopping down on the chair.

"He did. Seriously, Tahira. *Dasha Payne.* Why weren't you scream-ing for joy? Why aren't you packing your bags right this minute?"

I shrugged.

Gia shook her head, clearly unbelieving. "You're way out of touch lately, girl. I can't even process that *we* can be in one of her fashion spreads. And she wants to do an article about *you*. My own best friend. And my cousin, but he's still the black sheep of the family, so whatevs."

"I didn't agree to do it, Gia. We'd have to drop out of the Bloom."

Gia flopped onto her bed. "So?"

"So people are counting on us. And what about my Plan? Being in the competition is to catch the attention of Christopher Chan, remember?"

"A profile on your design work on Dasha Payne's site will catch Christopher Chan's attention. I checked, T—he totally interacts with her on Insta all the time."

I exhaled. That, I hadn't known.

"This is it, T," Gia continued. "Everything we've been working toward. All those hours learning photography, you with the designing, the hours we've spent on photo shoots, the lighting, the editing, the scouting the best locations. We're finally there. We could be famous before we're even eighteen."

"I'm not doing all this for fame! It's supposed to be about the designs, G," I said, curling my legs under me on the pine chair.

"And don't you think people are going to want more House of Tahira shirts when you're famous?" She paused. "This isn't because of Rowan, is it?"

I shrugged. "I haven't told him."

Gia shook her head. "You need to get your priorities straight, girl. Don't let a gardener hold you back from your dreams. Actually, don't let *any* guy hold you back. That's not you."

I didn't know what to say. I wasn't letting Rowan hold me back, was I?

Gia sighed. "Tahira, you're my girl, so I'm going to be straight with you. I know I'd just be riding your coattails, but Dasha doesn't want Matteo and me unless you do it. You're the star. We're just the sidekicks. If you don't do this, we'll lose the opportunity."

I looked up at her.

"Don't forget who's been there for you," she continued. "Matteo and I have been modeling for you for months. I'm always there to take pictures when you need them. When you found out you'd be stuck in this shit town all summer, I quit my job to come with you."

Yeah, Gia had done all that.

"It sucks to upset Rowan and Juniper," Gia said, "but you'd be letting down your older friends if you stay here. The ones who've done a hell of a lot more than just teach you about flowers."

"What about Shar and the store?" I asked. We both had Friday and Saturday off for the Bloom, but we were supposed to work Thursday and Sunday. The photo shoot was early Friday morning, and the rooftop party late on Saturday night.

"I talked to Shar," Gia said. "The light was on when Cam dropped me off. She thinks we should go."

"You spoke to my aunt behind my back?" I crossed my arms, annoyed.

"Yeah." Her jaw was set. "My best friend taught me to go after what I want, and I did. Shar is fine—she already hired a temp for Friday and Saturday, and she can ask her to work a couple more days. My dad agreed to drive us back here Sunday, so we'll be fine to work Monday. Matteo borrowed his brother's car and can pick us up here on Thursday morning, so we can still work our shift tomorrow. Everything is sorted, Tahira. All you have to do is say yes."

I blew out a puff of air. She made it seem so easy. Go get the exposure that could make my career, or stay here for . . .

For what exactly? I wasn't going to New York unless we won the Bloom. But . . . I really *did* think we had a chance to win. And even if we didn't win, I was going to use pictures of the sculpture in my portfolio, along with all the drawings I'd done beforehand.

Which option—staying and doing the Bloom, or going and doing the photo shoot—would be better for my career?

"Have you asked your parents?" Gia asked.

"It's late," I said. "I'll call them in the morning."

"You should talk to Nilusha Bhatt, too. Isn't a mentor supposed to, you know, help with career decisions?"

Gia was right. Nilusha and I had been talking about once a week since I got here, mostly about my designs (both fashion and floral). She had returned to Toronto recently. I sent her a quick email, telling her I needed to talk tomorrow.

"Okay." I got up from the chair. "I . . . I'm going to sleep." I headed back to my loft.

"You'll give this serious thought, Tahira? Matteo will need an answer tomorrow. Three, at the latest."

I nodded as I climbed the ladder to my bed. "Thanks for sorting out the details, G. I'll think about it." I'd probably do more thinking about this decision than sleeping tonight.

But I was wrong. I didn't think about it that much. I didn't sleep much, either. Instead, I spent most of the night trying to stop picturing the look on Rowan's face when he'd said good night earlier. I was terrified I'd be seeing more of that disappointment again tomorrow.

23

NOT A GOODBYE

I was sitting out on the outdoor sofa at eight the next morning with my chai and toast, waiting for Rowan. We had promised to be honest with each other, and I planned to keep that promise.

Rowan showed up five minutes later, coffee in hand. He sat across from me and rubbed his face. "Morning," he said. He looked like he hadn't really slept, either.

"Hi," I said. "We need to talk."

He sighed. "Yeah, I figured. So, you going to tell me what your ex wanted from you yesterday?"

I nodded. "I have a decision to make."

Rowan was quiet a second, then spoke. "Why would you have to decide anything when it comes to him? After the way he treated you?" There was anger in his voice. A touch of that old venom.

"It's not *him* I'm considering. It's an opportunity. This big-name style blogger is coming to Toronto and wants to do a profile on me and Matteo."

"You broke up. Why would the two of you be in a profile together? Have you still been talking to him?"

I recoiled. "Jesus, Rowan, no, of course not. I told you I blocked him everywhere. I promised you I'd be honest with you, and I have been."

"Okay, so then why a profile together?"

"Because we collaborated so much. He's an emerging model; I'm an emerging designer. The blogger is profiling the people she thinks will be the next big thing in fashion in major style cities across North America. It would be a ton of exposure for me. A real game changer."

He exhaled. "Okay, I get it. I do. I may not like it, but you should do this."

I paused. "It's this weekend. Gia was invited, too."

He shook his head and glanced toward the greenhouse, where the frame of our sculpture rested near the workbench. "This weekend."

"I wish it was any other time," I said.

He turned back quickly to face me. "So, you'd just leave the Bloom? Let down the team, and our chance of winning? I thought the Bloom was important for your career."

"Winning the Bloom *would* be great for my FIT application. Meeting Christopher Chan, going to New York, it would all be a *huge* boost. Even mentioning the Bloom in my application would help, I think. But this opportunity? This is about *visibility*. This is more about my whole career than just getting into FIT."

"Sounds like there's no decision here. You've already made up your mind." His jaw was tight.

"I *haven't* made up my mind. Not yet. I'm going to talk to my parents and Nilusha about it first. I might be able to do both. Maybe if I can convince Matteo to come up right after the Bloom closes, then—"

"Don't even bother."

I met his eyes. "What's that supposed to mean?"

He crossed his arms over his chest. "It means I should have *known* that all this was temporary. It means I *knew* you were only slumming it with us country folk, waiting for a better deal to come along. Honestly?

You told me about five minutes after we met that you didn't want to be here. I don't know why I thought anything had changed."

I blinked. That hurt. He was right, though. I had said that. But he knew I didn't feel that way anymore, right? I'd told him how much he, and Juniper, too, meant to me. All of Bakewell meant something to me. Whatever choice I made was going to hurt a friend, and he had to know how hard that was for me.

I shook my head. "Rowan, don't be like this. You *know* me. You're driven, I'm driven. You're trying to make something of yourself to prove you can be the best at what you want to do, and I am trying to do the same. That's why I'm considering this. Not because I don't want to be here. Not because I don't care enough about you." I sighed as I ran my finger over the flower design on my chai mug. "I admit, I do feel like this summer has changed me. It's going to be so fucking hard to leave Bakewell in two weeks. It's killing me that I might have to hurt you all right now. But that doesn't mean I care any less about my goals or my Plan than I did when I got here. I am still going to make my dreams come true."

He frowned, blinking.

And really, that was it. As much as my world had turned upside down and as much as I felt so different here, he was right about one thing: this *was* temporary. Just a summer job. No matter what, I was eventually going home. Old Tahira—*Toronto Tahira*—wouldn't have had to think twice about this; she would have just gone to the photo shoot. Was that who I was going to be when I was back in Toronto in a few weeks?

But one part of me that had not changed, that *would* never change, was that I still wanted my dream. I wanted it so bad I could almost taste it. There was nothing else I could imagine doing with my life but designing fashion.

And achieving success meant making hard choices sometimes, right?

Rowan didn't say anything, but he looked disappointed again. I hated that look on him.

I stared at my now-cold chai. "I don't know if I'll go," I said. "But if I do, you still have my design. The frame is done. Leanne can take our place on the team, mine and Gia's. Leanne'll probably be stoked to be back with you and June. You can still enter . . . still *win* without me."

"Leanne can't take your spot. She's going to a rabbit show on the weekend, remember?"

My heart sank. Damn. I'd forgotten. If I left, Rowan and June wouldn't have enough team members. They'd have to drop out.

"Then . . ." *Ugh.* I didn't know what to say. I thought for a few seconds. "I need to talk to my parents and Nilusha. I'll figure something out. Maybe I can—"

"Don't, Tahira." He ran his hand over his face. After closing his eyes briefly, he shook his head. "Just don't. I don't want to be the reason you don't do this. If this thing is that important for your career, then you should go." His gorgeous eyes were so sad and resigned.

"But the Bloom is important for *your* career!"

We stared at each other for several long seconds. Finally, I spoke quietly. "I know this is a decision I have to make by myself. When I couldn't face all the stars in the sky, you held my hand, and I . . . I'm so grateful to you for that. But now I need to face them alone, with my eyes open." I looked down. "Matteo is calling me this afternoon. I'll call you and let you know what I decide."

Rowan nodded. "I'm working late tonight. To make up the time I took off for the Bloom."

"I'll call you anyway."

He nodded. "Okay. Have a good day, Tahira." He got up and walked into his house. No hug, no kiss, not even a goodbye.

But that was good. Because I didn't want him thinking of this as a goodbye. I wasn't ready for that yet.

After Rowan was gone, I had a few minutes before we had to leave for the store, so I called Mom. I told her the whole situation.

"That's excellent news, Tahira! *Dasha Payne!* All that hard work is really paying off. I'm so proud of you."

"So you think I should come home for this? I'd be disappointing my friends."

"If they were really your friends, they'd understand how great this is."

I exhaled. Rowan and Juniper *were* really my friends. I didn't question that for a second.

Mom continued. "I agree you should talk to Nilusha about this first, though. She'll be able to tell you how influential Dasha really is in the industry. Because maybe she'll think the connection with Christopher Chan would be better for your application."

"Yeah, I'm hopefully going to talk to her today," I said.

"Excellent. Let me know what happens. Oh, by the way, in case you come home, I'm going to Hamilton for a few days because of a new hotel opening, and your father's been working long hours on a new case. We'll be home late Friday night, though. It would be great to see you!"

I agreed and said goodbye, promising to call later.

When Gia and I got to the store to work with Shar, I didn't really think much about anything until my phone rang around noon. It was Nilusha. Shar let me go outside to take the call. I walked around to the side of the building as I answered.

"What's going on, Tahira?" Nilusha asked, breezily. "You need any help with that amazing design you showed me for your competition? If you need somewhere to put the sculpture after you're done with it, my studio is a little bare—just saying . . ."

"What? No . . . I have a dilemma and I need advice." I exhaled. "I'm thinking of pulling out of the competition." I couldn't believe I was saying this.

"Why? You've been working so hard!"

239

"I know, I know. I . . . I was invited to do this photo shoot and in-depth profile for Dasha Payne—you know, that stylist turned—"

"Oh my God, I know who *Dasha Payne* is, Tahira. I'm doing that photo shoot with her, too!"

"She's doing a profile on you, too?"

"No, not a profile. But I'll be in a group spread on Friday, and at the swank party on Saturday. They asked me for a profile, too, but after talking to them, it was clear they wanted to focus on the fact that I'm using a cane right now. That kind of put a bad taste in my mouth, you know? I'm only *temporarily* disabled—if they're going to do a spotlight on a disabled fashion designer, then it should be someone who isn't going to be getting better in four to six weeks. I gave them the name of a former classmate of mine who's hard of hearing. Oh, did I tell you I hired a disability consultant to help me adapt some of my designs for people who use mobility aids?"

"That's cool." I paused, thinking. "Do you think they only asked me because I'm brown and Muslim?"

"Maybe. Is that a problem for you? I mean, you really are brown and Muslim. It's not temporary, like my disability."

I guess it didn't bother me. I mean, I'd been held back from fashion opportunities because of my religion, and I had no doubt I would be seeing a ton of racism and religious intolerance when I started working for real. So was it a big deal to get an opportunity thanks to something that would probably be more of a liability later? I leaned my head against the brick wall.

"But listen, Tahira," Nilusha said, "even if they asked you so they could tick off a box, it's also because you're amazing. It's a great opportunity for someone starting out. And selfishly, it'd be awesome to see you there."

"I haven't decided if I'm doing it yet. I have the Bloom this weekend."

"It's your decision, but the people at the *DashStyle* party I would introduce you to! We need to decide what you're wearing. Any chance you'd wear a Bhatt original?"

"Rowan can't be in the Bloom if I leave. He won't have enough team members."

"He looked so dazzling on your Instagram last week. Bring him along! I can get him into the party. Hell, even without you and me, that jawline could get him into the party."

I couldn't imagine it. Rowan and his plant T-shirts and flip-flops at a fashion party? Of course he'd let me dress him however I wanted, but still. Being surrounded by hundreds of people like Gia and Matteo would be his idea of hell.

"No, the Bloom is too important to him. Also, it was supposed to be important for me, too. Remember? Christopher Chan is going to be at the Grand Floral Cup?"

"Oh, he's still doing it? I was going to ask you about that. I read yesterday that Christopher Chan was taking this designer-in-residence post for some art museum in Helsinki in the fall, but I suppose—"

"What? Let me check . . ." I switched my call to speaker and went to the Grand Floral Cup site. And yup. There had been a judge change. Christopher Chan was out; some bridal florist to the stars was in.

"Shoot," I said. "You're right. He's not even going to be there."

"I'm sorry, honey. But that should make your decision easier, at least?"

Did it? It didn't feel any easier.

"Tahira, you're in a hard spot," Nilusha said. "If you feel it's important to stay and do your flower competition, then other opportunities will come up. But honestly? You can make some killer connections here this weekend. What do your instincts tell you?"

My instincts told me there was nothing more important than my Plan. My goals.

I sighed. "You're right. My career comes first. I'll come to Toronto."

It was the right choice. Even if it made me feel terrible. Even if I would be letting down Rowan and June.

"I'm really sorry about the timing, sweetie, but it will be grand. Let's find time to hang, just us. Bring your FIT portfolio and everything you've done this summer."

After chatting a few more minutes, we hung up. Nilusha was right. It probably *was* going to be great.

I glanced down the street. Bakewell was busy. Tourists, locals, and, of course, flowers everywhere. I'd thought the aesthetic of this town was both way too much and lacking in variety when I first got here. It was so strange how comforting Main Street had become to me now.

The Lilybuds door opened, and Shar came outside. "Just wanted to see how you—oh, Tahira, have you been crying?"

I shook my head, wiping a tear. "No, I'm fine."

She tilted her head, concerned. "That face doesn't look fine. Is this about the weekend?"

I exhaled. "Yeah. I'm stuck. I do need to go to Toronto to do this thing, but if Gia and I leave, Rowan and June will be short a team member."

"Why don't they find someone else?"

"It's two days before the Bloom. Who would drop everything to help them like that?"

"There has to be someone. Rowan and Juniper are so well liked."

Wait. Leanne couldn't do it because she was going to some rabbit thing, but she'd also said she wished she could spend the weekend with Rowan and June. Leanne thought of Rowan as her brother, and she thought of June as her . . . well, I didn't know what she thought of June, but she *did* give her flowers on Tuesday. It couldn't hurt to ask her.

"Hey, Shar," I asked, "is there a bus or a car service or something that could get me to the Langston farm today? I need to talk to Leanne. In person. It's an emergency."

Shar chuckled. "Of course not. This is Bakewell. We don't even have Uber. Why do you need to see Leanne?"

"I just do."

Shar looked at her watch. "The store is pretty slow—how about I drive you? We can ask if June will come in for a few hours to help Gia."

"You'd drive me all the way there?"

"Of course! You're my favorite niece! Call Leanne, see if she's home. I'll call June. I wouldn't mind saying hello to Joanne Langston, anyway. I need to thank her for those tahini cookies she brought me last week. They were so delicious!"

Thirty minutes later I was in Leanne's barn with her. June had agreed to come in to Lilybuds for a few hours to cover for us. Shar was in Leanne's mom's kitchen talking recipes or something.

"I wasn't surprised you wanted to talk to me," Leanne said. She was cleaning out one of the rabbit hutches, somehow with the rabbit still in it. "We're not really the 'hanging out alone' kind of friends, but apparently we are the 'ask to fill in for me at the Bloom so my boyfriend won't be upset that I'm hanging out with models and my ex-boyfriend' kind of friends."

I cringed. "Rowan told you."

She raised a brow. "You do realize he and I are best friends, don't you? He tells me everything."

"I'm sorry," I said. I was saying that too much lately. My eyes watered. "Damn rabbits."

She blinked at me a few seconds, then motioned me outside. "C'mon, let's get you away from these biological warfare bunnies."

We sat on the boulders outside. It was quite a different view during the day. The brilliant sun made the neighbors' crops seem to glow yellow.

"So, was I right?" Leanne asked. "You *are* here to ask me to take your spot in the Bloom."

Leanne had always seen right through me. I couldn't impress her with my popularity or my followers, or charm her using compliments. I had no choice but to be honest. But I wanted to be.

I nodded. "You said you wished you could see Rowan and Juniper at the Bloom."

"And that's true. But I can't say I'm excited to step in for you here—remember, *I pulled out* so you and your friend Gia could have a team for the competition."

"I thought you pulled out because of your rabbit show?"

Leanne paused a few seconds, then shook her head. "You know, I told Rowan not to get involved with you."

"You did?" I'd never gotten the impression that Leanne didn't approve of me dating her friend.

"I thought for sure that he'd get hurt. That something new and sparkly would come along and you'd forget all about him." She sighed. "I didn't think you were capable of seeing that there is no one more sparkly than Rowan. He's the best. He deserves someone who's all in for him. He's had a really tough year. I think he's ripe for being taken advantage of right now."

"I wasn't taking advantage of him."

"Yeah, well, he obviously didn't listen to me, did he? He's completely under your spell. But it's his life—I didn't even say 'I told you so' when he told me you were leaving him."

"I'm leaving the *Bloom*. Not Rowan."

She crossed her arms. "You promised him you wouldn't flake out on him or make him regret inviting you on the team."

I exhaled. "Look, Leanne, you can play the intimidating best friend game with me all day. You're probably right. I'm terrible for Rowan. He deserves someone who can commit to the things he cares about, and maybe I've got too much going on in my own life to do that. But right now all I need is to make sure Rowan and June don't miss out on the

Bloom. I honestly don't care if you like me or not, but I know you care about Rowan. I *know* you care about Juniper."

Leanne gritted her teeth. She blinked at me for a few seconds. There it was. Leanne totally had feelings for June.

"Don't you even bring Junebug into this," she said, sternly. "First you begged her to be in the competition, and now you're just abandoning her? You also promised you wouldn't hurt Juniper. They both deserve better than you."

"Exactly. They deserve *you*."

She glared at me again, then sighed, uncrossing her arms. "I have a confession. I'm not going to the rabbit show this weekend."

"What? You're not?"

She shook her head. "I think Daphne wants to retire. She's been even flightier than you, lately. So, fine. I'll take your place in the Bloom. But I have two conditions."

"Whatever you want."

"Don't call Rowan. Or text him or anything else while you're gone. Let him focus on the Bloom—this is important for him. You two need to take a break."

I didn't like that, but what choice did I have? "Okay. What's the second condition?"

"While you're in the city, you have to go to this book signing downtown on Saturday at three and get a signed copy of Lexi Greer's newest Silverborn book for Juniper."

I blinked. "Is that where you were *really* going this weekend?"

Leanne looked out into the distance again, and nodded. "Don't tell anyone."

I still didn't know exactly what was going on in Leanne's head where June was concerned, but one thing was clear. She didn't want to talk about it—at least not to me. Which, fair. But this was something I could do. I'd be downtown anyway for the profile with Dasha at one.

"Done," I said. "Send me the details. I'll get her the book. And I'll keep it on the down low, if that's what you want."

She nodded, then shook my hand. "We have a deal, then."

After leaving the farm, I texted Matteo that I was coming to the Dasha Payne photo shoot. Then I called Rowan to tell him Leanne had agreed to take my place on the Bloom team. He couldn't talk long since he was at work. I suggested we meet in the yard when he was done, but he said it was going to rain and he had to work early again. He didn't mention having breakfast together. He didn't want to see me.

I exhaled as I put my phone in my pocket. I was doing the right thing. I wasn't going to let myself regret this choice, no matter what.

∼

I woke up even before dawn the next day. I wanted to change up a sweatshirt to wear for the photo shoot so it wouldn't be a repeat on my feed. After pulling up the original design on my iPad, I played around with cropping the length. I also drew in some epaulets on the shoulders and metal studs on the neckline. Perfect. I had all the supplies to do this. I pulled out my notions box and the white and gray sweatshirt and started working.

It was so great to be engrossed in a sewing project again, but I made sure to go outside at eight for breakfast with a faint hope that Rowan would be there. He wasn't, but Juniper was.

"Row told me to tell you he went to the nursery early," she said, sitting across from me.

I sighed. "He's mad at me. Are you mad at me, too?" I didn't think I could handle both Johnston kids being upset with me.

"No. Not even a little bit. I mean, I'm sorry we won't get to hang out at the festival, but this whole photo shoot and interview sounds fantastic. Of course you need to go."

I smiled with relief. "Yeah. I *am* sorry, though."

"It's fine." Juniper smiled. "Maybe we can enter the Bloom together next year."

That wasn't likely. I needed a fashion internship next summer, according to the Plan. "You're way too nice, Juniper. What about Leanne? You okay with her on the team?"

Juniper nodded. I tried to read her expression, but I couldn't figure it out. "Totally fine," she said. "I realized something Tuesday. Leanne's always been so great to me, and like a stupid kid, I just saw more in that than what there was. I'm over it."

I watched her closely. I couldn't forget that Leanne had planned to drive all the way into the city just to get June a book. "She gave you flowers. I think there's something more there, June."

"No. Absolutely not. She's leaving in, like, a week. The flower thing is because she knows I love them. She wants to make sure there are no hard feelings between us before she leaves. Anyway," Juniper said, waving her hand, "I've figured out that if you remind yourself over and over that you're not into someone, you will eventually start to believe it."

I blew out a puff of air. I might need that trick when I left Bakewell. Because everything would be much easier without these pesky feelings for Rowan Johnston.

Juniper's face was full of concern. "Are you okay, Tahira?"

I chuckled, looking down. "Yeah, I'm good. I'm just annoyed I have to leave the Bloom. I'll be back, though. I'm not giving up my last week in Bakewell for anything."

"We'll stay in touch after you leave for good, right?"

I nodded. "Absolutely." I meant it.

We were all packed and ready to go by 1:30, and Gia and I were sitting on Shar's front porch waiting for Matteo. We needed to get on the road as soon as he got here because Gia had made an appointment in Toronto to get her roots done. I was checking my Insta when I heard a car turn onto the street.

Good. Matteo was early.

But instead of the blue Mustang, Rowan's Subaru pulled up. What was he doing home? He didn't even park in his own driveway, instead stopping in front of Shar's house, and he got out. He was carrying a bundle of flowers in one hand.

"Ooh, nice," Gia said. "Why doesn't Cameron ever bring me flowers? He works at the nursery, too."

I stopped listening to Gia, though. I was watching the most beautiful guy in the world come straight for me with a bouquet of flowers. I met him at the bottom of the stairs.

"These are for you." He handed me the flowers. "'I'm on lunch . . . can we talk for a few minutes?" I couldn't read his expression.

I nodded. "Yeah, but my ride will be here soon."

He took my hand and pulled me over to an ornate garden bench near the Bloom bunny in the middle of his yard. We sat.

"I didn't want you to leave without seeing you," he said.

I squeezed his hand. "I'm glad you came."

"I should apologize." He took his hand back and ran it over his head. I *could* read his expression now. Still sadness.

I looked at the bouquet, and noticed the sunflowers first. Small ones, brightly colored and contrasting against the blue and purple of the other flowers in the bundle. Heather and hydrangea. I knew exactly why he picked these flowers. The sunflowers were for our first kiss. The hydrangeas for the day we met, and the day we painted that mural together at Lilybuds. And the heather? The heather was because he was a designer down to the bone—big blooms like hydrangeas and sunflowers needed something tall and slender for balance.

I understood him. He understood me.

"Last night my mom really laid into me. She said I was being selfish," he said. "She said I needed to let you shine. It's a big deal, this photo shoot; I get that. I'm sorry I didn't support you."

"That sounds more like your mother's words than your own."

He squeezed his lips together. "I do mean them, though. I told you I can be tunnel minded, and maybe I needed her kick in the ass to see your perspective. This is your *dream*. Your life is out there, not hanging out in gardens and greenhouses with me."

I blinked. There was a lot of finality in his voice. "I'm only leaving for two days," I said. "When I come back on Sunday, we'll still have a whole week left in Bakewell to hang out in the garden." I wanted that. I wanted to lie on the grass and stare at the stars. I wanted to go hang out in flower fields and maybe finally try the marshmallow ice cream on Main Street. I wanted to talk for hours about art and design and flowers and beauty. I wasn't ready for all this to end.

Rowan smiled small. "I know." He pointed over to Shar's driveway. "Your ride is waiting." Sure enough, the blue Mustang was there.

I couldn't see Matteo from here, but I did see Gia's impatient face in the passenger-side window. "Thanks for these," I said, indicating the flowers. "And for, you know, coming to see me."

Eyes serious, he reached out and put his hand on my cheek. The calluses there, they gave me shivers like they always did. His hand was warm in the late-summer sun.

He leaned forward and kissed me gently. So soft. So right. I wanted more.

But of course I had to leave. I squeezed his hand. "I'll be back on Sunday," I said.

"Goodbye, Tahira. Go be amazing."

I was almost okay when I reached Matteo's car. Rowan wasn't angry with me. He was supportive. Maybe everything would be fine between us. I said nothing to Matteo as I got in the car, hoping he'd do the same.

Annoyingly, he didn't. "So, you *are* seeing that guy from your Insta?"

"Yes."

"How long has that been going on?" There was plenty of challenge in his voice. Asshole. He was the one who cheated, not me.

I don't know how I expected to feel the first time seeing my ex after our breakup, but I didn't expect what I was feeling now. Nothing. No hatred, no anger, no disappointment. A touch of annoyance, but that was it. He didn't even look that hot to me. I mean, yeah, he was good looking in a generic kind of way. Mediocre—compared to Rowan, at least.

Hallelujah. If nothing else, how great was it that I was already completely over this douche?

He snorted. "Giving you flowers. What is this, the nineteen fifties?"

I held Rowan's bouquet close.

"He *works* with flowers," Gia said. "In fact, he and his sister do the sweetest thing—they pick flowers based on their meanings. What do those flowers mean, T?"

It didn't matter, but Rowan had picked these particular flowers for sentimental reasons, not for the meaning behind them.

But then suddenly, I wondered, and I quickly pulled out my phone and searched up the meanings of the three flowers.

"They probably have the most romantic meanings," Gia said. She was laying it on a little thick for me, probably because she could see how annoyed Matteo was. "He's telling her how much he cares, and how he can't wait for her to be back so they can be together again."

Matteo scoffed.

I looked at the flowers. And no, that's not what these meant. There were literally a ton of flowers that stood for love. Red roses. Or tulips, for that matter.

But these ones? Rowan had chosen these flowers because they promised friendship. Respect.

This wasn't a bouquet of love or passion. And in retrospect? That kiss hadn't been, either.

It was over. Rowan was telling me it was over.

I leaned back in my seat and closed my eyes.

24

AWKWARD DRIVES ARE AWKWARD

I didn't say much on the drive to Toronto. Matteo and Gia caught each other up on family gossip, but I played mindless games on my phone or watched the farms pass by out the window. I wasn't regretting this trip—I still totally understood how important it was for me—but that didn't mean I wasn't allowed to be miserable about all I'd lost. I was certain I'd never feel as comfortable and content as I did staring at the stars with Rowan.

I sat up straight, scolding myself for that train of thought. Everything would be fine once I was back in Toronto. The tall buildings. Busy sidewalks. Street art. It was enough for me before, and it would be enough for me again.

We reached the city, and Matteo drove Gia straight to her salon for her hair appointment.

"Thanks," she told Matteo, jumping out of the car. "I'll take an Uber to my parents' when I'm finished here."

Matteo leaned back to look at me sitting in the back seat. "You want to come up here, or you gonna make me drive you around like I'm a chauffeur or something?"

I sighed and took the seat that Gia had just vacated.

"That's better," he said as he got back on the road. "You're looking good, Tahira. I think the country was good for your skin."

I didn't say anything.

"I expected you to post pictures from out there more often," he said. "I mean, Gia posted so much flowers and crap on her page, but yours was pretty empty."

"My feed is to show off my *designs*, and I was too busy to design much this summer."

"You did have those shots with your new guy, though. Loved the ones in that glass building. You take pictures of him a lot?" His tone had completely changed since I first got in the car. He seemed to be trying to be nice now. I didn't trust his motivation.

"No. Not really."

"He take pictures of you?"

I turned to look at him. "What's your point, Matteo?"

He chuckled. "Just talking. Nothing else."

I snorted. There was a time when I thought I could see through this person to his inner self. Now I knew there wasn't much worth seeing in there. "Bullshit," I said.

He rubbed the back of his neck. "Okay, I deserved that. I know you're pissed at me, and I don't blame you. I just . . ." He sighed. "I regret breaking it off with you."

I blinked. "*I* broke up with *you*, remember? When you cheated on me, and claimed we weren't exclusive when we *were*."

"I know, I know, I'm sorry." He bit his lip. "Alyssa, she trapped me. You know how it is, fame, followers, being recognized. She tempted me with parties and being seen with the right people."

"Inviting you to a party is not *trapping* you."

"It is, though. I lost sight of who I wanna be."

I raised a brow. Now Matteo was having an existential crisis? I didn't think he had it in him.

"But you and me," he continued. "We were *more* than that. It was, like, real. I know you felt it, too."

"What actually happened to your other girl?"

"Nothing happened. I broke it off because she wasn't you."

I turned to him. Back then I had felt it, too. Yeah, Matteo and I mostly were about the photo shoots and the fashion scene, but we were honest to each other about our dreams and about our insecurities that we wouldn't get where we wanted to be. At least I was honest. And there were moments with him in the city when all the pressure and the drive faded, and we were just us, together. He was the first person I ever had that with. But maybe I hadn't actually been real with him. Because I'd been a lot more open with Rowan than I ever had with Matteo. I never really told Matteo *why* I wanted to be in fashion, though. Like I'd told Rowan.

"You got all sides of me," he said. "You understood this life and all that, but you also understood more." He rubbed the back of his neck again. "Shoot, I'm not saying this right. I guess I'm wondering how serious you are with that guy?"

I exhaled. I had not seen this coming. Matteo? Self-reflecting and contrite?

But the truth was, Matteo and I *did* make sense on many levels. He understood how important it was to have the right shade of lipstick in a picture, and how amazing it was to look flawless without a filter. He understood what I was working toward and was helping me get there. He wouldn't have been grumpy about me leaving for this photo shoot the way Rowan was.

"Rowan and I haven't been together that long," I said.

"But you're really into him, aren't you?"

Yeah, I was. Right now, it felt stronger than it ever had with Matteo. But was there a future for Rowan and me? I couldn't forget what Leanne had said. Rowan deserved someone who was all in. And if I went all in, what would happen to my Plan?

And also? After that goodbye, I was pretty sure that it didn't matter what I wanted, anyway. Rowan had already tapped out.

"You and me? We got a few days together now," Matteo said. "Like old times. I'm not going to pester you for a chance or anything, but now you know where I stand. Maybe you'll feel the same."

"I don't think that will happen," I said. But then again, I hadn't thought I'd fall so hard for Rowan Johnston, of all people, back when I first met him two months ago. But even if I hadn't fallen for Rowan, Matteo no longer had any appeal for me. Because when things got hard and the stars closed in, I didn't picture Matteo as the one holding my hand.

~

As expected, my parents weren't home when Matteo dropped me off. My sister was playing video games in the living room.

"Hey, Samaya," I said, dropping my bags on the floor.

Samaya was a year younger than me but looked nothing like me. She was kind of tiny, with eyes that were borderline too big for her face. She usually kept her hair no longer than chin length, which gave her a vague Dora the Explorer innocence, even though her attitude was saltier than poutine. Most people were surprised I had a sister so close to my age. They were even more surprised when they met her.

Samaya's already ridiculously wide eyes went wider, and she spoke into her headset. "Gotta go, crew. A living ghost just walked in."

She took off her headset and stared at me.

"Nice to see you, too, sis," I said sarcastically, plopping on the couch next to her.

She was still staring at me. "I guess I forgot what you look like," she said. "Or sound like."

"What? We've FaceTimed this summer," I said.

"Yeah, you've answered maybe every third time I've called you."

"I've been busy!"

"Why are you home? I thought you had another week over there in . . . where was it? Bakingville?"

"Bakewell."

She shrugged. "Geography isn't my thing."

"I told Mom and Dad yesterday that I'd be home for a few days . . . they didn't tell you?"

"That assumes I saw them yesterday. Mom only texted me when she left on that business trip. I'm pretty sure they're avoiding me. Mom's got it in her head that I should be applying for this Oxford bursary or something. I am so done with their inane pressure, so I've been exclusively speaking to them with a British accent so they know what to expect if they ship me off to the UK." She demonstrated: *"Pip, pip, cheerio!"*

I chuckled. Samaya had the driest humor for a math nerd. Self-proclaimed math nerd, by the way. She actually had several shirts identifying herself as such. I wondered if she bought them at the same ironic-shirt store Rowan shopped at.

"So why are you here, anyway?" she asked.

I leaned back on the couch. "I have a photo shoot. I'm here until Sunday. How's math camp?"

"You know. Math-y. I'm also taking grade-twelve algebra online so I can switch to college level when I'm in grade twelve. Oh, and Devin and the crew and I started playing this new online role-playing game."

"That sounds cool. How are Devin and your friends?"

Samaya shrugged. She'd been seeing Devin, her boyfriend, since grade nine. He was just like her—obsessed with math and science. All her friends were academically inclined. Honestly, sometimes I was low-key jealous of Samaya's little crew. They were such a tight group. I was sure none of them would ever use one of their friends for their influence, or for anything else.

She indicated her game. "Were you, like, looking to have a Hallmark sisters' moment or something? Because I can tell them all to hold tight until later so you and me can have our bonding. You usually don't have time to talk to anyone but your model and influencer-y friends, but I'm game."

I cringed. "Am I that bad?"

She laughed. "Eh, you can be. But it's not like I've been around much, either. No worries. You do you, and I do me. You mind if I get back to my game? You're welcome to watch. Or I could set you up with a character. There's a weaver class that would suit you."

I stood and brushed Samaya's hair off her face. "Nah, maybe another time. It's good to see you, though. Let's try and squeeze in time for coffee or something while we're here. Seriously. Without Mom and Dad."

"Yes, please," she said, putting her headset back on. "The British accent is getting tedious to keep up, honestly."

I grabbed my stuff and went upstairs. I loved my room—but it seemed strange to me now. Yes, Ruby my dress form and my sewing machine weren't here, but other than that, it looked just the same. The simple modern furniture. The black accent wall, which had been a royal pain to paint. One wall covered with the best sketches I'd done last year. Big plastic bins of fabric and sewing supplies lining another wall. My low platform bed. My closet still full of clothes, even though I'd taken so much with me to Bakewell. It was like everything here had been stuck in time, while I hadn't.

I dropped the bags on my bed and pulled my hair into a bun. The most important photo shoot of my life was tomorrow morning, and I didn't have the time to mope, be sullen, or cry. It was already past four—I only had a few hours tonight to prepare. I pulled pieces out of my closet and my bags. I'd come this far. I'd left Bakewell and the Bloom. I needed to make this photo shoot worth my while.

25

THE MEGA PHOTO SHOOT

The group photo shoot for the most important style influencers in Toronto was being held in the Distillery District, a cute little shopping area downtown with cobblestone streets, old-timey brick buildings, and cafés with patios spilling out onto the sidewalks. It was a popular place for fashion spreads, if a little predictable. Gia and I took an Uber downtown to the meeting place and easily found the group. It wasn't hard—twenty people wearing clothes that to the uninformed would look like regular upper-teen, lower-twenties casual wear, but we recognized them as some of the hottest brands right now. Matteo spotted us immediately and came over.

Thankfully, I didn't have to talk to him long.

"Tahira! Look at you, gorgeous!" Nilusha said, hobbling toward me while managing cobblestones and a cane with no problem. Probably thanks to her weeks in Paris. She kissed both my cheeks and stood back, looking at me while holding one of my hands. "Did you make that shirt? I *adore* it."

I grinned. The sweatshirt had turned out so cool. I'd cropped it really short (I was wearing it with a tight cami underneath) and used bright-green grosgrain ribbon for the epaulets on the shoulders. "Of course I did."

She shook her head. "To think, I could have had all that talent working for me this summer. Instead, all I have is a designer walking cane."

"Your cane is designer?"

She shrugged. "I'm a designer, and I designed it."

I laughed. I introduced her to Matteo and Gia, who both complimented her outfit and her fashion line right away. To be fair, Nilusha was absolutely stunning in a tight black scoop-neck top paired with loose black trousers. She'd cut her hair. It was now above her shoulders with a cute flip out at the bottom, and she was wearing a black beret.

"I like that hat," I said.

"I'm making berets for the fall. Seriously, my whole line will be Paris inspired next season. Come, let me introduce you to Dasha Payne."

"Oh, I already know her," Matteo said as he followed me anyway. Gia squealed with glee, and I stopped myself from rolling my eyes.

Dasha Payne was a tall white woman with wavy brown hair, wearing a bright floral oversize blazer and matching ankle-length pants. After Nilusha introduced us, Dasha told us how thrilled she was that we were here. She was gorgeous, of course, and friendly enough. I could see why she was the hottest thing right now. She had the attention span of Strawberry the bunny, though.

"Tahira! I'm so excited to hang out with you tomorrow—I need you to be my tour guide." She turned to the person standing behind her. "We have to make sure we get to that haberdashery Amber mentioned." She turned back at me. "I've been stalking your Insta. I'm going to need you to tell me where all that street art is. And that sunflower field. Is that near where we're shopping?"

I shook my head. "No. The sunflowers are a few hours away. I've spent the summer in a small town near a bunch of flower farms."

Her face brightened. "Seriously? Oh, that reminds me." She called out to another person behind her. "Did you call the aquarium to see if we can use it after closing?" Then she was back to me. "Florals are hot next season, but, like, you know, done modern. Urban."

"Tahira doesn't use natural stuff in her designs," Matteo said. "Her aesthetic is more industrial, you know?"

Dasha nodded. "Fish are happening, too. Flowers and fish. But not, like, to eat. I do ketogenic but with intermittent fasting. I have no idea what I'll eat tomorrow. Do they have keto in Canada? Oh, there's Savannah!"

Dasha wandered away without another word. She was actually far from the flightiest person I'd met in fashion.

But interesting that she'd noticed the sunflower pictures. Now that Rowan and I were . . . whatever, should I have taken those pictures down from my Insta? I mean, the whole flower thing *was* against my aesthetic, and I needed to keep my design sensibilities consistent. Plus, at this point there were a few too many ex-boyfriends on my feed.

And I didn't love being reminded of that perfect day every time I looked at my page.

I stayed true to my promise to Leanne last night and didn't text Rowan. Part of me expected him to contact me—but he didn't. Nothing this morning, either.

"What do you think, Tahira?" Nilusha asked.

Jolted out of my thoughts, I turned to her. What were they talking about?

"Wow, you were out of it there." Nilusha smiled. "We were trying to figure out what Dasha meant when she said fish are happening. Like, aquatic prints? Or, like, fish scales? I've never heard of this trend. Have you seen any fish stuff?"

I shook my head. I needed to get a grip. This was important. I needed to stay focused right now, or the Plan would come apart.

~

The shoot was fine, I guess. I managed to stay mostly out of my head. It was great to get a picture with Nilusha. Less great that Dasha insisted on a shot of Matteo and me alone to use for our interview for her site tomorrow. Also, it was annoying to have to listen to Gia go on about how she wished someone had told her we'd be on cobblestones because her shoes were all wrong.

Both Matteo and Gia were kind of sucking up to Dasha. Gia told her three times how great the *DashStyle* site was, and Matteo wouldn't shut up about how stoked he was to hang with her tomorrow. He even told her to let him know if there was anything special she wanted him to procure or make happen, because he knew all the right people in this city.

I understood why they were sucking up—I mean, we were all here because Dasha was so influential. But they seemed to be so extreme about it. Was that what I seemed like with people I looked up to? I remembered Rowan calling me pouty and Thirst Trap when we met. And, of course, Samaya's comment about me only having time for models and influencers. Matteo's and Gia's behavior shouldn't have bothered me so much, but it did.

The photo shoot was as long and tedious as these things usually were. By the time we were done, it was past one and I was irritable and tired. The stunning day in Toronto surrounded by so many cool people (Matteo excluded) should have been a dream, but it wasn't.

After the shoot, we were all treated to a buffet on the patio of this Mexican restaurant in the middle of the Distillery District. It was really swanky—low tables with brightly colored bench seats and enormous urns filled with hibiscus flowers. I took a picture with my phone and almost sent it to Rowan because he'd love the hibiscus, but I didn't.

We were all sitting together at this huge table. I had Gia on one side of me and Nilusha on the other, with Matteo, Dasha, the photographer (Angie), and this guy Marcus near us. He'd introduced himself to us earlier today by saying he had fifty thousand followers on Instagram and even more on TikTok. Since then, he'd been following Gia around like a puppy.

"This place is so beautiful," Nilusha said, snapping a picture of the patio. "It makes me miss Paris, though. There was this one bistro where I had the most amazing little pistachio falafel . . . Tahira, you would have loved the floral arrangements there. It was a complete explosion of flowers in the planter boxes, like so many Paris patios, but they were all monochromatic white like the stuff you've been designing. It was such a departure from the more colorful arrangements everywhere else."

"Oh," Dasha said, smiling at me. "Are you into floral design? I thought Matteo said you weren't into naturals?"

Gia snorted before I could answer. "She's totally not normally into flowers, but when in Rome! We've been roughing it in the sticks all summer. Seriously, a total cow town. We came back for this shoot."

I frowned at Gia. Yeah, I'd thought the same thing about Bakewell at first, but I knew she didn't still think about it that way.

"And you've been flower arranging there?" Dasha asked me.

"Yeah," I said. "My . . . friend has been teaching me. I kind of love it." I looked again at the hibiscus arrangements. The big blooms were accented with philodendron leaves, but I thought the large greenery didn't do anything for the flowers. I would have used more delicate ferns.

I smiled at Dasha. "Mostly I've been working in my aunt's boutique, though. She wanted to bring in a new younger line, and I was helping her roll it out. Branding, buying, merchandising. It's been fun."

"Totally fun," Gia said. "And I feel like we've, you know, reconnected with a simpler life. A couple of days ago, we were even hanging out at a farm! Can you imagine? But I'm glad to be back to the city. Those rural communities are so monolithic, you know? Everyone is the same. There is no originality. I'm glad to be around, you know, *cool* people again." She smiled at Marcus.

"You mean everyone is white and straight out there," Angie said, dipping a tortilla chip into a green salsa.

I shook my head. "Actually, it's pretty diverse for such a small town."

"Yeah, but they're all into the same thing," Gia said. "*Flowers*. Like, seriously—I know florals are hot right now, but in *design*. Not actual flowers. We were even supposed to be doing this flower-arranging thing this weekend." Gia grinned at Marcus again. "This is so much better. Flower nerds have no chill. I'm glad to be back with people who know how to enjoy themselves."

Who exactly was Gia talking about? Cameron? Juniper? Rowan? Was this just to look cool in front of these people, or did she actually believe these things?

"Seriously, Gia?" I asked. "You were all about taking pictures of flowers from the moment we got there. And you didn't seem to have an issue spending all your time there with locals." One, in particular, but I doubted she wanted me to mention Cameron now that she was flirting with this guy.

Gia gave me her sweet smile. "I was trying to help you make the best out of a shitty situation." She turned to Dasha. "It's all good now, though. We have one more week there; then we'll be back to civilization."

"I love those cutesy small towns for the aesthetic, but the people are just exhausting," Dasha said.

"Exactly," Gia agreed.

"I thought you made friends there, Gia?" Matteo asked. Even he seemed to notice how ridiculous his cousin was being today.

Gia snorted. "With who? Addison, the bitchiest, meanest *mean girl* I've ever met? Or Juniper, real name, by the way? The girl only talks about three things: flowers, books, and her dead grandma. Yet her mouth never stops moving. Then there's Leanne. She's a unique one. Bit of a hillbilly. Obsessed with her rabbits and teaches them to jump through hoops, which must be some sort of animal cruelty. Only thing interesting about Juniper and Leanne is that they are secretly totally into each other, but like everyone else there, they're so backward they won't act on it."

I blinked at Gia. She was going way too far.

Matteo laughed. "Everyone couldn't have been bad, considering you and Tahira both hooked up there."

Gia gave Marcus a flirty giggle. "Nothing serious. Just a fling to get me through the summer." She winked at him. "A girl has needs, you know? And you can't blame Tahira for claiming Rowan for herself. I mean, did you *see* the guy on her Insta? He's hotter than sin, and he's a gifted artist. Too bad he has the personality of a . . ." She looked at me. "What was it you said? He's got the personality of a garden slug?" She laughed. "But oh my God, the engagement on her page from those pictures. *Phew.* He even got her into that sunflower field before it was open to the public. Worth it, I'd say."

What. The. Hell. Did Gia seriously think I was *using* Rowan for my Instagram? I wanted to tell her off . . . she *knew* that wasn't true. She knew how much Rowan and Juniper meant to me.

Or did she? That first day Rowan kissed me, I'd really wanted to talk to Gia about him. Even before that, I'd wanted to talk to her as soon as I noticed that I'd caught feelings for the guy. But she hadn't been around. She'd been with Cameron, who I'd thought she was actually really into but who she now was ready to dump for this guy who had fifty thousand followers.

But even if she didn't know how much Rowan meant to me, she did know I would *never* use someone like that. I mean, she knew I dumped Matteo as soon as I found out he was using that Alyssa person for her party invitations.

I didn't know what to say. I wanted to yell that yes, Bakewell started out being torture, but it turned out to be wonderful. I wanted to say that Juniper was sweeter, kinder, and more loyal to her friends than any of the phonies at this table. That being alone in a sunflower field was a more transcendent experience than any photo shoot or rooftop party.

That I'd take a flower nerd any day over a flighty, opportunistic, long-waisted, gaslighting cheater.

But this wasn't the right crowd to hear me admit that I really wasn't feeling this life anymore.

Nilusha started talking about the Paris streetwear scene, which was a bit different from the North American scene. I struggled to pay attention. I wanted to leave, but I couldn't, because this—the recognition, the networking, the ass-kissing—was all necessary to get where I wanted to be.

I loved fashion. I loved design. I wanted that feeling of being completely engrossed in the perfect flow of creating something. Seeing something go from a two-dimensional drawing to a three-dimensional garment and, finally, seeing it on a real person.

My work. My *designs*. Becoming a tool someone used to express their true selves.

I still wanted that.

But I also wanted to lie out on a clear night with so many stars in the sky that I could barely keep my eyes open. I wanted to watch sunsets in the middle of farmers' fields with my friends. I wanted to take pictures, of gardens, of cities, of people I loved. I wanted to stop and smell the flowers a little more often.

Problem was, I had no idea how to have it all. Or whether it was even possible.

26

CHOCOLATE, CHURROS, AND HEART-TO-HEARTS

After we finished eating, everyone talked about heading to a lounge of some sort, but I didn't feel like going, so I made an excuse. Matteo and Gia seemed super enthusiastic, though, so I resigned myself to taking the subway alone back to Scarborough. After saying a quick goodbye, I headed toward the nearest streetcar stop.

But Nilusha called out: "Wait up, Tahira!" She tapped her cane on a nearby light post. "I'm not in the mood to join the others if it means navigating those narrow 'lounges' with this. I told everyone I'd see them at the party tomorrow. Want to have that coffee before you head home?"

I wasn't sure. Nilusha wasn't annoying me like Gia and Matteo were, probably because she didn't need to suck up to these people, but she was a part of this whole scene that was getting under my skin today. Still, she was my mentor, and I knew what Mom would say: that an existential career crisis was exactly the stuff you were supposed to talk to your mentor about.

"Okay."

"C'mon," Nilusha said, motioning for me to follow her back into the Distillery District. "There is a place over here which has chocolat chaud almost as good as Paris."

The hot chocolate smelled good. The place was adorbs. Nilusha was as warm, open, and kind as ever. But still. I wanted to go home. Maybe watch Netflix and chill. Maybe stare at those pictures from the sunflower field. Maybe wait for my phone to buzz with a text from Rowan that would never come.

Pretty pathetic.

"Here, share with me," Nilusha said, holding her plate out to me. "I didn't realize an order of churros would have so many."

I shook my head. "No, I'm fine."

"I miss the patisseries in France so much," she said, taking a churro for herself. "Didier sent me some pictures of beautiful pâte à choux puffs that were decorated with gold leaf yesterday."

"Are you still seeing him?" How could they possibly still be together? A nurse in a busy Paris hospital and a Toronto fashion designer were about as far apart as you could get. The only thing they seemed to have in common was their love of pastries.

"No, not technically." She waved her hand nonchalantly. "Just friends now. It would be nice to keep someone as steady as him around, but I'm honest with myself. I don't have the time to devote to a relationship when I'm getting my brand off the ground. It was a holiday fling, like yours with that garden boy."

A holiday fling. She made it sound so insignificant.

Nilusha tilted her head. "I detected a bit of tension between you and your friend there—what's her name, Gina?"

"Gia." I blew out a puff of air, looking at one of the old French chocolate posters on the wall. "What she said was wrong. There *are* a lot of cool people in Bakewell. And I wasn't using Rowan for hits on my social."

"No, you don't seem the type." Nilusha dipped another churro into her single-origin steamed chocolate.

"Yeah, well, I didn't think Gia was the type, either. She was all over this guy in Bakewell. Why make it seem to Dasha like there was no one there of any substance? I mean, I know she can be a bit extra, but I've never seen her *that* phony. I don't know why she was acting like that."

Nilusha tilted her head. "Don't you?"

"You think she was just trying to be, I don't know, cool for the cool kids or something?"

Nilusha smiled, shrugging. "This industry brings out the worst in a lot of people. You must have seen that before."

Of course I had. I'd seen backstabbing when I was working on Yorkville or applying for internships. A girl intentionally spilled foundation on another girl's dress at the audition for that TV show. And I'd heard stories much worse. People would throw their own grandmother under a bus if it meant they could be a little closer to fame and the limelight.

But I wasn't like those people. And I didn't think my friends were, either.

Nilusha sipped her chocolate. "It's such a shame you and I couldn't work together this summer. I could have helped you figure out who is genuine. Let me give you a hint . . ." She leaned in close. "None of us are."

"That can't be true. You're not like that."

She nodded. "I am when I need to be. Sometimes it's hard to notice because we're all so friendly and affectionate, and we all party together. But I see those people as my *colleagues*, not friends. This is a cutthroat industry, and to get ahead, you need to be looking out for yourself first. People who get discouraged when people act fake aren't looking at it with the right lens. Everyone's using each other."

"That's awfully pessimistic."

Nilusha shrugged, smiling. "You do have to be real with some people so you don't forget how to do it. That's why I like mentoring interns. They keep me grounded." She smiled warmly. "The good interns, at least. You remind me so much of me at your age, so you're extra special."

"Gia *is* real. With me, at least. We've been friends for years."

"All I know is that girl was saying nasty things about what sound like good people just to impress Dasha. And she was saying it as if *you* felt the same way. She sounds super insecure, if you ask me. Sucking up to Dasha today isn't even going to make any difference for her, because Dasha only cares about what someone can do for her, and your friend is a nobody, no offense to her."

I mean, yeah, Gia was insecure. What seventeen-year-old girl wasn't? Especially one who wanted to be a style influencer and an actress. But now it was hard to accept this behavior of hers—projecting superiority over others because of her own insecurity. When would this become who Gia was, and not just a game she played?

I swallowed. Did Gia assume I'd play along with cutting up our friends to look good in front of Dasha? Or maybe she was trying to take *me* down a peg in Dasha's eyes to make herself look better. After all, it was *my* boyfriend, his sister, and his best friend Gia had insulted.

My stomach soured. Whether it was true or not, the very idea that Gia's antics today were an intentional attempt to make me look bad . . . *ugh*. I hated everything about this game. I loved fashion, not backstabbing and intrigue.

I turned my hot chocolate cup on the saucer, having no appetite to drink it.

"Also," Nilusha said, "just because you *were* friends, doesn't mean you *always* have to be friends."

I chuckled, feeling a little exposed. "Are you sure you're a fashion designer and not a therapist?"

"Maybe that's my true calling." Nilusha smiled as she sipped her hot chocolate. "So other than your friends getting under your skin, what's going on with you? Are you regretting leaving that flower contest?"

I exhaled. Was I? "No. I'm not." Being here was important. I had to succeed. This was how I was going to do it. "I'm just . . ." My voice trailed off. "I'm exhausted."

"Oh no, sweetie. Why? What's exhausting you?"

I looked out beyond the patio. There was a big statue in the middle of the courtyard—the letters *LO*, with *VE* under them—and a long line of people waiting to take a picture with it. Cheesy as all hell, and about as basic an Instagram shot as possible. But the girls posing in front of it now were having the *best* time. Laughing. Making silly faces, putting their arms around each other. Complete and utter joy. I sighed. "All of it's exhausting me. I'm always thinking about how to make a name for myself. Get more followers, get the best internships, get into FIT. Be noticed. Not to mention this backstabbing and sucking-up game. Don't get me wrong: I *want* to be a designer. I love designing and making clothes. I love styling, and I even love merchandising and fashion photography. But I'm so tired of always having to be . . . on."

Nilusha shook her head. "Tahira, you don't *have* to do any of that. Look, I'm not going to say it's easy. I *love* my job—that's why I do it. But there's a lot of noise I tune out. You don't have to be seen, now. That can come later. It *will* come later—organically. There is no point spending so much energy on a following until you've at least started design school and have a better idea of where you want your career to go. And I've always wondered, Why are you only focused on one school? There are lots of great fashion programs out there—even here in Toronto. Ryerson University is fantastic for fashion. So is the Ontario College of Art and Design."

I shrugged. "FIT is the best."

"That doesn't mean it's the best for *you*."

"Everyone says it's the top school. It's my parents' dream for me to be the best."

Nilusha chuckled. "Ah. Desi parents. I have a couple of those myself. You know my dad sends me the application package for engineering school every year? He says it's never too late."

I looked down at the table. "I'm not going into business like my mom, or law like my dad. I'm not even going into math like my sister. I want to be an *artist*. But I still want to make them proud."

"Tahira, with all due respect for what sounds like supportive parents, but if you're already exhausted and jaded about schmoozing, then New York might not be for you. It's *a lot*. There are a lot of people with talent, and a lot of people with connections. I have no doubt you can do it, but you know that as a person of color, you'll have to work twice as hard at everything to be seen there. It's *competitive*. Maybe you'd be better off as a big, fabulous fish in a smaller lake?" She laughed. "Oh, I think I just found Dasha's fish!"

I chuckled. Of course I didn't doubt that I'd have to work harder than everyone else—this was something Nilusha and I had talked about in our mentoring meetings. And I didn't mind working so hard at the designing work . . . but the thought of working harder at the other stuff—the fighting to get noticed, the schmoozing, the sucking up. Maybe she was right, and I would be better in a smaller lake?

But why was it so terrifying to even think of exploring other options?

I didn't want to upset Mom and Dad. They would absolutely not be happy if I didn't go to FIT. This had been the Plan for years.

But it was *my* life. Didn't I trust myself enough to forge my own path?

"I can put you in touch with some friends who work at those two Toronto schools," Nilusha said. "Just talk to them. Explore your options."

I had no idea what I'd tell Mom and Dad, but this was just research right now. "Okay. Thank you."

"Excellent." She held out the plate of churros to me again. "Now, tell me what happened with that garden-oriented boy. I'm in a problem-solving mood—maybe I can help there, too."

I chuckled, took a churro this time, and dipped it into my chocolate. "Okay. I guess I'll start from the beginning."

Nilusha and I spent the rest of the afternoon dipping churros into hot chocolate and talking about how Rowan and I went from dreading the sight of each other to spending hours talking under the stars. She couldn't really help me figure out what he was thinking or help me decide if I should fight to keep our relationship in Toronto, but this was the first time I'd really told someone how I felt about Rowan, and it was nice to say aloud how much he meant to me.

Nilusha smiled. "He sounds utterly lovely. And now I miss Didier. There is something so affirming about being with someone from outside your industry who still respects your abilities, you know? It's too bad mine lives in Paris." She exhaled. "It's those quiet moments that really feed your soul." She took a big bite of her churro drenched in chocolate. "That, and chocolate, of course."

I agreed, licking the chocolate off my fingers.

I eventually headed home, taking the streetcar and then hopping on the subway, and got there as Dad and Samaya were setting the table for dinner. I could hear Mom in the kitchen.

"Hey, I thought you and Mom were going to be out until late tonight."

"Your mother came home early from Hamilton so she could make you dinner, and I'm officially taking the weekend off. I've barely seen my firstborn all summer." He kissed my forehead. This was really rare—all the Janmohammads at home for dinner.

Mom brought the food to the table. She'd made my favorite, her famous kuku paka—East African chicken in coconut gravy. I poured a big ladleful on top of the basmati rice on my plate.

"So how was the photo shoot today?" Mom asked.

"It was fine."

"The profile is tomorrow, right?"

I nodded. "I'm meeting Dasha at that gelato place at Queen and Spadina at one."

"What are you wearing?"

"My black biker jacket with those yellow wide-leg trousers I made."

Mom nodded. "That would work. Make sure you wear a House of Tahira blouse, too."

I shrugged.

Dad looked at me carefully. I hadn't really seen much of him this summer, since it was usually Mom who FaceTimed. It was always harder to hide what I was thinking from him, especially when he was watching me like that. "What's wrong? You don't sound excited about this photo shoot today."

I exhaled. I'd thought about my conversation with Nilusha the whole way home. And about how I would bring it up with Mom and Dad. I took a deep breath. "Guys, what if I don't go to FIT?"

Mom put her spoon down. "You *will* get into FIT. Your grades are high enough; Sharmin's been telling me about the success at the store. Even if you didn't redo Lilybuds, I think it would work to focus your application on the success of the Lily line. You'll have to do a real deep dive—"

"No, Mom. I'm not saying I won't get in, but . . . would you guys be okay if I chose *not* to go there? If I went to another school for fashion?"

Samaya whistled the sound of a bomb dropping.

Mom glared at her, then turned to me. "But FIT has always been what you wanted," she said, straightening her spine to look down at me. "It's the best fashion school in the world."

I rubbed my hand. "It's the best, but the biggest, too. In a new city—a new country, even. I'm just . . ."

Just what? I wasn't afraid of not being good enough for New York—that wasn't it. I didn't really know how to explain it. All I could think about was how Gia was acting today. Putting others down so she could stand out as a model in a shoot with twenty-five other models.

I tried to smile. "Have you guys ever looked at the stars outside of the city?"

"The stars in New York are pretty much the same as here," Samaya said. "Same hemisphere."

"No, I'm talking about out in the country, not New York City. Where there is less light pollution, and you can see hundreds more stars. Thousands."

"Of course," Dad said. "Remember when we rented that cottage in Muskoka a few years ago? The night skies there were spectacular."

I smiled. "Bakewell's like that. It freaked me out at first—I didn't think it was right for there to be so many stars. But . . . those stars, they're here in the city, too; you just can't see them. Because there is so much else going on, these ridiculously bright things can't even be seen. That's what I'm afraid of in New York."

"But, Tahira, the brightest stars will always be seen," Mom said. "You have to believe in yourself."

I shook my head. "This isn't a low-self-confidence thing. It's just . . . the fashion world is cutthroat. I know that with hard work and hustle, I can make a name for myself. But all that hustle—for fame, followers, for bigger platforms—none of that is why I want to be a designer."

"Of course it's not," said Mom. "But it's how the game is played."

I sighed. "Maybe. But after talking to Nilusha today, I'm wondering how necessary it is to be already playing that game. Or if it's necessary at all. People do make it in fashion without thousands of followers first. I was *so* excited for the Bloom with my friends this weekend. Dropping out upset people I care about. And what did I do it for? To be seen. Not for what I actually want—to design." My voice cracked. "I disappointed people I care about because I thought I needed to be seen, but my friends, the people who matter right now, already saw me."

Mom reached out and took my hand. "Tahira. I know it's hard, but you'll have more time with your friends later. Everyone has to make sacrifices—"

Dad put his hand out, stopping Mom. "What *do* you want, Tahira? From deep within?" He touched his fingers to his heart.

I shrugged. "I want to maybe explore different schools."

Samaya made an explosion sound, and I glared at her this time.

273

"Which schools?" Dad asked.

I didn't even look at Mom. "Nilusha went to Ryerson. There's also OCAD in Toronto. LaSalle College in Montreal is excellent, too."

"This isn't because of your new boyfriend, is it?" Mom asked.

I frowned. "No. We're not really . . . I'm pretty sure we're done. But it *is* because my family is here. I'd like to be closer to home. And if I stay, maybe I can work with Nilusha while I'm in school." I looked at my sister. "I can spend more time with Samaya, too. Honestly, I shouldn't have left the Bloom. I'd made a commitment to my friends, and I don't even know where my career will be in the future. A bunch of urban style influencers might not matter to me."

They were both quiet for a bit.

Mom shook her head. "Tahira, you can't do this halfway. No success comes without hard work. I thought this was what you wanted."

"Being a designer *is* what I want. Honestly. I'm not doing this for the platform, or for followers, or fame. And I have every intention of working very hard at the part that matters. Design. The actual art. The flow. Losing myself in a project. Seeing something in my head and watching it become a real thing. Other people expressing themselves using my clothes. I still want that."

My parents were both quiet for a while.

Those were all the same reasons why I'd fallen in love with floral design this summer, too.

"How can we help you now, Tahira?" Dad asked. "We can worry about college later, but what about the competition? Is it too late to go back?"

I hadn't even imagined that as a possibility. "Probably. The competition is tomorrow morning."

"Tomorrow morning." Dad checked something on his phone. "Bakewell is only an hour and a half from here, and I love night driving. It's been a while since we had a Janmohammad mini vacation. Sabina, Sharmin has a spare room, doesn't she?"

"Um," Samaya said. "Do I have to go?"

I straightened. "You guys would be willing to take me back to Bakewell *tonight*?"

Mom checked her phone. "I don't have any meetings tomorrow."

Samaya raised a brow. "Tomorrow is Saturday, Mom."

"Yes, and I work for a hotel company. Hotels are open Saturdays." She nodded at Dad. "We can go to Bakewell for the weekend."

"All of us?" Samaya asked again.

Dad glared at her. "Yes, all of us. You can survive one weekend without your video games."

I shook my head. "I can't—I need to go to this bookstore at three to get a signed book. Leanne was going to drive to the city to get it tomorrow because it's Juniper's favorite author, but since I asked Leanne to take my place in the Bloom, I said I'd do it."

Samaya's hand shot to her mouth. "Oh my God, that's adorable. She was going to drive all that way to get her friend a book?"

"Just call the bookstore," Mom said. "They can have the author sign it and then mail it to you. They do things like this all the time."

That would solve that problem. I assumed Gia would want to stay and still go to the rooftop party tomorrow night, though. I doubted Dasha would go ahead with the interview without me, so Matteo would lose that opportunity, but I honestly didn't care if the guy who cheated on me lost a Dasha Payne profile. "But would the team even want me back?"

"Tahira—come on." Mom smiled. "Call your friends! The worst they can say is no, and then you'll be no more miserable than you are now."

If I asked Rowan to take me back on the Bloom team and he said no, I *would* be even more miserable than I was now. But if he said yes—

Janmohammads always succeed. And we couldn't succeed if we didn't even try.

27

THE BEST OF BOTH OF US

I could hear Mom phoning Shar as I walked to my bedroom. I closed
the door and plopped on my bed. I knew I'd promised Leanne I
wouldn't contact Rowan if I left the Bloom, but there had to be an
exception for calling because I wanted to come back.

I phoned him.

He didn't answer.

I texted him.

Tahira: I need to speak to you. It's important. Can you call me?

There was no response for a while. Then I saw the three little dots
appear under my message for what felt like hours. Finally the text came.

Rowan: I'm at work getting more plants.

Tahira: It'll be quick.

My phone rang. "What's up?" he said when I answered. He didn't
sound thrilled to hear from me. My heart sank.

"I won't keep you long," I said. I wanted to say that I missed him,
even though I'd only been gone a day. I wanted to tell him about the
photo shoot, about how weird Gia was being, and about how I was now
questioning if I even wanted to go to FIT. I wanted to tell him about
the hibiscus in the distillery, and about the churros dipped in chocolate.
About how Matteo had the nerve to say he regretted cheating on me

and he wanted me back. I wanted to tell Rowan that I shouldn't have left Bakewell yesterday. I wanted to say so much, but I couldn't. "About the Bloom. Can I come back?"

"What did you say?" There was a lot of noise in the background. I wondered if he was at the back of the greenhouse, where we took those pictures.

"Can I come back to your Bloom team?"

He didn't say anything. Maybe he didn't hear me again? "You want to come back," he finally said. I could hear the disbelief in his voice. He was bitter. I didn't blame him. "What happened to your fashion profile? I thought it was 'important for your brand'?"

"I'd rather come back to Bakewell."

It got quieter. Maybe he went outside. "I don't get it, Tahira. You made it seem like this thing in Toronto was essential, and now you're leaving it? This isn't guilt or pity, is it? Because I—"

"It's not guilt. I'd rather be in the Bloom than the fashion profile. Leanne can stay on the team if she wants—it would be just me coming back. Gia's staying here."

"Then why did you leave?" Rowan asked. "And I'm supposed to just *take you back*, just like that?"

Was he talking about the Bloom or our relationship? I understood his bitterness. He had taken a risk on me from the beginning. His first impression of me was that I was a flighty, social media–obsessed influencer thirsty for fame. He didn't want me on his team. And the first chance I got, I dropped him for "exposure."

The flowers he'd given me when I left were his goodbye.

I took a deep breath. "I get why you don't trust me after flip-flopping like this. I'm not asking you for anything else. Not friendship, not more. Just this. Let me be in the Bloom. That's all I want. Just the Bloom."

"But why?" he asked.

"I'll explain it to you when I get there, but trust me. The Bloom means more to me than staying here."

Rowan was silent a few seconds, then sighed. "Our team needs to be at the festival grounds early tomorrow. Can you be here at the house by eight?"

I did a silent happy squeal. "Yes. My dad offered to drive me to Bakewell tonight, so I can easily be there by then."

"Fine. June would have my head if she found out you asked me and I said no. Be in the garden by eight tomorrow. Oh, and the petal tips snapped again when we did another test run today. There's just too much pressure on them. We've switched to my design. We built the chicken wire frame earlier, and I'm picking up the colored flowers now."

"No problem. I loved your design. It's going to be amazing. Make sure you get lots of colorful primroses and begonias. Thank you. I'm sorry . . ." My voice trailed off.

"We'll talk tomorrow." He disconnected the call.

He said yes. It wasn't a lot, and he was clearly bitter, but he still said yes.

I needed to pack my things. I was going back to the Bloom.

~

I waited until we were on the road to Bakewell to call everyone. I called Dasha first. She was nice enough—all *It's cool, shit turns up*. She promised we'd do something next time she was in Toronto. Or that I could call her whenever I was in LA. The offer sounded pretty fake, but the fact that she was being fake nice told me Dasha considered me someone she might need something from in the future. I called Matteo next. He was furious, of course. Without me he wasn't getting the interview. I couldn't make myself care too much, though. If he'd wanted to ride my coattails long term, his first mistake had been cheating on me.

Gia was surprised. "Why are you going back to *Bakewell?*" She said "Bakewell" as if it were Kansas or something. Which, I realized, was how I'd talked about the place when I first got there.

"I decided I'd rather do the Bloom than the Dasha Payne thing. You can stay and hang out in Toronto, though, if you want."

Gia snorted. "Well, duh, I'm going to stay. Didn't you hear who's going to be at that pool party? I'm going bikini shopping tomorrow. Oh, you'll never guess what happened after you left . . . Marcus asked for my number! We're meeting up before the party tomorrow!"

"What about Cameron?"

"What about him? He was a summer fling. The summer is over. Hey, can you ask Shar if it would be okay if I don't come back on Monday? I mean, there's, like, only a week left anyway. I brought most of my stuff home this weekend, and you can bring the rest when you come back."

Nilusha was right. Spending the day with twenty-plus *influencers* had brought out the worst in Gia.

"I'm not doing your dirty work for you. If you want to quit early, G, *you* call Shar."

"Fine. I will. All right. I need to go. Byee!"

She hung up and I shook my head.

"I don't get why you've been friends with that girl so long," Samaya said.

I turned my head sharply. I'd forgotten my sister was sitting beside me in the car. I nodded. "Yeah, lately I've been wondering the same thing," I said.

Lastly, I called Nilusha. She actually approved of me leaving. She made me promise to send her lots of pictures of the sculptures at the Bloom and told me we were going for churros again when I was back in Toronto for good.

After that call, I tossed my phone in my bag. I didn't even want to look at it until I was back in Bakewell.

"Honestly, Tahira," Samaya said, "when I get famous, I'm hiring an assistant to make all my phone calls for me."

"I'm not famous."

Samaya raised a brow. "Um, *yeah*, I know. I said when *I* get famous."

I rolled my eyes. "How is a mathematician going to be famous?"

"Girls. Stop fighting," Mom said from the front seat. "You'll both be famous, and I'll hire your personal assistants myself. Your dad will draw up the contracts."

I laughed because it was so rare for the four of us to be in a car together. It was kind of nice.

Samaya pulled out her iPad.

"Whatcha doing?" I asked.

"Trigonometry."

"You have, like, a week between summer school and real school, and you're doing trig?"

"You're not in any design classes right now, and you're still designing."

Touché.

But now that she said that, I pulled out my own iPad to refamiliarize myself with Rowan's sculpture design. I'd loved it when I first saw it a few weeks ago, but I wanted to take a closer look now that this was the design we'd be building tomorrow.

It was, of course, striking. I'd made a minimalistic lily, while Rowan had made an extravagant iris. It had Rowan's signature sculptural look, with twigs and lots of long grasses for balance. Filled with purple, white, and magenta begonias and primroses, and even some white hyacinths. At the time I'd preferred my sculpture, but now? I was glad we were doing the iris instead.

"That's what you designed for the contest?" Samaya asked.

I shook my head. "No, this is Rowan's. We each made a design, but we're using his."

Samaya shook her head, looking impressed. "Wow. You're dating someone who is a better artist than you?"

I snorted. "Supportive sisters are really the best."

She put her hands up, laughing. "Kidding, kidding. I personally like to surround myself with people at my level of genius at all times. Let me see your design."

I brought up my flower on the screen.

"Ooh, I like that, too. I like how it's kinda hourglass-y, but not. It looks like a dress."

"A dress?"

"Yeah, look, turn it upside down."

I did. And yeah, I could see what she meant. The lily blossom did kind of look like an upside-down abstract-ish minidress, with the petal tips at the hem.

"Always designing clothes," Samaya said with a grin.

I laughed, but my mind was swirling with another image. I went back to Rowan's design and turned it upside down. It sort of looked like a skirt. Moving quickly, I did a little bit of cut-and-pasting on the graphics app, splicing my upside-down lily over his upside-down iris.

It was a stunning gown. My slim, white flower was the bodice, and Rowan's huge bloom was the skirt, with the longer iris petal as a train. I added some vertical striping to the bodice to simulate the stamen and pistil of the lily.

"Ooh, *that*," Samaya said. "Can you make me that dress for prom? Except out of fabric, not flowers."

It was *gorgeous*. With my stylus moving quickly over the iPad screen, I added more long grasses to give the impression of movement in the skirt, and some yellow primroses to the bodice.

"I like that better than both the other designs," Samaya said, watching me work.

"So do I," I said. It was strange—this was nothing like my, or Rowan's, original design, but somehow it evoked the feel of both. "It's too bad we can't really make this for the competition."

"Why not?"

I shrugged but kept adding details. "A little late to change the design. The competition is tomorrow."

Samaya studied the screen, head tilted.

"What are you girls talking about back there?" Mom asked.

"Tahira drew this really cool flower sculpture that looks like a dress. It's way better than the design they are actually doing for the competition."

"Then why don't you make it instead? You should be putting your best foot forward at all times!"

I sighed, shaking my head. "I know, Mom," I said.

Samaya shrugged. "You could at least try. I think this is a winner." She mouthed the words "Janmohammads always succeed," eyes twinkling.

I exhaled, looking at the design. Samaya might have been right.

But of course, I couldn't ask Rowan to change the Bloom design now. Not after everything that had happened for the last few days. I was lucky he was letting me back on the team at all. Still, I opened a new page on my iPad to redraw this dress-sculpture design from scratch. I couldn't help it. Even if this sculpture was never built, I couldn't get the image out of my head.

28

RUBY TO THE RESCUE

It was almost ten p.m. by the time we got to Bakewell. The whole family was tired and crabby, and to be honest, I was probably the worst of us all. It had been a long day. A long, emotional, *exhausting* day.

Shar was waiting for us. She showed Mom and Dad to her guest room in the main house while I took Samaya through the backyard lit with Rowan's garden lights and showed her the tiny house, since she'd be using Gia's bed.

Samaya laughed when I opened the door. "Seriously, Tahira? How have you and Gia been living *here* all summer? Hey, if you're used to small spaces now, can we switch rooms at home? Yours is twelve percent bigger."

I snorted. "My sewing supplies take up, like, half of my space, though."

Truth was, I didn't even mind the tininess of the tiny house anymore. Yeah, it would be great to walk three steps without bumping into pine, but it was worth it to be practically living in the garden, which had become my favorite place in the world this summer.

"You sleep here," I said. "Bathroom's back there. Help yourself to any skin care you see. Gia took all her skin care home with her, so it's all mine."

Samaya dropped her bag on the daybed. "You going to bed, too?"

"I will in a bit. I just want to . . ."

What did I want exactly? I wanted to find Rowan and put my head on his shoulder. I wanted to tell him how much I hated that fashion shoot in Toronto. I wanted him to see the design I'd done on the way up. But he'd made it clear on the phone that he didn't like the change of plans that had me back in Bakewell.

I did need to see the garden, though. So, after taking an antihistamine, I went out into the dark night.

Some new boxes and a wheelbarrow full of floristry supplies and chicken wire were near the workbench, along with rows and rows of plastic flats of vibrant plants, ready for the sculpture. The twinkle lights on the roof of the greenhouse were on, and I could also see the chicken wire frame of Rowan's iris.

I knew I shouldn't, but I couldn't stop thinking about the sculpture I'd drawn on the drive up. Was it even possible to create it?

I scrutinized the chicken wire iris. Right now, it just looked like a big ball of wire, and I could only tell what they were going for because I'd seen the original sketch. They'd done a great job. Without really thinking about whether I should've been doing this, I carefully flipped the frame over. It totally looked like the skirt of my design. I unrolled some new chicken wire and cut off a piece with wire snips from the greenhouse. I rolled it into a loose tube and placed it above the upside-down flower as the bodice for the dress. It did work in terms of the scale, but my tube of chicken wire didn't have the curves of a real body. I put it on the workbench, nipped in the waist, and tried to mold breasts, but it didn't go well. I was so terrible at sculpting with chicken wire.

Ugh. This was not working. What I needed was to mold it on a form. Like designing clothes by draping.

I almost pulled my sweatshirt off right there so I could wrap the chicken wire around myself to make the shape, but then I remembered Ruby, my dress form.

Samaya was getting into bed when I came in the house to get Ruby. "What are you doing?" she asked.

I unlocked the casters on Ruby's base. "Nothing. Just . . . working on something in the garden."

Samaya snorted. "With your dress form? You're in your obsessive designing mode, aren't you? You do that when you're avoiding real stuff."

I chuckled as I wheeled Ruby out the door. It wasn't fair that my sister was so perceptive.

I pushed the dress form over to the workbench, turned on the light on the bench, and inspected her.

Ruby was a professional-grade half-body double with an iron base on casters. She was covered with a thick off-white canvas and was more or less my size, instead of sample size. I unrolled the chicken wire bodice I'd made and wrapped it around her. This was ridiculous—the wire would probably ruin the canvas cover. What was I doing all this for, anyway? I should be getting some sleep so I'd be alert tomorrow.

But I wouldn't be able to sleep now, anyway. Not when I was so anxious about what was going to happen when I saw Rowan. Not when each time I closed my eyes, I imagined his expression when he'd said, "Am I supposed to just take you back?"

I needed a way to affix the chicken wire at the back of Ruby so I could mold it tight against her body. If this were fabric, I would pin it. I could attach it with floral wire, but that would be annoying to remove once I had my shape. Ah! I had some little clamps in my sewing box that I used instead of pins when sewing leather or vinyl.

I rushed to the tiny house to get them.

Then, clamps in hand, I paused in the doorway of the house to look at the garden. Ruby was lit almost as if by a spotlight from the work light on the bench, and the twinkle lights on the greenhouse shimmered. It was all surrounded by flowers illuminated by Rowan's garden lights.

It was ethereal. How was I going to leave this place in a week?

I then noticed that Ruby wasn't alone. Rowan stepped out of the greenhouse. When he saw me, he tilted his head toward Ruby. "This thing scared the crap out of me. I thought there was a ghost in the garden."

"Oh, hey. Sorry."

He was in his pajamas. Plaid flannel pants and a long-sleeve gray shirt. A plain one, no cartoon plants in sight. I kind of missed his bright colors, but it was so good to see him.

The look on his face told me he didn't feel the same. He would have preferred I stayed in Toronto. I almost turned and went back into the tiny house.

"Why is your mannequin here?" he asked.

"She's a dress form, not a mannequin."

He didn't say anything. Just waited for me to answer the question. I sighed. "Can I show you something?"

He shrugged.

"Give me one second," I said.

I hurried back into the tiny house to get my iPad, apologizing to Samaya when she grumbled something about trying to sleep.

His expression was blank when I returned. "What do you want to show me?"

"This," I said, bringing up the sketch of the flower dress on the iPad. I handed it to him.

I let him look at it for a few seconds, zooming in, studying the design. "This looks a bit like my sculpture design. And yours."

I nodded. "Exactly. On the way here my sister pointed out if we flipped them and put them together, it kind of looked like a dress." I pointed out the parts that came from his Bloom design and mine, showing him the flowers and extra grasses I'd added for movement. I was getting louder and talking faster as I explained it. "I brought my dress form out to see if I could drape the chicken wire onto it to make the bodice. The skirt part is easy because you did such an amazing job—"

"Wait, Tahira." He shook his head, looking incredulous. "Do you seriously want to change the Bloom design *now*? The night before the competition?"

"No, I'm just trying something . . . you know, like, proof of concept . . . I just need to clip the back . . ." I turned the dress form. "Tahira, look at me."

My arm dropped and I turned to him. He still had that intense look of . . . annoyance?

He ran his hand over his head. "You're a very frustrating person, you know that?"

He was right. What was I thinking? I really shouldn't have even been on this team. I definitely shouldn't have been playing with his sculpture frame the night before the competition. "I'm sorry," I said. "I'm getting in the way. Never mind. I'll try this out later on my own time."

I turned the chicken wire iris right side up and unlocked the wheels on Ruby with my foot. I rolled her over the uneven grass back toward the tiny house.

As an artist, I was used to some people not appreciating my work, but I still had to push down the stomach sourness that came with every rejection. But this was worse, because the rejection was coming from someone I was most likely in love with. But maybe being in love with Rowan was beside the point right now.

Or was it the entire point?

I squeezed my eyes shut. Samaya was right. This—obsessing over this design—was avoidance. I just didn't want to face the hard truth about Rowan and me. That my feelings were much stronger than his.

I continued pushing the chicken wire–covered dress form like a fool. No doubt she'd already left dents in the lawn. I couldn't seem to stop ruining everything.

"Wait, Tahira," Rowan said.

I sighed and turned around.

"You're frustrating." Rowan shook his head. "But you're a genius." He looked back down at the iPad. "A literal genius. This is amazing. Also, I've never met another person who gets so excited about an idea that they have to build it right away."

I gave a tiny smile. "You live in a small town. Wait until you're surrounded by creatives next year. They're all intense like you and me."

Still not meeting my eyes, he nodded. "I've spent the last two days convinced that you and I were way too different."

"We're not different."

He took a breath. "So, explain it to me. The mannequin would be the frame for the sculpture?"

I blinked a few times, then wheeled Ruby back to him. "No. I'm only using her to shape the chicken wire for the bodice. Here, look."

I showed him how I was using draping techniques to mold the chicken wire into shape. And then explained how I could attach it to the iris sculpture frame to make a complete dress that could be filled with moss and then plants.

I pulled the chicken wire taut over Ruby's chest. "The clips will hold it in place while I shape it."

He took the clips and started attaching them to the back. "Ouch. The edges of the wire are tearing the fabric back here," he said. "Your dress form will be damaged."

"Don't worry about it. It's nothing that can't be fixed. Right now, this is more important."

I hadn't realized the significance of what I'd said until the words left my lips, but it was true. Right now nothing, not my dress form, not even fashion design, was more important than the Bloom. I had nothing to gain from it professionally anymore, but I was more dedicated to this floral sculpture competition than I ever had been.

We worked together, me draping chicken wire and forming the shape, while he clipped, trimmed, and wired to create a woman's bodice made of strong chicken wire.

"How are we going to take it in here?" I said, pinching the extra under Ruby's bust. If it were fabric, I'd be sewing darts.

Rowan bit his bottom lip, thinking. And I completely forgot what we were supposed to be doing because he looked so incredibly hot. *Stay on task, Tahira* . . . Just because he was helping me now didn't mean he wanted things to be back to the way they were.

He raised his brows. "Staples?"

I laughed. "That could work."

He grinned as he headed to the greenhouse, returning a few seconds later with a staple gun, staples, and pliers. "These are rustproof, so they'll be fine once we stuff this with wet moss."

"Wait, Rowan." I stopped him. "You said 'we' . . . does that mean . . ."

A small smile transformed his face. "I think this is amazing. I think we should do this for the Bloom."

The smile just for me was back. I wanted to jump for joy.

"But what about the rest of the team?" I asked. "We can't make this decision ourselves."

He squeezed his lips together a second, then shrugged. "June and Leanne will agree."

"But we have to at least ask them."

He shook his head. "They'll love it. I don't want to bug them now. They're . . . out."

I grinned. "*Together?* Where are they?"

He shook his head. "Don't read into this . . . but they went to hang out after the three of us finished working on the sculpture earlier, and they're not back yet. Let's not bother them. They said they were leaving the design up to me, anyway."

I laughed, giddy. This was excellent. Yes, Leanne and June needed this time alone.

Rowan gave me that secret, just-for-me smile. "Let's make this happen. You and me."

I grinned so big I thought my face would split. "Yes. Let's do it."

～

I stepped back to look at Ruby with a critical eye. The bodice piece looked more or less like a metal tank top right now, but I hoped it would be less like casual wear made of chain-link fencing and more like an avant-garde ball gown once it was attached to the skirt piece and filled in with plants.

I squinted and tilted my head. "I'm not feeling that neckline."

I picked up the iPad and used the eraser tool to delete one of the shoulder straps. "If we go one-shoulder, then we can add big blooms on the strap. It will tie in to the front-to-back asymmetry on the skirt."

Rowan nodded. "Yes. And the big blossoms can be the nod to the theme, 'Things in the garden.'"

I nearly dropped my iPad. "Crap." I turned to Rowan. "I forgot about the damn theme. The sculpture is supposed to be of something you find in a *garden*."

Rowan waved his hand. "It's fine. It's covered in flowers, and people wear dresses in gardens, right? For, like, weddings and garden parties."

"Yeah, but *this* dress is not for gardens. It's for the red carpet at the Met Gala." I pictured the finished sculpture in my head. How could I make this work for a garden party? The floor-length hem and the small train were the problem. I inspected the chicken wire iris upside down on the grass. What if it was shorter? I lifted it up a foot off the ground. "We can take some of the length off the top before we attach the bodice. Then it would be tea length, which is totally perfect for a garden party."

Rowan frowned. "Yeah, but how're you going to keep it there? You can't hold it up like that all day. What if the sculpture had legs?"

Legs without a head would be creepy as hell. I wasn't looking to make a sculpture of a person, just the dress. But the dress needed to be *on* something.

I smiled at Ruby, an idea coming to me. "We can use Ruby's base." I rushed and sat in front of her, inspecting the base. "The body part is just screwed on. We can take it off and figure out a way to attach the skirt at the right height for a tea-length dress!"

Without speaking, Rowan went into the greenhouse to get tools, and we worked together to unbolt the chicken wire–wrapped body from the base, carefully setting it on the workbench. We were left with the iron base: basically a pole, with four legs on casters. After attaching the bodice to the skirt, we stapled a piece of a two-by-four inside the skirt and screwed the base into the lumber.

It was well past midnight when we were done. I was tired. I was sore. But I hadn't had such an inspired night in a long time. I was creatively recharged.

This was what I loved about designing. About creating. Figuring out how to make an image in my head a reality.

Satisfied, I sat heavily on the garden sofa. Rowan sat next to me. Not too close—there were a good six inches between us—but this was the closest we'd been, both literally and figuratively, in days.

"So, this is good?" I asked, indicating the now-complete frame. To anyone who didn't know better, it would've looked like nothing but barely shaped chicken wire and wood on a heavy base. But that's not what I saw. I saw the colors of the blooms and the plants we'd cover it with tomorrow. I saw what we were creating, not what we'd made so far.

And so did Rowan. Because he was an artist like me.

"It's great," he said. "We have a really good chance if we can pull this off."

"We'll pull it off. We just have to hope others recognize our genius." He chuckled. "Same old Tahira."

"Full of myself?"

"Confident." He gave me the warmest smile. And I gave one right back. We gazed at each other like that in the dark night, and I didn't know what it meant, but after spending most of the day convinced I'd never see that expression in his eyes again, I soaked it all up.

"Brilliant, too," he murmured, leaning in.

I inched even closer to meet him, but then I stopped. I *wanted* to kiss him. I wanted to slide back into how we were before I'd left, but first, I needed to know where we stood.

I exhaled, my hand on his chest. "Tell me what's going on with you," I said softly, his face still inches from mine. "I get why you were upset that I left, but you gave me those gorgeous flowers, then you made it clear that you didn't *want* me here today. What's been in your head?"

He blinked. "You, mostly. You've been in my head."

I smiled, running the back of my hand over his cheek. He leaned into my touch. What was I going to do with my sweet Plant-Boy?

"I know we have a lot to talk about," he said. "I'll be honest, I didn't want you to come back. I knew you'd come with another tsunami of big feelings, and mind-blowing creativity, and huge inspiration. I was scared I'd grow even more addicted to you and then just get left behind again when you went on to shine somewhere else. I'm used to looking at stars that are far away, Tahira. Not blindingly bright right in front of me."

I shook my head. "We're both brilliant, remember?"

He inched closer, his eyes full of intensity. "Only when you bring it out in me. I couldn't have done anything like this without you."

"You taught me everything I know about flowers, remember?" I put my hands behind his neck, pulling him closer. "We're a team."

I kissed him.

And kissing Rowan Johnston was perfect. My skin erupted in goose bumps like it always had. He immediately put his hands around my waist and pulled me even closer. His mouth was soft, but needy. He missed me as much as I missed him.

I managed to get even closer. If I could somehow meld us together forever right now, I would've been all over that idea.

Finally, we pulled away, but I kept my hands on the back of his neck to keep him close.

His eyes were dark. Lips pursed. Jaw twitching. He leaned forward, catching my lips in one more tiny kiss. "What now?" he whispered.

"I'd love to invite you to the tiny house, but my sister is sleeping in there."

He chuckled, leaning forward and resting his forehead on mine.

"That would have been great," he said. "But that's not what I'm asking."

I knew what he was asking. What was going to happen in the future? Would we stay together? When he started university in a week and I was back in high school in two? Was this connection even possible outside this garden? Outside Bakewell?

"Let's get through the Bloom," I said. "Can we wait and have this conversation after the competition?"

He nodded, then caught my lips for another little kiss. "Okay. I can live with that."

"Want to look at the stars?" I asked. "I can tell you why I left Toronto."

So that's what we did. Lay back on the grass talking, with my head on his chest, looking at millions of stars in the sky.

29

BUILDING OUR BLOOM

E ven though Rowan and I were up so late, I was showered, dressed, and ready before eight for the Bloom. I left the tiny house quietly, since Samaya was still sleeping. She'd be coming to the festival later with Mom and Dad. Rowan was already at the workbench, packing up the flowers and moss. I smiled, heading toward him.

But before I reached him, June and Leanne came out of the greenhouse wearing matching T-shirts with some floral design on them.

"There you are," June said, her hands on her hips. "I knew you had to be the one behind this." She waved her hand in the general direction of the sculpture frame Rowan and I had made last night.

"Hi, Juniper!" I said. Leanne was frowning behind her. I bit my lip. I probably should have told Leanne privately that I'd returned.

Rowan grinned at me. "My sister was just laying into me for not telling her you came back."

Juniper slapped her brother on the chest. "Of course I was laying into you! I mean, it's not like I don't love this new design, because holy crap, it's *spectacular*, and we're fine with changing our entry to this. But you can't just hog her for yourself because y'all are playing tonsil hockey these days! We're a team!"

"You got home so late. I didn't want to bother you," Rowan said, glancing at Leanne.

"Where did you go?" I asked Leanne. She still seemed mighty irritated to see me. I didn't blame her.

"We were getting T-shirts," Leanne said, pushing a white T-shirt at me. She looked at June. "Tell 'em how we got them, Junebug."

Juniper smiled proudly. "Leanne and I went for burgers yesterday while Rowan went to pick up the plants, and I had the idea to get shirts while we were eating. It was, like, super last minute to get custom tees, but then Leanne remembered there's a twenty-four-hour Staples print shop in Saint Catharines. Her dad once had to get brochures printed in the middle of the night because the ones he ordered said BEE LAND LANGSTON, instead of Leeland Langston, which, I mean, c'mon, I would have changed the whole business name to Bee Land because it's hilarious. Anyway, Leanne and I designed these on her phone, and they printed it on these iron-on sheets for us. But then we had to get the T-shirts to iron them onto. Do you know how hard it was to find blank T-shirts at midnight? These are from a grocery store, believe it or not. They're men's undershirts! They had books, too! Can you imagine being able to buy books in the middle of the night?"

I was looking at Leanne while June was talking, and she was looking at Juniper with so much . . . *liking*. Like, serious affection. I raised a brow at Rowan. What else had happened in Saint Catharines?

I held up the shirt to look at it. "Why'd you make me a shirt if you didn't know I was here?"

"You're one of us," June said, smiling. "Even if you needed to leave for that fancy photo shoot, you're still on the team."

The shirt was gleaming white, with a big rectangle in the middle filled with flowers of every color. Sunflowers, daisies, violets, cornflowers. In the middle, with white blocky letters, it said BFFs. Above those letters, with a smaller print, it said BFF.

"Get it?" June squealed. "We're the BFF BFFs. The Bakewell Flower Festival's Best Friends Forever. I know flowers aren't, like, what did you call it, your *aesthetic*, but for the Bloom, flowers are good, right? You only have to wear it today."

I grinned. "I love it. Seriously. It's perfect. I'll go change." I went into the tiny house and texted Leanne right away.

Tahira: I hope you trust me and we can work together today. And don't worry—I worked it out. June's still getting her signed book.

Leanne: June and Row are happy, so I can't be mad, as long as June gets the book. Don't hurt them. Welcome back.

I put on my flowered shirt, finally ready for the Bloom.

~

The Bloom was being held on a big grass-covered field next to the main festival grounds. The festival itself wasn't open to the public yet, but we had an hour to work alone before spectators were allowed to watch us. I was surprised to see how many people were already there. I rolled Ruby's wheels over the grass toward our assigned spot. There were about thirty other teams scattered over the field, and a stage area set up in front. We weren't near anyone I knew—but I could make out Addison and her team in the distance.

Before the competition officially opened, a judge with an impressive handlebar mustache visited our station to make sure our frame followed the rules. It was approved, thankfully. Soon after, that judge, and a bunch more people, climbed the stage.

A woman in a fifties-style pinup dress in a peony print said a little speech about the history of the Bloom (super long and auspicious, apparently) and the rules (super strict and unclear, if you asked me), then introduced another judge to officially open the competition—a sturdy woman in a floral button-up and unironic mom jeans. After a short inspirational speech, the judge pressed a button on a loudspeaker and proclaimed the Bakewell Bloom officially started.

The judge in jeans waved and winked at our team as she walked off the field. Leanne grinned and waved back.

I raised a brow. "What was that about?"

"That's Agnes Chiu," Leanne said. "She was my Girl Guides leader, and she's the one who got me into rabbit agility shows. She has three English lops—the sweetest things ever. They always trip over their ears when climbing the little ramps."

Ah. Hopefully, we had a small advantage thanks to the bunny-loving judge.

Rowan wheeled over the wagon of moss. It was time to start building our Bloom sculpture.

After making sure the skirt was well secured to the base, we started lining the chicken wire with moss. The moss could hold twenty times its weight in water, so we packed it very loosely to give it space to expand. With luck, once we wedged the plants in, it would look fuller.

The frame was holding its shape pretty well. We had to be careful to stuff the breasts evenly so she wouldn't be lopsided, and the narrow shoulder strap was a bit tricky. But overall, the sculpture was coming together. Not quite the magical gown of flowers she'd be later, but more solid at least.

Leanne was securing moss with floral wire when she sighed. "This almost makes me want to put on a dress again. Rowan, wouldn't a dress have been better for our prom pictures?"

Rowan laughed. "You looked fine in the green pantsuit. Very Hillary Clinton. I haven't seen you in a dress since—"

"Grade-eight graduation," Juniper interrupted. She covered her mouth, clearly mortified that she'd admitted to cataloging her brother's best friend's formal-wear history.

I had no idea what exactly was going on between the two, but there was a different vibe between them today. June was a touch less awkward, and Leanne a bit more natural with June. I wanted to respect them, and respect Rowan when he said I shouldn't pry, but I was dying to know. Had they had the heavy talk yet?

I glanced at Rowan. We, of course, were also due for a heavy talk. We'd agreed to a kind of holding pattern today, even though last night had been so spectacular. I felt closer to him than I ever had. Emotionally, I mean. He'd been so great when I told him about my existential crisis in Toronto. He listened and understood why I had needed to go to that photo shoot. And he understood why I came back. We talked about my struggle to decide what to do about college, and he gave me some great insights without trying to influence my decision.

I knew more than ever that I couldn't let this summer fling end when the season changed. And I was 90 percent sure he felt the same way.

But it was that last 10 percent that was freaking me out whenever I let myself think too much.

So I focused on the Bloom. I might not have had that much to gain by winning, but Rowan *did*. I planned to give everything to this competition, because that's what I did.

I pushed out some of the wire that had collapsed on the skirt and added more moss.

"Wow," June said. "It's finally looking like a dress. I love this thing."

About half an hour into the competition, we were ready to add the most important element of our Bloom sculpture—the flowers. We started with the darkest-magenta begonias at the bottom.

"What do you think?" I asked Rowan when I was halfway around the skirt. There were a few gaps between the flowers, but we could fill them in with clumps of sod or more moss. I thought the ombré effect was working.

He nodded. "She looks good."

"She looks like a headless nymph floating through the garden," Leanne added, which made Juniper give her a curious glance.

I studied the sculpture through narrowed eyes. "It's probably too late to give her a head, right?"

Rowan laughed. "She's fine. It's a sculpture of a dress, not a person. Like a dress on a dress form."

I nodded. With it on Ruby's base, it looked pretty much like a dress in a designer's studio.

We kept adding flowers. So far, the heavy metal base and the sturdy wire we'd used were holding the weight fine. I was feeling seriously optimistic about winning. Even with flowers only one-quarter of the way up the skirt, this gown was dazzling.

I was sitting on the ground, adjusting a coreopsis that wasn't sitting right, when the woman in the fifties dress approached. All I could see were her pink satin pumps.

"Stop. The prop on this entry is illegal."

Damn it. Everything had been going too well today. The woman loomed over me. Her dress looked like an authentic vintage piece up close. "Who authorized you to use this prop for your entry?" she asked me.

I blinked. She'd sounded nice in her welcome speech. Now? Not so nice. Also, she was with Mrs. McLaughlin, Addison's mother. Extra not nice.

"What exactly is the problem?" Leanne asked, coming around the sculpture to face the women. I stood.

"Leanne, I just asked your friend who authorized the use of this . . . prop?" She flipped through the pages in a clipboard. "Props are against rule twenty-four. Didn't you read the rule booklet?"

"They probably don't even have one," Mrs. McLaughlin added.

"We don't have a prop," I said. "Our frame was approved by a judge."

Vintage Dress Lady kicked the cast-iron base with her satin pumps. "This is a prop. It's used to enhance the sculpture instead of being a part of the frame."

"I have the booklet right here," Rowan said, pulling a brochure out of his back pocket. "Props are accessories. Like an umbrella or a hat. This isn't an accessory; it's *part* of the frame."

Vintage Dress tilted her head in a patronizing gesture. "The judges should be the one to decide that. Come, Melanie. Who knows what these kids told Albert when he inspected the frame? Let's speak to him ourselves. I'm sure this isn't—"

"Are we allowed to defend ourselves?" Leanne interrupted. "Or, just because the Bakewell desperate housewives have it in for us, we have to roll over and cower."

"Leanne!" the woman said. "The disrespect! I don't understand why anyone calls you one of Bakewell's brightest young students."

Mrs. McLaughlin tutted past her partner-in-privilege and waved a finger at me instead of Leanne. "I'll have you know that the Bloom is a long-standing tradition in Bakewell. Long before *you* arrived. If it was up to me, outsiders wouldn't even be allowed to enter."

Rowan's jaw twitched. "There is no residency requirement for the Bloom. There never has been. And all of us, other than Tahira, have lived here our whole lives."

Mrs. McLaughlin just glared. Why did she have it in for me? Was this because her daughter saw me as competition? Or because I was dating Rowan?

I pointed to one of the other entries. "That team's rabbit sculpture has a whole chair in it. Your own daughter is using a . . ." I glanced over to Addison's and Cameron's . . . "What is that exactly?"

"It's a wrought iron headboard," Mrs. McLaughlin said. "But those are their *frames*. This is a prop because it will be visible in your finished design."

Leanne, Mrs. McLaughlin, and Vintage Dress Lady continued arguing the semantics of a prop versus a frame while other contestants wandered over to see what the commotion was.

I rubbed my temples, stepping away from the crowd. Rowan was by my side in seconds. He put his hand on my lower back.

"You okay?"

I nodded, looking into his eyes for strength. "This is my fault."

"No. They're doing this because they're *intimidated* by you. By us. Seeing us succeed makes them feel like we're taking their spot."

I smiled. "You sound like your father."

"The design is spectacular, Tahira. Honestly, I don't even care if they find some silly loophole to disqualify us. They'll look closed minded, and we'll look brilliant. We're still the ones shining."

He was right. "We always shine," I whispered.

He wrapped me in a hug, and I sank into it.

"And now look at those two!" Mrs. McLaughlin shrieked. Rowan and I pulled apart to see her pointing and frowning at us.

"What now?" Rowan asked, rolling his eyes.

"They're not taking any of this seriously. I don't know how we can allow these hormonal teenagers—"

"Mom, just shut up." Addison had arrived at our little three-ring circus.

"Addie, go back to your station. This isn't about you."

Addison blinked, looking at Rowan and me. "Mom, this *is* about me. You're my mother, and you're embarrassing me. All this is because part of their frame is visible?"

Vintage Dress pointed to her clipboard again. "It's against rule—"

"Why don't you just cover it up?" Addison said to our team but mostly to Rowan.

"We could," Rowan said slowly. He walked over and bent to inspect the stand. "It's solid metal, though. How?"

Addison shook her head. "It's not rocket science. Cover it with sheet moss."

It could work.

"We didn't bring any sheet moss," Rowan said. "Only the sphagnum moss we lined the frame with."

"Well," Vintage Dress Lady snapped. "You can make do with what you have, or you can go purchase what you need, but they're not going to give you any extra time."

Mrs. McLaughlin crossed her arms and smiled smugly. "Those are your options. If you'd like to leave, then—"

"We have a ton of sheet moss," Addison said. "We're covering our whole headboard with it. You can have some."

Addison's mother turned sharply to her daughter. "Addison, if they aren't following the rules—"

"This is a dumb rule! We both know you're just trying to sabotage them because you don't want them to beat me! But it's not going to work, because they're going to beat me no matter what. This is Rowan! And his girlfriend is a real-life fashion designer! They worked harder and are just better at this than me. Stop being a stage mom and deal with it."

Wow. I had no idea Addison McLaughlin had that in her. I smiled at her, feeling a little overachieving-mother solidarity, even though my mother would never sabotage someone else to get me ahead. As much as my parents were intense sometimes, clearly I could've had it so much worse.

"You're being serious? We can have the moss?" Rowan asked, looking at Addison carefully.

"Yeah, totally." She indicated our sculpture. "This is gorgeous. It should stay in the competition. And . . . you're an old friend."

Everyone dispersed at that. Even Mrs. McLaughlin and her mean-lady lackey left with their proverbial tails between their legs.

Addison winced at me. "Sorry about my mother. It took me way too long to realize how toxic she is. Congrats on your sculpture—it's really amazing."

I tilted my head. "Thanks."

"You and Rowan are cute together. Love the shirts. Come grab the moss whenever." She turned to June. "Hey, Juniper, my mom gave me some advance copies for books coming out next year that she got from the library. I thought you might want them for your Instagram."

"Oh, wow," Juniper said. "I've never had an advance copy before. I . . . what's the catch?"

Addison shrugged. "No catch. Call it an apology for that stuff before. I don't even listen to my mother these days. And she doesn't know about your Instagram. Byee!" She flipped her shiny hair over her shoulder and went back to her team.

I looked at Rowan, but he just shrugged. Was it possible that Addison's *mother* was also commenting on June's YouTube? I exhaled. And . . . now that I thought about it, that day at Hyacinth's when Addison bugged June to help her with her Bloom team, it was her mother who'd pushed Addison to talk to us. Mrs. McLaughlin clearly wanted her daughter in the limelight.

I shook my head. We weirdly had a lot in common. "I'll get the moss in a bit. Let's get the rest of these begonias in."

30

AND IT ENDS WITH TULIPS

After that drama had faded, we got back to our sculpture. Covering the stand with moss worked fine. Personally, I liked it better with the metal base than this weird furry green, but whatever. The dress itself was coming along perfectly, and from the looks of it, we were ahead of the other contestants, timing wise.

Soon, the festival opened to the public, and spectators started wandering through the Bloom grounds. They didn't really bother us—most people who came to our station just asked a few polite questions about what we were making and then moved on. My parents and Samaya eventually showed up, each with large tote bags in their hands.

"I love country festivals," Mom said. She pulled something out of her bag. "Look at this apron I found!"

The apron was navy with a floral print and a large llama on it, along with the words No probLlama. I groaned. One day in Bakewell, and she was all into puns. She was going to love Rowan.

I finally introduced Rowan to my parents, and they subjected him to a full desi-parent interrogation with questions like *What do your parents do? Where are you going to university? What are you studying? What are your goals after school?* He of course passed with flying colors, just like I knew he would. They must have remembered when I told them yesterday that I didn't think the relationship would last, though, because they skipped the "What are your intentions with my daughter?" questions, thankfully.

"This is quite beautiful," Dad said, pointing at the sculpture. "I think yours is the best we've seen here."

Samaya grinned. "I'm totally taking credit for the dress idea."

"Are you taking pictures of it for your Instagram?" Mom asked.

I shook my head. "No," I said. "I've been too busy building it."

Samaya gasped dramatically.

"I'll take some," Mom said. "Turn around, Tahira; there's a dirt stain on that side of you. Don't you have a clean shirt?"

I groaned.

After some pictures, Mom and Dad started talking about the other competitions in the festival. "The floral arrangement contest had some lovely pieces," Mom said. "Reminded me of the ikebana class I took when I was in school. Rowan, I was surprised that you didn't enter your garden in the Best Garden contest. Your yard is much nicer than the pictures I saw of the winners."

Rowan shrugged. "It never occurred to me to enter. I only wanted to do the Bloom."

"Well," Mom said. "It's good you have Tahira now because she'll help you strategize which opportunities can help with your long-term—"

"Mom," I interrupted. I needed to get my family off the Bloom grounds. "Can I walk you back out to the festival? We really need to finish this."

Miraculously, they agreed, and I walked them to the front of the field.

"Did you call the bookstore for that book?" I asked once we were out of hearing range from the others.

Mom shook her head. "I tried, but the person in charge of the signing wasn't in yet. I'll try again later."

"Okay. Let me know when you have it confirmed. Leanne's going to kill me if June doesn't get the book."

Samaya's eyes brightened. "Are those two dating? Because Leanne was totally looking at Juniper with gaga eyes."

"No . . . at least I don't think so. But . . . they are . . . something."

"Adorable. I'm shipping them."

I laughed, shaking my head. "We all are. I need to go. Talk to you guys later."

I waved goodbye and went back to my team.

The loudspeaker letting us know our time was up sounded just as I was adding some final golden grasses to the bodice. I put my hands down and took a breath. We were done.

The sculpture wasn't perfect, but it was pretty damn good. Actually, it was spectacular.

Arms came around me. Rowan. I leaned back, wedging my head between his neck and shoulder. "You did it, Tahira."

"*We* did it," I corrected him.

He kissed the side of my neck, and I closed my eyes. "We're a great team," he whispered.

I couldn't agree more.

~

Bloom contestants and spectators were banished from the Bloom grounds so the judges could deliberate. We were told to wander around the rest of the festival and come back in one hour, at 2:00 p.m., when they would announce the winners.

"Okay, what now? Funnel cake?" Leanne asked, clearly still hyped up on adrenaline. She did not need funnel cake.

My sister came toward us, a clear plastic tray of mini Bakewell tarts in her hand. "Have you guys tried these things? They're phenomenal!"

I chuckled, taking a tart. The others did the same.

Samaya turned to me. "Mom just called the bookstore again, and they're not doing personalized signing unless you're *in* the store. She needs to know if you want her to order a nonpersonalized one." She put another tart in her mouth.

Oh no. Juniper wasn't going to get her signed book. My heart sank. I felt terrible.

I frowned at Leanne. "I'm so sorry."

Leanne crossed her arms on her chest. She didn't look impressed with me. Honestly, I didn't blame her. This was completely my fault.

"What book?" June asked.

"Oh," Samaya said, "they were trying to get this signed book for you." She grinned at me. I suspected she'd brought this up in front of June just to see what would happen with Leanne.

June blinked. "You were getting me a book?"

"Yeah," I said. "I was supposed to go to that signing for the Silverborn book while I was in Toronto. But since I ended up coming back here, my mom was going to buy it over the phone and have it mailed. I'm so sorry. I know you wanted that book."

Rowan, who had no idea what any of this was about, still defended me. "It's not your fault."

I shook my head. "No, *it is*. Leanne was planning to go to Toronto to get it, but I told her I'd do it if she took my place in the Bloom. But then I waffled and came back, and now June can't have the personalized book." I sighed, looking at my feet. "I haven't been a good friend to any of you this summer. I kept putting myself first, even though y'all have been so great to me."

"Tahira!" June said, shaking her head. "Don't you *even*. Do you think I'd rather have a signed book than *you* here for the Bloom? You've been a great friend! You've taught me about fashion, and merchandising, and I had the best summer ever because you were here!" She gave me a hug. Pulling back, she smiled. "I don't even care if the book is personalized! I really just wanted one of the limited editions with the silver foil on the eyes. They're only available on this book tour. I don't know why I didn't think to just call in to buy one—"

"Wait," I interrupted. "Did you say silver foil on the eyes?"

June raised a brow. "Um, yeah, the main character in the Silverborn books has silver eyes. You really should read them. I know urban fantasy's not your thing, but—"

"Oh my God." I pulled out my phone. "Give me a second. I need to make a quick call."

Rowan raised his brow at me. I smiled at him reassuringly while the phone rang.

"Hi, Kayla," I said when my neighbor picked up.

"Tahira! Did you get that last drawing I sent you? Evan hasn't taken the pencil crayons you gave me, so I did so much shading! They are so much better than the ones I used to—"

"Kayla, we can catch up later. I know this sounds super weird, but where are you right now?"

"I'm at a bookstore waiting in line to have the next Lexi Greer book signed. Why?"

I grinned huge. "Awesome! That's what I was hoping you'd say. Any chance you could grab an extra copy for my friend? I'll pay you back for the book."

Kayla was with her mother, who took the phone. I explained everything to Kayla's mom, asking her if she could have Lexi Greer sign the book to Juniper Johnston. I promised I'd e-transfer her the money right away, and I'd babysit Kayla's brother if she'd mail the book to Juniper.

I smiled as I hung up the phone. "There. She'll get the personalized book mailed off to you as soon as possible."

Juniper did a little happy dance, then hugged me again. Leanne smiled.

"So, no hard feelings, Leanne?" I asked.

"No hard feelings, Tahira," she said. "Junebug gets the book. And we all got to be in the Bloom."

June suddenly turned to Leanne, tilting her head. "Wait, did Tahira say you were going to go all the way to Toronto just to get me a *book*?"

Leanne shrugged. "I mean, I would have preferred we went together. That would have been a much better first date, don't you think?"

June's eyes widened. "Better first date than what?"

"Better than burgers at Henry's on Main last night?" Leanne said, slowly.

Samaya snorted behind me, so I elbowed her to shush.

June's hand shot to her mouth. "Was that a date? That wasn't a date!" She looked panicked. I wondered if I should step in to help her somehow. "That was just burgers! We're friends! We ate hamburgers! And we made T-shirts. We're not dating! You told me in December that you didn't see me that way!"

Leanne stared at June for a few seconds, then let out an exasperated sigh and stepped closer to her, eyes focused on June's shell-shocked face. "Juniper Jessica Johnston, I'm going to be super clear now," she said. "You're right, I *didn't* feel this way in December. I *do* now." She took June's cheeks in her hands and paused, looking into June's eyes. "Was that clear enough for you? Or, how's this: May I kiss you right now?"

June's eyes got even wider, but she let out a quiet, clear yes.

And Leanne planted a kiss on Juniper's lips.

I squeezed my hands together, trying really hard not to clap.

June's lip was trembling when Leanne pulled away. "You really want to date me?" June asked.

Leanne smiled again. "I've been trying to show you that all summer. You haven't made it easy. But maybe we should *actually talk* now?"

June nodded, still staring into Leanne's face. Leanne took June's hand in hers and waved at the rest of us with her other hand. "Catch up with y'all later!" she said, pulling June away from the Bloom grounds. June didn't even look back.

Samaya sighed happily. "Tahira, you need to do fan art of those two."

I laughed and looked at Rowan to see what he was thinking about his sister and best friend possibly, *finally*, figuring themselves out. He was also smiling. "I can't tell if they will have the most stable or the most chaotic relationship ever," he said.

I raised a brow. "And you're okay with it?"

He nodded. "I'm okay with it. I was the one who pushed Leanne to ask June out last night. Of course, I assumed she would do it in a way that would make it clearer to June what was going on." He laughed again and put his arm around my waist.

"Well," Samaya said. "I was a fifth wheel; now I'm a third. I'll go find Mom and Dad. Catch you later."

She disappeared toward the vendor area of the fair.

Rowan tightened his arm around me. "Can we talk now, too, Tahira?" he asked. "Alone? We can walk over to the midway . . ."

The fair was busy by now, and the midway was really hopping. Rowan bought a container of s'mores doughnuts—fresh mini doughnuts covered with marshmallow cream, chocolate sauce, and graham cracker crumbs. We sat on the grass overlooking the famous spinning-flower ride. It was pretty much identical to the spinning-teacups ride at every amusement park, but with flowers instead of teacups.

"These are good," I said, about the doughnuts. "They remind me of this barbecue place my dad likes in Toronto that has little doughnuts. They even make a milkshake with blended doughnuts in it."

He made a face.

I laughed. "It's surprisingly good."

He was quiet for a few minutes, enjoying the food, then grinned at me. "You looking forward to going back for good?"

"To Toronto?" I asked.

He nodded.

I shrugged. "I guess. I'm not *not* excited, but . . ." I sighed. "I think the whole photo shoot scared me. The people were so insufferable."

"But you don't need to see those people again."

"I know. But . . . they weren't really different from how those kinds of people always are. I'm afraid I'll find what I used to love insufferable now."

"Do you think *you're* a different person?"

"That's probably what you want me to say, right? That I'm not the same old Thirst Trap I used to be?"

He cringed. "I shouldn't have called you that. I'm sorry."

"No. That's just it. You weren't wrong." I sighed. "Sometimes I get so focused on a goal that I get tunnel vision. And this summer, I forgot to see that bigger picture. Forgot to step back and really look at what's important to me. Art means more to me than anything. Not chasing fame. Not even recognition, or being on top. I need to be around artists who see the big picture, so I don't lose sight of that again."

He smiled warmly. He was the artist I wanted to spend my time with. I took another bite of doughnut.

"What about you?" I asked. "You'll be in Toronto soon, too. How are you feeling about that?"

He exhaled long. "I have a confession. Or I should say, an explanation—for why I was so terrible to you when we met."

I shook my head. "You weren't really, but okay."

"I was . . . I *am* . . . terrified of moving to Toronto."

I shook my head. "You? No. You're not scared of anything. And you've been there loads of times."

"I've never *lived* there. I've visited lots of big cities because my parents didn't want us only seeing our own backyard, but I've never lived anywhere but here. Every time I've been in Toronto, it's just been so . . . much. There are people everywhere. The subway is confusing. Everyone is dressed better than me, and they all seem so cool. People have loads of friends, and they always say the right things. Remember when you said I beat to my own drum? What if I never fit in there? What if people think I'm weird—"

"Toronto is going to *love* you, Rowan." I might love him, and I *was* Toronto.

He shrugged.

"But I get it," I said. "Honestly, I'm scared, too. Because I've just realized I may not fit into the world that's so important to me like I used to."

I'd changed. How was I going to deal with the fashion show committee, and my photo shoots, and my Instagram when I got back? Or would I even bother with those things anymore? Could I do them, but more casually? Maybe just for fun instead of always trying to be the best?

But this conversation wasn't about my insecurities right now.

I took his hand. "So you were mad that I showed up in your life representing everything you were anxious about in the city," I said. "And I was shallow, and judgmental, and superficial. No wonder you hated me."

He swallowed. "No. That's just it. I was anxious about moving *until* I met you. You represented everything I *love* about the city. Ambition. Art. Culture. Breathtaking beauty. You reminded me that I needed all that in my life, and that little bit of discomfort when something is new is worth it. I never hated you. You drove me nuts a little bit, but I admired you so much."

I didn't even know what to say. He was the breathtaking one.

He fed me a mini doughnut with his fork. "My own backyard is comfortable, but I'm ready to move on." He sighed. "But for the last two days, I've been convinced this relationship wouldn't work in the city. You'll be so far ahead of me there, and I have no intention of asking you to stop to let me catch up."

I squeezed his hand. "I need to slow down a bit, anyway." I exhaled. "Do you still think this won't work?"

He chuckled, shaking his head. "I don't think I even have a choice. I'm *going* to keep crashing into you, Tahira. I have since the day we met.

315

Last night when you said you were coming back, I wanted to establish boundaries because I didn't want to get hurt. That went out the window as soon as I saw your new Bloom design. Your art, your passion, your brilliance. I will always be drawn to the brightest light in the universe. It's inevitable. I'm just hoping you want it as much as I do."

Oh. My eyes welled up. My sweet, sensitive Plant-Boy. I took his head in my hands and kissed his forehead.

"You and I are the most determined people I know," I whispered. "We can make this work if we want it."

His face was inches from mine. He smelled like marshmallows and chocolate, and he was wearing jorts and a soil- and moss-stained T-shirt covered with flowers and the letters *BFF*. He was perfect.

"I want it," he said before kissing me briefly.

I wanted more, but of course I couldn't make out in front of a novelty carnival ride. My parents were at this festival somewhere. I squeezed his hand, gazing into those beautiful brown eyes.

In a million years, I couldn't have imagined that this would be how my summer in Bakewell would end. With this amazing, kissable guy who inspired me to create more, appreciate more, and be the best me I could be.

"So, we're still going to be a thing, then? Totally exclusive, even in Toronto?" he asked, touching my cheek.

I nodded. "This summer fling just got a major upgrade." I smiled goofily, because how could I not?

Someone yelled my name. Samaya was standing on the other side of the ride, waving her hands frantically to get my attention.

I mouthed, "What?"

"They're announcing the winners soon!" she yelled. She pointed at the ride. "Grab those two and meet us at the stage."

What two? I looked at the ride.

And sure enough, Juniper and Leanne were sitting on the tulip seat of the spinning-flowers ride. June was holding a bunch of deep-red tulips. And her and Leanne's lips were locked in a kiss.

I smiled, feeding Rowan the last doughnut from the box before standing. It was time to go see if we'd won the Bloom.

EPILOGUE

BACK IN THE GARDEN

Two months later

We didn't win the Bloom. Neither did Addison and her squad, much to Mrs. McLaughlin's disappointment. The team with the rabbit sculpture made out of a chair won, which made me think that, yeah, Agnes Chiu was a bit biased, but not in a direction that helped us. Also, I kind of side-eyed Rowan and Leanne's second-place win last year.

I was disappointed for Rowan, though. He was about a month and a half into the landscape architecture program now, and the win would have meant a lot to him. But he said that realistically, he couldn't take time off school for a trip to New York. He'd known the architecture program would be a lot of work but hadn't realized just how ridiculously intense it would be.

And as for me, without Christopher Chan judging, there was no benefit to entering the Grand Floral Cup, anyway. Plus, it turned out I was also incredibly busy with my final semester of high school and with a new job in Toronto. I was taking a full course load at school plus one credit in online school so I could still graduate a semester early, and I was working twice a week at Nilusha's studio, helping her with a new line she was developing. I'd sent her a picture of me next to our finished Bloom sculpture, and I had to admit, it made me laugh that it wasn't the stunning garden-party gown made of flowers and greenery that I'd designed that inspired her new line, but instead the T-shirt I was wearing, the one Leanne and Juniper had made at Staples in the middle of the night using stock images and totally the wrong font.

Basically, Nilusha's new BHATT line was T-shirts, sweatshirts, joggers, and loose dresses with modern lines and busy floral prints. She said no one but me could help her with it, and she wanted me as a full-time intern from when I finished school in February until I went to university in September. She said together, we were going to make serious waves in the Toronto fashion scene. She was even helping me with a fun little side gig.

Gia had called Shar to tell her she wasn't coming back to Bakewell after the Dasha Payne photo shoot. She apparently dumped Cameron by text. I still saw her around school, and we weren't exactly enemies or anything, but we weren't really friends, either. We said hi in the hallways, and we had an awkward conversation when I dropped off the few things she'd left behind in the tiny house. She messaged me on Instagram a few times, but once she found out I wasn't designing or doing photo shoots of my own stuff anymore, and that Nilusha used real fit models instead of random friends for her fashion shoots, she stopped contacting me. I had no idea how or what Matteo was doing, since I didn't follow his Instagram. As for Dasha Payne, another hot new influencer had taken her throne as the one everyone sucked up to the most, but I wasn't interested in that game anymore.

I was still planning to apply to FIT in New York but had also researched, and was planning to apply to, Ryerson University and Ontario College of Art and Design, both in Toronto, and LaSalle College in Montreal. After a recent campus tour, my top choice was OCAD. But I was leaving my options open.

Juniper and Leanne were officially dating, and very happy, much to Samaya's and my utter delight. June was keeping Strawberry the rabbit in Rowan's greenhouse, which, to be honest, I thought was a pretty big commitment so early in their relationship. June had recently asked Leanne to come back to town for prom in the spring. I was planning to make June's dress. Not the yellow one she'd wanted as a child, but a deep-purple gown that was a similar shape to our Bloom sculpture. I'd also been assigned to make, or at least to help source a tailor for, Leanne's outfit—a tailored suit in a floral fabric I'd designed that had little white bunnies popping up between flowers. Last I'd heard, they were reading each other chapters of fantasy books over FaceTime, and June was holding her phone up to Strawberry's hutch so Leanne could say good night to him.

And June's brother? He and I were still dating, too. Rowan had settled in well in Toronto, like I knew he would. He proudly wore his plant shirts on campus, and it took him only three tries to take the subway to meet me in Scarborough without getting lost. I tried to visit him whenever I was working at Nilusha's studio downtown, since his dorm wasn't far from there, but sometimes he was working late in the architecture lab. We did manage to get together most weekends, though. We went to museums, galleries, and movies and shopped together. We talked about school, our families, our futures, and everything else. I'd honestly never been so close to another person. Ever. Rowan fast became the best friend I'd ever had—as well as the best boyfriend, of course.

Mid-October, I got my parents to agree to let me go to Bakewell with Rowan to have dinner with the Johnstons for the Canadian Thanksgiving holiday. We weren't really a turkey family, anyway—Mom had tried to make a tandoori turkey once, but it was so dry she said we'd go back to kuku paka the next year.

I wanted to stay in the tiny house while there. Both Shar and the Johnstons insisted I could stay in their warm indoor guest rooms, but I needed to be as close to the garden as possible.

And yes, even though it was October, and probably too cold for it, Rowan and I met in the garden at eleven on Friday evening after we drove up from Toronto in his car. He had a blanket under his arm, and I brought my camera with the new fifty-millimeter lens I'd bought specifically for taking pictures at night, and a tote bag that held a surprise for him.

He grinned huge when he saw me. "You and your camera. Isn't this how we met?"

I put my camera and tote down and put my arms around his neck so I could kiss him. I could never get enough of kissing him. I still couldn't believe that this guy, this brilliant, sensitive, wickedly talented flower-loving guy, was mine. Not to mention he was hot as all hell.

After Rowan helped me get some night shots of the garden, we lay back on the blanket in our heavy sweaters under the stars. The stars didn't overwhelm me anymore. But I still held his hand. Things were just better that way.

"Rowan?" I asked.

"Mmm?"

"When we first met, did you ever imagine we'd be back here for Thanksgiving together?"

He chuckled. "When we met, all I could think was, *This beautiful girl is covered with manure.* I wasn't exactly thinking about Thanksgiving."

"And all I could think about was that your face was *wasted* on those clothes."

Rowan leaned over me and tickled my side. "The nerve!" he said. "And you won't even give me that Stormtrooper shirt back!"

Of course I wouldn't. It was my favorite now.

We play-fought for a bit, which evolved to making out for a bit more. I finally pulled away, grinning. "Speaking of shirts, I have a surprise for you." I got up, turned the light in front of the greenhouse on, and grabbed the tote bag. I handed it to him. "This is for you," I said.

He grinned as he opened it. It was a gray T-shirt with an art image printed on it of mostly stylized flowers in lots of muted colors, with a brown-skinned couple in the foreground gardening and tall buildings in the background. I'd drawn the image myself, and Nilusha had helped set me up with a supplier to get it printed onto shirts.

"You made me a T-shirt?"

"No. Well, yes, you can have this one, but look." I handed him my phone so he could see my first-ever e-commerce site. "House of Tahira has officially opened for business," I said. "So far only one collection—a line of T-shirts with prints inspired by urban gardening. Some proceeds from their sale will go to a collective that teaches gardening to kids in at-risk neighborhoods in Toronto."

His face was full of awe. "That is so cool, Tahira."

"Read the name of the collection."

"Rowan Tree Collection." He beamed. "I have my own T-shirt line!"

"You do! You can even help me pick some pithy sayings to put on some of them."

He admired the T-shirt again. "You're amazing. I have tons of ideas." He reached over to kiss me, pulling me down so we were lying on the blanket, his arms around me, and my head on his shoulder. I nuzzled into his University of Toronto sweatshirt.

He sighed happily. "You know I love you, right?"

He said it often, but I liked to hear it as much as possible.

I squeezed him. "Yeah, and I love you, too."

He held me tight. "I know."

ACKNOWLEDGMENTS

For me, some books grow like wildflowers . . . where just the hint of a seed is all that's needed for a beautiful, miraculous story to emerge. Others need a spark of inspiration and then care, cultivation, and nurturing to bloom. Those books can grow into something more complex than I thought was even possible, maybe because of the extra tending they needed to grow. This book definitely needed that extra care. Maybe because it was such a departure for me.

I'd always seen myself as an adult romance writer. But I have a reader in my house who craves love stories with swoony happily ever afters even more than I do. Problem is, that reader is my thirteen-year-old daughter, and I'm not okay giving her my adult romances yet, despite the fact that my adult books are not explicit and are probably PG-13. Also, despite *me* reading adult romances by the time I was thirteen. And those were *not* PG-13. (Shhh . . . don't tell my mom.)

But anyway, my daughter wanted a book about kids like her—third-generation Canadian brown kids with immigrant grandparents instead of immigrant parents. Kids who aren't struggling with culture clashes or dealing with conservative families, but who are still finding out where they fit in the world. She wanted their warm, happy love stories. So thank you to Anissa for being the spark of inspiration for this book.

Thank you to my agent, Rachel Brooks, who was incredibly excited and supportive when I came to her with the wild idea of writing something in a new age category. Her editorial feedback on my submission was invaluable. Thank you to my editor at Skyscape, Carmen Johnson, for her unwavering passion and commitment to this project from day one. To Susan Hughes for her detailed and thorough edit, and to Bill Siever for the copyedit. And thank you to the rest of the team at Skyscape, from the art team, to publicity, to sales and marketing—it was comforting to know I was in such good hands for this book. Thank you to my friends who beta read, Roselle Lim and Laura Heffernan, for being there for me when I needed feedback. I couldn't have done this without you. And a special thank-you to my desi writing crew: Namrata, Mona, Nisha, Falguni, Suleikha, Sophia, Sonali, Kishan, Suleena, Sona, and Annika—we are changing the landscape in romance . . . and I am proud to be a part of it.

Thank you to my parents; to my kids, Khalil and Anissa (who, yes, I thanked above, too, but she's going to be thrilled to be mentioned twice); and most of all, to Tony. He's my partner, my brainstorming buddy, my coparent, my everything. Behind this author is a husband holding her up and making sure she's getting enough sleep.

ABOUT THE AUTHOR

Photo © 2021 J. Heron

After a childhood filled with Bollywood, Monty Python, and Jane Austen, Farah Heron constantly wove uplifting happily ever afters in her head while pursuing careers in human resources and psychology. She started writing her stories down a few years ago and is thrilled to see her daydreams become books. The author of *Accidentally Engaged* and *The Chai Factor*, Farah writes romantic comedies for adults and teens full of huge South Asian families, delectable food, and most importantly, brown people falling stupidly in love. Farah lives in Toronto with her husband and two teens, a rabbit named Strawberry, and two cats who rule the house. She has way too many hobbies, but her thumb is more brown than green. For more information visit www.farahheron.com.